D0349944

THE ROWAN

Other books by Anne McCaffrey

RESTOREE
DRAGONFLIGHT
DECISION AT DOONA
ALCHEMY & ACADEME (compiled by Anne McCaffrey)
THE SHIP WHO SANG
MARK OF MERLIN*
DRAGONQUEST
RING OF FEAR*
TO RIDE PEGASUS
OUT OF THIS WORLD COOKBOOK
A TIME WHEN
KILTERNAN LEGACY*
DRAGONSONG
DRAGONSINGER
GET OFF THE UNICORN
THE WHITE DRAGON
DINOSAUR PLANET
DRAGONDRUMS
CRYSTAL SINGER
THE COELURA
MORETA, DRAGONLADY OF PERN
DINOSAUR PLANET SURVIVORS
STITCH IN SNOW*
KILLASHANDRA
THE GIRL WHO HEARD DRAGONS
THE YEAR OF THE LUCY*
NERILKA'S STORY
THE LADY (aka THE CARRADYNE TOUCH)*
DRAGONSDAWN
RENEGADES OF PERN
SASSINAK (with Elizabeth Moon)
THE DEATH OF SLEEP (with Jody-Lynn Nye)
PEGASUS IN FLIGHT

*not science fiction-fantasy

THE ROWAN

Anne McCaffrey

AN ACE/PUTNAM BOOK

Published by G. P. Putnam's Sons

New York

Respectfully dedicated to
Jay A. Katz
because we enjoy a meeting of minds
(well, most of the time)

An Ace/Putnam Book
G. P. Putnam's Sons
Publishers Since 1838
200 Madison Avenue
New York, NY 10016

Printed in the United States of America

Quality Printing and Binding by:
Berryville Graphics
P.O. Box 272
Berryville, VA 22611 U.S.A.

PROLOGUE

During the late twentieth century's exploration of space, a major breakthrough occurred in the validation and recording of extrasensory perceptions, the so-called paranormal, psionic abilities long held to be spurious. An extremely sensitive encephalograph, nicknamed by critics "the Goosegg," had been developed originally to scan brain patterns of the astronauts who suffered from sporadic "bright spots," temporarily diagnosed as cerebral or retinal malfunction.

The alternate application of the Goosegg was inadvertently discovered when the device was used to monitor a head injury in an intensive-care unit of Jerhattan. The patient, Henry Darrow, was a self-styled clairvoyant with an astonishing percentage of accurate "guesses." In his case, as the device monitored his brain patterns, it also detected the minute electrical impulses discharged by activated extrasensory perceptions. The delicate instrumentation registered the discharge of unusual electrical energy as Henry Darrow experienced a clairvoyant episode. For the first time there was scientific proof of the extrasensory perception.

Henry Darrow recovered from his concussion to found the first

Center for Parapsychics in Jerhattan and to formulate the ethic and moral premises which would grant those with valid, and demonstrable, psionic talents certain privileges, and responsibilities, amid a society basically skeptical, hostile, or overtly paranoid about such abilities.

When worldwide disarmament finally followed the numerous Summits of the late '80s and '90s, governments turned to other researches and the western world's space program began to catch up with Soviet experiences. What few people knew was that Talents were instrumental in the promulgation of *honest* monitoring of the disarmament and monitoring processes, thwarting many attempts to subvert the program. Many Talents lost their lives to secure the world peace which enabled humans to turn their energies and hopes to space exploration.

More Talents were mustered to colonize this solar system and to bridge the gap between this and other systems with habitable planets.

When young Peter Reidinger made the first mind-machine gestalt, pushing a light spacecraft by telekinesis from orbit to Mars, a new era dawned for the parapsychic Talents in which they found themselves celebrated instead of shunned, admired instead of feared, and necessary to every aspect of the surge forward from the crowded and resources-poor planet Earth.

To extend the interstellar gestalt, special installations were built for the Talents, terraformed habitations on Earth's Moon, Mars's Demos, and on Jupiter's Callisto. From these stations were kinetically launched the great survey and exploration ships that colonized the nine stars that had G-type planets, suitable for humans.

Though the Talents abhorred notoriety and opted for political neutrality, it was inevitable that their abilities should contribute to the stability of the interstellar government. "Probity and neutrality" was both motto and method and a new kind of honest diplomacy resulted in spite of attempts to subvert the Talents. Many Talents died rather than dishonor their calling: the few who were corrupted were so swiftly disciplined by their peers that such treachery was eschewed as profitless. The Talents became incorruptible.

The need for Talent became chronic, far outstripping the supply. For those potential few, the training was arduous; the rewards did not always compensate Talent for the unswerving dedication required by their taxing positions.

PART ONE
ALTAIR

Torrents of rain covered the western side of the great Tranh mountain range of Altair, streaming in muddy runnels down slopes already saturated with nine days of steady precipitation. The sturdy *minta* trees were bloated and their root systems bulging to the surface, adding the slime of their overload of sap to the rivulets which increasingly dislodged the shallower root systems of the few brush varieties that could flourish in such rocky soil. Little brooks matured into streams, then rivers, into cascades of increasing volume and force, filling up blind canyons until such deposits also overflowed. And the *minta* slime seemed to grease the watery ways.

After seven people had slipped and broken bones on the main street of the Rowan Mining Company's small settlement, the manager had ordered miners and their dependents to curtail all outdoor activities and arranged door-to-door deliveries for supplies, using the Company's sturdy hopper vehicles. Operations in the several producing shafts had already been suspended when the pits began filling. When the unceasing torrents began to interfere with transmissions, there weren't even entertainment circuits to amuse those immured in ever-dampening and cramped quarters.

In the same lugubrious vein, Met reports gave no hope of an alteration in the deplorable conditions. The records show that, on the tenth day, the mine's manager asked his home office in Altair Port for permission to evacuate all nonessential personnel until the weather improved. His report pointed out that the accommodations were rather primitive and had not been constructed with excessive rainfall in mind. He cited an alarming number of respiratory ailments among his people, almost epidemic in proportion. Enforced idleness and substandard conditions had also seriously undermined morale. He put in an urgent order for pumps to drain the shafts when, and if, the rain ever did stop.

The records showed that the directors debated withdrawal. That particular installation of the Rowan Company was only just showing some profit which would be wiped out by the cost of a perhaps unnecessary expense. Meteorology was duly consulted and long-range satellite forecasts indicated that the rains were to abate within the next seventy-two hours, though arctic and antarctic pole conditions did not suggest any break in generally overcast weather, much less sunny intervals, within the next ten days. Approval to evacuate was withheld but advice on treatment of the respiratory complaints and appropriate medication was dispatched immediately to the Rowan Company's coordinates by the FT&T Prime.

It was early morning when the mudslide began, so high above the plateau on which the Rowan camp stood that it was not detected. A few people were already cautiously abroad, using their assigned hour with a hopper to do necessary errands, to the small infirmary for medicine for their sick, to the commissary for supplies. By the time the instrumentation in Operations registered the incident, it was already too late. The entire western face of the *minta*-clad slope was in motion, like a tsunami of mud, rock, and pulpy vegetation. Those outside saw their fate bearing down on them. Those inside their homes mercifully were unaware. Only one, a child still in the hopper while her mother carried her parcels quickly through the unabating rain to the house, escaped the disaster.

The sturdy little hopper was borne up on the lip of the sludge river, its ovoid shape an advantage, its heavy plastic hull slipping over, under, and along the inexorable slide of heavy, wet mud. Its occupant was bounced about, bruised, and knocked unconscious as the hopper rolled and caught, was freed and carried over a precipice, its fall cushioned by the mud that had preceded it. Nearly a hundred kilometers from the Rowan camp, it became wedged on an outcropping, covered by the vast river of sludge as the slide flowed on until its impetus was dissipated into the long deep Oshoni valley.

The crying began sometime after the mud ceased its downward

flow. A pleading, quavering appeal to a mother who did not answer. An announcement of hunger and hurt, sporadic at first, then increasingly insistent. Abruptly the cry was cut off, and a whimpering took its place, a whimpering which rose in volume and intensity. Was silenced again, during which time everyone with a psi rating of 9 or more experienced relief, for the nondirectional sound grated on the mental ears of the sensitive.

Throughout the settlements of Altair, a search was conducted to discover the injured, abandoned, or abused child whose distress was being broadcast planetwide.

"I've children of my own," the Secretary of the Interior Camella told the Police Commissioner as the Colonial officials met the Governor's office in emergency session, "and that is the cry of a frightened, hurt, hungry child. It's got to be somewhere on Altair."

"We've done street searches, checked the hospital records of any potential psi children born within the last five years . . ." He shook his head over failure. He didn't himself have any Talent but he had a great respect and admiration for those who did.

"The crying pattern, the incoherency, the repetition, suggests an infant of two or three years," said the Chief Medical Officer. "Every sensitive on my staff has been trying to make contact."

"What I don't understand is why it cuts off so suddenly," the Commissioner said, riffling through the reports he'd brought with him to show the extent of the search.

Opened for colonization a scant hundred years before, Altair did not have a large population the present density surrounding Altair Port and City amounted to some five million, two hundred and fifty-three thousand, four hundred and two people. Another one million, seven hundred thousand and eighty-nine people were beginning to carve additional settlements, generally mining concerns exploiting the mineral and ore wealth of the great planet, across the planet's immense main continent.

"Reports are a bit slow coming in from all the Claims," Secretary Camella said, her voice puzzled. "That freak weather pattern is moving eastward towards us. But we must identify the child: Someone this strong so young must be carefully monitored."

Involuntarily she glanced out toward the FT&T installation at the far edge of the Port Space Field. A puff of dust, followed rapidly by half a dozen more, indicated that the incoming freight was being racked up by the kinetic abilities of Altair's major asset, Siglen, the T-1 Prime. Her mental kinesis augmented by a gestalt with the powerful generators that encircled her installation, Siglen could pick up messages from as far away as Earth and Betelgeuse, could locate and land freight drones as easily as others lifted the ordinary artifacts of everyday living.

Mankind's exploration of Space had become feasible because the major psionic Talents of telepaths and teleporting kinetics were able to span the vast intersystem distances, providing reliable and instantaneous communication between Earth and its colonies. Without the Primes in their tower stations, constantly in mental communication with other Primes, able in the gestalt to shift both export and import materiel, the Nine-Star League would have been impossible. The Primes were the kingpins of the system. And such Talents were rare.

Without the Federal Telepath and Teleport network, Mankind would still be trying to reach its nearest spatial neighbors. The Earth Government, once a centralized, worldwide authority had finally been achieved, had ordained an irrevocable autonomy to FT&T, thus ensuring not only its impartiality but its effectiveness in keeping contact with the now far-flung colonies of Mankind. When the Nine-Star League had been formed, it had ratified that autonomy so that no one Star System could ever hope to control FT&T, and with it, the League.

Most communities took pride in the number and variety of Talents among their inhabitants. The fear and distrust of paranormal abilities had been submerged by the obvious benefits of employing Talented folk. There were, of course, many degrees of Talent, with micro- and macro-applications. Naturally, the stronger Talents were the most visible and the rarest. The strongest in each area of expertise were accorded the title of "Prime." The rarest of Primes were those who combined telepathic and kinetic abilities and became the main link between Earth and the planet on which they served.

"We may well be witnessing the emergence of a Prime!" Interior couldn't quite stifle that burgeoning hope and the somewhat vain dream that this new Talent might eclipse Siglen. She might be Altair's greatest asset but a prickly one. Camella had to deal with her and found no joy in that aspect of her duties. Her predecessor, now happily fishing in the eastward foothills, had christened Siglen "the space stevedore," an epithet which Interior tried very hard to forget in Siglen's more trying moments.

For Altair to have produced a Prime Talent so soon would be most prestigious. If the child's potential was properly developed, and the strength inherent in its manifestation augured well, Altair would attract the best sort of colonist, hoping that something in the atmosphere of the planet nurtured Talent. (No one had ever proved that connection. Or disproved it.)

Altair had been fortunate enough to have a reasonable range of

Talents in the original complement of settlers: precognitives; clairvoyants; "finders" with strong metal and mineral affinities who had discovered the high-assay ores and useful minerals, increasing Altair's exports; the usual range of minor kinetics, macro and micro who could shift, connect or manipulate things; a good range of the healing Talents, though no Primes yet, in the medical field, and the more ordinary empaths who were invaluable in any sort of employment which might generate boredom or minor dissension. Empaths and precogs were also members of the Constabulary arm of Civil Government, not that there was much criminal activity on Altair: people were generally far too occupied in carving out their personal bailiwicks on Altair's broad and fertile acres, or exhuming its hidden treasures. The planet was too new to have developed the "civilized" crimes of densely populated and deprived urban areas.

Altair was lucky in its spatial position in the Nine-Star League and, because it was central to several new colonial ventures, had been one of the first colonies to receive a full Federal Telepath and Telekinetic Station with a Prime telepathic kinetic, Siglen. That advantage had greatly boosted Altair's appeal to both individuals and industrial concerns. To have developed a Prime Talent would fill the Governmental cup to overflowing. So the Secretary of the Interior turned to the Medical Officer.

"That's all well and good, but first we have to have the child," the Medical Officer said, voicing her very thought though the man was unTalented. Then he cleared his throat testily. "My advisors suggest that the child is injured—yet there's been no report anywhere in the medical system of a wounded or shocked infant victim."

"Demonstrably there IS one," the Governor said, bringing his fist down on the table. "We'll find it, and know why an infant was allowed to cry so long without attention. New lives are the most valuable resource this planet has. Not one should be squandered . . ."

A wail, a piteous, mind-scoring wail cut through his rhetoric. *MOMMEEEEE! MOMMEEE! MOMMEEE, WHERE ARE* . . . The plaint was abruptly severed.

In the ensuing silence, the Secretary pressed careful fingers against temples which still reverberated from that mental shriek. The most perfunctory of knocks was made at the Council Chamber door which opened to admit an anxious administrative assistant.

"Secretary, Siglen wishes urgent communication with you."

Interior exhaled in relief. Siglen could as easily have inserted her message into Interior's mind but the Prime was a stickler for protocol—for which the Secretary now blessed her.

"Of course!"

The screens all around the Council room came on, lending considerable immediacy to this event. Siglen made few demands on the Council. Now, as the angry woman stared out at them, her eyes seemed to penetrate deep into the thoughts of each of those present. Siglen was a slab of a female, soft from a sedentary life and a disinclination to exercise of any kind. She was in her Operations room, the hum of the gestalt generators a background noise.

"Interior, you are to find that child wherever she is, and discover who has abandoned her and deal with them to the full extent of the law." She had large eyes, her best feature, and they were wide with indignation and frustration. "No child should be allowed to broadcast on such a level. I cannot keep interrupting my flow of work to deal with what is clearly a parent's responsibility."

"Prime Siglen, it is fortunate that you are free to contact us . . ."

"I'm not at all free. I'm falling behind on today's shipments . . ." She gestured impatiently behind her. "That simply is not good enough. Find that child. I can't waste time silencing her."

Interior muttered something dire under her breath but composed her expression, and sank her thoughts. "We were about to ask you to help us find . . ."

Siglen's indignant expression interrupted her. "I? . . . assist . . . in finding a child? I assure you I am no clairvoyant. I will endeavor to keep her *quiet* enough to allow me to discharge my duties to this planet and the service to which I have committed my life. Buy *you* . . ." and a bejeweled finger, its tip enlarged by perspective so that the whorl pattern was clearly visible, "will locate that appallingly bad-mannered infant!"

The contact was abruptly cut. The child began to whimper and that was also abruptly cut.

"If she keeps shutting the child up, how are we going to find her?" Interior asked sourly. "You've had your clairvoyants on it, haven't you?" she asked the Commissioner.

"Indeed I have, but you know as well as I do," he replied somewhat defensively, "that a clairvoyant requires 'something' on which to focus."

"Yegrani didn't," the Medic said ruefully.

"Yegrani's been dead for years," Interior said with real regret and then caught a look on the Commissioner's face.

The wail began again, piteous, gasping, begging for help. They could hear it falter, pick up again with an overtone of outrage.

"Ha! Siglen's met her match. She can't silence the brat."

"It's not a brat," Interior said, "it's a frightened child and it needs all the help we can muster. Look, these days children are simply not left alone for . . ." she checked the digital on the wall, ". . . days. There has to have been an accident. You have no reports of any in Port or City, let's concentrate on the Claims. There are quite a few isolate mining settlements on this planet where a child might be left alone. Don't we have reports of an unseasonal rain in the west?"

"Five thousand miles is a long way to 'throw' a mental cry," the Governor remarked, then looked startled at what his own words implied. "My word!"

"Indeed there could have been an accident. Earthquake, or flood perhaps with the recent appalling rainfall." Interior rose resolutely, nodding courteously to the Governor. "We have the resources, people—let's use them."

As they all left the chamber for their own offices, Interior caught the Commissioner's arm.

"Well? Is Yegrani still alive somewhere?" Being careful to check that no one had heard her or paid them any particular attention in the general departure, he gave her an almost imperceptible nod. "Surely she would help us save a young life?"

"Under the circumstances, she might very well, but she's outlived Methuselah by another lifetime and hasn't much strength. We'd best try to narrow the search down to one area."

That took less than an hour once every element of civil service became involved. First satellite pix were reviewed and the 150 kilometer-long swathe of destruction could not be mistaken. Interior herself phoned the industrial concern which had laid claim to that section. They were swift to open records to the Incident inquiry. They had not heard from the mine manager and were beginning to be concerned.

"Not concerned enough to send us an alert, I notice," Interior remarked caustically. Then she turned to the Commissioner. "What I don't understand is why you didn't have a registered precog on this disaster."

"It isn't what could be called a gross personnel disaster," he replied with a look of chagrin. "I mean, I know a substantial number of people have obviously lost their lives but their deaths don't affect all Altair in a knock-on situation. Unfortunately. Then, too, most of our precogs have urban affinities," he added apologetically.

"I think I'll introduce a fine for companies that do not keep in twenty-four contact with their field installations," muttered Interior, jotting down a note in capital italics.

"Say again?"

"Look!" she said as the Company's personnel files scrolled past.

"Fifteen kids between the ages of one month and five years. How much detail does your clairvoyant need?"

"I don't even know if she'll help us," the Commissioner said ruefully. "She hasn't opened a connection to my calls."

The crying started up again, was cut off, and continued with a desperate edge to the wail.

"That child is growing weaker," the Medic exclaimed as he barreled into the Incident room. "If she's buried in a mudslide, she's got no food or water—and maybe not much air left."

The printer murmured to itself, smoothly extruding new copy. Interior bent over it, groaning with a note of despair in her voice.

"I ordered a comparison survey of the terrain before and after the slide. There're ravines fifty-meters deep now with mud and debris. The slide is sixty-klicks wide in places. If she's buried in any depth of mud, she'll be asphyxiated soon. Particularly if she keeps crying like this, using up her oxygen."

The Commissioner moved to a console, gesturing for the others to step back. "I'm adding a Mayday to her private code but whether she'll answer or not . . ."

"Yes?" The guttural voice dwelt on the sibilant. No picture appeared on the screen.

"Have you heard the crying?"

"Who hasn't? I could have told you Siglen wouldn't help. It's beyond her capabilities. Bouncing parcels from place to place requires no finesse, since the gestalt does all the work."

As there was no visual contact, the Commissioner rolled his eyes at the bite in Yegrani's tone. For years, there had been enmity between the telekinetic and the clairvoyant, though the Commissioner happened to know the original fault was more of Siglen's making than Yegrani's.

"There is a fear that the child is running out of air, Yegrani. The mud is fifty-meters deep in places along a 150-klick swathe. We've plenty of . . ."

"Look to the left above the Oshoni valley, on a ledge, approximately two klicks from the tongue of mud. She's not deeply entrenched but the hopper skin has been fractured and sludge is oozing in. She is frantic. Siglen has done nothing to reassure the child as a sensitive, caring person would have done. Guard this one well. She has a long and lonely road to go before she travels. But she alone will be the focus that will save us from a far greater disaster than the one she has escaped. Especially guard the guardian."

The connection severed but as soon as Yegrani had "sighted" the child's position, the Secretary of the Interior had forwarded a printout of the conversation to the rescue teams, waiting in their special vehicles. The Governor himself requested the launch and gave Altair's Prime the coordinates. She did not ask how they had been obtained but faultlessly sent the mission speeding to its destination.

"Did she mean 'left' looking at the bloody thing, on *its* left?" demanded the captain as the rescue team emerged after their journey. Their shells had slid to a halt on the valley floor, just where the outthrusting "tongue" of mud ended. "Phaugh!" he pinched his nostrils, "the stench of *minta*'s enough to choke you! Lemme see that geo print."

"The ledge should be there!" his second in command exclaimed, pointing to their right. "Solid ground, too, from which to work."

"Get the two klick fix," the captain ordered, pointing to the scan operator. "Stay off that mud! Anyone who falls in has to walk home."

The team scrambled to the stone outthrust above the ledge and brought their detectors to bear in careful sweeps. An intrusion was detected approximately ten meters out in the mud. The medic extended his sensitive equipment and caught vital signs. The digger boom was rigged and swung out. Two volunteers, on cables linked to the boom, descended into the ooze above the point of detection and began to shovel the muck away. As fast as they shoveled, the uncooperative sludge slid back in.

"I want that suction tube and now!" cried the captain, inwardly well satisfied with the instant obedience to that order.

The hopper, wedged onto the outcropping, was not deep and once a large enough surface was cleared, the tractor beam was attached. It fought the suction of the mud while the shovel team worked with desperate speed, muttering about kinetics never being where you needed them. Suddenly sufficient air got under the hopper to break the seal, and only the quick reflexes of those on the bank kept the craft from colliding forcefully with the tractor arm. The little vehicle swung and bumped about before finally settling to solid ground.

Mud sheeted off the hull and oozed from the fracture, as the entire team watched anxiously. How much of that stuff had seeped into the interior? Everyone was immensely relieved to hear a thin, tremulous cry, mental and physical. As one, the team attacked the battered door to wrench it open.

"Mommie?" A tattered, bruised, mud-encased child crawled to the threshold, sobbing with relief, squinting in the sudden daylight. "Mommie?"

The team medic leapt forward, radiating reassurance and love. "It's all over, honey. You're safe. We've got you safe." She pressed the hypno spray to a muddied arm before the child could realize that her parents were not among those clustered around the hopper. At that, the sedative was not quite fast enough to allay the anguished mental yowl which all Altair heard from the orphaned Rowan child.

"We've done as much as we can," the Chief Medical Officer said in a slightly defensive tone.

"We know you have," Interior replied, radiating all the approval she could project.

"The fact remains that the Rowan child is not cooperating," the Governor remarked with a rueful sigh.

"It's only ten days since the tragedy," Interior added.

"And there are definitely no relatives to take charge of her?" the Governor asked.

Interior consulted her records. "We have the choice of eleven parents of similar genotype because many of the miners were from the same ethnic background. The Company headquarters did not keep backup files of the infirmary records, so we don't even know how many children have been born since the camp was established ten years ago. So, no immediate relatives. There are doubtless some back on Earth."

The Governor cleared his throat. "Earth has more high-ranking Talents than any other planet."

"We do indeed need to guard our natural resources," Interior replied with a slight smile.

"Let it be noted and so stipulated in the records of this meeting that the . . . Rowan child," he had paused for someone to supply a name, "is henceforth a Ward of the Planet Altair 4. Now what?" and he turned to Interior.

"Well, she can't stay indefinitely in the Pediatrics Ward," she replied and turned to the Chief Medical Officer.

"My chief therapist says she's basically recovered from shock. The lacerations and hematoma sustained in the slide have healed. She has also managed to block all memory of the disaster but she can't quite delete the fact that the child had parents, and possibly siblings." He nodded as the others murmured against more repressive measures. "But . . ." and he spread his hands, "she is parentless, and although the T-8 junior therapist has managed to . . . to deal with the general telepathic 'noise,' the child's control is limited and her span of concentration woefully short."

Everyone grimaced, for the entire planet was still favored with outbursts from the Rowan child.

"Does she receive as well as broadcast?" the Governor finally asked.

The Medic shrugged. "She must or she wouldn't hear Siglen."

"Now that is something that has to be stopped," Interior said, setting her lips in a firm line before she went on. "Slapping the child down for perfectly normal . . ."

"If loud," the Governor amended.

". . . exuberance—which you must admit is a welcome change from the crying—is going to inhibit what Talent the child has," Interior went on. "Siglen may be a Prime T&T but she doesn't possess a single neuron of empathy, and her insensitivity to the child's situation borders on the callous."

"Siglen may have no empathy," the Governor said, a thoughtful look filming his gaze, "but she has great pride in her profession and she has already trained two Primes to their current responsibilities at Betelgeuse and Capella." Someone grunted cynically. "She's the most logical person in this system to undertake the Rowan child's education."

"She's been made a Ward of Altair," Interior stated, sitting erect with opposition, "and no one's likely to contend that. She'd have more kindly treatment on Earth at the Center. They'd care about her. I vote we send her there. And as soon as possible."

Lusena had the task of explaining it all to the Rowan child. The T-8 had been working steadily with her, playing games to get her to speak with her physical voice, rather than her mental one. Once the child was recovered from the physical effects and the sedative dosage had been reduced, Lusena had taken her to select a pukha toy from the hospital's supply.

Pukhas, deriving their name from the imaginary companion discovered by needful children, had become widely used in pediatrics. They could be programmed for a variety of uses, but more often were used in surgical and long-term care with great effect and as surrogates for intense dependency cases. The Rowan child needed her own pukha. Considerable thought had been given to its programming: its long soft hair was composed of receptors, monitoring the child's physical and psychic health. It could, receiving danger signals from the Rowan, initiate pacifying sentiments, encourage conversation and, of paramount importance, moderate the little girl's mental "voice." It also responded with its soothing, rumbling purr when the little girl became restless or distressed. Although Lusena and the pediatrics staff would adjust the pukha's programs throughout its usefulness, every sensitive on Altair knew when the Rowan christened it "Purza." Her silvery laughter was a great improvement over whimpering, and almost everyone was sympathetic to the little orphan.

Siglen's personal assistant, Bralla, a T-4 empath, certainly was and did her best to soothe her mistress—who could, Bralla had admitted to the stationmaster, be more juvenile at times than the Rowan child.

"Siglen might benefit by having a pukha herself," Bralla told the stationmaster, for Siglen had been extremely irascible when the Rowan child's babble intruded on her concentration.

Gerolaman snorted. "The kind of cuddling she wants she'll never get." And snorted again as Bralla frantically signaled him to guard his sentiments.

"She's really not a *bad* person, Gerolaman. Just . . ."

"Far too accustomed to being THE most important person on the planet. She doesn't like competition, not no way, no how. You remember that dustup with Yegrani?"

"Gerolaman, she's not deaf!" Bralla rose, "She's about to need me. See you later."

Purza was not always the key to exemplary behavior for a three-year-old. Siglen's intolerance, even with Bralla's discreet assistance, fell all too frequently on the Rowan child. Finally, the Secretary of Interior decided that someone had to do something about Siglen, and it was going to give her intense personal and official satisfaction to do so.

"Prime Siglen, a matter of urgent importance," Interior said as soon as the T-1 came on screen. "We have been able to divert a passenger ship tomorrow to collect the Rowan child."

"Collect her?" Siglen blinked in astonishment.

"Yes, we shall get her out of your hair by noon, so you will kindly see that her remaining hours on Altair are not punctuated by your reprimands."

"Remaining hours on Altair? You must be insane!" Siglen's eyes widened with shock and horror, and her fingers stopped fondling her sea-jewel necklace. "You can't expose a child . . . a mere infant . . . to such a trauma."

"It seems the wisest course," Interior replied grimly, shielding the real reason.

"But she *can't* go. She's Prime potential . . ." Siglen stammered, her complexion ashen. She released her necklace to grip the edge of the console. "She'll . . . she'll die! You know as well as I do," and Siglen's words crowded each other out of her mouth, "what happens to the truly Talented in space . . . I mean, look at how ill David became. Remember how devastated Capella was. To subject an infant . . . of unknown potential . . . to such mind-destroying trauma! Why, you must be mad, Interior. You cannot! I will not permit it!"

"Well, you're not permitting the child to exercise her Talent. She'll get expert attention and training on Earth at the Center."

"You'd abandon that child of Altair, you'd send her away from kith and kin . . ."

"She doesn't have any on Altair," Interior heard herself saying, and then realized that Siglen was about to launch into one of her attitudes. "Prime Siglen, it is the order of the Council that the Ward of Altair be transported to the Earth Center—with your well-known delicacy of kinesis —on the passenger ship which has been diverted to Altair for that purpose. Good day to you!"

As soon as the image on the screen was erased, Interior turned to the Medic and Lusena. "I'd've thought she'd flip the kid out to the ship without its having to land!"

"Is there any foundation in what she said about David of Betelgeuse and Capella?" asked the Medic frowning. He'd been a minor medical administrator ten years ago and not privy to details of that period.

"Well, none of the Primes travel well, and none of them ever teleport themselves any great distance," Interior replied thoughtfully. "But the Rowan child will be a lot better off away from Siglen's sort of discipline."

"I'll just get back," Lusena said, rising and looking apprehensive. "She was napping but I'd hate for her to wake up and find me gone."

"You've done marvels with her, Lusena," Interior said warmly. "You'll find a tangible reward from the Council when you've delivered her safely to Earth."

"She's a taking little thing, really," Lusena said, smiling with affection.

"A bit odd-looking with that whitened hair and those enormous brown eyes in that thin face," and the Medic looked uncomfortable.

"Gorgeous eyes, lovely features," Interior said hastily to cancel Lusena's dismay at the Medic's blunt description. "And you'll be all right with her tomorrow?"

"I think the less fuss made the better," Lusena replied.

All the fuss the next day was due entirely to the Rowan child's total reluctance to enter the passenger vessel. She took one look at the portal of the ship and dug her heels in, literally and mentally. From her mind came a single high note of abject terror. From her lips a monotonous "no, no, no, no, no." Purza, clutched so tightly around its middle that Lusena feared for some of its programming, was purring in loud response to the little girl's distress.

"Sedation?" the ship's medical officer suggested to the distraught Lusena, who vainly tried to persuade her charge that no danger existed on this ship.

"We might have to keep her sedated the entire trip," Lusena murmured. "Even the most intensive therapy does not seem to have significantly reduced her trauma. It's entering a ship that's upset her so. Not that I blame her."

One moment she had her arms wrapped about the struggling body, the next moment the Rowan child had disappeared, even the pukha discarded in her haste.

"Oh, my word, where can she have gone?" Lusena cried in panic.

I warned you, came the ominous voice of Siglen. *The child shouldn't leave Altair.*

Lusena's attention was caught by Siglen's phraseology, mindful of Yegrani's clairvoyance. 'She has a long and lonely road to go before she travels.' "Oh, lords above," Lusena murmured, her sympathies entirely with the child.

Nor will you force such a young and powerful mind to leave the planet of her birth, Siglen intoned. Then she added, sounding almost sympathetic, *especially as she has just proved that she is telekinetic as well as telepathic.*

"But that child has got to receive proper training," Lusena cried, suddenly fearful for her.

And I, mindful of my responsibility to my Talent and to preserve this planet's resources, will undertake her education.

"Not if you treat that child the way you have been, Siglen," Lusena cried, startling the people on the boarding way as she waved her fist in the air.

There was an audible pause, a thickening of the air about the small group, a palpable silence.

She has been a very naughty, badly behaved little girl, was the somewhat chastened reply. *She must learn manners if she is to be my pupil. But I will not have her terrified out of her mind by traveling in space. You will be reassigned as her companion, Lusena.*

"Guard the guardian," Yegrani had said. Lusena had not had the slightest notion that events would conspire to appoint her to that gratuitous position. She sighed but, when Secretary Camella implored her to be the Rowan's nursemaid, she agreed. She genuinely cared for the little orphan who needed a staunch friend to deal with the stresses and tensions which Lusena could foresee without a vestige of clairvoyance in her Talent.

Go and collect her from your room in the hospital, Siglen told her, but rather more politely than she usually delivered orders. *That seems to be the only place she knew to go.*

"I'll collect her," Lusena said, scooping up the pukha. "But you had better be kind to her. Don't you dare be anything but kind to her, Siglen of Altair!"

Of course, I will be kind to her, Siglen said, chidingly. *What is her name?*

"She calls herself," and Lusena paused significantly, "the Rowan." She felt the slightest resistance and opened her mouth to retort.

She'll find something else more suitable when she has been in my Tower awhile, was the soothing answer. *Kindly bring the Rowan to me now, Lusena. She is weeping on a very broad band.*

In point of fact, the Rowan child did not take up residence at Siglen's Tower for nearly nine years. Lusena had two children of her own —a girl nine and a boy fourteen with minor but valid Talents. Lusena urged the Secretary of the Interior to let her keep the Rowan at home, taking a temporary leave of absence from the Port Hospital. It was a pleasant enough house which was, as most Talent residences were, already shielded. Lusena distrusted Siglen for no reason she was ever able to articulate so she accepted, even encouraged the procrastination for a variety of excuses: hers and Siglen's.

"The child isn't really settled yet after that fright." "She's just getting over a cold." "I'd hate to disturb her just yet, she's integrating so well with her play group." "Her current teaching program ought not to be interrupted." "She would miss the support and companionship of Bardy and Finnan. Next year."

Siglen never protested too hard: adding her own delays. There would have to be a suitable apartment for her student, as she felt the child would be more comfortable away from the busy-ness of the Tower and all the bustle of her support staff coming and going. When Interior ordered plans to be drawn up for the facility, Siglen found exception with each submission, sending the plans back for minute revisions. The exchanges continued for nearly two years before the foundations were laid.

Meanwhile the Rowan became integrated into Lusena's family, for Bardy, the daughter, and Finnan, the son, were old enough to be kind and naturally caring of the waif. The Rowan played with non-Talented children her own age in a specially supervised group and learned NOT to manipulate her peers. Most of them were so "deaf" they were unaware of her subconscious attempts to control them. Their unawareness also resulted in making the Rowan vocalize in their presence. Toward the end of that first year, the Rowan would occasionally prop Purza on the sidelines of particularly active games but otherwise the pukha was within fingertip reach. Three times the feline had to be peeled from the sleeping child to replace its furry covering, worn or damaged receptors, and to update its programming.

Siglen did keep her promise about not suppressing the Rowan, though she sent pointed enough reminders that she was keeping her word and that Lusena and the others had best see to it that the Rowan did not distract her. As the Rowan matured, outbursts diminished. Gradually, Purza spent more and more time on a shelf in her room, but was always on the pillow beside the Rowan at night.

On the day that the Rowan finally came to live with the Prime, she did not appear to be in awe of Siglen. She clutched Purza tighter to her side as the Prime towered above her, smiling in the fatuous way of someone unaccustomed to young persons. Secretary Camella of Interior, who had driven Lusena and the Rowan to the Tower in her own vehicle, wanted to strangle Siglen.

"Aren't we a little old to be dependent on a stuffed animal?" Siglen asked.

"Purza is a pukha and she's been mine a long time," the Rowan answered, hefting the pukha behind her in a proprietary way.

Both Lusena and Interior tried to warn Siglen, but the woman was concentrating with formidable intent on the Rowan. Lusena caught Bralla's eye and the woman raised her eyebrows in a despairing arc. But she stepped forward.

"Siglen, do show the child the quarters you have arranged for her. I'm sure she'd like to get settled."

Siglen flapped one beringed hand to silence Bralla.

"A pukha?"

"A specially programmed stabilizing surrogate device," the Rowan explained. "It's not a stuffed toy."

"But you are twelve now. Surely too grown-up to need that sort of infantile pacifier."

The Rowan was polite—Lusena had drilled her in courtesies, vocal and mental—but she could be as stubborn as Siglen, though she would never be as insensitive.

"When I no longer need Purza, I will know." Then she adroitly added, "I really would like to see my room." And the Rowan smiled hopefully. She had a particularly endearing smile and harder hearts than Siglen's had been beguiled by it.

"Room?" Siglen was affronted. "Why, you have an entire wing to yourself. With every amenity that I myself enjoy. State of the art, as well, though some of my equipment will soon need replacement." She gave Interior a pointed glance. Then she led the way, heaving herself from side to side in a most remarkable gait. Siglen was quite tall, dwarfing the slender child beside her. Nine years had added more soft flesh although the increase was not apparent with the sort of loose garments she wore. But it showed when she moved, making an effort of even a short walk.

Interior mused that Siglen was putting herself out in this initial contact and hoped that the child, who displayed considerable empathy, would be responsive. As she fell in step with Lusena and Bralla, she was uncomfortably aware of the ludicrous comparison between the rake-thin Rowan and the massive Siglen and hastily recited a mind-clogging nonsense verse. Hopefully, Siglen was too busy impressing the child with her generosity—all paid for by the Treasury—to hear peripheral thoughts. Neither Siglen or the Rowan had communicated on a telepathic level, but then it had been drilled into the Rowan that, vis-a-vis, she must use voice address.

"You will report to me daily now, between 10:00 and 14:00 for instruction. I have had a special room added to my Tower where you can observe without interfering in the daily routine. It is most important . . . what is your name, child?"

"The Rowan. That's what everyone calls me," and Lusena knew that the girl had picked up Siglen's not so carefully concealed disapproval, "the Rowan child. My name is therefore the Rowan."

"But surely you know what name your parents gave you? You were old enough at three to know your own name, for goodness' sake."

"I forgot it!" And the Rowan made that a positive enough termination of such questions that Siglen was taken slightly aback.

"Well, well, well!" She repeated that word a few more times before they all reached the entrance to the Rowan's wing.

The Rowan's startlement was apparent in her rigid posture as she peered through the door panel Siglen opened. Interior and Lusena hurried up and were equally stunned.

The entrance hall was grand—that was the only word for it, with hidden lighting to emphasize its opulence, the formal, rigid chairs made of exquisite woods, the equally fragile tables set with either statuary or arrangements of static flowers, picked at the moment of bloom perfection and held eternally at their peak. Walking carefully across the intricately mosaic floor, the amazed trio entered the reception room, its walls adorned by the sort of gaudy, big floral print that Siglen preferred. The room, which would have been spacious if it had not been so cluttered, was crammed with twisted-ware stools, two- and three-seat couches, arranged in conversational groupings: tables set everywhere, squatting in corners, nestled against the couches, their surfaces and shelves filled with what looked like Interstellar Bazaar items, some undoubtedly valuable enough, Interior thought, but none of it the sort of furnishing or adornment suitable to a young girl. The walls were hung with artwork from every star system, judging by the variety of styles and mediums, but crowded frame to frame so that the eye could not fasten on anything. Down one corridor was a small kitchen, an ornately claustrophic dining area, and two guest bedrooms en suite. Down the other was an almost barren "library" with shelves and worktops, and a swimming pool, plasglassed, far too shallow for an active and accomplished swimmer like the Rowan.

With a final flourish and in anticipation of effusive praise, Siglen waved her large hand across the admit-panel of the bedroom she had created for the Rowan: a yellow-and-peach confection box of frills, doodads, and so many embellishments the necessary pieces of furniture were disguised.

"Well?" Siglen demanded of the Rowan, having taken the silence for amazement but needing some verbal gratification.

"It is the most incredible apartment, Prime Siglen," the Rowan said, turning slowly around and clutching Purza to her breast. Her eyes were wide, glittering with an emotion that Lusena hoped the child could contain. The Rowan swallowed noticeably but managed to say clearly, "I appreciate all your efforts. This is worth waiting for. Really, you have been extremely generous. It is all too much!"

Lusena shot the Rowan an alarmed shaft of appeal, hoping the girl would stop there. Twelve-year-olds are not the most tactful creatures. The Rowan was avoiding Lusena's eyes. Indeed she kept looking around her, as one item after another caught her attention. Lusena was counting heavily on the Rowan's empathy.

"You have been exceedingly thoughtful and kind," the Rowan went on and approached a low bed, smothered in bright satin pillows, some of which colors clashed with the yellow and peach of wall, carpet, and furnishings. She rearranged one pillow and planted Purza on it. "We shall be immensely comfortable here, won't we, Purza?"

Thus addressed, the pukha whirled and made a sound that was certainly not a purr, definitely a comment. Eyes dancing with mischief and suppressed laughter, the Rowan swiveled to Lusena. "I think the power strands need replacing. That's no purr!"

At once Lusena and the Secretary of the Interior distracted Siglen, who looked about to say more on the subject of dispensing with the pukha, by effusively complimenting her on the magnificence of these quarters, so much time spent on thoughtful details, and where did Siglen manage to find so many unusual things.

Just then, a porter brought in the trolley containing the Rowan's effects, two carryalls, and five cartons of books and educational disks.

"Ah, are these all you have?" Siglen asked in a disparaging tone, glancing accusingly first at Lusena and then at Secretary Camella.

"The Rowan was awarded an adequate stipend above and beyond her living expenses but she doesn't make use of it," Camella said defensively.

"She isn't an acquisitive child," Lusena said at the same time.

Siglen made a noncommittal noise. "I shall leave you to get settled."

She patted the Rowan on the head and turned, so she did not see the expression on the girl's face although both Lusena and Interior did. Lusena moved to the girl and Interior thought she'd better make certain that Siglen left before the Rowan exploded. Hastily, she closed the bedroom door behind her.

When Interior got back, the Rowan was howling with laughter, rolling on the bed, clutching a now purring Purza in her arms. Most of the satin pillows had fallen to the floor. Lusena was collapsed on a chair, tears of laughter streaming down her face. Secretary Camella, who had expected rather a different scene, sank to another chair, grinning with relief.

"I simply don't believe that woman," Lusena finally managed to gasp. "This . . . this bordello ambience . . . is suitable for a twelve-year-old girl?"

"Don't worry, Rowan," Interior promised, "you can sleep in the library until we clear out this . . . this . . . bazaarity."

Waving one hand in agreement, the Rowan continued to burble.

"Well, at least you can see the amusing side of it," Interior added and could not resist chuckling, too.

"Purza says it wasn't fair of you not to program her to laugh," the Rowan said and kissed her pukha fondly.

Lusena and Interior exchanged startled looks and Lusena mouthed "later" over the child's head.

"Maybe Siglen was right and it's time to remove the pukha," Interior said in a low voice to Lusena while the Rowan had been set to unpacking her booktapes in the library.

"This really IS the first time Rowan has claimed a spontaneous response from it," Lusena said, her fingers fiddling with the cuff of one sleeve. She frowned down at her hands. "At least in my hearing. Of all the freakings!" Lusena was clearly upset. "We gave up monitoring her room a long time ago. She's adapted well: she has no trouble interacting with either the Talented or the normal."

"Start recording again. The child cannot develop any aberrations."

Lusena almost exploded, gesticulating toward the main Tower. "With *that* as an example? I'd say she'll need the pukha now more than ever before!" Abruptly, she subsided. "Perhaps we're borrowing trouble. The pukha could be invaluable now to monitor the Rowan's adjustment to Siglen."

Interior gave a heartfelt moan of sympathy. "Why did I let Siglen talk me into this?"

"Planetary pride?" Lusena asked drolly.

"Probably. Be a dear and, when the Rowan's asleep tonight, rig the pukha for monitoring, will you?" Then Interior looked around her at the incredible array. "And how are we going to get rid of all this?"

"I'll think of something!"

The Rowan anticipated the need. A troubled security guard reported that an empty warehouse in the Port facility appeared to be used as the cache of pilferers, although he couldn't find a single one of the items listed on the stolen property lists published by the Constabulary.

With considerable discernment for a youngster, the Rowan stripped her apartment down to basics, unerringly retaining the most valuable and appropriate of the artifacts. To Lusena's immense surprise, the Rowan had also managed to alter the color of the walls to soft shades of green and cream.

"How'd you repaint?" she casually asked the girl.

"Purza and me thought about it," the Rowan replied with one of her inimitable shrugs. "D'you think it's an improvement?"

"Oh, vast, vast improvement. I didn't realize you knew how to paint."

"That was easy. Purza was in the house the day you had your place done. She remembered."

Lusena managed to nod understandingly. "Well, do you think you're settled in enough now to begin to learn your business?"

The Rowan shrugged. "She's got a mass of pods to shift today. I don't think she'll want me around."

Lusena phoned Interior later, while the Rowan was swimming under the watchful eyes of Purza.

"She has verbalized many things to the pukha over the years," Lusena said slowly. She found it very difficult to understand how she could have overlooked the Rowan's subtly reinforced dependence on the pukha. "Most of it perfectly consonant with the doubts and fears of any normal child. But she AND the Purza personality had a long discussion about color and the mechanics of painting: together they looked up and discussed interior decoration. Purza evidently has considerable acumen on which objcts d'art and paintings are likely to be valuable, and those were the ones they kept. Purza seems to have discovered the empty warehouse although it was clearly the Rowan who did the shifting. I know she has great telekinetic potential and nothing was very heavy or awkward, but she cleared most of the drek overnight. And repainted the next one—with Purza's encouragement. I'll send you a transcript of the conversation—no, it's not a conversation, that takes two intelligences—the monologue with interesting pauses for the Purza contributions."

"Send me the transcript file," Interior said, trying to keep the panic out of her voice, "and I'll set up an in-depth psychiatric study."

"Oh, would you?" Lusena was weak with relief. "This is far beyond anything in my training."

"Now, don't start feeling inadequate on me, Lusena. You've coped magnificently with the child. She's just . . . just . . ."

"One step ahead of us?"

"That's better," Interior said, approving the wry tone of Lusena's voice.

The conversations between the Rowan and her pukha became fascinating auditing for her guardians and any pediatric psychologist granted the privilege of listening.

"Purza, Siglen's silly. I've done that sort of lifting, placing, and putting since I was a baby!" the Rowan was heard to say after her first day's tutelage. "I can't very well tell her I shifted everything out of this apartment, can I? Well, yes, I know, you helped, and even told me where the space was. You're a very clever pukha, you know. How many would have been able to estimate the volume of that warehouse so precisely? There was just space left for an aisle when you'd finished. Yes, they know. The man is supposed to check that the stuff doesn't *leave* the premises but how were you to know that he'd object to having an empty place used? Yes, people are funny about such details. *She* did give them to me so I may dispose of them as I see fit. Oh, you think I should have asked her first? Yes, but asking would have wounded her feelings because she really did think she'd done a marvelous job in the decorating. Only, Purza, how can *I* do good work when she considers me such a baby?"

"Yesterday was bad enough, Purza, a whole day spent making knots of straight lines! But I had to do it all over again today! Yes, actually I thought of doing that, but she was with me every second and when I tried to deviate, she just pulled me back on line and said that I must concentrate harder. Concentrate? Who needs to concentrate on that ol' baby stuff! Did you hear her?" The Rowan then produced such an accurate imitation of Siglen's fruity tones that the clandestine auditors were astonished. " 'We must proceed carefully, step by step, until you become so totally aware of your Talent that its use is instinctive, efficient, and energy-saving.' "

"Energy-saving? I ask you, Purza, with all the energy available on Altair, we could never use it all up. She what? I know history as well as you do. So what if she did grow up on old Earth when their energy sources were stretched to the limit, but we're here! There's unlimited power in just the winds and the tides, not to mention the fossil fuels. . . . Siglen ought to update herself. And if she says 'waste not, want not' one more time, I'm going to puke. It's near as bad as 'Always Be Careful'—ABC—" the Rowan dropped into the devastatingly accurate Siglen voice for the maxims. "And I *am* thrifty." Now the Rowan giggled. "I saved all that awful stuff she crammed into my place. Crabs, Purza, I'm so boooooooooored!"

That complaint became more and more prevalent in the pukha conversations.

Bralla did her best to assist, tactfully mentioning to Siglen that the Rowan showed great application and dexterity with the basic kinetic exercises.

"But then, she has the best of teachers in the entire known galaxy," Bralla had added when she saw Siglen bridle. "Of course she would grasp the basics quickly. You explain things so succinctly even the dullest wit would understand."

It took three days for the notion to be absorbed and then suddenly Siglen began the Rowan's lesson with a new exercise, designed to strengthen her "mental muscles."

"It *is* a nice change," the Rowan confided in Purza that night and then spent time rearranging the furnishings in her apartment with her "mental muscles," "to explain the technique to the pukha."

Gerolaman, the Station manager, took his turn in suggesting more challenging tasks for the Rowan.

"I need a bit of help in Stores, Siglen. It'd take this li'l girl a couple of hours while you're busy with the batch coming in from David. It's more or less what you've been doing with her only more practical because she can't break anything, yet she'll get the practice. Whaddya say?"

"It'd be a thrifty use of my time and energy, Siglen," the Rowan added casually, pretending indifference.

"I dislike interrupting the flow of your lessons, Rowan child," Siglen temporized.

"Same thing, different objects," Gerolaman remarked as if he couldn't care less. And the Rowan was excused to his care. "You're a clever one," he told her when they were on their way to Stores. "Good shot Siglen's not got an ounce of empathy: You were leaking a little of what you felt in there and that's not good."

"I was?"

"You're getting careless. Don't! Siglen's got faults, the Good knows that, and we all suffer from them from time to time. The main thrust of her Talent is the gestalt. Most of us here," and his gesture took in the entire Station, "can bounce things from a place we can see to a place we know about. But she can juggle objects she can't see and get them where they're supposed to go even if she's never been there. Nor likely to go. So you study her, Rowan, and get to hear underneath what she says. Lusena says you've a high empathy rating. Let it work *for* you. I don't say you should attempt to manipulate her moods but you could sort of ease her along now and then and she wouldn't get suspicious. That way," and Gerolaman gave her a shrewd sideways glance, "you won't get so bored, working several levels in that white head of yours." He ruffled her hair affectionately.

For some reason that casual caress had more effect on the Rowan than Gerolaman's spoken advice.

"He touched me, Purza. He put his hand on my hair and messed it up, just like Finnan does. That must mean he likes me. Is it because he understands Talents? . . . Oh, he's not a pervert, silly Purz. It *wasn't* that sort of a touch. I'd recognize the slimy kind from what Bardy told me. Gerolaman's got children of his own. He treats me like one of them, Purza. Fatherly. It would be nice to have a father, Purz."

Gerolaman was instructed to act as paternally as circumstances permitted.

"But she's a Prime Talent!" Gerolaman had replied, surprised, pleased, and nervous. "I can't just treat her like I do *my* daughter."

"That," Lusena said firmly, "is exactly what she needs! A little fatherly affection! Bardy and Finnan had their father during their early childhood. Rowan's never had a father figure. Since she has now realized it, we must provide a suitable substitute and you're it, Gerolaman!"

"Sure I'll do what I can. The Good knows she'll get no love and affection from the Prime."

Gerolaman often prevailed on Siglen to lend him the Rowan for more "muscle" exercise. These tended to be dispatched quickly enough so that the Rowan would have time to have a snack or "tea" in Gerolaman's office. On those occasions, he would explain other aspects of the Tower responsibilities, its administration, how cargo was routed from one Prime station to another, the "windows" to other systems and moons, how to connect with mid-space drone shipments, the major mid-points all around the Central Worlds' sphere of business and colonization. In a relaxed atmosphere, she developed the spatial sense she would require when, if she came into Prime status, she would need to know how to scan the instrumentation in the Tower that kept track of all matter in the Altairian sector of the galaxy. She learned to appreciate and how to adroitly assist the lesser kinetic Talents who did not have the gestalt faculty but nevertheless handled the traffic of message capsules constantly shunted about the Nine-Star League.

Gerolaman would often take her out of the Tower and into the freight yards so that she became familiar with the variety of carriers, freight pods, drone vehicles, specialized cargo carriers for live or inanimate freight. He took her on inspection tours of the powered ships from scout vessels and shuttles to the great passenger and immense bulky freight containers. He had her memorize the major trade routes and lines, the space stations and other Nine-Star League facilities until she knew the furniture of space as well as the things in her own quarters.

"You should know every aspect of this business," Gerolaman said, "not just how to sit in that Tower couch and bitch when there's an equipment failure."

There had been one recently and Gerolaman had borne the brunt of Siglen's outrage and fury, for she felt that she would be held responsible for a failure that interrupted the smooth function of Altair's FT&T Station. The Rowan had been in his office when the Number 3 Generator had overheated and started shedding parts. She had seen how quickly Gerolaman had patched in the spare and then ordered an investigation of the accident. When it appeared that poor grade oils had been at fault, he canceled the supplier's contract and took tenders for a new source. That morning provided the Rowan with a new insight into her own problems with the Prime. The next day provided yet another. A T-8 stormed into Gerolaman's office, threatening to resign and leave Altair altogether to get away from "that woman": Siglen had taken out her frustration with the brief lapse of service on the first person to irritate her.

"I didn't realize, Purza, that others have problems with Siglen," the Rowan told the pukha that night. "I made myself as small as I could and I don't think the T-8 even saw me. I liked the way Gerolaman talked to Macey, kindly like, as if he was as deeply hurt as she was. He got her an accommodation at Favor Bay for a week off, though her annual holiday is not for another three months. I wonder if we get holidays. It'd be nice to get away from the Tower for a while. Lusena used to take us all on trips when I lived with her."

Lusena, Gerolaman, Bralla, and Interior put their heads together to figure out how they could grant that wistful desire.

"I didn't realize so much time has passed but the Rowan's been here for two years," Interior remarked. "Everyone gets holiday time."

"Except Siglen," Gerolaman said gloomily. " 'And who could possibly take over if I went on vacation'?" Gerolaman's falsetto was a poor imitation of Siglen's fruity tones. "Even I get away. Maybe that'd be the answer. Siglen might give her leave of absence if I promised to keep up her exercises. My family's got a nice cabin in the woods . . ."

"No woods," Lusena interrupted, holding up a warning hand. "For the Rowan, mountain and forest might be traumatic. I always kept to the plains and the seaside when she vacationed with us."

"Well, then," Interior began briskly, "there's a Cabinet guesthouse, spacious, but not too grand, which can be made available to her. At this time of year, there aren't all that many vacationers at Favor Bay." She gave Lusena a significant look.

"I'd gladly accompany her," Lusena replied with a long sigh. "I could use the break myself. And I've nieces, my brothers' children, who are the Rowan's age. She's had no peer group contact since she came here and she shouldn't get so far out of touch. She may be Prime material but she's also a young girl and that side of her development shouldn't be neglected as . . ." Lusena tactfully broke off.

"I think a few words in the ear of the Medical Office might produce some results—especially if Bralla," and Interior winked at the woman, "and Gerolaman notice that the Rowan is becoming listless, with no appetite . . . you know the sort of thing that can afflict the overextended youngster, Lusena."

"Indeed I do."

"Ill?" Siglen's eyes enlarged while she also appeared to compress herself. "How is the child ill?" Rarely indisposed herself, Siglen had no patience with sickness.

"Well, as you know, Siglen, girls her age are prone to minor ailments and I do think she's sickening for something," Bralla remarked. "Why, you know yourself that her appetite's been poor these past few days. You might suggest to Lusena to remove her until the symptoms disappear."

"To the infirmary?"

"Well, a full medical check never hurts," Bralla replied. "I'll make arrangements immediately."

So the Rowan was given an official leave to improve her health: Siglen practically ordering her out of the Tower.

Favor Bay was essentially a family resort, with an excellent crescent beach of fine powdery sand: a marina catered to water sport enthusiasts and the bright, clear water encouraged them. There was also a small fair with a mechanical amusement park and an aquarium situated on the northern tip of Favor Bay's crescent. The Cabinet guesthouse was set up on the southern hill surrounding the Bay, in its own grounds, neatly obscured from public view by shrubs and trees of Terran origin which had adapted to Altair and flourished in the mild climate of that part of the coast.

"Not a *minta* among 'em," Interior had remarked in an aside to Lusena. "Doesn't grow in that sort of soil."

An official air carrier whisked Lusena, her ecstatic nieces—Moria, Emer, and Talba—and a subdued Rowan to the resort. The driver saw the party safely installed, good-humoredly hauling in the many pieces of luggage which the nieces had brought. The Rowan managed her one small carisak, and Purza, quite handily by herself. She was, however, given the grandest room where a balcony gave her a splendid view of the sea and coastline for miles in all directions. That was the first bone of contention.

Although each child had a luxurious bedroom with adjoining bath, comparisons became inevitable as the amenities were discussed at great length over the afternoon snack. At first Lusena dismissed the arguing as part and parcel of normal maneuvering of status-conscious thirteen- and fourteen-year-olds. The Rowan merely listened, more interested in the delicious foods arrayed on the table than power plays.

Until Moria remarked that she ought to have Emer's room, since the closet space was better and she really hadn't enough room for her clothes.

"Fabrics must breathe," she explained in an arch manner. Then, seeing the Rowan's surprised expression, found a ripe target for her effusions. "Garments need to be refreshed by circulating air, you understand. That's even more important than proper cleansing and pressing, particularly with expensive gauzes." Moria shifted her attention to her aunt. "Is there someone to tend to our wardrobe?"

Lusena was nonplussed by such a question. Her brother was exceedingly well connected with the mercantile bankers of Port Altair, and the girl was accustomed to a more sophisticated life than Rowan, whose social life was nonexistent. Lusena had no idea if Moria's household included any indentured colonists, working out the expense of their transportation to Altair in menial capacities but, judging by Moria's question, there probably were.

"Did you bring any gauzes with you, Moria?" was what Lusena asked to give herself time to think. "I did tell your mother that this would be a low-key holiday."

"I looked up the A-Z and it specifically mentions evening dances at the Regency Hotel where formal attire is de rigueur," Moria replied in a tone that suggested Lusena should know.

"We have no escorts."

"There is also an agency which supplies escorts of impeccable character," Moria replied and Emer giggled. She and her sister exchanged anticipatory looks. Their parents did not entertain on the same level as Moria's but that was by choice, certainly not necessity.

"Who are unlikely to wish to escort a thirteen . . ." Lusena said severely.

"I'll be fourteen in three weeks' time . . ." Moria was persistent.

". . . Thirteen- or fourteen-year-olds to any Regency ambience."

"I was certain that Rowan would *want* to dance," Moria retorted, eyeing the Rowan with a penetrating stare. "She's old enough to know how." Her tone implied that anyone who didn't was deprived, underprivileged, and asocial.

"Talba and I can dance," Emer hastily put in.

Lusena was beginning to regret the notion that her nieces would be suitable as friends for the Rowan.

"Dancing is not a recreation in which I have any interest," the Rowan replied casually, with a mild hauteur and indifference that quite shot the wind out of Moria's sails. "I am here to enjoy the sportive, not the cultural aspects of the resort. You did bring appropriate attire for swimming and boating, did you not?" The Rowan's tone was more coolly dismissive than Moria's, but then, Lusena thought, Siglen was a mistress of the put-down.

Emer and Talba goggled but Moria blushed and sulked for the rest of the meal. Lusena wondered what was going through the Rowan's mind. Would she make an adjustment or might she, tempted by Moria's example, respond by manipulating the others: something the Rowan was quite able to do, consciously or unconsciously. And that was not what this holiday effort was about.

Lusena sighed. Her timing was wrong. A year or two at this age could produce such astounding swings in attitudes and standards. The Rowan had left her schoolmates as a child with childish interests and concerns. Now, hovering at the edge of the major physiological and psychological adjustments in a young girl's life, a perilous rite of passage might be forced.

Lusena pressed briefly, cautiously, against the Rowan's mind but the girl's immediate thoughts were of satiety with the excellent meal just served and a mental debate over which area of the resort to explore first.

"I see no reason," Lusena began briskly, hoping to alter the mood of the afternoon, "why you can't all change into swimsuits. We can explore the beach while our lunch is being digested and then we'll be ready for a dip. Moria, as the oldest, you're in charge of water safety. I know your family often holidays by the sea whereas Emer, Talba, and Rowan haven't done very much sea bathing."

Moria's manner altered with the possession of even this nebulous superiority and, forgetting her sulk, she ran up the stairs well ahead of the others in order to be the first changed.

It turned out to be a very pleasant afternoon for the water was cool enough to give a brisk tingle, the sun warming, and the beach deserted. Having marshaled her young charges into the water until they were exhausted with their exercise, Moria stripped to allow the sun full access to her already tanned skin. The Rowan watched with discreetly averted eyes. Moria had a splendid start on a feminine body. The still juvenile Emer and Talba also slipped out of their suits, oiling their paler skins with a sun block and then, suddenly, the Rowan was lying supine on the beach blanket as if she was a frequent sunbather. While Moria chattered away about the merits of various tanning preparations, Lusena was positive that the Rowan must be making some bizarre internal adjustments for in the space of about fifteen minutes, she acquired a nice sun-burnishing.

Moria stopped mid-spate and stared at the young Prime. "I don't recall you having a tan, Rowan?"

"Oh," and the Rowan opened one eye drowsily to regard the older girl, "I've always tanned easily."

Now that, my girl, is coming on too strong! Lusena said, for once bending the Talent's rule not to communicate telepathically.

You might even say I was doing it up too brown, Luse? and, eyes closed, the Rowan smiled ever so slightly.

That evening when the girls had settled to sleep, Lusena opened the line to Purza.

"I think she's a spoiled snob of a prig," the Rowan was saying to her pukha. "She apes mannerisms and pretends to be far more mature than she is. Trouble is, Purz, she *believes* she's acting properly. Acting is exactly what she's doing. Acting. Silly bouzma!"

Lusena wondered where the Rowan had acquired that term until she remembered that some of the cargo handlers around the Tower facility came from mixed cultural backgrounds. The Rowan had been eavesdropping again.

"Emer's okay and Talba'll do whatever she's told," the Rowan went on, more musingly than critically. "I'm glad I'm not Moria's kid sister. She'd be a pain in the arse! Yes, yes, I know that's cant language and Siglen would have a fit. But she's not here and I am, and Moria *would* be a pain in the arse!" A giggle came through clearly. "And I got a better tan than she has and it took me a lot less time and perspiration at no cost. Imagine having to smear such expensive gunk on my skin. All I had to do was alter the absorption level of the epidermis. Simple! I wonder how tan I should get! Don't be silly, Purza. Pukhas don't need tans. You'd scorch your fur and blow all the circuits."

That sentence caused Lusena some intense cogitation. In the mention of its circuits, was the Rowan accepting the fact that the pukha was only a therapeutic device? But by being concerned that "you'd scorch your fur" was she attributing some degree of anthropomorphism to it? Animals did not tan: humans did. Use of the pronoun implied a recognition of the pukha as an entity. Her conversations with it indicated a subliminal response—her alter ego speaking through the pukha? So far there had been no conflict with established ethics and morals.

Although constant discreet psychological testing revealed that the

Rowan was basically a well-adjusted personality, the continued dependence on a pukha, which was usually abandoned once a child reached adolescence, could indicate a possible instability. A proven instability, even a suspected one, might put the quietus on any hope that the Rowan would make Prime. Lusena couldn't bear to think of the procedures that would ensue should the Rowan be considered an unstable Talent.

Not that dependence on a pukha was a real cause for alarm. Lonely children of ten had imaginary friends—it was a healthy developmental stage that should be passed through without trauma. The Rowan's pukha had certainly been a boon to the child and to her preceptors. Once the holiday was over, Lusena decided she would have to discuss a weaning process with the Medical Officer.

The next day dawned so bright that Lusena immediately arranged for a sail down the coast to a sea garden where the girls could safely indulge in some underwater exploration. Moria fretted during the short training session because she'd "done all this sort of thing so often before."

Turian, the instructor, was handsome and far too intelligent to respond to Moria's coy attempts at flirting on the trip down. He pinned her with a cold stare and remarked that in his experience it was those who didn't listen to safety precautions who invariably made the mistakes underwater.

Once they had all submerged and were following Turian through the sea gardens, Lusena lightly touched the Rowan's thoughts and felt the girl's utter delight and pleasure in the experience. The Rowan was a strong swimmer. Clear, bright water was unlikely to summon memories of *minta*-stained mud.

It was exceedingly unfortunate that it was Moria who was caught by the sting-sheet which Turian had particularly warned them all against. It was equally unfortunate that the Rowan was closest to her and remembered the first-aid measure. She rubbed Moria's stings with handsful of sand. (And that had been done kinetically though Lusena hoped she was the only one who noticed *that* at the moment of panic.) When the Rowan began the metamorphic massage which Lusena had taught her as being useful in reducing shock, Moria complained that the Rowan was deliberately bruising her feet. The accident put an end to the expedition and was, when Lusena reviewed the week later, the beginning of the trouble.

If Moria was somewhat mollified by being taken up in Turian's arms and jetted back to the sloop, it didn't help that he treated her like a silly, thoughtless adolescent. Fuel was poured on her wounded pride when he complimented the Rowan on her quick thinking and apt use of first-aid measures.

Lusena perceived that the Rowan was surprised at praise from any quarter and shrugged it off, but Lusena could tell the girl was pleased. Unfortunately, Moria noticed, and affected a little squeal as Turian, his expression worried, rubbed lotion on the long, thin sting welts. Also unfortunately, Moria proved to be one of the nine out of a thousand who had an allergic reaction to sting toxins and Turian cranked up the engine to get the girl to hospital with all dispatch. The others took turns applying cool sea-water compresses to the malevolently swollen flesh. Moria had good reasons now to moan.

"I think she did it on purpose," the Rowan confided to Purza that evening after Moria had been treated and then sedated. "I don't know what she's trying to prove, except that she's real silly, because Moria's no match for the woman Turian's living with."

Lusena was a trifle surprised that the Rowan had dipped into Turian's mind that way. Or maybe she hadn't. Turian had allowed her to take a turn at the sloop's helm on the return voyage. They had been deep in discussion which might have covered more than the mechanics of powered sailing. The Rowan seemed to elicit information from a wide range of personalities.

"Moria's stupid," the Rowan remarked to the pukha, "but she's determined not to be limited to childish activities. Maybe I should warn Lusena to watch out. No? You don't think I should. Yes, I suspect you're right. Lusena doesn't miss much, does she?" And the Rowan giggled sleepily, for that moment very much a young girl.

That was the end of that evening's monologue. And Lusena had been warned. Moria was much improved the next day but quite genuinely not up to much activity. Though the inflammation was reduced, the welts were raw and red. Moria quickly became bored with her invalid state and Lusena suggested games. If Moria won she avidly wished to continue but once she started losing, she wanted to try something else. Emer and Talba were amenable, so was the Rowan during the morning. But, after lunch, in a partnered computer game which Moria and Emer lost to the Rowan and Talba, Moria accused the Rowan of cheating!

"You couldn't win by that much of a score unless you were cheating somehow. Talba's no good at this, so how could you possibly win?" Moria complained in a carrying snarl which brought Lusena instantly into the room.

None of the girls knew that the Rowan was Talented. That had been one of the reasons Lusena had picked children who hadn't previously met the girl.

"Talba is so good at Fighter Pilot," the Rowan replied, putting a comforting arm about the younger girl. "You're just not able to adjust to having a partner: you want to dominate and you don't win this game by dominating."

"You did cheat! You did!" Moria screamed, her face reddening and the sting marks turning dark suddenly. Talba stared at them, horrified.

"Oh, you're really quite stupid, you know," the Rowan said in a tone that bore a strong resemblance to Siglen's. "There is no way to manipulate the components of this program from an external source and there's absolutely no point in cheating in a childish game."

Moria stared at her, too infuriated to do more than stutter. Then abruptly she got control of herself, her color abated, and she leaned forward in an ominous threatening posture. "How do you know there is no," and then her tone and accent mocked the Rowan's cool speech, "way to manipulate the components of this program from an external source if you didn't try?"

The Rowan stared at her with contempt and pity, and then she took the distressed Talba by the hand. "C'mon, we'll go for a walk on the beach until certain tempers calm down."

Lusena recognized that as a suggestion out of her own book but she decided to deal with Moria now, and comfort Emer, who was as upset as her sister. "Rowan is quite accurate, Moria, that there IS no way to cheat at Fighter Pilot. It's a matter of cooperation and fast reflexes."

It was possible, Lusena thought optimistically, that the drugs had had an adverse effect on Moria to make her act in such a volatile manner. Before the evening meal, she was contrite and managed a creditable apology to the Rowan on those grounds. The Rowan accepted—unfortunately almost too casually, for Moria hated to admit she might be in the wrong to a younger person—and appeared far more interested in the dinner menu.

Sometimes the Rowan could be extremely adult in her attitudes and perceptions, and then revert to childlike indifference. In this instance, she ought to have used more empathy with Moria, and didn't. Lusena caught the expression on Moria's face and maintained a stronger presence when all four girls were together.

Moria was able to swim the next day and that evening they all went to the amusement park. The amenities for young people included a carousel which enchanted the Rowan: horses and biffs and lionets and catarons and two amazing sea creatures that even the attendant could not identify. But the outside circles of beasts rose up and down with the motion of the carousel and if a rider caught ten of the brass rings, he won a free ride.

Moria insisted on riding just behind the Rowan who caught every ring she reached for. The mechanism did not recharge fast enough for

Moria to acquire one. She changed places on the next ride but she was not as agile as the Rowan. By now Lusena was aware of the tension and watched both girls closely. The Rowan was not using her kinetic ability to catch rings, of that Lusena was positive: the girl was simply more deft, with excellent timing so that it didn't matter if her cataron was up or down or midway, the Rowan collected a ring with each circuit.

Nothing would do then but for Moria to insist they go onward to one of the other rides.

"Rowan's got enough rings to do two free circuits," Emer pointed to the rings Rowan played with, her index fingers touching and her hands tipping the roll of rings up and down.

"Oh, I'll go on if you want to," and with that the Rowan tipped the rings into the collection maw. "Where will we go next?"

Why her willingness should infuriate Moria, Lusena couldn't understand. The rest of the excursion was somehow colored by Moria's seething fury which communicated itself to Emer and Talba. The Rowan seemed oblivious.

"That girl wants for manners," the Rowan told Purza that evening. "She made Emer and Talba miserable and Lusena's worried. Should I find out what's bothering Moria? No? Well, I *know* it's not done but I really don't want to spend the rest of my holiday appeasing that old bouzma. I have to do *that* all the time with Siglen. If I just . . . No? I can't? Even to lighten up our holiday? Can I not just *lean* on her a bit when she gets particularly antsy? Just a little! It'd make things a lot easier all 'round. Okay! I promise. Just a little!"

Most of that night went by sleeplessly for Lusena as she reviewed that conversation. The Rowan had clearly displayed an understanding of Talent ethics. Leaning wasn't a violation exactly, nor even a genuine intrusion of mental privacy, Lusena conceded: a little leaning often did a lot of good and she had applied leans on the Rowan in her early years. It was the most minor of infractions of the basic Law but she would monitor the Rowan. Talents, particularly Primes, had to be so careful of their interactions.

The Rowan did *lean* on Moria the next morning at the first note of petulance. It was adroitly done, Lusena thought, and it certainly did improve the atmosphere at the breakfast table. The morning was spent pleasantly in swimming on their private beach. The Rowan was careful to keep her "tan" slightly less bronze than Moria's and to comment wistfully that she would never attain the lovely shade Moria had acquired.

That evening Lusena took them all to a concert in the open air amphitheater, a re-creation of an ancient structure with brilliant acoustics.

The program was varied, suiting many tastes in a vacationing public. At the conclusion, an announcement indicated that the last group would be playing dance music at the Regency.

Naturally Moria begged to be allowed to go. "Who needs a partner? There's sure to be some unaccompanied boys wanting to dance. I just know it. There were hundreds in the audience. Oh, please, Lusena. The others can sit and listen. Emer adores this group anyway. She wouldn't mind. And if Rowan's never been to a dance, this would be an intro. Please, please."

Moria might come from a sophisticated household but Lusena did not believe her parents would condone her attendance at a hotel dance no matter how the girl pleaded. So she flatly refused and took the girls home, Moria coming up with more and more reasons why they should attend. Lusena was so worn out by her whining that she almost leaned on the girl herself and wondered why the Rowan didn't.

Lusena was startled then, two hours later, when the Rowan knocked at her door.

"She's gone!"

"Who's gone?" Lusena exclaimed inanely. "Why? Were you peeking?"

"I didn't need to, not with her climbing down the trellis and making a lot of noise," the Rowan said. Then, looking Lusena straight in the eye, went on. "She was also broadcasting as loud as if she'd Talent. She doesn't like me, you know."

"Moria's at a very difficult stage in adolescence," Lusena felt obliged to explain.

"Well, she's NOT an adult. She's far too silly and she could get in a lot of trouble at the Regency. The boys she wants to attract were popping junk at the concert. They won't know one end from another by now." The Rowan paused, concentrating, scowling. "They don't. She'll be in big trouble if she meets them. She's wearing gauzes."

"How much of a headstart does she have?" Lusena zipped herself into the nearest clothes to hand.

"You should catch her on the main road. Unless she gets a ride but I don't see any vehicle going her way along that road."

A very sullen Moria was retrieved. When she quite accurately blamed the Rowan as her informant, Lusena did her best to center Moria's thoughts on her willful disobedience, detailing the consequences of such irrational behavior. Moria smarted under the lecture, though when Lusena mentioned that the boys at the concert had been popping, the girl did pause thoughtfully.

"I'm not a parent, Moria," Lusena said sternly, "but I am in charge and you are grounded!"

When Moria raised her head challenging that authority, Lusena *leaned* and Moria's eyes widened with surprise.

"You're a Talent!"

"It runs in the family," Lusena remarked drily. "Or doesn't your father ever mention his?" Moria stared at Lusena as if she'd sprouted wings or horns. "The more fool he," Lusena muttered and gestured firmly for Moria to get into her room. "You'll be staying there tomorrow!"

Because she intended to enforce that punishment, the original plans for the next day had to be altered. Lusena said that Moria would be keeping to her room and neither Emer nor Talba questioned it, completely ignorant of the early-morning episode. The Rowan announced that she wanted to swim as the waves looked energetic enough to surf on.

Lusena joined them later, having checked that Moria was still deeply asleep. She kept in touch with the girl's mind when she did wake, listening to the grousing and complaining as Moria ate the meal left for her and idled about the room. Lusena caught a glimpse of her on the balcony, observing the others down on the beach and then the girl withdrew, her thoughts most uncomplimentary and her resentment aimed at the Rowan. Lusena wondered if she would have to send Moria home prematurely. The holiday had been arranged for the Rowan's benefit—not Moria's.

The Rowan had caught the knack of riding the rolling combers back to the beach. The sea was rough but not overly so and there was no undertow on this beach so when the girls clamored for Lusena to join them, she did so, keeping a light touch on Moria's mind.

They were all riding the crest of one large wave when Lusena heard the Rowan give a terrible shout. There was a look of agony on her face so intense that Lusena probed to find out what had injured the girl. But the pain was psychic. Frantically propelling herself through the comber, the Rowan staggered onto the beach and started running for the house, mentally broadcasting a shout that nearly deafened Lusena.

DON'T! YOU CAN'T! YOU MUSTN'T! YOU'RE KILLING HER!

Shrieks now came from another source—Moria!

ROWAN! YOU CAN'T, YOU MUSTN'T DESCEND TO HER LEVEL! Lusena tried to free herself from the wave, was tumbled about roughly and came up, gasping for breath. She wasn't kinetic but somehow she was on the path with no recollection of having reached it and running as fast as she could toward the house. She saw the Rowan on the balcony outside her room and then a final shriek from . . . . Lusena could not immediately identify the source but the pain came from an anguished soul.

Panting with exertion, she finally reached the Rowan's room. Moria was crouched in one corner, knees drawn up to her head, her arms wrapped over it, whimpering in jagged little cries. The Rowan stood in the center of her room, her face a mask of grief, of unimaginable sorrow as she stood, clutching the Purza's head, its fur shorn in hunks about her, its dismembered limbs cut into many pieces.

Some force prevented Lusena from entering and she sagged against the threshold, trying to find some way to comfort the Rowan, knowing there was none. Then, as she regained her breath after her exertions, she blinked to clear her eyes, thinking at first that sweat clouded her vision. But no, slowly the hacked pieces of the pukha were reassembling themselves in a feat of kinetic reconstruction that Lusena doubted few but a potential Prime could have managed. The Rowan knelt, placing the pukha head where the rest of its body could rejoin it. She knelt there stroking the length of the creature, crooning to it.

"Purza? Purza? Please speak to me. Tell me you're all right! Purza? Purza! Please, it's Rowan. I need you! Talk to me!"

Lusena bowed her head, tears streaming down salt-encrusted cheeks, knowing the magic, and the Rowan's childhood, were gone.

"I was under the distinct impression that this holiday would have brightened the child," Siglen said, rattling her necklace of thick blue beads irritably. Her heavy face was drawn down into petulant lines. She didn't like hearing that her magnanimity in permitting the Rowan to take such an unprecedented holiday had not been a complete success.

"Unfortunately," Lusena began uncertainly, "I erred in my choice of companions. There was a serious confrontation between the Rowan and one of the girls. Up until that point, the Rowan was thoroughly enjoying the respite. My niece is at a very difficult age . . ." She faltered.

"A childish spat? Which results in four days of melancholic behavior?" Siglen was disgusted.

"Girls verging on puberty are so vulnerable, so easily upset. And," Lusena went on quickly, for Siglen's face was falling into a pontifical mode, "ridiculous things can sometimes get magnified all out of proportion to their true significance. The Rowan is, as you know, basically a sensible and well-balanced youngster. But . . ." and here Lusena faltered again. Siglen had always been contemptuous of the Rowan's dependence on the pukha. Siglen's fingers made the rhythmic rattle of impatience on the hollow beads. Lusena took a deep breath and plunged on. ". . . the wanton destruction of the pukha was devastating."

Siglen's eyes bulged with indignation. Her fingers gripped the necklace so hard that Lusena worried that the chain would snap.

"I told you that pukha should have been phased out long ago. Now you see what comes of ignoring my advice! I will have no more temperamental fits from the Rowan. She's to be on duty in the Tower at the usual hour tomorrow. I'll tolerate no further delinquency. Especially for such a specious reason. As it is, I shall have to report her dereliction to Reidinger. Primes *must* be responsible. Duty first! Personal considerations come a long way down the list. Now, try to imbue that in your charge. Or," and Siglen shook an ominous finger at Lusena, "you will be replaced."

Shaking with outrage at the woman's insensitivity, Lusena stalked down the ramp from Siglen's Tower. She was so upset that she almost didn't hear Gerolaman's "hsst!" He looked ill-at-ease—no, conspiratorial—for there was a decidedly wicked gleam in his eyes. Mystified, she followed him to a small closet.

"Look, it isn't the pukha, Lusena, but, with a bit of luck, it'll be something to help her," the stationmaster said and flipped up the cover of a caribox.

Lusena exclaimed in amazement and a sudden spurt of hope. "A barquecat? Who did you bribe to find one? They're unobtainable!" She peered in at the mottled bundle of the curled-up cub and drew back the hand that inadvertently went to stroke it. "It's the loveliest colors," she said, admiring the pattern on the tawny fur ends and the deep creamy base that highlighted the markings. "How did you find one so like Purza's fur? Oh dear," and Lusena dropped into anxiety again. "Maybe that wouldn't be such a good idea right now."

"I thought of that aspect myself, but this was the only cub left and only because I wanted it for the Rowan would they give me the option. Of course, I have to give him back if he doesn't take to the Rowan."

"Will it adapt to surface life?" Lusena asked, having to hold her hands tightly behind her in her overwhelming desire to stroke the sleeping beast. Barquecats had that effect on people.

"No fear. It's cruiser bred so it's more accustomed to gravity than most but it'll have to be sequestered in the Rowan's quarters. One, the mutation's never been cleared for Altair and two, they absolutely cannot be allowed to crossbreed. I had to swear an oath of blood to neuter him when he's six months just in case he did get out. He's got a clean vet-cert because the rest of the *Mayotte*'s litter was still in quarantine, pending dispersal. They're just weaned."

"You are a real gem, Gerry. I've despaired. She just sits and looks at the pieces of Purza, tears streaming down her face. She hasn't said a word since she got back. I've even tried some pretty severe metamorphics on her which usually restore balance but they didn't dent her depression this time."

"And her?" Gerolaman jerked a thumb over his shoulder in the direction of Siglen's Tower.

"Siglen wouldn't know an emotion if it bit her. She put me down smartly because the holiday was my idea."

"Don't blame yourself, Lusena."

"I do. I *thought* I was a good judge of character and compatibility. And my own niece, at that!"

"Trouble is, the Rowan's not around her own age often enough . . ."

"The Rowan acted with great dignity and common sense. My niece is wretchedly spoiled, self-centered, arrogant, envious, and determined to have the last word. It was NO fault of Rowan's."

Gerolaman patted Lusena's shoulder. "Of course not."

Lusena groaned, shaking her head. "And Siglen's reporting the Rowan's *delinquency,"* and she grimaced over the word, "to Reidinger!"

Gerolaman raised his eyebrows high and gave an amused snort. "That might just be a blessing in disguise, you know. Reidinger's got more sense than Siglen. Always had. That's why he's Earth Prime. You did know, didn't you, that Siglen fancied herself for the job? Well, she didn't get it and it rankles her mortal soul. Don't you fret her telling Reidinger." He gave Lusena a final pat on the back before handing her the covered barquecat box. "Try this and see. You'll know quickly enough if the critter won't accept her." He winked. "I don't think I'll need to bring it back to the *Mayotte."*

Carrying the box with great care, Lusena hurried down the corridors to the Rowan's quarters. At the very least the Rowan would appreciate the honor she was accorded in having a chance to acquire a precious barquecat.

They were as special as pukhas, only alive and as independent as the bobcat, from which they had mutated in the century of space exploration and travel. Some say they had evolved from those early felines as far as man had evolved from the ape. And with a suitable increase in intelligence. There was a widespread notion that barquecats were telepathic but no Talent had ever had communication with them, not even those with strong empathies to animals. Barquecats were equally comfortable in free-fall or gravity. Most marked was their ability to adjust to sudden alterations. Barquecats had been known to survive space wrecks which killed all humans aboard.

Scouts or small crews insisted on having a barquecat as companion on cruises of any duration beyond the range of a Prime Station. Some likened them to the canaries ancient colliers had carried deep into shafts, for the barquecats invariably noticed pressure alterations too minute for humans, and instrumentation. They were said to be responsible for saving thousands of lives with this faculty and they could lead repairmen unerringly to the source of a leak, ping, or fracture. Traditionally, they lived on the vermin that infested every type of commissioned vessel but in fact they were the first to be fed in the galley. Their breeding was carefully monitored by their shipcrews and the progeny were scrupulously registered. The placement of barquecat cubs took as much time, discussion, and power plays as ancient historical marriages between heads of state.

Despite that, adult barquecats were laws unto themselves, bestowing affection and favors in whimsical fashion. To be accepted by a barquecat was considered a mark of esteem.

As she hurried to the Rowan's quarters Lusena fretted briefly. It could be traumatic if the barquecat didn't accept the Rowan. Possibly it could complicate the Rowan's melancholy to be rejected again so soon after Moria's antic. Something had to happen to break through her self-absorption. And the girl knew all about the peculiarities of barquecats.

"It's worth the risk," Lusena muttered to herself and touched the doorpad. It swooshed open and Lusena had to blink to adjust her eyes to the gloom. Once again the Rowan had reduced the illumination to a funereal level. Ruthlessly, Lusena spun the rheostat to a bright daylight. "Rowan? Come out of your bedroom this instant! I have something to show you!" Lusena infused mind and voice with nebulous hints of surprise and anticipation. The Rowan was still young enough to have an insatiable curiosity.

She placed the box on the low table between the main seating units and dropped with a sigh of relief onto the one facing the Rowan's room. She let her pleasure at her surprise ripple through her thoughts as she waited. In part, Lusena agreed with Siglen that this melancholy had gone on quite long enough. Loss is measured on varying personal scales, but loss was still what the Rowan had unquestionably suffered in Purza's destruction.

Lusena continued to wait, rather longer than she expected, until the door opened and a wan Rowan appeared.

"Gerolaman has indentured his mortal soul for you," Lusena told her charge in a conversational tone of voice. "It'll be up to it," and she pointed to the box, "whether or not it'll take to you. Especially as you're not really yourself at the moment. So I don't know if I'm doing you a favor or not."

Lusena was pleased to see that she had fired the Rowan's interest, if not enthusiasm. The girl took slow steps into the room, raising her chin slightly to peer over the back of the couch to see what was on the table. Lusena waited until the Rowan came round before she motioned her to sit. Still moving like a badly lubricated android, the Rowan flopped down. She looked at the box and then at Lusena, who felt the first pressure of query against her mind.

Lusena flipped back the cover and the Rowan's response was all that Lusena could wish: delight and incredulity.

"Is it really a barquecat?" she asked, her eyes flicking up to Lusena's face with the first glint they'd held since that morning at Favor Bay. Impulsively she reached out and then secured her arms to her rib-cage, knowing better than to disturb a barquecat's slumber.

"A really truly live barquecat cub. Even if it doesn't like you, remember to be very grateful to Gerolaman for the chance."

"Oh, it's so lovely. I've never seen a fur so spectacularly marked and lustrous. Tawny tips and creamy base and such an unusual pattern on the tips! There wasn't one like that in the Animal Index of the Galaxy. It's simply the most lovely creature I've ever seen." Once again her hands fluttered over the caribox. "Lusena, when will it wake? What do we feed it? How can we *hide* it from *her?*"

"I don't know, it's omnivorous, and she never intrudes on your quarters." Lusena answered all the questions in one breath, immensely relieved at the girl's resurgence. "So as long as it doesn't escape, Siglen's not likely to know it's here." Even if they had to return the cub, its presence had shaken the Rowan into some awareness beyond her loss.

"Oh, look, it's stretching. What do I do now, 'Sena? What if it doesn't like us?" Her face suddenly went dull again. "Purza had to like me but the cub doesn't . . ."

"Well, we'll just have to hope it finds merit in you, then, won't we?" Lusena was certain that she had struck just the right note in her reply. For all her Talent, for all the potential of her ability, and despite more frequent glimpses of maturity, enough of the child still remained in the Rowan to require support and reassurance. Could a tiny bundle of fur provide that need?

It stirred. The tiny mouth opened and the white fangs were visible around a pale pink tongue curling in a yawn. The dainty seven-fingered toes of the front paws extended the tiny blunt claws of the breed. Its back

arched and it twitched its full banded tail before rolling onto its stomach. Then it opened its silvery-blue eyes, the pupils mere slits in the bright room.

It looked with momentary disdain at Lusena whom it was facing before it turned its classic head toward the Rowan. With one of the grating cries for which the breed was famous, it rose to all fours and with great deliberation padded over to the girl. Lifting its forepaws to the edge of the box, it tilted its head inquiringly at her.

"Oh, you darling!" the Rowan said in a whisper and slowly extended a finger for the barquecat to sniff. It did so and then promptly butted the finger with its head, turning slightly so that the Rowan could scratch behind the delicate ear. "Lusena, I've never felt anything so soft. Not even . . ." she broke off but more because the barquecat was insisting on an energetic caress than because she couldn't finish the sentence. "It wants to drink. Water." The Rowan blinked.

"It didn't ever *speak* to you, did it?" Lusena was astonished.

Quickly the Rowan shook her head. "No, it didn't speak to me. I felt no mind-touch at all. But undeniably I know that it is thirsty, specifically for water."

"Well!" and Lusena brought both hands down hard on her knees and rose. "If that's what that rascal wants, then water it shall have." She tried to keep the elation she felt within bounds as she headed for the kitchen alcove.

"I have been awful, haven't I, Luse?" asked the Rowan in a soft, apologetic tone.

"Not awful, Rowan, but terribly bruised by Purza's loss."

"Silly then. Mourning the loss of an inanimate object."

Lusena returned with a bowl of water which she handed to the Rowan. "Purza was never an inanimate object in your eyes."

Just as the Rowan put the bowl in the caribox, there was a quick rap on the door. She had the lid down when the door slid open and an anxious-faced Bralla came in.

"I was so positive we had one that I never thought to really look . . . sorry to be so abrupt but she's in such a state . . ." Bralla looked from one face to another, her body in a posture of entreaty.

"What are you talking about, Bralla?" Lusena asked, for the T-4 often forgot to project.

"You DO have a recent hologram of the Rowan, don't you, Lusena? Surely you took *some* at Favor Bay?"

"I did, but why the flap?" Lusena had no trouble finding the holograms which she hadn't even unpacked from the caricase. There were

several very good ones of the Rowan. Lusena picked one of her, smiling, standing alone by the stern of the boat, her silver hair wind-whipped like a bright, ragged ensign.

"Oh thank goodness," Bralla stopped fluttering for a moment. "Reidinger insists on having a recent hologram of you, Rowan. It has to be dispatched immediately and I can tell you, Siglen's in no mood on account of that, too. Oh, now that's a very nice one!" She threw a pleased smile at the Rowan who was trying as unobtrusively as possible to keep the barquecat from poking the lid up with an importunate head. "This is perfect. Though I don't know as you'll ever get it back. Shall I copy first?"

"If you would . . ." and Lusena wasn't sure if Bralla heard the request for she was out of the door as if 'ported away.

"Why would Reidinger want a recent hologram of me?" the Rowan asked, hastily lifting the confining lid over the now squalling barquecat. It was not the least bit interested in leaving its box but it evidently resented being covered. After a cursory look about the room, it went back to drinking.

"I'm not really sure," Lusena said, covering her thoughts because she knew exactly why Reidinger wanted one: he could then focus his thoughts directly to the Rowan. Oh dear! Would she be up to the sort of a searching interview for which Reidinger was famous? Lusena looked down at her ward, at her total absorption in the barquecat and gave a discreet sigh of relief. If Reidinger gave her even half a chance . . .

When the cub had finished drinking and had eaten sparingly of milk-soaked bread, it preened briefly and then curled up for another nap to rest from such arduous exercise. As soon as its breathing settled, the Rowan made for the keyboard and accessed information on barquecats, fact and fiction.

"What he should eat," she said, handing Lusena the first few pages, "and what he is likely to want to eat. I want to catch Gerolaman before he leaves for the day. Be right back."

She was out the door before Lusena could protest. Oh, Lord, what time was it on Earth? Lusena ground her teeth. She wanted to be near the Rowan when—and if—Reidinger did contact her directly.

By that evening, there was no doubt that Rascal approved of the Rowan. Waking from his second nap, the cub had looked around for a litter box (for Lusena had thought to provide a temporary affair) and then

hauled himself up her arm, settling companionably on her shoulder, claws hooked into the fabric of her shirt.

"Don't fuss, Luse," the Rowan told her, "he's not sinking them in deep." She giggled and gave a funny shudder. "But his whiskers tickle. There, now, Rascal."

Although the cub appeared to be settling down for a lengthy residence, he suddenly vaulted from the Rowan's shoulder to the back of the couch, running along it to the opposite end. He turned then and sat glaring at the girl accusingly.

"What on earth did I do?"

"Why . . ." Lusena began in surprise and then saw the Rowan suddenly tense to an erect sitting position.

"Yes, Prime Reidinger?"

I've been meaning to address you directly, Rowan, the deep voice said as clear as if he had been beside her on the couch and speaking audibly. *Even I,* and Reidinger added a chuckle, *require a talisman on which to focus and I have added your hologram to those on my special access list. I have, by the way, informed Siglen that you are to take whatever regular holidays are current in Altair's schooling system. She may drive herself but there are rules which apply to minor children that must be observed.*

I haven't minded, Prime Reidinger. There is a lot to be learned . . .

A loyal child, too. The discussion I just had with Siglen should clear the air over several misapprehensions on her part. And about your future training. Let me make this plain to you as well. Rowan: you have the right to contact me directly on any question you might have. A suitable hologram is on its way to you to make that contact easier. You have the range. The Rowan heard the smile in his voice. *Use it. You should also be receiving holograms from David of Betelgeuse and Capella. It won't hurt for you to get to reach them mentally from time to time. Good practice as well. They both studied with Siglen.*

The Rowan caught the dry note in his mental tone and wondered about it.

One more thing: Gerolaman is to conduct a Tower Basics course and I wish you to join his students. Tower management is not merely mental, you know. There was a distinct pause and the Rowan wasn't sure if she should respond with thanks for his intercession or what. *You have a barquecat cub? Well, my dear young lady, you have been honored.*

Yes, sir, I think so, too. And thank you for the holidays and the Basics course and . . . and everything.

Never fear, Rowan. I'll take it all out of your hide at a later date.

Then the space he had occupied in her mind abruptly became empty and the Rowan blinked with surprise.

"Rowan?" asked Lusena tentatively, leaning across the table to touch her hand.

"Earth Prime Reidinger was speaking to me," she replied and then she looked down the length of the couch to the tawny cub. "He knew about Rascal," she added in a mystified tone.

"Reidinger probably would," Lusena remarked caustically, glancing quickly at the cub as he now marched toward the Rowan again along the back of the couch.

"How could he?"

Lusena shrugged. "The Reidinger Family have always had unusual Talents and perceptions. They've been Talents for centuries. What else did he say?"

The Rowan grinned with pure malice. "I'm to have the same holidays that schools give here. And I'm to join Gerolaman's course on Tower Basics."

Lusena paused. "I didn't know he was giving one."

The Rowan laughed. "According to Reidinger he is."

"Then he is."

When Gerolaman arrived late that evening to check on the cub's settling in, he was looking exceedingly pleased with himself. He accepted the brew that Lusena offered and sat opposite the Rowan, whose lap was occupied by a fist-sized ball of fur. He raised his glass to her.

"I thought you'd make the grade. I'll make it official and you'll get the papers direct from the Captain of the *Mayotte.* He said to tell you Rascal is from a line of real champions."

"I can see that," the Rowan replied, smiling fatuously at the sleeper. She hadn't so much as twitched a muscle since Rascal had curled up after his supper.

"It's been a good day," Gerolaman said, stretching comfortably. "Placed a barquecat and got notice that a fully subscribed class of young T-4s and 5s are arriving next week all the way from Earth, to learn what there is to know about Tower management and maintenance. Siglen says that it's a mark of *her* standing in FT&T that Altair has been chosen." Gerolaman winked at Lusena who chuckled. "You're included, Rowan. I was told to inform you myself. You'll be in the Tower as usual in the mornings, but you'll attend my classes in the afternoon and evening. Okay?"

The Rowan nodded acknowledgment and Lusena silently applauded her discretion.

"I haven't taught you all I know yet by a long stretch, but now it's official. You mind yourself with these imported Talents, girl. It's a mixed bag, T-4s, 5s, kinetics, empaths, a couple of mechanicals, but only one true telepath. Still, it'll give you more insight into some of the other manifestations of Talent. And perhaps a friend or two your own age."

"How many?" Lusena asked, noting the Rowan's sudden wariness.

"Eight, I'm told."

"That many? Surely Siglen won't permit them to be quartered at the Station?"

"Not *on* Station. Over at the guest facility," Gerolaman replied with a knowing grin. "My wife's moving in to keep them under control. Not much gets past Samella even if she is only a T-6. Strong empathy, especially for teenage nonsense. Smells it before it can happen." He drained his brew and rose. "I've got a lot to organize before they get here so I'll leave you, ladies. Oh, and I'll get you what you need for the cub on my way home. The *Mayotte* Captain gave me a list. Bring it in tomorrow."

The Rowan once again expressed her deep gratitude for the barque-cat.

"I should have thought to get you one a long time ago, Rowan," Gerolaman said in a gruff voice and, with a curt nod of his head at Lusena, left.

The next day the Rowan found that Siglen was by no means delighted with the thought of *her* Station as a training facility. But this distracted her to the exclusion of any other topic, including the Rowan's recent behavior. Siglen fired orders to Bralla and Gerolaman who, the Rowan observed, both pretended to be disgruntled over the "invasion." They had so many complaints to lodge with Siglen over suitable accommodations, lecture room, which part of the big landing field beyond the Tower would be a far enough away to avoid interference with these lamebrained numskulls that they'd have to pamper and instruct. By midday, Siglen got so flustered that she rounded on Bralla.

"If Earth Prime Reidinger has chosen Altair for this course, then we must cooperate with him in every possible way, and I am heartily tired of listening to your laments. Prime Reidinger knows exactly what he's doing. And that's the end of that."

The Rowan could not help but notice the sly and secret glint in Bralla's eye: the diversion was successful; Siglen had had to resort to upholding Reidinger's decision. The Rowan began to look forward to having company in her lessons.

Later, when she asked Gerolaman, he handed her the ID file on his prospective pupils.

"Facts and figures and holograms," he told her with a grin. "Get to know them a little. They won't know you're not the same general level as they are: Reidinger's orders," he added when she stared in surprise. "That's why there're no indigenous Talents in the course. Make it easier for you to integrate in the group."

She took the file back to her quarters and ran it. Each entry included a hologram, academic record, and a coded strip, obscuring private details from prying eyes but the open information reassured the Rowan. Three boys and one girl were Earthborn: the twin brother and sister who were only a few months her junior, came from Procyon, the other two girls were Capellans.

She called up the holograms and sat for a long while examining the likenesses and trying to imagine the personalities. She stared longest at one of the Earth boys because Barinov was as handsome as a tri-d performer, with blond and curly hair that he wore long to his bare shoulders: he'd been hologrammed in swimming briefs. He deserved to be. He was as muscular and gorgeous as Turian. And only three years older than she. It was just as well Moria wasn't Talented. Then Rascal managed one of his incredible leaps from her tapeshelf to her shoulder, demanding attention now that he had awakened from his latest nap.

The students all arrived on the same official passenger shuttle which the Rowan and Gerolaman met. They had obviously had a chance to become acquainted during the short transfer. They were in high spirits as they crowded through the doorway, laughing and joking, their personal effects bags bobbing behind them in a display of kinetic skill. Then one of the boys noticed Gerolaman and the Rowan and two of the bags dropped to the ground.

"Tsk, tsk," Gerolaman said, grinning a welcome. "Stationmaster Gerolaman, T-5, and your instructor in this course." He nudged the Rowan discreetly who was staring at Barinov. He was even more handsome in the flesh, even flesh covered by casual clothing.

"My name is Rowan," she said. "I hope you'll like it here on Altair." She berated herself for her lapse in manners and smiled impartially around. She felt two, no, four distinct mental touches, more like handshakes than intrusions. She let them see her excitement at meeting new Talents and deflected.

"Sure beats gloomy old Earth," one of the boys said, raising a hand in greeting. The Rowan recognized him from the hologram as Ray Loftus, born in the South African megacity. He shaded his eyes with one hand as he looked across the flat landing field toward Port's low skyline and whistled. "Is that all the city you folks got?" he asked, adding a low disparaging whistle.

"Abort, Ray," laughed Patsy Kearn. "Don't let him make fun of your city, Rowan. That's all he's used to, cities."

"Not cities, Pat, ci-ty, a proper high-tech skyscraping city," Joe Toglia said, making outlines of huge buildings with a flailing of arms. "I'm as much citified as he is even if my folks live at the perimeter of Midwestmetro. Hi, there, Rowan."

The Rowan responded to the friendly warmth emanating from the two Procyons, Mauli and Mick, the twin empaths. Theirs was a curious Talent since it had an echo effect: the second mind reinforcing what the first mind projected. They weren't even attempting to shield so anyone could hear them.

No one quite knows what to do with that trick, Mauli told the Rowan.

They would like to very much, Mick spoke almost simultaneously. *They're certain we can be extremely useful.*

If they can only figure out where, how, why.

"That's enough of that," Gerolaman said, scowling in mock reproof at all three. "Not all of us are telepaths. But every one of you knows the proper manners to display, don't you? Now, whichever of you is kinetic, bring the gear and we'll get you settled in your quarters." He shooed them toward the big passenger land vehicle.

The Rowan clambered in last and sat next to the tall thin dark-haired Capellan, Goswina, who had a very private air about her. There was the faintest tinge of green to her skin. Her eyes were also greenish, but closer to yellow. Seth and Barinov appeared to be continuing an argument but Barinov looked right at the Rowan and winked. She wasn't quite sure what she should do. She certainly wasn't going to imitate Moria's arch coyness.

"Altair is a lovely planet," Goswina said in a gentle voice and the Rowan was grateful for the interruption. "Capella is a very harsh place. Are those really trees?" She pointed toward the wooded hills rising behind Port Altair.

"Oh, yes."

"And people can visit them?"

"Oh, yes," although the Rowan realized that she'd never been to the forest. An uneasy memory stirred in her mind but she lost the thought as she saw the rapt expression on Goswina's face as she continued to gaze in that direction.

"Will we be allowed to visit the forest?"

"I don't see why not. You're eighteen and old enough to go unescorted anywhere."

"You don't have problems with indent gangs?" Goswina looked mildly relieved.

The Rowan lifted the explanation of this phenomena from Goswina's public mind: *indent* meant indentured, and on Capella groups of indentured persons would often indulge in unlawful activities once their worktime was over.

"Not on Altair. We don't have that many indentured people here yet."

"You're lucky! When there are a lot of them, they display the only talent they have: a propensity for violence."

Then the land vehicle drew up in front of the guest accommodations and Ray Loftus whistled again, this time in appreciation.

"Hey, not bad! Not bad at all. Glad I came!" He grinned broadly and hopped out of the vehicle, to be the first inside the facility.

Samella was there and Ray's grin faded a little as he immediately recognized her supervisory attitude.

The Rowan remained through introductory remarks from both Gerolaman and Samella on privileges, the conduct expected of the students, and handed out daily schedules. Then each was assigned a room and told that they were free until the evening meal.

"Aren't you staying, Rowan?" Goswina asked her as she turned to follow Gerolaman.

"I have to stay in the Tower but I'll be back after supper."

The Rowan suppressed the fierce urge to teleport herself because Barinov was looking in her direction just then. But, just in time, she remembered Gerolaman's warning. A fourteen-year-old T-4 wouldn't be able to pull that sort of stunt yet. Among other Talents, she didn't have to be quite so careful of using her abilities but it would be stupid to show off. Although she had been completely at her ease in that interview with Reidinger, it occurred to her that everyone else scrupulously obeyed him and she'd better, too. If he wanted her to act no more Talented than a T-4, she would oblige.

She was a bit surprised then when Gerolaman took her by the elbow and steered her back to the land vehicle. He wasn't upset with her, his mind-touch the usual calm blue, with the yellow of laughter threading it, and the tang of him at a normal level.

"No funny stuff, Rowan. That's not part of this drill. Reidinger's orders! Most of all, you don't swat an insect with a fifty-pound sledge, m'girl," he murmured, grinning down at her. But he ruffled her hair before she climbed into the vehicle.

"Gotcha!"

And she kept that advice firmly in the forepart of her mind over the next two months. In the mornings while she was assisting Siglen, teleporting basic supplies to the outlying Claims, Gerolaman had the rest of them doing exercises she'd long learned and passed beyond. She listened in and once in a while, when her stomach roiled with exasperation at Ray's awkwardness or Seth's incompetence, she'd give things a discreet push. She didn't think Gerolaman noticed her minor interferences.

She joined them in the afternoon for Gerolaman's lectures which covered every mechanical aspect of a Tower, including dismantling and reassembling of every piece of equipment and the diagnostic tests that would isolate a dysfunction. Barinov and Seth were the mechanically apt Talents. Gerolaman paired them with Ray and Goswina, timing them in reassembly. Patsy Kearn was deft at micro-kinetics so she was teamed with Joe Toglia for computer-board repairs. Then each of the students had to duplicate what others had done. The Rowan had never had to work micro before and she found the exercise far more exhausting than assisting Siglen. But she also found it exhilarating.

Then Gerolaman set up situations which produced dysfunctions and each student had to write down ("and no peeking in anyone's head while you write," Gerolaman warned) what she thought was the matter and how to repair it.

It annoyed the Rowan that either Barinov or Seth finished their analysis first and smugly waited while the others thought the problem through, but she was more often correct than they were.

"Arriving fast at the wrong answer can be more of a setback to a crippled Tower than taking that little bit longer and being accurate," Gerolaman told the two, frowning at them. "You two are supposed to be the mechanical Talents but Rowan's got a higher average of correct answers. Tell the class exactly what led you to think this problem was caused by corrupted circuitry, Rowan."

She stammered at first in her explanation because Barinov's handsome face was sullen from the reprimand. Seth didn't mind as much but he wasn't the one that the Rowan wanted to attract. Back in her own quarters after the session, she could not settle to anything, even to playing with Rascal who was in a vivacious humor, attacking pillows and rugs as if they were hostile enemies. Ordinarily his antics would have amused her. She went to bed, still haunted by the sullen face of Barinov.

To her complete surprise, the young man smiled broadly at her the next afternoon. She was tempted to 'path him to find out what had occasioned the sudden alteration, but Siglen's training was too strong. And the Rowan was half afraid to try for fear of what she might learn. It was enough that he had smiled at her.

She could and did keep from competing so accurately against him, pretending that she hadn't taken metal fatigue into consideration on that day's problem. She didn't miss Gerolaman's surprise and decided she'd better "pretend" a little less obviously. However, when Barinov came over to sit by her at supper that night, smiling and friendly, she felt she had acted with discretion.

"Look, we're all going into Port for a concert. The twins are allowed so you should be able to come, too. And we've talked Goswina into venturing forth so you'd be the only hold-out. You haven't been grounded or anything, have you?" he added, noticing her hesitation. She also felt his mind push at hers and let him see that she wanted to come very much. "So, ask Samella. She cleared me for driving the landcar."

"I see no harm," Samella said with a shrug. "It's a group activity."

The Rowan had to dampen her elation and was rather put out that there wouldn't be time for her to go back to the Tower—not unless she teleported—and Samella's knowing glance canceled that notion. Even if she just "lifted" a change of clothing from her closet to a toilet stall, there'd be questions. But she was feminine enough to want to freshen up.

"Don't delay, Rowan," Barinov called after her. "You look fine just the way you are."

She wondered about that when she saw the smudges on her face and hands in the rest-room mirror. Impartially, she examined herself: her dratted hair. It just wasn't logical to be fourteen and silver haired, though there were other mutations that seemed less bizarre and no one commented on them. Her face was far too thin, narrow, with a pointy chin. Her very thin high-arched eyebrows were at least fashionable but her eyes were too large for her face. But she had a figure now: not much bosom but a big one would have made her look top-heavy. Why had Barinov smiled at her? Especially after yesterday? Maybe he wanted to figure out how she managed a higher percentage of correct answers. Well, two years in a busy Tower under Siglen's tutelage had not been useless even if Siglen still kept her to baby exercises. Maybe when she finished this course creditably, Siglen might give her more responsibilities.

The concert was very good indeed, with three bands and some

extremely clever light and sound variations: much more sophisticated than the Favor Bay recital. Barinov sat very close to her for the first part, his muscled thigh pressing against hers. His energy was a rusty-brown, which surprised her, and his aroma was indefinable, not unpleasant, exactly, but not reassuring.

What she really didn't like was the way he kept nudging her mind, poking here and there, trying to find a way in. In the first place it was very bad manners and in the second she did not like his insistence. His intrusions increased when the light, sound, choreography, and lyrics combined into erotic suggestiveness: not highly erotic, just enough to get positive hoot-holler and whistle reactions from the audience. They were sitting well up in the amphitheater so she couldn't miss seeing some couples, and several groups, moving into the dark outer corridors. She knew such things occurred for Lusena had completely briefed her on sexuality and sensuality but this was the first time she'd witnessed it in public. On her other side, Goswina squirmed nervously. Those furtive leavings distressed her.

Subtly, the Rowan emanated a soothing empathy to ease Goswina and that seemed to help.

The finale of the concert, however, was a deliberately sensual construction, ending on a triumphant blare of sound, spectacular light effects, and everyone on stage in frankly sensuous postures. Goswina rose from her seat—to leave, not to cheer and shout approval. The Rowan followed for she caught the girl's choked exclamations.

" 'Wina! It's only a show!" the Rowan said, catching her up in the crowded parking lot.

"Do they have to be so . . . so disgustingly vulgar? Suggestive displays are simply not condoned in public on Capella." Goswina's voice was low and taut with disgust and she was actually shaking in fury. "I just hate it when it's so very obvious. It's supposed to be a very private, wonderful experience. Not cheap, tawdry and . . . and public."

Without meaning to pry, the Rowan "knew" that Goswina had had an attachment which had been deep and meaningful, which she had had to leave behind her for this course. That she missed her friend with an intensity that surprised her for she felt she was too young to have a lifetime commitment. Fortunately, Goswina was too involved in her own emotions to have been aware of the Rowan's trespass. And the Rowan was involved in extricating herself so that she was not as aware of externals as she might have been.

Moving shadows became the solid figures with imperfectly shielded intent. Goswina let out a little scream before her mouth was covered and her arms pinned tightly to her sides just as the Rowan felt herself attacked.

"Oh no, you don't!" She snarled aloud, but mentally stabbed out, exerting a kinesis in all directions for she wasn't sure how many attackers there were. Indiscriminately she sent them all spinning away from Goswina and herself. She didn't bother to limit the push she exerted and had the intense satisfaction of hearing soft bodies meeting solid objects with considerable force, inflicting pain and damage. Ruthlessly she closed her mind, sparing herself their anguish and, for the time being, any immediate sense of guilt at having injured another human being.

"Rowan!" her companion gasped. "What did you do?"

"Only what they deserved. Let's get out of here," and the Rowan grasped Goswina and pulled her out of the shadows and into the more brightly lit parking field. "There'll be public cabs at the entrance."

"But . . ."

"No buts, no explanations and don't tell me you want to be involved in those!"

"Oh, no! No! Oh, dear! We should have stayed with the others."

"We should have, but we didn't." The Rowan was getting exasperated with Goswina. *Ray, Goswina's taking me home. I feel sick.* Ray Loftus would be less likely to question a 'pathed message from her. And right now, she didn't want anything to do with Barinov's curious interest. "I've told Ray that we're going back separately. Now, c'mon. There're plenty of cars."

Goswina was quite willing to let the younger girl take the initiative. She collapsed into the corner of the car which monotonously inquired the destination.

"The Tower."

"The Tower is restricted."

"I am the Rowan."

The car responded by lifting from the road and smoothly turning southeast, gaining altitude quickly and speeding toward the now visible configuration of lights about the Tower complex.

"You're not a T-4, are you, Rowan?" Goswina asked in a quiet voice.

"No, I'm not."

Goswina sighed then, relief and satisfaction emanating from her. "So you're the reason this course is being held on Altair. You're a potential Prime so you can't travel."

"I don't know that I'm the reason . . ."

Goswina uttered a noise of disbelief. "You'll need a Station support team. You'll need people you can trust and empathize with. Building a team takes a lot of time and experimentation. I know. My parents are Capellan support personnel. That's why they let me come, in the hopes that I'd be acceptable . . . to you when you're Stationed."

The Rowan could find no immediate reply. But Goswina's explanation made a lot of sense. How many of this group had guessed the purpose? And her real Talent stature. Barinov? That made more sense than his developing a true attachment for an odd-looking adolescent.

"Please, Rowan. I like you very much and I'm very grateful to you but we would not work well together. I . . . I frighten easily and you're very strong. That's good," Goswina said hastily, lightly touching the Rowan's arm and the girl could see Goswina's gentle smile, "for you. You *must* be strong. I don't honestly think I'm the sort of person who should *be* in a Tower. But my parents wanted me to have this chance. My younger brother, Afra, he's only six but he's already shown considerable potential. At the least, T-4, in both 'path and 'port. He adores going to the Tower with my father and Capella's always teasing him that he's going to take over from Father."

The Rowan chuckled and briefly clasped Goswina's fingers in hers, emphasizing her appreciation and friendship. Goswina was delicate blue and florally fragrant.

"I think we'd better deal with the present, Goswina. Now, you're not to say anything when we get back 'cept that I didn't feel well. The place got so loud and stuffy . . ."

"It was open air, Rowan . . ."

"The noise! And all that lighting gave me a headache. That's what you're to say."

"But those . . ."

"Thugs?" the Rowan filled in wryly.

"They'll know they'd been acted against. And you hurt them."

"Let them explain why—if they give anyone the chance to ask." The Rowan refused to relent. She was furious that, having assured Goswina that Port Altair was a safe place, they had actually been assaulted. And Goswina, too, whose empathy made her the least able to have to cope with nastiness.

"You were much braver than I would have been."

The Rowan snorted. "Not brave. Angry. Here we are."

"Occupants: identify."

"The Rowan here and Goswina of Capella," and the car was permitted through the security web.

"Now, you see me to the Tower, Goswina, and then the car'll take you to your quarters. That way we keep to the story," the Rowan said, giving the necessary directions. "Remember now, Goswina," she said as she got out at the Tower entrance. "And when he's old enough, I'll make sure Afra takes the course here, too."

"Oh, would you?" Then the car carried her away.

The Rowan told Lusena about her headache caused by the blinding flickering lights and meekly agreed to having her eyes tested the next day. While Barinov was concentrating on the problem that Gerolaman had given them to solve, she had no compunction about probing in past his public mind. She didn't know his source but it was clear to her that Barinov was deliberately cultivating her because he'd learned that she was a potential Prime. She had no further hesitation then about competing against him, or any of the others. A Prime ran the Station: sentiment did not enter into its management.

So, during the last week of the course, she ran Barinov a very subtle dance which occasionally caused the gentle Goswina to flush.

Over the next four years, other courses were given by Gerolaman at Altair which the Rowan was not specifically required to attend. She often dropped in when it came to the troubleshooting: She liked matching wits with the other students but she never permitted herself to become too friendly with any of them. She ignored overheard insinuations that she was cold, aloof, too haughty, conceited, stuck-up. She was pleasant enough to everyone, even those she genuinely liked, but she kept those preferences to herself. Sometimes Gerolaman would invite her into his office to have an informal chat and discuss her opinions about this or that student.

At some point after each course had finished, Reidinger would contact her for a talk, discussing various aspects of the material covered, and the problems proposed and solved.

The Rowan told Lusena that she felt as if she was being given a long-distance final exam.

"Well, I'd say you were lucky, young lady, to have his personal interest. Bralla says," and here Lusena grinned with some malice, "that he expects monthly reports from Siglen about your progress."

"Oh, is that why she suddenly allows me to handle the ore drones?" The Rowan was not completely satisfied to be given the chore since the routing was usually pretty basic transferral. "How many years will she keep me on inanimates before I'm allowed a real job?"

Lusena had no adequate consolation. Instead, backed by Reidinger's authority, she could and did arrange for the Rowan to take time away from the Tower. When Tower traffic was very slow, they went camping on long weekends on Altair's scenic Eastern Shore and several times on the Great Southern Wasteland which, the guide showed them, was teeming with all sorts of insect and invertebrate life forms, fantastic flowers that bloomed at night or in the dawn-lit hours, drooping and dying once the blazing Altairian primary seared the planet's equatorial areas. The Rowan enjoyed water sports the most so that the executive house at Favor Bay was a frequent holiday site: Bardy and her husband, or Finnan and his wife and young children joining them.

The summer of her sixth year at the Tower coincided with the scheduling of a larger than average group, some of whom were older personnel from planetary as well as interior stations, taking the course as a refresher. By this time, most of the students knew that the Rowan was an unusually strong telepath and teleporter: the likelihood was that she would make Prime.

Where, in the Nine-Star League, was the real quandary. Plainly, it would not be Altair for there was no diminution of Siglen's sure handling of her Tower; David was firmly entrenched at Betelgeuse, Capella at her Station. Procyon's Guzman was aging but still years away from retirement. There was no possibility of her acceding to Earth Prime but the rumor strengthened that Reidinger might settle some of his more onerous duties on her. Or that League Council might be considering a Station at Deneb, one of the newest colonies, though that was most unlikely. A colony had to have both exports and the credit to purchase imports from League members as well as sufficient off-planet correspondence, or a trade route, to justify the expense of establishing a Tower. Right now, Deneb had no surplus of materiel or credit.

"I've told Reidinger," Gerolaman said to Lusena the evening before the new group was to arrive, "something's got to be done for the Rowan. She'll get stale, bored, and while she's a sensible kid, it's not right to keep her twiddling her thumbs. She knows far more about Station mechanics and operational procedures than Siglen ever did. She's fully capable of Prime responsibilities right now and she isn't even at full adult strength." He shook his head slowly, fretfully. "And that woman never gives her any *real* work."

"Humph. She's jealous of the child, and you know it as well as Bralla and I do."

"She's always going to be a *child* in Siglen's lexicon. I often wonder," and Gerolaman scratched his jaw, "if it wouldn't have been better to have sedated the child and taken her to Earth when you had the chance."

"Oh, no," Lusena said, sitting upright in contradiction. "You weren't there. You didn't see the terror in her face when we tried to get her to board the shuttle. And her mind was chaotic with fear. That's why Siglen intervened. She wouldn't have otherwise, I assure you. That was the only time I've ever seen Siglen worried about someone other than herself! And you know that Primes are agoraphobes. Look at the breakdown David of Betelgeuse went through. And Capella! They had awful voyages to their stations."

Gerolaman scratched his head thoughtfully. "Well, Siglen sure was sick. I came on the same ship and there was more medical staff than Station personnel, from the Moon onward. Though I thought at the time, she was hoping they wouldn't send her to Altair. She was so sure that she'd be Earth Prime if she just hung around long enough down at the Blundell Building," he said in a dissatisfied grumble. Then he picked up the sheaf of hard copy, the records of the incoming group. "I think something's going to happen soon, though. Look, every one of the repeats is someone the Rowan worked well with in the courses. Ray Loftus, Joe Toglia: they've been transferred from Capella with excellent ratings. Reidinger's tagged three for me to vet as potential Stationmasters. He hasn't done that before. Devious, that man is. Pure devious."

"If only he'd tell the Rowan, maybe she wouldn't spend so much time fretting."

"You take her off to Favor Bay, just as you planned. Give her a good break, and come back in time for her to show these lamebrains up in the troubleshooting phase."

Lusena started to smile at the relish in Gerolaman's malicious anticipation and then sighed. "If she were just a little more subtle with her corrections, a little less forceful in her opinions . . ."

Gerolaman raised his eyes in surprise and waggled a finger at the woman. "Station crew measure up to their Prime, you know that, Lusena. That's what all this is about. They support the Prime, they assist the Prime and the Prime calls the plays. Primes aren't in it for popularity awards. They've got to be tough on everyone and are usually tougher on themselves." He made a slicing motion with his hands. "That's the way it's got to be or FT&T falls apart. Let that happen and then the League has a wedge to gain control. FT&T won't function half as well as a bureaucracy, with this system or that system throwing its weight around and demanding preferential thises and thats. FT&T is strictly first-come, first-served: high, low, or middle men get the same considerations."

"I do," and Lusena gave a rueful sigh, "but I don't forget that she's a lonely child, and always has been."

"But not for *always*. Yegrani promised."

"A promise which is a long time coming." With that Lusena left the Stationmaster's office. "And I have guarded the guardian," she muttered to herself with considerable satisfaction.

Favor Bay in the full height of spring was glorious and Lusena noticed that the Rowan began to brighten as soon as she stepped from the groundcar.

"The only thing wrong with this place," the Rowan said, glancing about and then pulling windswept silver hair off her face, "is that I can't bring Rascal with me."

"He doesn't seem to mind being left with Gerry," Lusena replied.

"True cupboard love," the Rowan said with a wry grin, "so long as you feed me, I love you."

Lusena laughed. "Partly, but he is affectionate with you and runs to the door whenever he hears you coming. He never notices me even when I feed him and he only tolerates Gerolaman."

The Rowan made a skeptical noise in her throat, and turned to 'port first Lusena's baggage and then her own up to their respective rooms. "Someday it would be nice to have something who loved *me!* Not the Rowan Prime, not the provider, but *me!* Some*one* preferably."

Lusena replied in the same objective tone of voice. "You're eighteen now . . ."

"Are we sure of that?"

"Medically, yes," Lusena said with a tartness in her reply. The Rowan still yearned to discover the minor details most people grew up knowing: birthdate, family name, family background.

"Not many people here in Favor Bay know that you're Talented, much less Altair's coveted young Prime. You've always been here as part of a family group. You're fully old enough to do a bit of private research."

The Rowan regarded Lusena with a wide-eyed smile. "Siglen would have apoplexy if she heard you say that! Persons with our Talents and responsibilities cannot indulge in gross physical activities." Her mimicry was devastatingly accurate.

"Gross physical, indeed," and Lusena laughed. "Oh, I shouldn't laugh at her, but really, Rowan, Siglen is not temperamentally, or physically, suited to enjoying the 'finer emotions in life' . . ."

"Even if she recognized them . . ."

"Whereas you're a slender young . . ."

"Fey-looking, isn't that what that redheaded Earth kinetic in last year's course called me?" The Rowan shot Lusena a challenging look.

"Fey is attractive." Lusena refused to budge from that interpretation.

They were in the house now and the Rowan peered at her features in the hall mirror. "I could dye my hair!"

"Why not?"

"Indeed, and why not?"

They tried several shades but, although the Rowan would have preferred to wear long black tresses, she didn't have the right skin tone to go brunette. So they settled on a mid-blonde. For summer wear, the Rowan decided to have short curly hair as well and the result pleased them both.

"Any improvement?" the Rowan wanted to know, twisting a curl to curve down onto her brow.

"Piquant! Fashionably sensible. Now, go enjoy yourself. The color's guaranteed not to fade in sun or sea."

"I'll just swim and sun a bit: to make sure the claim is accurate. Coming along?"

"Not today," and Lusena shooed the Rowan on her way. There was a good deal to be ordered for the food preparation unit. Some visitors were not as scrupulous in replenishing stocks when they left.

A leisurely swim, time to adjust her skin tone to a decent tan, greatly improved the Rowan's mood. She and Lusena dined out and several men cast admiring looks in their direction.

"You're sure no one here knows who I am?"

"Not likely. Besides, even Gerolaman would have to look twice to recognize you right now. Oh," and here Lusena shrugged her shoulders, "it's suspected that you might have some Talent, but then a third of the planet can lay claim to some sort of minor Talent."

"It'd even be nicer to be me and not have to worry about that sort of thing at all."

Lusena wasn't sure if the Rowan had spoken that wistful sentence aloud or not. Over the years, Lusena had occasionally "heard" purely mental comments but she'd never mentioned it to save the Rowan any embarrassment at having been overheard. On the other hand, it signified the girl's complete trust in her. Lusena had never regretted these fifteen years, though now and then both Bardy and Finnan had unkind words about her dedication.

That was why, two days later, when Bardy's husband, Jedder Haley, vized that her daughter had gone into an early labor, Lusena felt obligated to leave immediately to Haleys' claimsite on the eastern edge of the Great Southern Wastelands.

"If I tag along, Bardy'll be upset," the Rowan told her firmly. "Bardy needs you by yourself. You said I'm old enough to manage for myself. And you did say," the Rowan went on, overriding Lusena's objections, "that no one knows exactly what or who I am so I'm perfectly safe. Frankly, I'd welcome the idea of a few days alone. Most kids are out on their own at sixteen. I can't be vacuum-wrapped all my life." The Rowan had read deeply enough in one quick shot to perceive all Lusena's reservations and her dilemma over her daughter. "It isn't as if I can't keep in touch, dear Lusena. I'll behave. I'm not Moria!"

"Indeed you're not!" Lusena had never forgiven her niece even if her brother remained unaware of why the holiday had been shortened by several days.

"We might as well use Camella's shuttle since it's at the airfield for our use. You'd have no delays getting there then," the Rowan continued, rapidly but neatly filling Lusena's travelpak with items from her drawers. "You'll be on your way in ten minutes. Bardy can't ask for a better response than that!"

"Oh dear!" Lusena's mobile face shadowed with regret.

"Nonsense, dearest friend," and the Rowan embraced her, wrapping Lusena with love, affection, and understanding. "I did monopolize you, and you know I did. Bardy has every right to resent me deep inside but she was generous enough never to chide me for it out loud. I needed you far more than she did. Until now. She needs you now."

As the Rowan stood on the verandah, she felt the oddest exhilaration: a curious sort of release, even though Lusena had always been discreet and subtle in her care of the Rowan, so that there had never been a reason to resent the supervision. But she was alone—alone for the first time in fifteen years, since that famous miraculous escape of hers. Not even a pukha with her.

She spun on her heel and went back into the house, slapping her hand against the door, running fingers along the hall table, pinging the vase with its fresh spring blossoms, twirling into the sitting room and stroking the polished wood, the brocade of a chair, as if to establish their inanimacy and that she was the only living being in the house. She whirled in a wild pirouette and then collapsed onto the sofa, laughing at her own whimsy.

What a wonderful feeling. To be alone! To be on her own! At last.

She reached out for Lusena's mind: The poor woman was still dubious about the wisdom of leaving her charge all by herself, but she really *had* to respond to Bardy's appeal. The Rowan softly and gently lifted the anxiety from Lusena's mind, setting up a diversion anytime Lusena might start to worry about the Rowan who was going to thoroughly enjoy her first really true holiday from her previous regime.

Favor Bay took on a *glamourie* that it had never before had for the Rowan. She ate only when she felt hungry, with no Lusena to remind her of "normal" mealtimes. Especially with no Siglen encouraging her to eat this, or have more of that, or please to finish the food she was given since there were many in the world who were starving for a taste of such magnificent cuisine. By the time she felt any hunger, she was ravenous indeed and took one of the cycles down to the main town, following her nose to the best of the many smells wafting about on the light spring breeze.

She parked the cycle in the rack outside a charcoal shop and glanced through the handprinted menu hanging from the ceiling. The smell of roasting fish tantalized her so she took her place beside the other patron in the grill shop. A second discreet look at his profile, and a light touch at his mind, and she recognized Turian, their captain and guide on that first Favor Bay excursion.

"What d'they do best here? It all smells so good," she asked.

"I'm having the redfish steak sandwich," he said, smiling down at her. "Pretty little thing," his mind was saying, "can't be a student as it's not holidays yet. A convalescent? Looks tired. Lovely eyes."

The Rowan wasn't sure that she was pleased or annoyed by the fact that he didn't recognize her. Well, he must have hundreds of clients in a single summer. Why would he recall one adolescent girl?

"Are they all redfish?" she asked.

"No, but that's the freshest," Turian replied. "I saw it unloaded from the dock a half hour ago."

"Then that's for me."

So when the attendant asked her choice, she pointed and had a hard time not listening in on Turian's stream of consciousness. He was mentally reviewing a list of things he had to do to get his ship back into commission and wondering if he had enough credit to do the jobs properly or where he could stint without risking the safety of his clients or his ship. He was hungry after a morning scrubbing the winter's grime from the hull and the aroma was increasing the saliva in his mouth. Or was it the proximity of the pretty girl? She was enough to make any man's mouth water. A little on the thin side: with that tan, she'd been here a few days at least. Strange! her face was oddly familiar. No. He had to be mistaken: he'd never seen her here in Favor Bay before.

"D'you come from around here?" he asked, to pass the time while his fishsteak was cooking.

"No. From 'Port."

"On holiday?"

"Yes, I had to take it early this year. Office schedules rarely give juniors a break." That should answer his questions. "And you?"

"I'm getting my ship ready for the summer."

"Oh, what sort of ship do you own?" Might as well start afresh with him. That way he was less likely to remember the details of the earlier acquaintanceship—and how old she really was.

He grinned. "Tour the sea gardens! Swim with the denizens of the Deep! That sort of thing." If I earn enough in the summer, I can sail all winter where I choose to go, was his silent addition.

"Always in Favor Bay?" She didn't recall seeing him last year, not that she'd been looking for him, or had revisited the sea gardens.

"Not always. Altair has some splendid harbors. I move around a lot but this is a good spot in the summer."

The attendant set their dishes on the counter and was asking for payment and, as the Rowan dug into the pockets of her light jacket, she flushed with embarrassment as her fingers touched only three small credit pieces. How could she have been so stupid? Always she'd had Lusena to remind her. On her first solo outing, she forgot the most basic requirement. She pulled out what she had, an inadequate sum for the meal.

"Ooops!" She gave the attendant and Turian an apologetic grin and thought hard as to where in the house she'd left her purse. She could 'port enough into the pocket of her shorts . . .

"Here! Let me," said Turian, smiling. It beats eating by myself and she's not on the take or make, not this one.

The Rowan's relieved smile was more for his charitable thoughts than the deed of paying for her meal.

"I insist you allow me to pay you back," she said as he motioned toward an empty spot on the deck overlooking the bay. "I left my credits at home. True holiday mindlessness."

"Tell you what. I'll spot you the sandwich for a couple of hours of not so hard labor. If your folks won't object."

"It's my holiday," she said. "But surely there're enough . . ." she gestured to the men and women walking up and down the street outside.

"Everyone's busy getting their own places in order. Mainly I need a couple of extra hands and someone who can take simple instructions." His grin told her she more than qualified. "I'll teach you how to rig sail. A skill guaranteed to be useful—sometime in your life again!"

The Rowan knew very well that he intended no more than that. Turian was still, as he had been four years before, a genuine and honest man.

"Done! A spot of hard work'd do me good and be a nice change from sitting on my duff in an office. Where do I report to work in the morning, sir?" And she flicked her hand in a nautical type salute.

"Cender's Boat Yard. Down there! Mine's the sloop rigged fifteen meter with the blue hull."

Grinning, she raised her sandwich and bit into the crusty bread and hot flaky fish. The piquant sauce she'd slathered on the fish flowed down her chin. She cleared the overflow with a finger and then licked it. Turian was doing the same thing and his grin was one of camaraderie.

When they finished their meal, he insisted on adding "afters" to her tab with him: a half melon full of fresh spring soft fruits and a cup of the local infusion. Then he asked her to arrive by 7:00 so they'd finish the heavy part before the sun was high and gave her a courteous farewell.

He went off, talking himself out of making any passes at such a young thing. He had the summer before him and he usually had many options.

Somewhat piqued, the Rowan cycled back wondering how to prove to him that she wasn't as young as all *that!* He was a good person, honorable and sensible, a capable seaman, and an interesting guide.

Back in the cottage, she decided to study tomorrow's tasks. She accessed information on sail-rigging, on seamanship in general, pausing long enough on the sections of refitting a ship that had been stored over the winter period to assimilate all the information available. Primes were generally blessed with photographic memories as perfect recall was a boon for the sometimes split-second decisions which their duties often required them to make. Not all those with the same basic Talents the Rowan possessed would be suitable as Primes.

She also checked with the Maritime Commission Records concerning the credentials of one Turian Negayon Salik and, using her Station password, looked over his personal records, finding nothing untoward. Turian was thirty-two years Standard. Sun creases made him look a few years older. (From comments made by some of the females on the various courses, older men were apt to be more considerate.) He was single, had never even filed an intent to marry, let alone a short-term parental contract. He did have a large number of siblings and immediate relatives, most of them involved in the sea enterprises.

Aware of a curious absence in the documentation of himself and other members of his family, the Rowan had to sit and think what *was* missing. Then it dawned on her: neither he nor any of his relations had ever taken a Talent test. This was most unusual since most families ardently looked for signs of such abilities, minor or major, in their progeny.

Recognizable, measurable Talent meant preferential schooling, and often grants-in-aid for the entire family. Not, perhaps, as necessary on a rich, fertile, mainly unsettled planet as Altair, but generally comfortable additions to incomes. There was no law requiring registration at a Talent testing center but it was an odd enough omission.

She checked on his ship, the *Miraki,* and had its voyages for the past four years graphed out so that she knew where he had sailed, anchored, and who his passengers had been. She learned that when he had finished his apprenticeship with a maternal uncle, he had been granted part of the credit needed to purchase the sloop, worked for the balance, and now owned her free and clear. The *Miraki* was licensed for charter, for trawling and for exploration, and in the eight years since her commissioning, had done about every job her size permitted. Her seaworthiness records had been scrupulously kept up to date and she had acquired no fines, penalties, or damages.

The Rowan woke at six, ate a hearty breakfast and was nearly late at Cender's Boat Yard because she spent so much time choosing appropriate clothing. That is, clothing appropriate for the end result she now wished. She was about to leave at fifteen minutes before the hour—the boat yard being downhill from the house—when she realized that Turian had been evading, or avoiding, the stalkings of many girls far more adept at this sort of flirting than she. He thought her a nice young girl, a bit too thin. Well, she'd start right there. And elaborate.

So she appeared at the boat yard, promptly at the tone of seven on the tri-d blaring from the boat yard office window, in workmanlike gear, and a change tied onto the handlebars of the cycle. Her review last night indicated she was likely to get wet and dirty. She also had a hefty handful of credits stuffed into her spare-pants pocket.

"Have you ever rigged sail before?" Turian asked halfway through the morning as yet again, she anticipated an instruction.

"Well, yes and no. Sailing's always fascinated me so I boned up on re-rigging sails. A good tertiary education teaches you how to find out what you don't know."

"I'll give you this: you're deft at putting theory into practice. Intelligent helpers are hard to get in any line of work. What do you do?"

"Oh, boring stuff, expediting imports and exports," and she added a diffident shrug. "But the pay's decent and the perks aren't bad. I'd need off-world training for any decent advancement. I'm being a good company person until they notice that I'm keen to advance."

This one has her head screwed on right, was Turian's thought. He wasn't a devious person so it wasn't as if she was invading his privacy: everything was right up front, like an unvoiced monologue.

As the sun reached its zenith in the brilliant cloudless skies, he called a halt and suggested they take a quick dip at the end of the boat yard wharf to cool off before lunch. She peeled to swim briefs and was into the water before him, laughing and splashing at him. He still had a finely made, strong body, enhanced by the deep bronze of his skin.

Refreshed after the swim, they climbed back onto the wharf and sat in the shadow of drying trawl nets.

"You're such a good worker, I'll spot you lunch," he said gratefully.

"One meal you may buy: two within twenty-fours is not on. I brought enough for both of us."

His sea-light eyes crinkled into the sun creases as he stood, dripping wet, hands on his hips and looked down at her.

"You're a smarty, aren't you?"

"Fair's fair. You helped me out of a spot: I paid my way out of the debt. Now I want to make it one up on you and the price is a sail when the *Miraki* is back in the water. Done?"

They shook on it, Turian laughing while his mind admired her independence. She wished he wouldn't think quite so loud: it gave her an unfair advantage over him. And yet, she seemed to be making all the right moves to prove that she was not as young as she might look.

It took them three more days to be sure the *Miraki* was seaworthy, with the Rowan working right beside him, trying not to anticipate prevocal orders too frequently. In the cool of the evening, as he checked off completed chores on his master list, he'd tell her what they'd be doing the next day. If she had to study up on something—varnishing required no mental effort at all, but she found the physical effort, especially through her shoulders rather a remarkable experience—she would access the proper authority before she went to bed. She was sleeping much better than she had in many months.

When Turian had every inch of the *Miraki,* hull, deck, bilge, boom, mast, sheets, rigging, engines, cockpit, galley, and living quarters, he had the Favor Bay Marine Engineer come to recertify her seaworthiness. She passed and the Rowan could not restrain the shout of triumph at what she considered a personal achievement.

"Now, do I get my sail?" she demanded when Turian returned from escorting the Engineer back to the wharf. "Weather report says tomorrow's going to be clear, with a fifteen-knot breeze nor'-nor'east."

Turian chuckled and reached out to ruffle her curls. She squashed the sudden surge of keen sexual awareness of him that his casual caress elicited. She mustn't overreact to a friendly touch. But his affectionate, half-fooling gesture had not surprised her as much because he had extended the caress as because physical touching was rare between Talents, and reserved for moments to reinforce mental bridgings. She didn't wish to prematurely give away her designs on one Captain Turian who still considered her as a "young" girl despite her attempts to educate him.

"Yes, you get your sail. Can you take a full day of it?"

"I've sailed before, Captain Turian," she said archly, "and I've a cast-iron stomach."

"I'll provision her if you'll take charge of the galley," he offered. "And bring a change of clothing and a stout windbreaker." He looked appraisingly up at the sky, squinting at its brilliance, his eyes narrowed. "I make it we'll have a change in the weather before the day's out."

"Really?" She laughed at his assurance. "Meteorology's pretty advanced these days."

Parting his lips in a wise smile that showed her white but slightly crooked teeth, he nodded. "Can you be down here at 4:00 AM to catch the turn of the tide?"

"Aye, aye, Captain," and she flicked an impudent salute at him before mounting her cycle and treadling off the wharf.

The first thing she did when she got back to the cottage was get an update on the weather pattern. She knew that he had not accessed his ship's facility so she was intrigued to find that a new low-pressure pattern was forming in the arctic. How in the name of all the holies had he *known* something which was happening thousands of klicks away? And his family had never tested for Talent? Curiouser and curiouser! The Rowan made up her sailing pack, and stuffed in wet-weather and a few non-essentials that might prove useful.

With her pack slung over her shoulders, she cycled down in the faint light of the dawn, grateful she now knew every rut and hole in the road to the main wharf. When she hailed the *Miraki,* moored fore and aft to the wharf and gently rocking in the outgoing tide, her voice seemed overloud.

"Stow that cycle and loose the aft line, mister," Turian said, emerging from the cabin and pacing to the cockpit. "Now, stand by the for'ard line and we'll get underway."

Laughing at how nautical Turian had become, the Rowan did as she was bid and neatly jumped to the deck to coil the for'ard line as the *Miraki* 's blades took hold and propelled her away from the wharf.

"Stow your gear, mister, and grab us both a cup of the brew. We'll need it," he said, "while we're clearing the harbor."

As she cheerfully did his bidding, she was positive that this was going to be a glorious day, certainly a highspot in the past year. She hadn't an ounce of precognition in her Talent but there were moments, and this was one of them, when you didn't have to be clairvoyant to know the auspices were good.

Once clear of the harbor and beyond the fishing boats chugging more slowly out to their day's labors, Turian ordered the sails hoisted. The exhilaration in being under sail in a stiff breeze and hull down in the sea thrilled the Rowan and she caught Turian's tolerant grin at her abandonment to the experience.

"I thought you said you'd sailed before," he said, half-teasing as they sat in the cockpit, Turian's capable hand on the tiller between them.

"I have, but never quite like this. Always on 'outings,' not adventures like this."

Turian threw back his head with a hearty guffaw. "Well, if a common ordinary shakedown sail is an 'adventure' for you, then I'm glad to have offered you this rare occasion." Poor kid, his mind said, though his glance on her was kind, if this is all the adventure she's ever had.

However, he intended to give her full measure of the experience and in doing so, forgot his own weather prediction. He had filed a day trip to Islay, the largest of the nearby coastal islands, but they made such good speed to their destination that he decided to continue on, picking up the Southerly Current. That should carry them neatly to the southern tip of Yona, then they'd swing nor'west and come up the coast back to Favor Bay. That would make it more of an adventure for her.

Meanwhile he took great pleasure in seeing the girl so eager and vivacious: She didn't relax much and, although he approved her diligence, she got far too tense doing the simplest jobs. The odd time or two she had spoken with an authority and maturity that surprised him yet at other times she seemed even younger than she looked.

The purple mountains of Islay Island, with Yona just south of it, were on the horizon when Turian sent her below to her galley chores. By the time they had sated their sea-sharpened hunger, he had steered in close enough for the settlement on Islay to be visible. They picked up the current and the girl's eyes widened at the way the *Miraki* drove now, spume flying from the bow, heeled over. He had her furl the jib and he close-hauled the mainsail. Just as she came aft again to join him in the cockpit, he heard the chatter of the Met-alarm.

"Grab the printout, would you, Rowan," Turian said, "and get us something warm to drink." He craned his head about, but there weren't many clouds yet on the northern horizon.

"You were right about a weather change," she said, coming back on deck with steaming mugs in her hands. "Low-pressure ridge making down from the arctic, crowded isobars so the winds are likely to be galeforce." She pulled the printed sheet out of her pocket and handed it to him. "But you knew about a change yesterday."

He laughed as he read the Met report, cramming it into his pocket to take the mug in his free hand. "My family have been seafarers for centuries. We've got a kind of instinct for the weather."

"You're weather-Talents?"

He gave her a very odd look. "No, nothing formal like that."

"How do you know? Didn't you get tested?"

"Why? All the men in my family have the weather sense. We don't need to be tested." He shrugged, taking a cautious sip of the hot soup in the mug.

"But . . . but most people *want* to be Talented."

"Most people want more than they need," he replied. "As long as I've a ship to sail and an ocean to sail her on, enough money to keep her safely afloat, I'm satisfied."

The Rowan stared at him, bemused by his philosophy.

"It's a good life, Rowan," and he gave an emphatic movement of his head. Then he smiled at her. "There have to be some like us on every world, who are content with what they have, and not bored by sitting on their butts all day in an office, shuffling papers about."

She caught in his mind an acceptance of that ineffable consciousness which was not at all a lack of ambition: but a totally different lifestyle. It was part of his innate honesty and ethics. Briefly she envied him his certitude. She had no argument against it though she could never have been allowed to live as he could. That she almost resented. From the moment she was rescued from the little hopper, there was no alternative path for her to follow.

"You're a lucky man, Captain Turian," she said, with a twisted envious smile.

"Why is it, Rowan, that sometimes you seem decades older than you can possibly be?"

"Sometimes, Captain Turian, I am decades older than I should be."

That puzzled him, and she smiled to herself. If naught else works, being enigmatic might.

"We'll have to alter our plans, however," he said, hauling out the sheet and rereading it. "We haven't a chance of making it back to Favor

Bay before those winds arrive. And I don't want to be caught on this side of the Islands. We have a choice, and I'll leave that up to you, mister," he shot her a challenging glance. "We can go through the Straits," he pointed ahead to the fast approaching end of Islay Island, "and shelter on the lea side of Yona. There's a nice little bay on Yona's Tail. We'll be safe there, and tomorrow we can make our way back. Or we can go back to Islaytown, moor her against the blow, and go ashore for the night."

"You're the Captain."

"Passage through the Straits can be hairy at high tide and that's what we've got."

"The *Miraki* would be safer on the lea side of the island, though, wouldn't she?" His smile answered her. "Then it's the Straits." Her grin answered his challenge.

Turian hesitated a moment longer. Islay Straits at high tide was a testing passage. She might have sailed a bit on her holidays, but she wouldn't have encountered the boiling cross currents and riptide. He'd done it often enough in the *Miraki* and had complete confidence in his own seamanship and his craft. She wanted an adventure: she was about to get one.

So, when the *Miraki* rounded the Gut Rocks that bordered the entrance to the Strait, he ordered her into her wet gear and life vest, stopping any argument from her by shrugging into his own.

"Prepare to tack, mister," he roared at her over the surf pounding the Gut Rocks.

By the time that was done, the Rowan had her first good look at the surf boiling through the Straits.

"We're going through *that?*" she demanded, and he admired the way she covered the sudden fright she'd experienced.

"You said you had a stomach of iron. I'm testing it."

As she made her way back to the cockpit, he grinned when he noticed how tightly she kept a hold of the life-rail, and how neatly she balanced in her bare feet against the plunge of the *Miraki.*

To himself, Turian thought that perhaps this had not been the kindest way to test her seamanship but he was as proud of her courage. She seemed undaunted until they hid the midpoint, and suddenly the *Miraki* was cresting a huge wave, plummeting down with stomach-churning abruptness, wallowing in the trough before being flung up again on the next wave.

The girl beside him screamed and he shot a glance at her, her face white as the sheet, eyes distended and staring straight ahead, in the grip of complete terror. He spared one hand from the tiller long enough to haul her as close to him as the tiller between them permitted. He grabbed her rigid hand and placed it under his on the tiller. Then he coiled his right leg around her left one, angling his body to touch hers at as many points as the rough passage permitted.

And it wasn't the sea that terrified her. How he knew that he never questioned. This was an old terror, somehow revived by their situation. She was struggling with her fears, struggling with every ounce of her. He kept as close a contact as possible, knew she'd have bruises on her hand from his pressure but that was all he had to reassure her.

Fortunately, for all the danger, the Straits were not long and though under these conditions, the passage seemed to last an unconscionably long time, he was very soon able to veer into the much calmer waters.

"Rowan?" He let go of the tiller for long enough to pull her over onto his knees, holding her tight against him, while he grabbed a line to secure the tiller on the new course. He cranked on the cockpit winch to trim the mainsail and then he was free to comfort the shuddering girl. Gently he pushed the wet curls back from her forehead. "Rowan, what scared you so?"

I couldn't help it! It wasn't the Straits. It was the way the ship bounced and rolled and surged. Just like the hopper. I was three. My mother left me in the hopper and it was caught in the flood, bounced about just like that. For days. No one came. I was hungry and thirsty and cold and scared.

"It's all right now, girl. We're past it now. Smooth sailing from now on. I promise you!"

She made an effort to push him away but Turian knew that she was far from over the shock of that revived terror and he continued to hold her gently but firmly against him. Casting his seaman's eye at wind and water, at the searoom between the *Miraki* and the shore, he was satisfied with their current course. Lifting the Rowan, light and shivering in his arms, he maneuvered her carefully down into the cabin and laid her down on the bunk. He started the kettle before he removed her life vest and wet gear. Her skin was chilled under his hands so he wrapped her well in a blanket before he made a restorative brew. Liberally lacing that with spirits, he handed it to her.

"You drink that down," he ordered in an authoritative tone that provoked a slight smile from her as she obeyed. Then he stripped off his own rough-weather gear, rubbed his hair and shoulders dry before he made himself a similar brew. He sat down on the opposite bunk and waited until she felt like talking.

"The ship?" she asked once between sips, hearing the rush of the hull through the water.

"Don't worry about her."

Her smile was less tentative. "Don't worry about me, then. I haven't had that particular nightmare in years. But the motion . . . ."

"Strange what triggers off a bad memory," he said easily. "Catch you unawares out of nowhere. I damned near lost ship and self in a strait similar to that one. Scared me shitless and not a clean, dry pair of pants in the locker. You might say," and he ducked his head a bit, affecting embarrassment, "I sort of try myself more often in the Islay Straits just to prove I can't scare anymore."

"I'm not sure," she said slowly but the color was back in her face again, "that I'd like to go back through today, if you don't mind."

"Couldn't anyway," he said with a laugh, and took the empty cup from her. "Tide's the wrong way right now for the westward passage."

"Now, isn't that a pity!"

Admiring her resilience, he gave her a mock cuff on the jaw and then tossed a clean towel at her. "Dry off, change, and get on deck again. You're standing the watch down to Yona's Tail."

Something to do, he was telling himself as he went topside, was much better for her than reliving that old scare. The Rowan was in complete agreement but she couldn't quite shake off her response to his immediate support of her in the depths of renewed terror. He might have mocked her lack of courage: He might as easily ignored her as a coward but he had read her correctly and given her exactly the physical reassurance she needed—and had needed as that three-year-old child.

Old terrors could indeed grab you at the most unexpected moments: this was the first time so much had surfaced past the blocks they had placed on that horrific experience. Her mind might not be allowed to remember but her body had. This time someone had been there to hold her hand.

She dressed in her spare dry clothes, donning the warm sweater against the chill of bones that not even the hot stimulant had dissipated. As she scrubbed her hair dry, she was wryly amused that Turian hadn't realized that her explanation of her terror had been subvocal. But then, so physically close, he didn't even need to be empathic for her to 'path to him.

His face brightened as he saw her emerge on deck. She smiled back.

"Helm's yours," and he pointed to the compass setting. "I'll run up the jib. That way we'll make our anchorage well before dark. I've changed our ETA with the Seaguards so they won't panic but d'you want to tell anyone at Favor Bay that you won't be back till noon?"

She shook her head, aware from his obvious thoughts that he

wasn't at all disappointed in extending the cruise. He had an edge of anger for people who had somehow put a three-year-old child in such peril. Turian was beginning to see her not just as another useful pair of hands, a workmate, but as a distinct and interesting personality.

She watched his lithe body as he hoisted the jib, coiled some lines that the rough passage had scattered, and generally checked port and starboard on his way back to the cockpit. As he settled in the corner of the bench, he squinted at the compass and then at the shoreline.

"Helmsman, set a new course, ten points to starboard." He raised an arm, pointing toward the distant tip of Yona Island. "We're making for an anchorage on Yona's Tail. Come morning, we can set a straight course back to Favor Bay."

"Aye, aye, sir. Ten points to starboard on a course for Yona's Tail. And I beg to inquire of Captain, if he brought along enough provisions for a starving sailor."

"No one goes hungry aboard the *Miraki,*" he said with an approving chuckle. "You can catch as much fish as you can eat, mister, and there's plenty to garnish with."

Thick clouds had begun to darken the skies before they reached the anchorage, a pleasant little crescent bay with a fine sandy beach. Yona was a popular summer resort with hundreds of similar strands along its eastern shore. They were the only vessel in those calm waters for the cradled sailing boats and the shoreline dwellings were still in their winter cocoons. As soon as the sails were furled, all lines coiled, riding and cabin lights on, Turian broke out fishing gear.

"No bait?"

He grinned. "Drop your line overboard and see what happens."

"Incredible!" was her reaction as flat fish seemed to leap onto the hook as soon as it dropped below the surface.

"Right time of year for 'em. Always plenty in this bay. Now, five minutes from sea to plate and eat as much as you can."

The Rowan did for she had never been so hungry, nor appreciated a plain meal more. As she washed plates, pans, and mugs after the meal, she was suffused with an unaccustomed sense of contentment. She was also tired, with a fatigue of body, not mind, that was as soothing as it was soporific.

"Hey, you're asleep on your feet, mister," Turian said, his voice warm with amusement but his brows were slightly puckered in concern.

"I'm all right, now, Turian, really I am. You were marvelous back there. If you'd been in the hopper with me, I wouldn't have been so scared." At the anger in his face, she held up a hand, "It wasn't anyone's fault. In fact, I survived because I was in the hopper. The only one who did." Then she wondered if she'd given away more than she intended. To hear Siglen tell it, everyone on the planet had been aware of her terror. Maybe he'd been at sea. He certainly wasn't insensitive.

"You've no family?" Somehow that distressed Turian most.

"I have very good friends who have cared for me better than family would."

He shook his head. "Family's best. You can always count on family. Surely you had kin left someplace?"

The Rowan shrugged. "You don't miss what you've never had, you know." She knew that upset him deeply, a man who knew every one of his blood relatives, to whom family ties were sacred. "I'll have a family of my own one day," she said as much as a comfort for his distress and a promise to herself. Maybe that's why Reidinger quizzed her so on the course students: he seemed to dwell more on the boys than the girls. Primes were supposed to form alliances, preferably with other high Talents, to perpetuate their own abilities. Was Earth Prime also a marriage broker?

With that running through her mind, she was unprepared for Turian's embrace. She clamped tightly down on her emotions as his arms enclosed her and drew her tenderly against him. She surrendered to the luxury of being caressed, the feeling of a warm, strong body pressed against her, of gentle hands stroking her head, rubbing up and down her back. She turned her head against his chest and heard a heartbeat, faster than normal and knew that Turian was reacting to his outrage over her orphaned state.

And suddenly the Rowan realized that this was decision time: without meaning to, she had achieved the desired effect on Turian. With only the slightest mental push, she could . . .

She didn't have to make a decision. Turian did it for her. A wave of tenderness, tinged only slightly with pity, but mainly comprised of approval for her courage and resilience, emanated from the man. She had never felt so appreciated, so comforted and . . . and wanted. Startled by the intensity of his emotion, she looked up and received his gentle but insistent kiss.

The Rowan had no time to do more than try to reduce the surge of her emotional response to an acceptable level. The past few hours had awakened many emotions long kept under strict control. To have contained them all would have had serious repercussions. She'd have enough, and so would the unsuspecting Turian, if she wasn't careful. And she didn't want to have to BE careful for once in her life. Sensuality flared into full awareness in mind, heart, and body and as Turian responded, she received his attentions with wholehearted honesty.

He did not expect her to have been untouched and she was aware of both anger at her deception and his inability to slacken the incandescent desire which now consumed him. So she encouraged him with body and mind, with her hands and her lips. The hurt was minimal to the blaze of passion that overwhelmed him which she experienced through his mind and touch. She cursed her own ineptitude which kept her from matching his release but the glory which awaited her the next time she made love with him was vividly seared in her mind.

The Rowan awoke suddenly, aware that the comforting, warm length of Turian was missing from the narrow bunk on which they had fallen asleep. It hadn't been the gentle slip-slop of waves against the sides of the *Miraki* which had roused her. It was Turian's mental distress. He was suffering intense feelings of guilt, self-castigating himself for the loss of control which had resulted in deflowering a virgin, anger with her for what he thought was a studied attempt to seduce him, and a terrible longing to repeat the act of love which had overwhelmed him with its intensity.

The Rowan felt keen remorse for his state of mind. What had begun for her as half-game, half-challenge had backfired with disastrous effect on an honest man, well content with his work and his life-style. She was little better than Moria!

She rose, dressed rapidly but the cold was pervasive so she wrapped the blanket firmly around her as she quickly made two mugs of a steaming stimulant. Securing the blanket about her with one hand while balancing both mugs with a touch of mental assistance, she went topside. Turian was slouched in the cockpit in a mind funk, shivering convulsively in a mental and physical chill of devastating proportions. His mind kept inexorably returning to the intense sexuality of their spontaneous union and his inability to control his participation.

"We need to talk, Turian," she said quietly, startling him. She handed him a mug and, throwing part of the blanket over his shoulders, deliberately sat close beside him. "You've no cause at all to feel guilty about last night."

He shot her a furious glance. "How do you know how I feel?"

"Why else would you be sitting out on a freezing deck looking as if you'd committed a major crime. Drink up, you need the warmth." She used the firm tone Lusena often adopted with her and he took a judicious sip.

"Now," she said firmly, giving it a mental accent, "let's come to an understanding. I didn't set out to have you seduce me." He snorted disbelief, hauling the blanket around his right shoulder, but he did not move his chilled body from her warmth. "But I did want you to stop looking at me as a kid, a young girl, an unperson. I wanted very much for you to see *me!* Me, the Rowan!"

Slowly he turned his head toward her, the whites of his eyes more visible in the dark as they widened in the surprise of recognition.

"I remember that name. I did meet you before. I knew your face was somehow familiar."

"I was with a party of four, three girls and my guardian, four summers ago. You sailed us about. At the sea gardens, one of the girls, a terrible flirt, got badly stung because she didn't listen to your warning."

"And you had, and treated the little bitch." Then he cocked his head a bit. "How old *are* you, Rowan?"

"I'm eighteen," she said, facetiously adding, "going on eighty. So I'm old enough to have an affair and to know when I should. But honestly, it just happened. I liked helping you fix up the *Miraki.* It's such a change from the sort of work I do all year long. That alone will make this the most memorable holiday I've ever had, Turian, and last night was pure serendipity. I don't see much of that, I assure you."

She was reaching him with her quiet explanation, for he was basically a sensible man. A hand, warm from the mug he'd been holding, covered hers. She could feel the tautness of body and mind through that contact and tried to find in his mind a clue to reduce that stress. He was still thinking in a circle that went from her youth to last night's eroticism.

"I've made love to a lot of women since I first learned how but I've never had it quite like you!" He let his breath out heavily. "Never like that before!" His mind paused once more on that unexpected blazing intensity that caused his frame to tremble at its recall. "You've about ruined me for anyone else." He resented that. He liked his affairs short and sweet and uncomplicated, affairs in which he was always the dominant partner and in complete control as he had not been last night.

"Me? the kid, ruining you, Captain Turian?" she asked with humorous skepticism. "I doubt that, though that's quite a compliment you've paid me. I'd no idea what to expect once we got started. You're a marvelously tender lover. Even if I have no other experience for comparison, I could appreciate that. And I know you for an honest, decent, caring man. But ruined? Highly unlikely. You couldn't ever settle to just one woman, or one port and one reach of the Altairian seas. If you want my opinion," and she had to phrase this carefully or give away her illegal prying into his personal files, "I don't see you as a family man though your kin mean much to you. But I just can't see you staying on the land to raise kids. The *Miraki* 's wife and child to you. I'm right, aren't I?" She rather hoped her sly cajolery would work and was immensely relieved to feel the shift in his thoughts at her candid remarks. "Even if we had a chance of some sort of an association, this ship would win in the end, and I'd be the one left high and dry."

He gave a wry laugh. She knew that he was within an inch of reaching up to ruffle her hair in that casually affectionate gesture, but his mental state was still inhibiting him. She took his hand and laid her cheek against it, to allow a healing anodyne of respect and abiding friendliness to seep through the touching.

"I shall never forget how you comforted me, Turian, coming through the Strait, and that you knew I needed comfort. That was so generous of you and it was a kindliness with which I am totally unfamiliar. It disarmed me completely, you know."

He nodded, understanding at several levels in his mind what she was trying to convey to him.

"What are you really, Rowan?"

"I'm an orphan, I'm eighteen, I'm a Talent, and I serve in Altair's Tower."

She heard the sudden intake of his breath and felt awe color his mental image of her.

"Like Prime Siglen?" For though he knew what Tower personnel did and how they did it, he couldn't quite place his companion in that context.

"Well, I'm not a Prime," she said with a laugh, hiding the half-truth. "But it's a lonely job and I've got to isolate myself from the people I work with. I can't be the sort of informal captain you are. Being your crew has been such a marvelous experience all by itself. Working with you to set the *Miraki* to rights, just the two of us, was as far from my life in the Tower as you can get. I haven't ever had such a wonderful week. I certainly didn't intend to repay your friendship with a sexual imposition."

"Imposition?" He almost shouted at her, and she knew she had struck just the right note. "I've heard it called many things, but not an imposition!" He gave a bark of laughter and suddenly all the tension and dismay dissolved from his thoughts. "Imposition, indeed."

The dawn was brightening the sky and she could see the amused expression on his face, echoing the recovery of his mental equilibrium.

"Well, then," she began in a meek voice though she was emboldened by his resilience, "without prejudice and seeing that this is a unique opportunity, unlikely to recur, could we impose on each other again?"

"If you've any Talent, Rowan," and his expression mirrored the desire in his mind, "you'll know I'd like that more than anything else right now." Then he smiled, ruffled her hair, and added, "except perhaps some breakfast to give us both the energy we're going to need."

It was late afternoon when they reached the wharf at Favor Bay. The Rowan could, and did, make certain that an easy companionship had grown up between them on the return voyage. He had talked a good deal about previous voyages around the planet, about his many relations, and, sitting as close to him as possible, she had learned more about her native planet than she had ever thought to know.

They were both silent as they moored the ship and did the final chores, setting the ship to rights, cleaning the galley, but there wasn't much more, or too much, to be said. She stuffed her salty clothes into her backpack, climbed onto the wharf, and collected her cycle. Turian stood in her way for a long moment and she knew he was equally loath for this idyll to end.

"I must leave, Turian. Clear skies and good sailing."

"Good luck, Rowan," he said in a low voice, heart and mind reaching out to her but he stepped aside and she cycled past him, feeling his regret as sharp as her own.

By the time she had cycled up the long hill from the anchorage, she was sweating so it didn't matter if some of what poured down her cheeks happened to be tears. It had been a beautiful interlude. Lusena had been right to suggest it, however obliquely. Would Lusena *know* what had happened? Lusena knew just about everything else about her. Such a magical incident would take a lot of camouflage from her eagle-eyed guardian. Did she really want to cover it all up? Wouldn't Lusena rejoice that she had met such a lovely lover?

She had entered the cottage, slung her backpack down the corridor to the laundry room before the sustained squeal of the answerphone penetrated her self-absorption. There was a sheaf of messages, curling down from the machine to the floor. So many in just thirty-six hours?

"Now what?" The Rowan resented the return of the pressures she had been able to forget. She tore off the final sheet and bundled the whole screed up, settling herself first in a chair before reading any.

The first, from Lusena, had arrived just after she had left the cottage for the *Miraki*'s journey and announced the triumphant arrival of twin girls and the prognosis of a speedy recovery of their mother from a prolonged and complicated labor. A second, also from Lusena, was a confirmation of Lusena's opinion that both babies had recorded high-potential Talent at birth. The third was her pleasure that Finnan had come to view his nieces and there had been a marvelous family reunion. The fourth was a query from Gerolaman about her lack of response to messages. The fifth which had come in the previous evening was an order from Siglen to contact the Tower immediately. The sixth, and the first words made the Rowan yearn for Turian's supportive presence, burst the fragile bubble of the idyll.

MUST INFORM YOU THAT LUSENA SHEV ALLOWAY KILLED IN GROUND VEHICLE COLLISION. REPORT IMMEDIATELY. SIGLEN.

The dateline was 1220 today as the *Miraki* had been plowing across the Southerly Current under full canvas through the seas still running high from the previous night's storms. She and Turian had been side by side in the cockpit, warm with companionship and shared love.

The tears streamed down the Rowan's face. "Must inform," she muttered. "No regrets, Siglen? No regrets at all that a fine loving woman is gone?"

She let grief take her then, vainly searching for a mind touch that was lost forever to her, lost as the comfort of the woman who had cared for her with such dedication. The ache expanded, closing her throat, pushing down into her belly, shoving upward to crowd into her brain and press behind her eyes. Tears flowed and the sobs wracked her body. Turian would comfort her. Surely she had the right to ask that of him. But why involve him in a private grief? It was something one had to live through; the ache of the heart, the fruitless searching of the mind, and the sorrow of the spirit. Lusena! Lusena! Lusena!

The comunit's piercing summons was a harsh intrusion. Irritably, she 'ported the connection open and the screen lit up. Fortunately it displayed a worried Gerolaman.

"Rowan! Where have you been?"

"I was sailing. We were weathered in last night in a deserted anchorage. I'm only just in the door. What's happening with . . ."

"Siglen had a fit when the accident report came in. She was positive you were with Lusena and she was in some state."

"Thought she'd got rid of me, huh?"

Gerolaman's scowl reproved her. "We were all worried, Rowan. Especially after Finnan said you hadn't accompanied her."

"Bardy needed her mother. She didn't need me hanging about and at eighteen I'm well able to take care of myself for a few days of holiday." She knew she sounded querulous but she couldn't help it. "Oh, Gerolaman, Lusena was . . ." and she covered her face with her hands, weeping bitterly.

"I know, honey, I know. It won't be the same. It's just that . . . we didn't know where you were. And you had to know."

"Siglen herself broke the news."

"Give her some credit, Rowan," and Gerolaman's voice was rough, "she was upset, too. And got worse thinking you might have been killed. Secretary Camella's handling arrangements which is very good of her. Now I know where you are, I'll come and get you."

The Rowan smeared the tears off her cheeks with both hands. "I appreciate it, Gerry, but there's no need. I'll be there as soon as I can close up this place." She cut the line before he could protest.

She ignored the comunit while she gathered up her belongings, showered and dressed, phoned the caretaker that she was vacating. From the porch she could make out the *Miraki,* moored to the wharf. She had that memory at least!

Then, for the first time, she 'ported herself directly to her quarters at the Tower. She'd had the range and strength to do so for several years but this was the first time she'd had occasion to make use of that ability. Rascal launched himself at her from the bookcase, muttering imprecations at her as he clung to her shoulder. She turned her head to bury her face in his soft fur, and felt the sting of tears again. She bit her lip and walked toward the kitchen to give him a treat for his welcome. She couldn't bear to look down the corridor to Lusena's empty room.

The comunit rang imperatively. "I'm back, Gerry," she said.

"It is not Gerolaman," Siglen's thick voice answered her. "Where have you been, you irresponsible child? Stand where I can view you. This instant."

"In a moment, Prime, I'm presently indisposed." The Rowan stroked Rascal as he happily munched his morsel before she complied.

"Where have you . . ." Siglen's protruberant eyes bulged still further as she took in the Rowan's altered appearance. "Your hair? You cut your hair? And it's the wrong color! What have you been doing? Where have you been? Do you not realize that Lusena is to be interred today and you must, in decency, attend."

"I'll go as soon as I've changed and as soon as I know where the ceremony will be."

"Secretary Camella is representing the Council and you will have to hurry to be ready. And really, you must do something about your hair before attending an interment."

"Why? My hair was Lusena's idea. Excuse me, Prime. If haste is the order, I have things to do."

"And you will report to me the instant you return, do you hear me, Rowan? You have tried my patience beyond all bounds . . ."

Unable to bear such recriminations, the Rowan cut and closed down the connection. *Gerry, tell me where. I want to go on my own!*

Gerolaman was not a sender but she felt him receive her message and knew he was acting on it. She didn't need another shower but after she had changed to suitable clothing for the sad duty, she bathed her face in cold water until he arrived. Rascal coughed a warning of his entry.

There was great pity in the stationmaster's face for her, and a sorrow of his own for the loss of a dear and valued colleague.

"Can I say anything to help, Rowan?" he asked, his hands held open in a gesture of helplessness. He was dressed with appropriate sobriety, his usually unkempt hair parted and flat on his skull. His eyes were red, too.

She shook her head. "You'll come with me?"

"The Secretary of the Interior . . ."

"Camella will be in floods: she was very close to Lusena . . ." it hurt even to speak her name. "I can't stand more emotional backlash, not all the way to the interment. If we can get to your office where I can use gestalt, I'll get us both there. I'll want to see Bardy and Finnan. At least, she was there when Bardy needed her."

"Now wait a minute, Rowan, you can't tap the gestalt without Siglen's permission?"

"Scared I'll misjump us?"

"No, trying to keep you acting sensibly!"

"There is nothing sensible about grief," she flashed at him. Then grimaced and added in an affected tone, a hand to her forehead, "I'm grief-stricken. I don't quite know what I'm doing. Will you come with me?"

"I'd better!" He turned and led the way down the corridor toward his office. She followed.

Once inside, she placed both hands on his shoulders. "Is there anything medium large in the cradles right now?"

"No. Not right now. Siglen is upset, you know," and his fierce expression surprised the Rowan. Gerolaman had several loyalties but the Tower was the top priority. "She hasn't been working well today."

"I can see that," the Rowan remarked flatly, glancing at the pressure idling in the generators. "What are the coordinates?"

Gerolaman hesitated but she hooked her fingers sharply into his flesh and he gave them in a grating voice. She leaned into the leashed power of the Tower's generators as she had done time and again over the past three years. She felt the surge through her and, making sure of her grip on Gerolaman, she 'ported them both.

She almost laughed at the relief on the stationmaster's face as they arrived, without so much as a landing stumble, in front of the Claimtown's one municipal building.

ROWAN! How DARE you! Siglen roared in her mind.

Leave me alone right now, Siglen. You can read me all the pertinent Rules and Regulations I've just broken when I get back to the Tower.

Siglen had no reply to such mutinous impertinence but the Rowan was aware of peripheral fuming and boiling fury.

The Rowan ignored that as she ignored Gerolaman's concerned expression. "C'mon. Bardy's house is down that way."

"Lusena'll be in there," Gerolaman pointed to the building.

"There'll be nothing of my Lusena in there. I'll remember her as she left Favor Bay. But I can help Bardy."

In truth, the Rowan was almost afraid of confronting her foster sister. She had monopolized so much of Lusena's life, never mind the fact that Lusena had willingly accepted the post. Bardy had been solicitous and kind to the fosterling but there had been times when both Bardy and Finnan had resented their mother's absorption in her charge. Why wouldn't they?

That's why she wanted Gerolaman with her, to see that she faced her foster sibs, to deflect any recriminations.

There were none. Instead Bardy, true daughter of a generous natured mother, comforted the Rowan who burst into tears at the sight of her. Finnan threw his arms about both women and, with Gerolaman, comforted them. Then there were the twins to be admired and one of them did seem to be a tiny replica of her grandmother which was both reassuring and saddening.

So it was as a family, united in their sorrow, that they all went to the interment. The Secretary of the Interior was there, obviously relieved to see the Rowan in attendance. It was a mark of considerable respect that it was the Secretary herself who read the eulogy but the Rowan "heard" more than the sincere words: She "heard" much from the others gathered there, and some of it was unkind, untrue, and specious. She closed those minds out and concentrated on the spoken words. The tears continued to fall into her hands. Then a large handkerchief was offered by Finnan, and Bardy's hand, so like Lusena's in shape, closed firmly on the Rowan's arm. Through that contact, she was one briefly with her.

By custom, interment was not a lengthy ceremony on Altair. Afterward the Secretary, firmly but kindly, insisted that the Rowan and Gerolaman accompany her back to Port Altair in her fast shuttle. Numbed by her acute loss, the Rowan acquiesced. Bardy and Finnan said they could keep in touch with her: they still considered her their little sister. But, on the trip back, the Rowan's emotions were so overloaded that she curled up in a chair and closed out even the tacit understanding sympathy of the Secretary and Gerolaman. As anodyne, she forced her mind to dwell only on the tranquil return voyage of the *Miraki,* cutting through the lucid blue waters, the gleaming whiteness of the sail on that dazzingly bright morning, the sensation of wind on her face, sun on her body, until the monotonous rhythm of the sea lulled her into an exhausted sleep.

She awoke, late the next morning, in her own bed, Rascal mumbling beside her head on the pillow.

Rowan? She recognized Bralla's tentative voice. *Reidinger has left word that you are to contact him as soon as you wake.*

Reidinger? Can't Siglen do her own chewing out?

I assure you, Rowan, and Bralla sounded prim with rebuke, *Siglen quite understood your state of mind yesterday and wishes to hear no more about it. We are all sympathetic to your terrible loss. But Reidinger was most emphatic about an immediate contact.*

He can speak loud enough to wake me.

No one was going to wake you up, Rowan, and again Bralla reproved her.

Sorry, Bralla.

That's all right, dear, and Bralla's tone was kinder by many degrees.

I'll get a brew and speak to Earth Prime immediately.

Rascal clung to her, claws uncomfortably latching into her new curls, as she got out of bed, tossed a robe about her, and went to make a stimulant. There'd been a note of sympathy from Reidinger among the pile on Bardy's table. Well, he owed her a lot.

She picked up the hologram that Reidinger had sent her of himself, to use as a focus. He'd usually contacted her. She took a long swig of the hot drink and arranged herself for the long mental leap to Earth. Reidinger's hologram had him seated in a chair, arms on the rest, hands relaxed, a position of repose which she secretly felt he had assumed only for the replication. Even so, his alert, heavy-featured face, the erect posture of his body, gave off clues of the tremendous energy and potential of the man. His dark-blue eyes seemed to spark—a trick of the holographer—as if, even over the light-years separating them, he had a total awareness of her, the Rowan.

Reidinger! She focused her mind on those large, bright eyes. She was about to repeat the call with more force when she felt his touch.

Awake, are you? He might have been in the next room so strong was the contact.

Did I wake you? I was told to make contact as soon as I could.

It won't be the first time and I don't use sleep much. Gerolaman tells me you haven't sat in yet on this latest course. Before she could frame a response, he went on. *I want you to sit in, sort out which personalities you like, with a view to a Tower staff of at least twenty. Gerolaman assures me that your judgment's good. It's much easier,* and now his tone was sardonic, *if we can start off a new Tower with a well-integrated staff, otherwise efficiency suffers. So take your time choosing.*

The Rowan shot upright in the chair. *A new Tower?*

Girl's quick. Yes, a new Tower. On Callisto so it's a terraformed Station. FT&T agree that Callisto can route a lot of the stuff that has had to come in System first before it can be rerouted. You'll be saving me a lot of headaches and give me time to acquire others that only Earth Prime can solve. You're young, I know, but you'll be under my supervision and if you think Siglen's been rough on you, you'll soon learn that she was really the lesser of two evils. As soon as you've assembled a crew, you and they will depart directly for Callisto. Check in with me tomorrow at precisely 9:00 Earthtime.

The gap left by his departure was almost palpable in the quiet room.

"A new Tower," she murmured, stunned. "On Callisto?" That was one of Jupiter's moons. Why there? Why not on the Earth's Moon? Surely that would have been feasible with all the terraforming that had been done to improve that satellite. "I'm to assemble a team? I'm to . . . . I'm to be a Prime!"

Gerolaman, Reidinger's assigned me to Callisto Tower!

I can't say that you deserve such a signal honor, young woman,

Siglen answered her. *At least you will be under his direct supervision and I must say, after the other day, that's exactly where you should be!*

Quite right, Siglen. Quite right. Not even Siglen was going to spoil her elation.

Lusena would have cheered! The Rowan closed her eyes over the pain the errant thought evoked. Lusena would never know that her charge had achieved Prime status. And the Rowan could not suppress her bitter tears which she wiped quickly away when she heard the rap on her door.

Gerolaman entered, his smile tentative until he saw her bravely smile back at him. "That's my girl. Put regret aside. She'd have been proud, no doubt of it, as I am but," and he shook the sheaf of hard copy he held, "we've work to do now in earnest, Prime Rowan. My pleasure and my privilege to assist."

Work did help: She had to concentrate on the reports first, and then had to match them up with the people on the course. Half a dozen times, she found herself thinking she must tell Lusena this or that, and the anguish would seize her momentarily until she relentlessly pushed it back. Sorrow was yesterday: today was for her future, the future which Lusena had cherished for her—her own Station and the title of Prime.

Four years on and she still liked Ray Loftus and Joe Toglia as technicians and maintenance personnel. Gerolaman approved for they had good records as assistants in their skills and had worked at Procyon, Betelgeuse, and Earth. Mauli and Mick were available for reassignment and they had always intrigued the Rowan. From the new people on this course, she chose a Bill Powers as assistant supercargo from his record as well as his calm, stolid manner and a slow smile.

"As good a reason as any," Gerolaman remarked, "considering you're going to have to look at his face a lot."

An older woman, a Capellan named Cardia Ren Hafter, might work out as Stationmaster. She'd temped in that position on Betelgeuse and Prime David recommended her. She wondered about the fifty-year-old scanreader, Zabe Talumet: His qualifications were sound but he seemed to have moved around a lot. But he had a good rating in his profession.

"You'll have to expect some shake-ups before you shake down, Rowan," Gerolaman assured her. "Personalities have to mesh and that takes time, trial and often error. Whatever crew you pick aren't set in plasglas forever, you know. It took nearly six years before Siglen was satisfied, and some of her choices have always astonished me and Bralla but we all work well when it comes to the crunch."

Reidinger sent four more T-4 and T-5 ratings from Earth Prime, and when she couldn't find a good life-support manager, bullied someone from the Moon into taking a promotion in the Callisto's system.

Three days later, Bralla earnestly requested the Rowan to have dinner with Siglen.

"She really did feel badly about Lusena. And she was terrified that you'd been in the crash, too. It took her a nervous half hour before she located the wreck and she scared the local officials out of their wits with a direct consultation. She's really thrilled for your promotion, Rowan, truly she is."

The Rowan entertained a niggle of suspicion about Siglen being thrilled for her sudden advancement by Reidinger. Altair's Prime had always maintained that the Rowan would not be ready for any responsibilities for years. Certainly the Rowan had never been called to account for her impertinence, and direct action, disregarding Siglen's explicit orders. Still there was little point in any unnecessary bad feelings between herself and Altair's Prime.

So, the Rowan purchased a plainly cut, flowing dinner dress in a pale gray—about the only color that wouldn't clash with the flamboyant colors in Siglen's dining area, with a silver torque, to make a subtle statement of her adult status. She presented herself at Siglen's suite to be greeted by Bralla who nodded approvingly and ushered her into the reception area.

Siglen had made significant inroads on the dainty canapés which accompanied the aperitifs. Three places at the dining table meant that Bralla was included, a fact which reassured the Rowan.

Siglen initiated the conversation with a long explanation of systems updates which Reidinger had discussed with her at length. The Rowan listened politely all through the first three courses of which she ate only enough to be courteous.

"It really is too mean of Reidinger to transfer you just when Altair will be upgraded. You could learn so much from the new equipment if you stay just a few more months here so that I can advise you."

"If it's all new equipment, Siglen, you'll be learning to operate it, too, won't you?" replied the Rowan logically.

She noticed the twitch of annoyance on the Prime's face but she could find no break in the woman's mental shield. The twitch expanded slightly into a weak smile.

"I do wish you ate properly, my dear. I gave a good deal of thought to this evening's meal. You are so thin and whatever will they think of me," a jeweled thumb pressed dramatically against Siglen's large bosom, "and the way I have cared for you."

"The medics say I have an active metabolism, Siglen, and I'm unlikely ever to put on much extra weight."

"But you will need it, my dear, to sustain you." Siglen's flabby face now registered extreme concern.

"To sustain me? I believe the hydroponics units at the Callisto Station are state of the art and can supply every known edible fruit and vegetable."

"I'm sure you'll be all right once you get to Callisto," and there was an ominous suggestion of imminent disaster in Siglen's round tones.

"Of course I'll be all right on Callisto."

"Yes, but you have to get there!"

Then, to the Rowan's utter amazement, Siglen burst into tears, covering her face with her napkin. She reached out a hand to grab the Rowan's and there was no doubt of the woman's concern and anxiety. The girl looked to Bralla for an explanation. Terror pulsed through Siglen's fingers to the Rowan who worked her fingers free, wanting no part, however vicarious, of that particular emotion. Bralla looked equally upset, her mouth quivering.

"What are you talking about, Siglen?"

Mopping her eyes, Siglen gave the Rowan a single woeful glance before propping both heavy arms on the table and once again giving way to noisy sobs.

"It's space, my dear," Bralla said, her expression rife with dread.

"What do you mean?"

"You know what travel in space does to Primes, Rowan," Bralla told her earnestly as if that explained everything. "David suffered agonies when he left here for Betelgeuse. He was so unwise to believe that a male Prime would be unaffected. Capella took three months to recover from her disorientation."

"I've 'ported myself from Favor Bay to Bardy's Claimsite without any disorientation . . ."

"But you were planet bound, with home gravity . . ." Bralla argued.

"And I've flown in shuttles all over Altair."

"Shuttles are not at all the same thing as being 'ported," Siglen said disputatiously. "Oh, I have dreaded this from the moment I heard the rumor about Callisto Station. I begged Reidinger to consider T-2s, any sort of combination but you, Rowan. I couldn't let you, a mere baby, go through that terror so soon after your hideous ordeal. Now you don't even have Lusena to support you in your hour of need."

The Rowan hadn't thought of that abortive attempt to send her three-year-old self to Earth for her training. But she did indeed remember the dark passage into the shuttle: into an enclosed space. The erratic motion of the *Miraki* through the Straits reinforced that ancient terror far too vividly.

"Nonsense. I'll be perfectly all right. I was a child and no one had explained anything to me. They just said I had to . . ." and she opened her eyes wide so as not to see the huge frightening maw they had been urging her into. "I do wish, Siglen, that you didn't make a mountain out of a molehill. I'll be perfectly all right."

"That's what David said when I warned him about spatial disorientation. Capella believed me and went heavily sedated but it still took her three months to reorient herself. I wish I could spare you this when you have so recently lost your confidante. There isn't one of the T-4s in Gerolaman's course who'd be any use to you. Bralla agrees with me."

Bralla nodded vigorously and the Rowan kept a tight grip on a growing vexation.

"If I don't find a T-4 from this group, I'm sure there'll be plenty more willing to accept a promotion to a new Tower. Now, do please stop overdramatizing a simple 'portation. I know that you'll make the shift with your usual skill, Siglen, so I've no worries at all."

She stayed only as long as minimum politeness dictated and then went in search of Gerolaman.

"Well, it's true enough about David and Capella and she went completely sedated and cocooned in a special shock capsule," Gerolaman said. "I know Siglen was so sick she lost 5 kilos. And no Prime I've ever heard of has ever been able to 'port himself or herself through space. Reidinger went to the Moon once and never stirred off planet afterwards."

"I'm the youngest Prime, and healthy, athletic . . ."

"Everything the others weren't," Gerolaman finished with a malicious gleam in his eyes. "I'll lay bets on you, m'girl. Now, what d'you think of that T-4, Forrie Tay?"

"I don't like him at all. He eyes me the way Siglen does a particularly creamy éclair and he won't meet my eyes. He slams up shields up against even the most courteous request. I'd never be able to work with such a closed mind."

"Procyon's sending over a T-4 female."

"I work better with a male pairing."

"Well, Siglen would have preferred to but Bralla was the only one to suit her, ever."

"Gerolaman, do I have to remind you that I am NOT remotely like Siglen."

"No, you don't, Rowan, but we still have to form the nucleus of a working team before you reach Callisto!"

"I'll try the woman."

Channi could not have been more of an opposite had a mad genetic scientist deliberately designed them. She was a half-meter taller than the Rowan, big-boned, a woman who moved with deliberation (probably because she was afraid of injuring someone smaller than her large self), and while she was tested as a T-4 rating in both telepathy and teleportation, the Rowan could not achieve any rapport.

"She slows me up as if I was trying to work through a wall," the Rowan said and began to worry that she'd never assemble a cohesive Tower staff.

Where Gerolaman kept reassuring her that there was no question that she would soon find appropriate matches of skills and Talents, Bralla would appear with suggestions from Siglen which invariably proved totally useless. The time for the Rowan's scheduled departure drew closer and she became more anxious to start out on the right note.

ROWAN! Reidinger's unmistakable tones roared through her skull. *Stop that fidgeting. You've got enough to run a Tower right now with the seven you've picked and the ten who're waiting for you at Callisto. You're going to have to relax. I don't want you in a muck sweat when you board the transport.*

And how are you betting on my survival? she demanded acidly.

On what? The genuine surprise in his tone reassured her more than the diatribe he launched when he understood what the bet was.

Mauli and Mick came to help her pack the things she would be transferring to Callisto. Their companionship helped ease the inevitable heartache as she came across gifts that Lusena had given her over the years. From his special caricase, Rascal alternated between acid comments on his incarceration and plaintive requests to be allowed out but he had proved too much of a nuisance, hiding in crates or attacking Mauli. When everything had been neatly stowed in the container, the Rowan with Mauli and Mick, 'ported it into its assigned space in the transport waiting on the cradle for the morning's lift.

"Are you sure you don't want to sleep in the guest house?" Mauli asked, looking about the rooms empty except for Rascal's case.

"I'll be fine. I'll just move a few things in from the stores," the Rowan reassured them and saw them firmly out of her quarters.

She put Rascal's cage safely in the food preparation area which was the only room that she and Lusena had not redecorated from Siglen's original offering. Then, working at top speed, the Rowan papered, painted, and restored the rooms just as they had been on the day she had moved into the Tower. For just this night, it wouldn't hurt her to sleep on that ghastly pink and orange bed. She was tired enough so she wouldn't even notice. But Rascal did and it took him a long time to stop his disgusted commentary.

If the Rowan could have avoided the farewell rituals, she would have. She hadn't had much sleep on that wretchedly soft bed and formalities invariably set her teeth on edge. All the Secretaries were there, each with something encouraging to say to her and a small present to brighten her new quarters. Secretary Camella wavered between radiant smiles and a teary face. Siglen wept copiously on Bralla's shoulder, moaning about the imminent tribulations and why wouldn't anyone listen to her and take proper care of her little pupil, the best one she had ever trained, and to have to endure what was before her . . .

Leading her Tower personnel up the gangway into the big and brightly lit transport, the Rowan ignored a flashback to the day it had been Purza she'd carried, not Rascal, up a ramp. She turned for one last wave at the assembled, and confidently followed the steward to her room.

"You've a barquecat?" the man exclaimed, noticing her burden.

"Rascal. The *Mayotte* let me have him four years ago. He's been a super friend."

"Mayotte, huh? You rate, Prime. You got to be real special to be voted a *Mayotte* barquecat."

"What do you have on board?" and the stimulating exchange lasted until he slid back the door of her cabin, explaining that it was larger than most accommodations and showing her the various facilities.

The Rowan pretended interest but she had to swallow frequently and she began to sweat even before she thanked the garrulous steward and finally managed to ease him out the door. The cabin was *very* small. She'd been in shower stalls that were larger. But then she wouldn't have to be in it long.

Now, please don't worry, dear. Really, there is absolutely nothing to worry about, Siglen's anxious tones blossomed in her mind. *It isn't the same sort of mind-wrenching trip that I had to take to get here the first time, you know, before Altair Tower was operational.*

Siglen's mind was roiling with fear for Rowan. The girl could easily visual the slab of a woman, supine in her couch, her eyes on the vessel's coordinates on the ceiling screen, her fingers checking and checking the gestalt thrust needed for the launch. It was a scene she had witnessed time and again, but not at this end of the operation. Bralla would be hovering in the background.

I do hope everything will go smoothly for you, dear, Siglen continued, her anxiety intensifying. *I've checked and double checked and everything is in perfect working order. I just wish I didn't have to be the one . . .*

The Rowan gritted her teeth. The last thing she needed was Siglen reminiscing over her tribulations on the journey from Earth to Altair. The woman meant well.

The Rowan urged the lift-off claxon to sound, signaling their imminent departure. Involved in gestalt, Siglen could not transfer mental garbage. What was keeping the woman from completing the lift?

Oh, oh, Bralla, and Siglen's wide open mind wailed as the Rowan child once had done. *How can I do this to her?*

The Rowan tried to close out a sudden whirling, mind-boggling disorientation.

Lift, Siglen! Now is not the time to dally! Get me off planet NOW! the Rowan cried, unwilling to endure any more delay colored by a cowardly old woman's ancient fears.

The Rowan leaned back against the door, closing her mind to Siglen's moans. Siglen was frightening herself. The Rowan wasn't at all frightened, even if the cabin suddenly seemed constricting. The cabin on the *Miraki* had been small but the *Miraki* had been on the sea which rolled around Altair. There was fresh air all over. She took deep gulps of air and it tasted properly. She knew from standard procedures that air was replaced between voyages so this wasn't stale recycled air she was breathing.

The passenger vehicle was not a large one: Siglen lifted far more mass without thinking twice about it. She had only to 'port the ship halfway to its destination where Reidinger as Earth Prime would catch and ease it into Earth's Star System. As it neared Jupiter, the ship would enter the proper orbit to land on Callisto's surface.

Once the Tower was in full operation, it would be the Rowan who would catch an incoming 'portation and land it neatly and without a bump into the cradle designed to receive it on Callisto. The Rowan fixed her mind on her future, her own Tower to run, free forever of Siglen's fussy peculiarities.

The claxon sounded. The Rowan found it oddly difficult to move from the door to the bunk. Even silly, but she lay down. She ought not to feel any motion whatever. Siglen was an experienced Prime. There would be no motion, nothing at all like the *Miraki* coming through the Straits, no bouncing, rolling, slewing.

Oh my dear child, brace yourself! Brace yourself! Siglen even managed to penetrate the Rowan's shielding but then she had the gestalt to magnify her telepathy.

But the Rowan knew the moment the 'port began: she knew it because the marrow of her bones vibrated with the generator gestalt.

Oh, Bralla, HOW could I do this to the child? How? Oh, what she'll suffer now!

There was no escape for the Rowan from Siglen's anguished keening. Nor would Siglen leave her alone, determined in her unnecessary solicitude to support her former pupil through this ordeal.

Then, just as Siglen had said it would, suddenly everything was spinning in her head: She was neither up nor down, nor sideways, but whirling in a desperate spiral to nowhere and she screamed and screamed and screamed and screamed, and heard Rascal shrieking with equal panic. Then she was falling into hands, hands that seized and held her down, down, down, forcing her into the vortex that reached out to envelop her and she descended, unchecked into the awful spinning, mind-wrenching blackness.

PART TWO
CALLISTO

When the Rowan came storming into Callisto Station that morning, its personnel mentally and literally ducked. Mentally, because she was apt to forget to shield. Literally, because the Rowan was prone to slamming loose furnishings around when she got upset. Today, however, she was in fair command of herself and merely stamped up the stairs into the Tower. A vague rumble of noisy thoughts tossed around the ground floor of the Station for a few minutes, but the computer and analogue men ignored the depressing effects with the gratitude of those saved from greater disaster.

From the residue of her passage, Brian Ackerman, the Stationmaster, caught the impression of intense purple frustration. He was basically only a T-9, but constant association with the Rowan had broadened his perceptions. Ackerman appreciated this side effect of his position—when he was anywhere else but at the Station.

At the beginning, just after the Rowan had been assigned to Callisto, he had tried to transfer with no success. Federal Telepathers and Teleporters, Inc. had established a routine regarding his continuous applications. The first one handed in each quarter was ignored; the second brought an adroitly worded reply on how sensitive and crucial a position he held at Callisto Prime Station; his third—often a violent demand—always got him a special shipment of scotch; his fourth—a piteous wail—brought the Section Supervisor out for a face-to-face chat and, only then, a few discreet words to the Rowan.

Ackerman was positive she always knew the full story before the Supervisor finally approached her. It pleased her to be difficult, but the one time Ackerman discarded protocol and snarled back at her, she had mended her ways for a full quarter. It had reluctantly dawned on Ackerman that she must like him, and he had since used this knowledge to advantage. He was also becoming proud of the fact that he was one of the longest serving members of the Callisto personnel.

Each of the twenty-three Station staff members had gone through a similar shuffling until the Rowan accepted them. It took a very delicate balance of mental talent, personality, and technical skill to achieve the proper gestalt required to move giant liners and tonnes of freight. Federal Tel and Tel had only five Primes—five T-1s—each strategically placed to effect the best possible transmission of commerce and communications throughout the sprawling Nine-Star League. It was FT&T's dream someday to provide instantaneous transmission of anything, anywhere, anytime. Until that day, FT&T exercised patient diplomacy with its five T-1s, putting up with their vagaries like the doting owners of so many golden geese. If keeping the Rowan happy had meant changing the lesser personnel twice daily, it would probably have been done. The present staff had been intact for over two years in spite of the Rowan's eccentricities.

The Rowan had been peevish for a week this time and everyone was beginning to smart under the backlash. So far no one knew why the Rowan was upset . . . if she did herself. To be fair, Ackerman thought, she usually *does* have reasons.

Ready for the liner! Her thought lashed out so piercingly that Ackerman was sure everyone in the ship waiting outside had heard her. But he switched the intercom in to the ship's captain.

"I heard," the captain said wryly. "Give me a five-count and then set us off."

Ackerman didn't bother to relay the message to the Rowan. In her mood, she'd be hearing straight to Capella and back. The generator board was ablaze with varied colored printouts and messages as the team brought the booster field up to peak, while the Rowan impatiently revved up the launch units to push-off strength. She was well ahead of the standard timing, and the pent-up power seemed to keen through the station. The countdown came fast as the energy level sang past endurable limits.

ROWAN, NO TRICKS, Ackerman said.

He caught her mental laugh and barked a warning to the captain. He hoped the man had heard it, because the Rowan was on zero before he could finish and the ship was out of the system, beyond com distance in seconds.

The keening dynamos lost only a minute edge of sharpness before they sang at peak again. The lots on the launchers snapped out into space as fast as they could be set up. Then loads rocketed into the receiving area from other Prime Stations, and the ground crews hustled rerouting and hold orders. The power note settled to a bearable pitch, as the Rowan worked out her mood without losing the efficient and accurate thrust that made her FT&T's best Prime.

Callisto Moonbase was not a large installation, but its position was critical. Most of the heart system's freight and passenger ships required the gestalt lift beyond the system where the hyper or drone drives could safely be activated. As such bases went, it was luxurious—once you got accustomed to the overhead lower of Jupiter, or its mass jutting up from the horizon. Terraforming the moon gave its workers psychological reassurance during the working "day" with trees and grass lawns and flowering bushes and plants under the main dome.

There were pleasant gardened accommodations for those staff that were on 24-hour duty, though most of the personnel—the Rowan willing—returned to their Earth surface or orbital homes. As befit her status as an FT&T Prime, the Rowan had a special double-domed enclosure, with gardens and a pool and rimmed with small trees and bushes to complete her privacy. Rumor had it that her quarters were rich with priceless furnishings, gathered from many planets, but no one knew for certain as the Rowan guarded her privacy even more than FT&T guarded her. The Callisto installation had been the engineering and scientific feat of the century, now commonplace since technological improvements outstripped that accomplishment as humans reached newer and more exotic planets in ever more remote star systems.

One of the ground crew toggled the yellow alert across the board, then red as ten tonnes of cargo from Earth settled on the Priority Receiving cradle. The waybill said Deneb VIII, one of the newest colonies, which was at the Rowan's limit. But the shipment was marked TOP EMERGENCY PRIORITY/ABSOLUTELY ESSENTIAL with lavish MED seals and stencils shouting "caution." The waybill described the shipment as antibodies for a virulent plague and specified direct transmission.

Well, where're my coordinates and my placement photo? snapped the Rowan. *I can't thrust blind, you know, and we've always rerouted for Deneb VIII.*

Bill Powers was scrolling through the Stardex which the Rowan suddenly tripped into a fast forward, the appropriate fax appearing on all screens at once.

Glor-ree! Do I have to land all that mass there myself?

No, Lamebrain, I'll pick it up at 24.578.82, the lazy rich baritone voice drawled in every mind, that nice little convenient black dwarf midway. *You won't need to strain a single neuron in your pretty little skull.*

The silence was deafening.

Well, I'll be . . . came from the Rowan.

Of course, you are, sweetheart—just push that nice little package out my way. Or is it too much for you? The drawl was solicitous rather than insulting.

You'll get your package! replied the Rowan, and the dynamos keened piercingly just once as the ten tonnes disappeared out of the cradle.

Why, you little minx . . . slow it down or I'll burn your ears back!

Come out and catch it! The Rowan's laugh broke off in a gasp of surprise, and Ackerman could feel her slamming up her mental shields.

I want that stuff in one piece, not smeared a millimeter thin on the surface, my dear, the voice said sternly. *Okay. I've got it. Thanks! We need this.*

Hey, who the blazes are you? What's your placement?

Deneb VIII, my dear, and a busy boy right now. Ta-ta.

The silence was broken only by the whine of the dynamos dying to an idle burr.

Not a hint of what the Rowan was thinking came through now, but Ackerman could pick up the aura of incredulity, shock, speculation, and satisfaction that pervaded the thoughts of everyone else in the Station. What a stunner for the Rowan! No one except a T-1 could have projected that far. There'd been no mention of a new T-1 being contracted to FT&T, and, as far as Ackerman knew, FT&T had the irreversible first choice on T-1 kinetics. However, Deneb planet was now in its third generation and colonial peculiarities had produced the Rowan in two.

"Hey, people," Ackerman said, "sock up your shields. She's not going to like your drift."

Dutifully the aura was dampened, but the grins did not fade and Powers started to whistle cheerfully.

Another yellow flag came up for the Altair hurdle and the waybill designated LIVE SHIPMENT TO BETELGEUSE. The dynamos whined noisily and then the launcher was empty. Whatever might be going through her mind at the moment, the Rowan was doing her work.

All told, it was an odd day, and Ackerman didn't know whether to be thankful or not that the Rowan wasn't leaking any aggravation. She spun the day's lot in and out with careless ease. By the time Jupiter's bulk had moved around to blanket the out-system traffic, Callisto's day was nearly over and the Rowan wasn't off power as much as decibel one. Once the in-Sun traffic had filled all available cradles, Ackerman wound down the system. The computer banks darkened and dynamos fell silent . . . but the Rowan did not come down out of her Tower.

Ray Loftus and Afra, the Capellan T-4, came over to sit on the edge of Ackerman's desk. They brought out the bottle of some home brew and passed it around. As usual, Afra demurred and took from his belt pouch a half-folded *origami,* his special form of relaxation.

"I was going to ask her Highness to give me a lift home," Loftus said, "but I dunno now. Got a date with—"

He disappeared. A moment later, Ackerman could see him near a personnel carrier. Not only had he been set down gently, but various small necessities, including a flight bag, floated out of nowhere onto a neat pile in the carrier. Ray was given time to settle himself before the hatch sealed and he was whisked off.

Powers joined Afra and Ackerman.

"She's sure in a funny mood," he said.

When the Rowan got peevish, few of the men at the station asked her to transport them to Earth. She was psychologically planetbound, and resented the fact that lesser talents could be moved about through space without suffering a twinge of shock.

Anyone else?

Adler and Toglia spoke up and promptly disappeared. Ackerman and Powers exchanged looks which they hastily suppressed as the Rowan appeared before them, smiling. It was the first time that that welcome and charming expression had crossed her face for two weeks.

The grin made you realize, Ackerman thought, very very softly in the deepest part of his brain, what a lovely woman she could be. She was slight, thin rather than slender and sometimes moved like an animated stick figure. She was not his notion of "feminine"—all angles and slight breasts—and yet, sometimes when she looked up at you out of the corner of her eyes, that slight smile tugging at the corner of a rather sensual mouth, she fair took a guy's breath away . . . wondering. And thinking about things no married man—or T-9—had any business reviewing, even in his head. Maybe it was her white hair—some said she'd had that since she was hauled out of the mudslide on Altair—others said it marked her as part alien. The Rowan looked different because—and Ackerman knew this for a fact—she WAS different!

She smiled now, not sly exactly, but watchful, and said nothing. She took a pull from the bottle, made a grimace, and handed it back with a thank-you. For all her eccentricities, the Rowan acted with propriety face-to-face. She had grown up with her skill, carefully taught by old Siglen on Altair. She'd had certain courtesies drilled into her: the less gifted could be alienated by inappropriate use of Talent. While the Rowan could be justified in "reaching" things during business hours, she was careful to display normal behavior at other times.

"Heard any 'scut about our Denebian friend?" she asked with just the right degree of "casual" in her voice.

Ackerman shook his head. "Those planets are three generations colonized, and you came out of Altair in two."

"That could explain it, but FT&T hasn't even projected a station for Deneb. They're still trying to find Talents for closer systems."

"And not for want of trying," Afra said.

"Wild Talent?" Powers helpfully suggested.

"At a Prime level? Unlikely." She shook her head. "All I can get from Center is that they received an urgent message from an inbound merchantman to help combat a planet-wide virus, including a rundown on the syndrome and symptoms. Lab came up with a serum, batched, and packed it. They were assured that there was someone capable of picking it up and taking it the rest of the way past 24.578.82 if a Prime would get it that far. Prior to this morning, what little goes to Deneb has been sent by cargo drone or rerouted. And that's all anybody knows." Then she added thoughtfully, "Deneb VIII isn't a very big colony."

Oh, we're big enough, sweetheart, interrupted the drawling voice. *Sorry to get you after hours, my dear, but I don't really know anyone else to tag on Earth and I heard you coloring your atmosphere.*

What's wrong? the Rowan asked. *Did you smear your serum after all that proud talk?*

Smear it, hell! I've been drinking it. No, lovey. We've just discovered that we got some ET visitors who think they're exterminators. We got a reading on three UFOs, perched four thousand miles above us. That batch of serum you wafted out to me this morning was for the sixth virus we've been socked with in the last two weeks, so there're no bets on coincidence. Someone's trying to kill us off. You can practically time the onset of a new nasty by the digital. We've lost twenty-five percent of our population already and this last virus is a beaut. I want two top germdogs out here on the double and say, two naval squadrons. I doubt our friends will hover about viral dusting much longer. They've softened us up plenty. They're moving in now and once they get in position, they'll start blowing holes in us real soon. So send the word along to Fleet Headquarters, will you, sweetheart, to mobilize us a heavy-duty retaliation fleet?

I'll relay, naturally, But why didn't you contact direct?

Contact whom? What? I don't know your Terran organization. You're the only one I can hear.

Not for much longer if I know my bosses.

You may know your bosses, but you don't know me.

That can always be arranged.

This is no time for flirting. Get that message through for me like a good girl.

Which message?

The one I just gave you.

That old one? They say you can have two germdogs in the morning as soon as we clear Jupiter. But Earth says no squadrons. No armed attack.

You can double-talk, too, huh? You're talented. But the morning does us no good. NOW is when we need them. We've got to have as many healthy bodies as possible. Can't you sling the medics . . . no, you can't, can you, not with Jupiter's mass in the way. Sorry, I just found the data on your station. Filed under Miscellaneous Space Installations. But, look, if six viruses don't constitute armed attack, what does?

Missiles constitute armed attack, the Rowan said primly.

Frankly, missiles would be preferable. Them I can see. I need those germdogs NOW. Can't you turn your sweet little mind to a solution?

As you mentioned, it's after hours.

By the Horsehead, woman! the drawl was replaced by a cutting mental roar. *My family, my friends, my planet are dying.*

Look, after hours here means we're behind Jupiter. But . . . wait! How deep is your range?

I don't honestly know. And the firm mental tone lost some of its assurance.

"Ackerman!" The Rowan turned to her stationmaster.

"I've been listening."

Hang on, Deneb, I've got an idea. I can deliver your germdogs. Open to me in half an hour.

The Rowan whirled on Ackerman. "I want my shell." Her brilliant eyes were flashing and her face was alight. "Afra!"

The station's second in command, the handsome yellow-eyed Capellan T-4, raised himself from the chair in which he'd been quietly watching her.

"Yes, Rowan?"

She glanced to the men in the room, bathing each in the miraculous smile that so disconcerted Ackerman with its sensuality.

"I'll need all of you to help me. I'll have to be launched, slowly, over Jupiter's curve," she said to Afra. Ackerman was already switching on the dynamos, and Bill Powers punched for her special shell to be deposited on the launch rack. "Real slow, Afra. Then I'll want to draw heavy." She took a deep breath.

Like all Primes, she was unable to launch herself through space. Her trip from Altair to Callisto had deeply traumatized her. Primes were the victims of particularly pernicious agoraphobia. Most could not tolerate heights either. There were some who said that the Rowan did very well indeed to climb the stairs to her "tower." Paradoxically, where the looming bulk of Jupiter gave others "falling" psychoses, it reassured her. With the planet in the way, she couldn't "fall" far into the limitless void of space.

As another necessary security measure—in the event of a meteor shower on Callisto—the Rowan had a personnel capsule, opaque and specially fitted, padded and programmed to reduce the paralyzing sensation of "movement." By the exercise of severe self-discipline, the Rowan had accustomed herself to taking short emergency drill trips.

As soon as she saw the capsule settle in the rack, she took another deep breath and disappeared from the Station, to reappear beside the conveyance. She settled gracefully into the shock couch of the shell. The moment the lock whistle shut off, she "knew" that Afra was lifting her, gently, gently away from Callisto. She wasn't aware of the slightest movement. Nonetheless, she clung firmly onto Afra's reassuring mental touch. Only when the shell had swung into position over Jupiter's great curve did she reply to the priority call coming from Earth Central.

Now what the billy blue blazes are you doing, Rowan? Reidinger's base voice crackled in her skull. *Have you lost what's left of your precious mind?*

She's doing me a favor, Deneb said, abruptly joining them.

Who'n hell are you? demanded Reidinger. Then, in shocked surprise, *Deneb? How'd you get out there?*

Wishful thinking. Hey, push those germdogs to my pretty friend here, huh?

Now wait a minute! You're going a little too far, Deneb. You can't burn out my best Prime with an unbased send like this.

Oh, I'll pick up midway. Like those antibiotics this morning.

Deneb, what's this business with antibiotics and germdogs? What're you cooking up out there in that heathenish hole?

Oh, we're merely fighting a few plagues with one hand and keeping three bogey ETs upstairs. Deneb gave them a look with his vision at an enormous hospital, a continuous stream of airborne ambulances coming in; at crowded wards, grim-faced nurses and doctors, and uncomfortably high piles of still, shrouded figures. That melded into a proximity screen showing the array of blips on an orbital hold. *We haven't had the time or the technology to run IDs but our Security Chief says they're nothing he's seen before.*

Well, I didn't realize. All right, you can have anything you want—within reason. But I want a full report, said Reidinger.

And patrol squadrons?

Reidinger's tone changed to impatience. *You've obviously got an exaggerated idea of FT&T's influence. We're mailmen, not military. I've no authority to mobilize patrol squadrons like that!* There was a mental snap of fingers.

Would you perhaps drop a little word in the appropriate ear? Those ETs may gobble Deneb tonight and go after Terra tomorrow.

I'm filing a report, of course, but you colonists agreed to the risks when you signed up!

You're all heart, said Deneb.

Reidinger was silent for a moment. Then he said, *Germdogs sealed, Rowan. Pick 'em up and throw 'em out,* and his touch left them.

Rowan—that's a pretty name, said Deneb.

Thanks, she said absently. She had followed along Reidinger's initial push, and picked up the two personnel carriers as they materialized beside her shell. She pressed into the station dynamos and gathered strength. The generators whined and she pushed out. The carriers disappeared.

They're coming in, Rowan. Thanks a lot.

A passionate and tender kiss was blown to her across the intervening light years of space. She tried to follow after the carriers and pick up his touch again, but he was no longer receiving.

She sank back in her couch. Deneb's sudden appearance had been immeasurably disconcerting. The strength, the vitality of his mind was magnetic. He had seemed to be inside the capsule with her, filling it with his droll humor and warmth. That was it! He was "warm" toward her and she had basked in that sensation like a sun-dodger. She had never achieved such an instant response to anyone since Turian, whom she often thought of wistfully.

Oh, she had always had rapport, contact, with others. In fact, with anyone the Rowan chose to, but, with everyone below her own capability, there had always been an awkwardness, a reluctance that had inhibited her overtures. Siglen certainly had thrown shields across her most private thoughts, explaining them patronizingly as "no need to put old worries on young shoulders." Siglen, to this day, still considered the Rowan "a mere child" despite the fact that she'd been Callisto Prime for nearly ten years.

There were still times when the Rowan wished that Lusena had not died in that crash, days before Reidinger had appointed her to the new base on Jupiter's moon. Lusena had been such a comfort, such a support, believing so firmly in her future, in the future promised by Yegrani: an ephemeral promise. So the Rowan had struggled to understand herself as she had earlier struggled to perfect control of her Talent.

"We who have been blessed with extraordinary powers," Siglen had been fond of declaring in a doleful tone, "cannot expect ordinary joys. We have an obligation to use our Talent to benefit all Humankind! It is our Fate to be singled out and single, the more to concentrate on our duties."

There had been only Turian to prove an exception. However, that had been ten long years ago now. And male Primes didn't have a problem finding suitable mates.

Reidinger had a score of children of varying degrees of competence. David on Betelgeuse was madly in love with his T-2 wife and concentrated on a duty to populate his system with as many high-potential Talent offspring as his wife would tolerate. The Rowan did not have any personal liking for David, though she could work with him satisfactorily. Capella was as eccentric as Siglen was conservative and her personality rubbed the Rowan the wrong way. For all the mental rapport the Rowan achieved with the other Primes, none of them were ever really "open" to her. Reidinger was usually at least sympathetic to some of her problems, but he had to be available every single moment to the myriad problems of the FT&T system. And the Rowan knew fully the loneliness that Yegrani had foretold with no diminution anywhere.

When the Rowan had first been assigned to Callisto Base, she had thought it was what the words of the Sight meant, for she was a focus. After some months of the routine, the Rowan was severely disillusioned. She was useful, yes: Even essential for the smooth flow of material and messages between the Nine Star capitals, but any Prime would have done as well.

Once her enthusiasm died, she fell back on Siglen's dogmatic training and tried hard to find satisfaction, if not sublimation, in doing a difficult and taxing job well, suppressing her increasing sense of unrelieved isolation. Quite aware of her devastating loneliness, Reidinger had combed the Nine-Star League to find strong male talents, T-3s and T-4s like Afra, but she had never taken to any of them.

She liked Afra well enough, and not just because of her promise to his sister, Goswina, but not that well. The only male T-2 ever discovered in the Nine-Star League had been a confirmed homosexual. And now, on Deneb, a T-1 had emerged, out of nowhere—and so very, very far away.

Afra, take me home now, she said, suddenly aware of physical and mental exhaustion.

Afra brought the shell down with infinite care.

After the others had left the Station, the Rowan lay for a long while in the personnel carrier. In her unsleeping consciousness she knew that Ackerman and the others had retired to their quarters until Callisto once more came out from behind Jupiter's bulk. Everyone had some place to go, someone waiting for them, except the Rowan, who made it all possible. The bitter, screaming loneliness that overcame her during her off-hours welled up—the frustration of being unable to go off-planet past Afra's sharply limited range—alone, alone with her two-edged Talent. Murky green and black swamped her mind until she remembered the blown kiss. Suddenly, completely, she fell into her first restful sleep in two weeks.

Rowan. It was Deneb's touch that roused her. *Rowan, please wake up.*

Hmmmm? Her response was reluctant for sleep had been deep and desirable.

Our guests are getting rougher . . . since the germdogs . . . whipped up a broad spectrum antibiotic . . . we thought . . . they'd give up. No such . . . luck. They're . . . pounding us . . . with missiles . . . give my regards . . . to your space-lawyer friend . . . Reidinger.

You're playing pitch with missiles? The Rowan came totally awake and alert. She could feel Deneb's contact cutting in and out: he must be deflecting the bombardment.

I need backup help, sweetheart, like you and . . . any twin sisters . . . you happen . . . to have . . . handy. Jump over . . . here, will you?

Jump over? What? I can't!

Why not?

I can't! I am unable to! The Rowan moaned, twisting against the web of the couch.

But I've got . . . to have . . . help, he said and faded away.

Reidinger! The Rowan's call was a scream.

Rowan, I don't care if you are a T-1. There are certain limits to my patience and you've stretched every blasted one of them, you little white-haired ape!

His answer scorched her. She blocked automatically but clung to his touch. *Someone has got to help Deneb!* she cried, transmitting the Mayday.

What? He's joking!

How could he, about a thing like that?

Did you see the missiles? Did he show you what he was actually doing?

No, but I felt him thrusting. And since when does one of US distrust another when he asks for help?

Since Eve handed Adam a rosy, round fruit and said "eat." Reidinger's cynical retort crackled across space. *And exactly since Deneb's not been integrated into the Prime network. We can't be sure who or what he is —or exactly where he is. I certainly can't take him at his word. Oh, all right. Try a linkage so I can hear him myself.*

I can't reach him. He's too busy lobbing missiles spaceward.

I'll believe that when I see 'em. For one thing, if he's as good as he hollers, all he needs to do is tap any other potentials on his own planet. That's all the help he needs.

But . . .

But me no buts and leave me alone. I'll play Cupid only so far. Meanwhile I've got a company—and seven systems—to hold together. Reidinger signed off with a blacklash that stung.

The Rowan lay in her couch, bewildered by Reidinger's response. He was always busy, always gruff. But he had never been stupidly unreasonable. While out there, Deneb was growing weaker. She left the capsule and made for the Tower. She should be able to do something once Callisto was clear of Jupiter and the station was operational. But when incoming cargoes started piling up on the launchers, there were no naval units waiting for a Deneb push.

"There must be something we can do for him, Afra. Something!" the Rowan said, choked with an unreasonable fear. "I don't care what Reidinger said: Deneb's genuine and Talents help each other!"

Afra looked down at her sadly and compassionately, venturing to pat her frail shoulder.

"What help can we offer, Rowan? Not even you can reach all the way out to him. And Reidinger has no authority to order patrol squadrons. What about focusing whatever other Talents there are on his planet? Surely he can't be the only one!"

"He needs Prime help and . . ." She dropped her head, self-defeated.

"And you can barely go past Callisto's horizon," Afra finished for her, "which is more than any other Prime can manage."

Keerist! Incoming missile! Ackerman's mental shout startled both of them.

Instantly the Rowan linked with the stationmaster and saw, through his eyes, the little-used perimeter warning screen, now beeping frantically. Rowan located and then probed out into space. The intruder, a sophisticated projectile, leaking lethal radiations, was arrowing in from behind Uranus. Guiltily she flushed, for she ought to have detected it before the screen had. There was no time to run up the idling dynamos. The missile was coming in too fast. Deneb was certainly going to prove his peril to Reidinger! She marveled at his audacity in spinning the ET missile into the heart system.

I want a wide-open mind from everyone on this moon! The Rowan's broadcast was inescapable. *Mauli! Mick! Go into action.* She felt the surge of power as forty-eight Talents on Callisto, including Ackerman's ten-year-old son, enhanced by the twins, answered her demand. She picked up their energy—from the least 12 to Afra's sturdy 4—and sent it racing out to the alien bomb. She had to wrestle for a moment with its totally unfamiliar construction and components. With the augmented capability of the merge, it was easy enough for her to deactivate the mechanism and scatter the fissionables from the warhead into Jupiter's seething mass.

She released those who had merged with her and fell back into the couch.

"How in hell did Deneb do that?" Afra asked from the chair in which he had slumped. "Reidinger won't like it!"

She shook her head wearily. "No, but it proves Deneb's problem!"

Without the dynamos there had been no gestalt to act as the initial carrier wave for her effort. Even with the help of the others—and all of them put together didn't add up to one-third the strength of another Prime—it had been a wearying exercise. She thought of Deneb—alone, without an FT&T station or trained personnel to assist him—doing this again, and again, and again—and her heart twisted.

Warm up the dynamos, Brian. There will probably be more of those missiles.

Afra looked up, startled.

"To illustrate the point Deneb's trying to make, Afra." *Prime*

Rowan of Callisto Station alerting Earth Prime Reidinger and all other Primes! Prepare for possible attack by fissionable projectiles of alien origin. Alert all space stations and patrol forces. She lost her official calm and added angrily, *We've got to help Deneb now—we've got to! It's no longer an isolated aggression against an outlying colony. It's a concerted attack on our heart world!*

Rowan! Before Reidinger got more than her name into her mind, she opened to him and showed the five new projectiles driving toward Callisto. *For the love of little apples!* Reidinger's mind radiated incredulity. *What has our little man been stirring up?*

Shall we find out? Rowan asked with deadly sweetness.

Reidinger transmitted impatience, fury, misery, and then shock as he gathered her intention. *Your plan won't work. It's impossible. We can't merge minds to fight. All of us are too egocentric. Too unstable. We'd burn out, fighting each other.*

You, me, Altair, Betelgeuse, Procyon, and Capella. We can do it. If I can deactivate one of those hell missiles with only forty-eight minor Talents and no power for help, five Primes plus full power ought to be able to knock any sort of missile off. Then we can merge with Deneb to help him, that'll make six of us. Show me the ET who could stand up to such an assault!

Look, girl, Reidinger replied, almost pleading, *we don't have his measure. We can't just MERGE—he could split us apart, or we could burn him up. We don't know him. We can't gauge a telepath of unknown ability.*

You'd better catch that missile coming at you, she said calmly. *I can't handle more than ten at a time and keep up a sensible conversation.* She felt Reidinger's resistance to her plan weakening. She pushed the advantage. *If Deneb's been handling a planet-wide barrage, that's a very good indication of his strength. I'll handle the ego-merge because I damned well want to. Besides, there isn't any other course open to us now, is there?*

We could launch patrol squadrons.

THAT should have been done the first time he asked. It's too late now.

Their conversation was taking but brief seconds, and yet more missiles were coming in. Earth itself was under attack!

All right, Reidinger said in angry resignation, and contacted the other Primes.

No, no, no! You'll burn her out—burn her out, poor thing! Old Siglen from Altair was babbling. *Let us stick to our last—we dare not expose ourselves, no, no, no! The ETs would attack us then.*

Shut up, Ironpants, David said.

It's our responsibility, Siglen, you know that! We simply must! Capella chimed in waspishly. *Hit hard first, that's safest!*

Siglen's right, Rowan, . . . Reidinger said. *He could burn you out.*

I'll take the chance.

Damn Deneb for starting all this! Reidinger didn't quite shield his aggravation.

We've got to do it. And now!

Tentatively at the outset, and then with stunningly increased force, the leashed power of the other FT&T Primes, augmented by the mechanical surge of five great station generators, siphoned into the Rowan. She grew, grew, and only dimly saw the puny ET bombardment swept aside like so many mayflies. She grew, grew until she felt herself a colossus, larger than ominous Jupiter. Slowly, carefully, tentatively, because the massive power was braked only by her conscious control, she reached out to Deneb.

She spun on in grandeur, astounded by the limitless force she had become. She passed the small black dwarf that was the midway point. Then she felt the mind she searched for: a tired mind, its periphery wincing with weariness but doggedly persevering in nearly automatic reactions.

Oh, Deneb, Deneb! She was so relieved, so grateful to find him fighting his desperate battle, that they merged before her ego could offer even a token resistance. She abandoned her most guarded self to him and, with the surrender, the massed power she held flowed into him. The tired mind of the man grew, healed, strengthened, and blossomed until she was a mere fraction of the total, lost in the great part of this immense mental whole. Suddenly she saw with his eyes, heard with his ears, and felt with his touch, was immersed in the titanic struggle.

The greenish sky above was pitted with mushroom puffs, and the raw young hills around him were scarred with missile craters that had been deflected from targets. Easily now, he was turning aside the barrage of warheads from three immense vessels.

Let's go up there and find out what they are, the Reidinger segment said. *Now!*

Deneb approached the three enormous marauding ships. The mass-mind took indelible note of the intruders, spidery forms that scrabbled about interiors resembling intricate webs. Then, offhandedly, Deneb broke the hulls of two, spilling the contents into space. To the occupants of the survivor, he gave a searing impression of the Primes and the indestructability of the worlds in this section of space. With one great heave, he threw the lone ship away from his exhausted planet, sent it hurtling farther than it had come, into uncharted black immensity.

He thanked the Primes for the incomparable complement of an ego-merge and extended in a millisecond the tremendous gratitude of an entire planet which had been so nearly obliterated. This incredible battle could never be forgotten, and future generations would celebrate the incomparable victory.

The Rowan felt the links dissolving as the other Primes, murmuring withdrawal courtesies, left him. Deneb caught her mind fast to his and held on. When they were alone, he opened all his thoughts to her, so that now she knew him as intimately as he knew her.

Sweet Rowan. Look around you. It'll take a while for Deneb to be beautiful again, but we'll make it lovelier than ever. Come live with me, my love.

The Rowan's wracked cry of protest reverberated cruelly in both naked minds.

I can't. I'm not able! She cringed against her own outburst and closed off her inner heart so that he couldn't see the pitiful why. Mind and heart were more than willing: frail flesh bound her. In the moment of his confusion, she retreated back to that treacherous body, arched in the anguish of rejection. Then she curled into a tight knot, her body quivering with the backlash of effort and denial.

Rowan! came his cry. *Rowan! I love you!*

She deadened the outer fringe of her perceptions to everything, curled forward in her chair. Afra, who had watched patiently over her while her mind was far away, touched her shoulder.

Oh, Afra! To be so close and so far away. Our minds were one. Our bodies are forever separate. Deneb! Deneb!

The Rowan forced on her bruised self the oblivion of sleep. Afra picked her up gently and carried her to the couch in the Tower room. He shut the door and went silently down the stairs. He positioned a chair so that he could prop his feet on the bottom step and settled down to wait, his handsome face dark with sorrow, his yellow eyes blinking away moisture.

Afra and Ackerman reached the only possible conclusion: the Rowan had burned herself out. They'd have to tell Reidinger. Forty-eight hours had elapsed since they'd had a single contact with her mind. She had not heard, or had ignored, their tentative requests for her assistance. Afra and Ackerman could handle some of the routine freight with generator support but two liners were due in and that required her. She was alive but that was all: her mind was blank to any touch. At first Ackerman had assumed that she was recuperating. Afra had known better and, for that forty-eight hours, he'd hoped fervently that she would accept the irreconcilable situation.

"I'm gonna have to tell Reidinger," Ackerman said to Afra, wincing with reluctance.

Well, where's Rowan? Reidinger asked. A moment's touch with Afra told him. He, too, sighed. *We'll just have to rouse her some way. She isn't burned out; that's one mercy.*

Is it? replied Afra bitterly. *If you'd paid attention to her in the first place . . .*

Yes, I'm sure, Reidinger cut him off brusquely. *If I'd gotten her light of love his patrol squadrons when she wanted me to, she wouldn't have thought of a merge with him. I put as much pressure on her as I dared. But when that cocky young rooster on Deneb started lobbing deflected ET missiles at us . . . Well, I hadn't counted on that development. At least we managed to spur her to act. And off-planet at that.* He sighed. *I was hoping that love might make at least one Prime fly*

Whaa—at? Afra roared. *You mean that battle was staged?*

Hardly. As I said, we hadn't anticipated the ETs. Deneb presumably had only a mutating virus plague to cope with. Not ETs.

Then you didn't know about them?

Of course not! Reidinger sounded disgusted. *Oh, the original contact with Deneb for biological assistance was sheer chance. I took it as providential, an opportunity to see if I couldn't break the agoraphobia psychosis we all have. Rowan's the youngest of us. If I could get her to go to him—physically—but I failed.* Reidinger's resignation saddened Afra, too. One didn't consider the Central Prime as fallibly human. *Love isn't as strong as it's supposed to be. And where I'll get new Primes if I can't breed 'em, I don't know. I'd hoped that Rowan and Deneb . . .*

As a matchmaker . . .

I should resign . . .

Afra broke the contact abruptly as the Tower door opened and the Rowan, a wan, pale, very quiet Rowan, came down.

She smiled apologetically. "I've been asleep a long time."

"You had a tiring day," Afra said gently, "day before yesterday."

She winced and then smiled to ease Afra's instant concern. "I still am a little frazzled." Then she frowned. "Did I hear you two talking to Reidinger just now?"

"We got worried," Ackerman replied. "There're two liners coming in, and Afra and I just plain don't care to handle human cargo, you know."

The Rowan gave a rueful smile. "I know. I'm all set." She walked slowly back up to her Tower.

Ackerman shook his head sadly. "She sure has taken it hard."

Her chastened attitude wasn't the relief that her staff had once considered it might be. The work that day went on with monotonous efficiency, with none of the byplay and freakish temperament that had previously kept them on their toes. The men moved around automatically, depressed by this gently tragic Rowan. That might have been one reason why no one particularly noticed a visitor. Only when Ackerman rose from his desk for more coffee did he notice the young man in plain travel gear, sitting there quietly.

"You come up in that last shuttle?"

"Well, sort of." He spoke with a modest diffidence, rising to his feet. "I was told to see the Rowan. Reidinger signed me on in his office late this morning." Then he smiled.

Fleetingly Ackerman was reminded of the miracle of the Rowan's sudden smiles that could heat the very soul of you. This man's smile was full of uninhibited magnetic vigor, while his brilliant blue eyes danced with good humor and friendliness. Ackerman found himself grinning back like a fool and stepping forward to shake the man's hand stoutly.

"Mighty glad to know you. What's your name?"

"Jeff Raven. I just got in from . . ."

"Hey, Afra, want you to meet Jeff Raven. Here, have a coffee. A little raw on the walk up from the launch yard, isn't it? Been on any other Prime Stations?"

"As a matter of fact . . ."

Toglia and Loftus had looked around from their computers to inspect the recipient of such unusual cordiality. They found themselves as eager to welcome this charismatic stranger. Raven graciously accepted the coffee from Ackerman, who then proffered his special coveted ginger cakes which his wife excelled at making. The stationmaster had the feeling that he must give this wonderful guy something else, it had been such a pleasure to provide him with coffee.

Afra looked quietly at the stranger, his calm yellow eyes a little clouded. "Hello," he said in a rueful murmur, his tone oddly accented.

Jeff Raven's grin altered imperceptibly. "Hello," he replied, and more was exchanged between the two men than a simple greeting.

Before anyone in the Station quite realized what was happening, everyone had left his post and gathered around the newcomer, chattering and grinning, using the simplest excuse to touch his hand or shoulder. He was genuinely interested in everything said to him, and although there were twenty-three people anxiously vying to monopolize his attention, no one felt slighted. His reception seemed to envelop them all.

What the hell is happening down there? asked the Rowan, with a tinge of her familiar irritation. *Why . . .*

Contrary to all her previously sacred rules, she appeared suddenly in the middle of the room, looking wildly about her. Raven stepped to her side and touched her hand gently.

"Reidinger said you needed me," he said.

"Deneb?" Her body arched over to project the astounded whisper. *"Deneb?* But you're . . . you're here! You're *here!"*

He smiled tenderly and slid his hand down her shining hair to grip her shoulder. The Rowan's jaw dropped and she burst out laughing, the laughter of a supremely happy, carefree girl. Then her laughter broke off in a gasp of pure terror.

HOW did you get here?

Just came. You can, too, you know.

No! No. I can't! No T-1 is able to. The Rowan tried to free herself from his grasp, as if he were suddenly repulsive.

I did, though. His gentle insistence was unequivocable. *You just jumped from the Tower to this level. If you can do that, why should it matter how far you go?*

Oh, no! No!

"Did you know," Raven said conversationally, grinning about him, "that Siglen of Altair gets sick just going up and down stairs?" He looked straight at the Rowan. "You lived with her, you should know. All on the one level, not so much as a step anywhere? That long padded ramp to her tower which is so hemmed by thick-leaved trees any glimpse of the outside is obscured? I know she told you all about that hideous, grim, ghastly, nearly fatal trip she took from Earth to Altair on—of all torture mechanisms—a spaceship? Especially when she had planned to stay on Earth as its Prime? Disappointment can have a weird effect on some personalities, you know."

The girl shook her head, her eyes wonderingly wide.

"No one ever asked why she had really rather unusual reactions to a deep space flight, did they? I did. Seemed damned silly to me when Reidinger 'explained' the problem." He held his audience's attention as he paused, his grin turning malicious. "Siglen has a massive neural deterioration of the middle ear, a genuine enough disability which does make for travel difficulties. She was so miserably sick in her first space voyage, she went into a trauma about any sort of travel without discovering the real cause. The worst of it was that she then imposed that trauma on everyone else she trained. Of course, it never occurred to *her,* or anyone else, that this wasn't part of 'the price the Talented must pay!' " He dramatically placed his hand against his throat, mimicking Siglen so aptly that Afra had to choke back a laugh. Then he shot a wicked grin at the appalled Rowan.

"Siglen . . . Oh, Deneb, no!"

Raven laughed. "Oh, Callisto, yes. She passed on the trauma to every one of you. The T-2 doesn't have it. Siglen wouldn't be bothered with training an inferior Talent. The proof of the matter is that she didn't train me." He opened his arms wide. "And I, bigod, got here under my own steam. The Curse of Talent!" He mimicked Siglen's deep contralto voice again. "The Great Fear! The great bushwah! You've no middle ear imbalance: you only 'think' you've got agoraphobia. Bad enough a thought to hold for long, I agree, but it's a rotten handicap for *you* to have, my love." Warmth and reassurance passed between them, and the Rowan's eyes began to shine. Her eyes shone.

Now, come live with me and be my love, Rowan. Reidinger says you can commute from here to Deneb every day.

"Commute?" She said it aloud in hollow astonishment. And stared at him in wonder.

"Certainly," Jeff said encouragingly. "You're still a working T-1 under contract to FT&T. And so, my love, am I."

"I guess I do know my bosses, don't I?" she said with a little smile.

"Well, the terms were fair. Reidinger didn't haggle a second after I walked into his private office at eleven this morning."

"But to commute from Deneb to Callisto?" the Rowan repeated dazedly.

"All finished here for the day?" Raven asked Ackerman, who shook his head after a glance at the launching racks.

"C'mon, gal. Take me to your ivory Tower and we'll finish up in a jiffy. Then we'll talk about it. I'm not pushing you, or anything, but I've got a planet to put to rights . . . *And a few million things to discuss with you . . ."*

Jeff Raven smiled wickedly at the Rowan and pressed her hand to his lips in the age-old gesture of courtliness. The Rowan's smile answered his with blinding joy.

The others were respectfully silent as the two Talents made their way up the stairs to the once lonely Tower.

Afra broke the tableau by taking a cake from the box in Ackerman's motionless hand. There was nothing in the cake to cause his eyes to water so profusely.

"Not that that pair needs much of our help, people," he said, "but we can add a certain flourish and speed things up."

The whine of the generations sobbed away into silence, a silence which was at first pleasant as the two Primes let the tension of their labors drain from them.

Jeff Raven broke the silence, giving a low grunt as he pushed his chin down to his chest to stretch neck and shoulder muscles. He had been sitting in the swivel chair at the console, so he hadn't had the full body support of a couch like the Rowan's. He swiveled about to face her now.

"I know you," the Rowan said shyly, suddenly unnerved by his presence and the end of known routines, "and I don't."

Gently then she felt the feathery touch of his mind in hers, withdrawn as gently but leaving behind it a sweet, spicy taste. That had never happened to the Rowan before in all her mental encounters, and she took a moment to absorb the sensation.

"There's a lot about each other that we're going to have to *know,*" Jeff Raven began to smile, a smile that was also tinged with a shy uncertainty. He ran his fingers through his shock of black hair. "And Lord above, woman, we've got a lifetime to learn." His smile broadened, and he cocked his head slightly at her, looking at her with warmly affectionate eyes that hinted of deeper emotions kept in firm check.

"Look," he said in a totally different tone of voice and he leaned forward in the chair, elbows on his knees, "it's been a rough few weeks for me and now we've met, we don't have to rush *anything.* In point of fact," he said, with a huge yawn, "I'll be candidly unromantic and admit that I'm whacked. I've been on the stretch since those ETs arrived." He gave her an ingratiating smile. "That rather romantic gesture of mine, to launch us to Deneb, is totally beyond me. I'm starving, I need a bath, and about twenty years' sleep!"

The Rowan began to laugh, more gurgle than chuckle, as practical considerations dissolved the moment of restraint and doubt. She rose and thrust out her hand to him. His was warm, calloused, and physical contact only reinforced mind and voice. "Then, tonight, you come home with me!"

Gently Jeff pulled her to him. *You're such a little thing!* He tucked her head under his chin and held her against his body. She put her hands about him with an experimental lightness. His body was firm. She liked it. *That's good!* She also felt the weariness permeating muscle, sinew, blood, and bone.

"Come!" she said and jumped them into the main room of her quarters.

"Rather special," Jeff said, looking about the spacious room with appreciative eyes. "I think you'll find it easier to shrug off Siglen's silly conditioning than you believe. Look, steps all over." He gestured at the various levels, for the dwelling had been built into Callisto's stony landscape.

"I designed it myself." She spoke with pride, sensing his flattering approval as she followed his gaze, from the small conversation pit around the archaic hearth with an imitation fire, to the dining level that had a three-sided view of the gardens and the little copse, to the sound and vision wall, to the corridor leading to the wing.

"Well done! Very well done! And it proves conclusively to me that your agoraphobia was Siglen's imposition. She didn't tolerate steps anywhere. As you must know." Then he yawned convulsively. "What a lover you chose!"

"You get the bath," and she pushed him in the direction of the bathing room. "I'll fix a meal guaranteed to raise all known energy levels. Then you may sleep as long as you need to."

She "saw" him as he shucked off his clothing: very privately she compared him to Turian's heavier build and the Captain's deep tan. Then she decided that she liked his spare build, lean, muscled back and narrow hips; bulky people irritated her.

With good reason, Jeff remarked as he eased himself into the steaming pool. She had half-expected him to dive in, for it was deep enough, and heard his denying chuckle. *Another time,* he told her with a sigh of total relaxation as he floated. *Fix me that food, love, or I'll starve to death in my sleep.*

She sent the water pillow to hold up his head and felt her lips tingle with an impressed kiss. She smiled as she collected the necessary foodstuffs from storage. Siglen may have adored eating for its own sake, but the Rowan had learned the fundamentals of good nutrition and the value of well-prepared and presented food.

"What will people think of me when they see you so thin, Rowan? Eat more! It's really delicious. If you'd only force yourself to eat . . ." Siglen's wheedling tone resounded in the Rowan's ears.

It was, however, infinitely more satisfying to prepare something for Jeff Raven. So involved was she in making certain that all nutritional elements had balanced tastefully that the Rowan was astonished to feel the rhythms of profound sleep emanating from her lover. A moment's pique was soothed by her realization that she would indeed have all the time in the world to prove her worth as a cook. Now she'd better keep him from inadvertently drowning. Unexpectedly she felt some fatigue from the day's excitements.

Gently she lifted the inert form of her lover from the water, swathed him in warm, soft, scented towels, and conveyed him to her wide bed. Being telekinetic had, for once, practical applications she had not heretofore considered, she thought, tenderly gazing down at his sleeping face. All the stress and fatigue lines were smoothing away and Jeff Raven looked younger.

His wasn't actually a handsome face: without animation, the harsh planes looked uncompromising, the nose prominent, jutting out from a wide and high brow. His eyes were far more deepset than she had realized. He had a very strong jaw—no getting around this man with specious argument. She wondered if he'd jut his chin out when annoyed. His lips, too, showed firmness for all they were well-shaped, if a trifle on the thin side, but he had smiled so often, that detail had escaped her. In all, a strong, vital face and exceedingly attractive to her.

Sternly she suppressed unusual clamorings of body and blood. Eighteen-year-old Rowan might have planned to challenge Captain Turian but she wouldn't ever be silly enough to dare Jeff Raven. She placed water, fruit juice, the "supper" she had made him in a heating cocoon, in easy reach on the bedside table.

What would their children be like? Despite her solitude, she suddenly blushed. Once Turian had been cajoled out of his regrets, they had enjoyed each other thoroughly. But no one since then had aroused her. Not even the high Talents Reidinger kept sending to Gerolaman's courses, or to Callisto Tower on specious errands.

For a long while, the Rowan had held the firm conviction that, once her long training had been accomplished, her "travel" would resolve all her problems. Instead, she had gone from one lonely tower to another Yegrani's "long and lonely road" had been before her a long and lonely time. Even the cryptic "seeing" seemed fulfilled. She had been the focus. Was her reward Jeff Raven? Would she "travel" now with him?

He stirred slightly, as if responding to her thought; her heart caught in her throat. Then, with a smile, he sank more deeply into his much needed rest. She curled beside him on the wide bed, not needing to touch, content to be in his presence. And then fatigue overcame all her new sensations and wonderings.

The startlement of being kissed woke the Rowan abruptly, and it took a moment to recall the extraordinary events of the previous day.

"Honey, I am sorry to the death to have to wake you, but duty calls!" Jeff's tone and expression were regretful—and so was the clinging touch of his mind in hers, all spicy.

"Why?" She resented "duty" with an intensity that blazed from every pore.

"Easy, girl," and Jeff chided her. "When we so blithely destroyed those ET vessels, we left a lot of debris at spatially unsafe distances for the good of my poor planet." She saw in his open mind the visual report from Deneb. "Some of it's extrapolated to come thunking down in settled areas. My kin are good, but not that good."

"Can I help?" She dressed quickly.

"You can, indeed, and I'm counting on it. Reidinger has got Earth to release our colony a lot of much-needed supplies, and I need you to relay them out to me without splitting the packets. The High Command also wants samples of what we so indiscreetly made piecemeal."

"But Jeff, what about *us?*" The sheer terror of renewed solitude sounded in her cry.

He pulled her into his arms, once again tucking her head under his chin. He rocked her slowly, wrapping her in such deep and tender regard that she truly realized physical separation was no barrier to their rapport. Then he tilted her chin up and kissed her lips, a contact that was made far more poignant by his mind-touch and the scenes he projected of how they would make love when "duty" permitted. She was vibrating with a sensuality which he then completed with an intimate mental touch, and she clung to him in amazed relief. He grinned down at her, pleased by the effect he had on her.

"The chemistry's right between us, love, and I can't wait to prove it time and time and time and time again. However," and his manner altered as, with deep mental and physical regret, he released her, "while I'm gone, work hard on overcoming Siglen's impositions. I'll be back as soon as I've done garbage detail. We'll be transporting some mighty queer stuff. I'd have a good look at it when it comes through Callisto were I you, honey. If there's one group of space traveling animosities, there may be more." He released his physical hold of her and guided her to the door. "We'll walk across this time. Gives us a few more moments."

She matched strides with him and was unaware of anything on the way to the Tower but the touch of his hip and thigh against hers, his fingers laced in hers. For once she wasn't even aware of the great generators' start-up whine.

"Who was Purza?" he asked suddenly, looking down at her.

The unexpectedness of that question at this moment made her lose step. She had been worried that he might have accessed her Turian memories. Maybe he had and didn't care to comment. After all, that belonged to the past.

"Purza was my pukha," and her throat still closed with a vividly remembered grief and outrage. *One is forced to put away childish things.*

Ah, love, and tenderness, spicy-sweet and gentle, laved her. *I don't think you were allowed to be a* child. *We'll assure our own of that privilege.* Then, with a mischievous note in his tone, he added, "And I'll prove that a Raven's a much more innovative companion than a pukha."

His eyes were intensely blue and a devilish smile curved his lips, and suddenly she was aware of renewed sensations, coursing through her, setting off unusual reactions until suddenly, from her loins, an incredible warmth began to expand in a sudden burst of exquisite pain.

And that is only a sample, my love. Only a sample! Jeff's voice seemed to be part of that sensation, and she had to cling to him to remain on her feet.

Then they were in the tunnel that led to the garage. With an effort she assembled her wits, aware that Jeff was very well pleased with his effect on her. She was grateful for the diversion provided by the strange personnel carrier in the launch cradle, the blazon of the Central Worlds on its nose, the paint still gleaming with Jeff Raven's code.

"New design, huh?" She ran tentative fingers down the shell. It had not yet acquired the static of well-used carriers.

"Only the very best for the newest, love," Jeff replied, lightly teasing though there was no sparkle in his deep-blue eyes. He pulled her into his embrace and kissed her long and deeply. She responded as intensely as she could. The twinkle was back in his eyes. He quickly settled himself in the carrier. The whine of the generators was keening up to launch power. "See you, love!"

It was astonishing for everyone in the Tower to launch Jeff's capsule. He was helping, laughing when the Rowan told him to save his strength for his day's work, teasing Afra and Ackerman in a casual way and then—abruptly he had separated himself from them.

The Rowan became far too busy to examine her feelings just then. A near invasion of pods and drones, of medium-sized personnel carriers were flicked out from Earth Prime en route to Deneb: experts in all fields to parse through the debris of the invaders to ascertain what was the most important for in-depth analysis to be sent back to the main Moon labs.

Every sort of information must be gleaned from that assault, analyzed, and neatly catalogued for future reference.

Whenever Deneb-cargo went off Callisto, Jeff and the Rowan exchanged kisses, and other caresses which made her glad she was alone in the Tower. It gave an unexpected fillip to intensive mental effort.

And, as he had asked, she did a quick look at some of the more unusual flotsam that came through: hull arcs, like the segments of fruit; packages of curious supplies (food?); shreds of metallic films—clothing?; some frozen specimens of alien parts. She did recall the look of them as she, with the focus meld of Prime minds, disassembled them and their ships. Not at all humanoid, rather a form of beetle, with carapace or chitinous wings, with multiple legs, with joined digits. Some of the creatures which had been standing erect at their control devices were approximately two-meters long. Those in the round access tubes through the long space vehicles had been smaller and scurried about on six of their ten legs. There had been a heavily guarded central feature with immature creatures, a startling number of egg cases and the largest specimen. A generation ship? Indicative of perhaps a cross-galaxy voyage of incredible duration?

The contents certainly gave rise to incredible speculations and overwhelming relief that the Primes had been able to destroy such an alien menace. And some rather silly minor hysterics from the nervous.

Not only was there the unusual traffic to Deneb, but over the next few days, the Rowan was called upon to dispatch naval reconnaissance vessels to the perimeter of the Central Worlds' sphere of influence. Massive amounts of equipment and personnel were shifted around in the panic following the Denebian Incident. Reidinger decided to increase the Talented complement of the main Prime Stations for the purpose of unceasing vigilance and to upgrade distant early warning beacons set beyond the perimeter. That left him short of experienced staff, and rather short on temper as a result.

"Reports of the Incident were toned down a lot," Ackerman told an exhausted Rowan at the end of that fourth chaotic day. "The public report," he added when the Rowan blinked uncomprehendingly up at him. He decided her mind was only half here. "They decreased the size and capacity of the ships, and the armaments and potential danger."

"Considering some of the stuff that we handled, I'd say that was discreet of them," Afra remarked caustically, his fingers busily constructing a paper shape remarkably like the aliens that had been destroyed. Then he casually crumpled the *origami* into a wad.

Afra was exceedingly different from his sister, the gentle Goswina. And the day had exhausted her.

Me, too, Jeff said softly in her head. *I've got just about enough energy to crawl into my lonely bed and remember how great it was to lie beside you. To know all through the night that you were there.*

When the Rowan realized that she was grinning foolishly, "Jeff!" she said enigmatically and both men nodded understandingly.

Loftus brought in a sheaf of hard-copy sheets. "They plan to work our butts off again tomorrow, too!" He shook out the ream-long manifests of projected shipments. "And a big mother of a battleship, complete with flag admiral. Where was he when he was needed?"

"D'you think he will be?" Ackerman asked, suddenly apprehensive.

Afra snorted. "With all the monitors, detectors, remotes, and junk we've had to parcel out? Highly unlikely."

"Nothing like locking the barn door when the horse is gone!" Loftus said.

"What on earth do you mean by that?" the Rowan asked. It sounded like something Siglen would come out with.

"Old saying! Procrastination is a thief! Here, Ackerman. You'd better analyze how we're going to shift all *that!"*

I can see you now. Jeff's loving voice came softly into her mind, *talking in the Tower. Why don't you go on home so I can see you in your own place and fall asleep knowing where you are?*

In a sort of trance, the Rowan excused herself, leaving the three men staring at the spot she had just vacated.

"I suppose we'll have to get used to her looking all starry-eyed and flicking out like that," Brian said, slightly envious.

"Has she gone to Deneb?" Loftus asked, his eyes bugging out.

"She's not quite ready for that yet, I think," Afra replied and tossed off the half-finished mug of stimulant. "I hope it's not a long time coming."

As the tall Capellan went back to his workspace, he was unaccountably depressed. In no way did he resent Jeff Raven's acquisition of the Rowan. Afra had long ago buried his tentative and unrequited attraction for the quicksilver girl. He had hoped that out of sheer need she might one day have turned to him, for he adored her in his own fashion. Since the day, as a very nervous eighteen-year-old, he had reported for duty at Callisto, they had shared a rapport, becoming stronger over the years, close enough so that he did not exactly envy Jeff Raven. Rather he worried for them both.

They ought somehow to have taken themselves to Deneb that first night. He had been surprised that they hadn't. And more concerned, though it was certainly none of his business, when he sensed that the union had not been consummated. If he'd been in Jeff Raven's shoes . . . Well, how the Denebian conducted his seduction of the Rowan was NOT the business of Afra, Capellan T-4. The Rowan showed no resentment; why should he?

While he could also understand the necessity of pumping men and material out to the other Primes, and the naval units, and whatever else was on tomorrow's dockets, why hadn't Reidinger sent out some T-2s or a few well integrated T-3 teams to assist Deneb. Why couldn't FT&T have given the Rowan and Jeff a few days together? Was Reidinger still playing games with the Rowan's space cafard? Reidinger might just find his strategy backfiring.

Though Afra had little clairvoyant capability, he had a sickening uneasy-making hunch that Reidinger was wrong to proceed as he did. The trouble with an undeveloped pre-science was that it was so fecking nebulous. He intended to push against it until something did clarify. Forewarned was forearmed. Or was it?

He was tired enough so that, when he got to his own quarters, he drank a formula meal and went immediately to bed.

Rowan, love!

Jeff's rich voice was tender and soft, gently rousing her from sleep. Phantom lips laid pressure on hers, and a phantom touch caressed her loverly in other places.

She so much desired his presence, was convinced that he had somehow returned, that when she realized that she was still alone in her bed, she almost wept.

Oh, Rowan, lovey, I am so sorry! I devoutly wish I was really there. And she experienced a jolt of his own sexual tension and was a little dismayed at its intensity.

The debris is still falling?

She caught the grimness—and the fatigue—in his mind. *Like rain!* He was also disgusted. *If any of us in that merge had had the sense God gave little green apples . . .*

He gave them some?

. . . we'd have made sure we scattered those hulks sunward!

Oversight!

Overhead, too. At least we have equipment now to monitor falls. The squadron's on twenty-four-hour duty lassoing the big stuff, packing it into drones for shipment back. We may think we're tired now, but you wait. She felt the unruly humor. *One basket's entirely full of eggs.*

Eggs?

Eggs, I said. Our biologists say that the beetles were reproducing for 1) a generation-type voyage 2) shortlived workers that had to be periodically replaced, or 3) stocking up for a population explosion on our planet. They want to do an in-depth examination and extrapolation of the life cycle. So don't make an omelette.

Not with frozen eggs, Jeff! Wouldn't it be a lot easier and more work- and cost-effective to examine everything there? The Rowan felt tired just thinking about the effort involved. Was Jeff warning her or complaining?

They "say" they have to do it in the big Moon labs—to prevent contamination or something. I *think they don't want Deneb to get such a juicy contract so early in its career as a colony. We could pay off our Central Worlds' Start-up debt if we'd that kind of investigatory work here.*

The Rowan thought about that. The Armed Services, naval and military, regarded Talent with deep suspicion—since generally speaking, those of a mind to make war were too prosaic to understand minds which eschewed physical violence. Except, of course, she reminded herself, when they needed an entire squadron dispatched to a far corner of the galaxy. THEN they remembered Talent quite well! She didn't trust bureaucracy either but regulations and rules did reduce chaos to mere confusion. She had come to respect regulations: she would never condone restrictions. Not being of an acquisitive nature, she also did not understand the economics involved: she had all the possessions she needed; she could purchase whatever she liked—within reason—and she was not covetous.

Jeff was another matter. And all that happened to Jeff.

How badly is your colony in debt to Central Worlds? And how HAD your governors decided to pay it off?

This planet's mineral rich: we're miners and engineers, with enough farmers thrown in to keep us locally supplied.

The Rowan pondered a moment, permitting the peripheral information she had absorbed in that merge to surface to her public mind. She *knew* he was an engineer in a farming family. She *knew* he had six brothers and four sisters, since increases in Deneb's population were as important as any other occupation. She *knew* that his oldest brother and his two older sisters with young families had been wiped out by the aliens, as well as his father and the two youngest siblings: that two younger brothers were medical personnel, that his mother would soon deliver a posthumous child. He had uncles, aunts, and cousins unto the third degree, and half of them had minor Talents. But Deneb, which was not scheduled to achieve full status in Central Worlds nor slated to receive a Prime in the next hundred years, had not organized its Talents until the imminent invasion had forced them into maturity.

Yes, you picked up a lot about us, didn't you, sweeting? Jeff sounded pleased and she felt him stretching . . . . the stretch of someone relieving aching, strained muscles. She sent soothing impulses, phantom hands to knead and smooth. She would much rather have had the genuine warm flesh beneath equally fleshy fingers. *I, too,* and the longing in Jeff's tone ran as deep as her own.

This can't continue!

That's for sure, but I also cannot leave Deneb. Jeff's tone took on an irritated resignation. *There's just no way I can permit myself personal time if my absence results in more destruction. Like right now. Be back!*

His presence in her mind was gone: not so much as an echo remained. She felt more bereft than ever, deeply dissatisfied. If she applauded his principles, she fumed at the circumstances. Which brought her to the nub of the problem: Siglen's imposed space fear. If Jeff could not, in honor, leave Deneb at this critical moment, it was up to her to break down her own resistance to space travel.

Afra!

The Capellan's mind-touch was instantly available. He always was, she realized. Afra was like a shadow—a loving shadow she also perceived with her newly expanded perceptions of loving and caring. She squashed that observation to save Afra's sensitivity.

I'll need to practice in my shell.

Not in the middle of night, Rowan, he came back, not bothering to mask his exasperation. *Believe me, I'm all for helping the course of true love, but trying to crack a trauma of such long standing is irrational when you—and I—are exhausted. Tomorrow morning. We'll have a few hours before Callisto clears Jupiter and Earth shipments arrive. This humble T-4 needs all the rest he can get to cope with you on the best of days and I don't count today one of them! Go to sleep, Rowan. I need mine!*

It was so seldom that Afra was adamant that the Rowan meekly broke the contact. He was right. It would be crazy to try anything in her state of mind.

State of mind! How did Siglen manage to condition her so thoroughly? Why hadn't anyone noticed it? Lusena had been so common sensible: why hadn't she spotted the neurosis?

BECAUSE Siglen harped on it so often, moaned about the Curse of the Primes so that no one thought to question her. And both David and

Capella had been woefully stressed on their flights. Who would have dared question Altair's biggest asset?

Ass was right, the Rowan thought, spotting anomalies that refuted Siglen's contention. She'd always been able to teleport herself about Port City and the Tower. She'd never experienced agoraphobia. The mechanics of teleporting oneself on a planet were no different than teleporting oneself from one planet to another. The Rowan was disgusted. *YEARS* had been wasted because of Siglen's stupid inner ear imbalance!

And yet, the Rowan distinctly remembered her own terror when, as a very little girl, Lusena was taking her into the shuttle that would have transported her to Earth. She had been so terrified at the sight of that portal she had even dropped Purza to teleport to the only place of safety she knew. Siglen had been raving then about the horrors of space travel, and sparing the poor child any further anguish. Just as she had in the act of teleporting the Rowan to Callisto! The Rowan shuddered remembering that nightmare: *why* did Talents have to have such perfect recall?

David of Betelgeuse could clearly remember being nursed at his mother's breast. Capella swore she remembered her birth trauma. Which, David had acidly remarked, was why Ironpants refused to mate, unwilling to inflict such horror on a child from her womb. Well, that was her excuse.

Once again, the Rowan tried to force her memory back, before that aborted departure. All she knew about her early childhood was what she had been *told:* that her parents had died in an avalanche, that she had been the sole survivor of the Rowan disaster. She had never questioned those facts. She had devoutly wished that she had known something of her background: her real name, what her family had been like, if she'd had any brothers and sisters. It hadn't been until she'd been in Turian's company that she realized what she might have been lacking.

She did remember being taken from the hopper, and immediately sedated. She most certainly remembered telling Siglen that she was the Rowan, because "they" all called her "The Rowan Child."

Now that she *knew* that this whole fufurrah about Primes traveling in space was an imposed neurosis, she was more than halfway to restoration. Or that was the often repeated theory. She stilled her restlessness, found a comfortable position in her half-empty bed, and initiated her sleep pattern.

The next morning she was awakened by the rumble of generators warming up.

We've two hours before we clear Jupiter, Afra said in his customary dry tone.

I know. Odd how she always did. Callisto's orbit in its relation to its primary was a permanent fixture in her consciousness. She dressed quickly, remembered to drink a sustaining meal, and jogged down the passageway to the bunker where the personnel carriers were stored, saw hers missing from its rack and went on to the launch cradle in which it now rested.

She didn't feel the least bit altered from the last time she had lain on the padded couch. Shouldn't she?

Feel different? Afra echoed and gave her a chuckle.

[Why had she never realized that Afra was warm brown, velvety smooth, and faintly citrony of scent?]

YOU yourself haven't altered, Afra went on through her private observation of him. *Just your perception of the process.*

Did you ever suspect that it was a psychosis engendered by Siglen's lack of equilibrium?

[Mental shrug.] *A T-4 does not delve into the exalted mechanics of the Primes, my dear.* Afra snorted at the mere thought of such blasphemy.

But what do you think about, or Brian Ackerman, or any of those I whip back to Earth, when they're being transported?

I don't listen in, and Afra added an admonitory chiding.

You're being obstructive. Well, be objective. What do YOU think about?

During a kinetic displacement? Generally, I concentrate on getting where I'm supposed to go. Where did you plan to go today, Rowan?

I would prefer to go to Deneb, she answered in a very meek and subdued voice.

Not unless Jeff Raven is there to catch you, and he isn't. And even with the gestalt, I can't send you very far. You're safe in that respect, he added quickly when he felt the first tinge of terror in her mind. *It will take time, you know, to condition you to space travel.*

I can't just sit here in the cradle . . .

You're not, you know, Afra said very gently. *You're hovering in Demos's orbit above Mars.*

WHAT? In her fright, the Rowan projected such an almighty scream that Afra slapped his hands, instinctively but ineffectually, to his ears.

WHAT are you doing, Rowan? came a roar from Earth Prime. *Afra, I'll flay your yellow skin and hang the meat from your bones out to dry! What ARE you doing with her?*

Leave him alone, Reidinger, was the Rowan's prompt and equally agitated response. *Afra's obeying my orders and your stated wishes—that THIS Prime will learn to travel in space. Stop blustering. Here I am orbiting*

Demos and that's further than I've ever been able to come before. But, and while she forced herself to admire the view, she found herself "looking" straight ahead, unable/unwilling to turn her eyes from the sight of Demos's pitted surface with Mars's red/orange bulk beyond. As long as she had only that view to contend with, she could manage it. Demos looked exactly like its hologram.

I think that's enough for now, she added, spacing her words carefully, as if one of them might alter her head a fraction, forcing her to see more of the open space all around her shell which could be a prelude to the godawful spinning she'd felt on her first space voyage. Shut up, Rowan, that was a Siglenish imposition. Nevertheless, she felt sweat trickling down her face.

You did very well, Afra said calmly and the next thing she knew she was back in the cradle.

Did you really send me all the way to Demos, Afra? She felt totally spineless and couldn't move a hand to blot the perspiration on her face.

I certainly did, and you suffered no significant trauma according to the monitors in the shell. Just stop thinking about Siglen.

Afra did not have to sound quite so smug, she thought deep inside her head. He had royally fooled her, that treacherous T-4.

"What's the Rowan's capsule doing out here?" Ray Loftus yelled and he had flipped up the canopy before he noticed her lying inside. "Hey—whaaaaat?" He stared down at her, his face gone white. "Are you all RIGHT, Rowan?" He didn't appear to know what to do, waving one hand impotently.

"Stop dithering and give me your hand," the Rowan said. "I've been to Demos and back—for my sins!"

Ray willingly assisted her out of the capsule and, then almost too solicitously for she was drained by the experience, supported her up to the Tower building. His incredulity and several odd, unsortable fleeting emotions were inescapably projected to her through the physical contact. But she also caught pride and relief.

Afra palmed open the door, took her hand and, with a brief kinetic surge, renewed her energy. Before she could read him, he had his shield up again.

You don't need to treat this as so commonplace an occurrence, you know, she added, piqued.

Why not? It should be! Yow! He sidled away from the pinch she gave him.

Now, if fun and games are over for this morning, can I please review the day's schedule? came the acid tone of Reidinger. *There are a few alterations.*

That night as the Rowan lay in her doubly lonely bed, she reviewed that lift. She *had* felt nothing: not even that spinning—once she'd shut her mind away from the notion—that had consumed her on the 'portation from Altair to Callisto. But, in the light of present knowledge, was it any wonder she responded as she had during her first space voyage? Hadn't Siglen wept and moaned and wrung her hands and carried on as if she was sending the Rowan to her death? And all those preventive shots and medicines which, since her middle ear was not impaired at all, had probably produced the nausea, the spinning and disorientation because she hadn't needed them. Siglen had done one fine job of preconditioning her to react exactly as she had.

She'd get Afra to take her back to Demos tomorrow and this time she'd look at it—and around her. There was absolutely no physiological or psychological reason why she should be affected by space travel.

No, there's not. Keep telling yourself that, honey. Keep saying it until you believe it with all your heart and mind, Jeff's voice said, gently inserted into her mind.

Oh, your touch is so fragile . . . She worried that the tasks set him were too much for his so recently acquired abilities.

No, not at all, he replied, deepening his tone. *I didn't want to startle you.*

Don't try to deceive me, Jeff Raven. I know you're exhausted. You shouldn't even be trying to contact me in that state . . .

Aren't you glad I have? [His mental smirk was accompanied by a very delicate caress.] *Wherever you are, no matter how tired I am, I shall always reach out to you. Though . . .* and now his tone altered suggestively, *it doesn't help when I am trying to get some rest. Sleep well, love.*

She sent a light kiss for his cheek, laughing as she did so and tried to calm his mind to the sleep pattern.

Granny! I can do that for myself!

Tired as she was, she was not quite ready for sleep yet herself. So often she used sleep as a method of interrupting negative mental patterns, of unproductive and circular thinking. Sometimes she could gain an insight into a problem by going over and over it again—then wake the next morning with the solution.

Tonight Purza appeared, not the remains that Moria had vandalized, but the comfort creature that had been her mainstay. The Rowan paused, thinking back to those last days of her childhood, of all the conversations she carried on with Purza, of the silly things they'd discuss . . . *They?* The Rowan caught herself up. She *had* believed, for many years, that Purza was sentient, despite the unalterable fact that the Rowan *knew* the pukha was NOT. She had imbued many qualities and characteristics into the comfort . . . toy, say it, Rowan, toy! . . . No, not a toy. Device! Monitor! Surrogate! The pukha had certainly been the receptacle of more confidences than any human being, even of matters she never could have discussed with Lusena. Yet the Rowan distinctly remembered Purza advising her against things which she, the Rowan, had particularly wanted to do. How could the pukha have such discretion?

The loss still rankled in the Rowan's mind and heart. She had succumbed to a deep melancholia which Lusena had been unable to lift despite metamorphic treatment. Siglen had been irritated, having realized just how much she was beginning to rely on her apprentice, but she was far more fearful of contracting even the merest sniffle. Then Gerolaman had acquired the barquecat. And that ungrateful scamp whom the Rowan had counted on as a companion in her Callisto quarters had refused to leave the *Jibooti* passenger vessel, to the intense delight of the crew. She'd had to let him stay, more angered than dismayed by his defection.

"When I was a child, I played with childish things!" That phrase, which had been well dinned into her head during that painful readjustment time, now came to mind.

The Rowan tossed restlessly in her bed, hating the phrase, and all the memories it evoked.

Why would Purza come to mind now, tonight? Except that Jeff had queried the memory. Jeff was more than a substitute for a surrogate . . . except that he couldn't even do his courting of her in person!

Why Purza? Why not Rascal? She had truly outgrown the need for the comfort surrogate! Or had she?

Puzzling through that, the Rowan fell asleep. In the morning, searching her waking thoughts for an answer, she found none. Instead she had an overpowering urge to seek Jeff. And resisted. She had set an additional clock to Denebian time and he would be hard at work. She had overslept her usual waking hour but Jupiter did not clear Callisto for three hours.

Listlessly she rose to face the day's routine. She and Jeff might have their lifetimes to get to *know* each other, but she'd rather start in earnest. Damn Reidinger! How could he! She'd like to tell him a thing or two!

In person.

Watch out! she heard Afra warn the Station staff. She wasn't sure if she was annoyed or amused that caution was given. She palmed open the door into the Tower and let it whoosh shut behind her as she observed the wary expressions.

I don't think you're ready for a jaunt to Earth yet, Afra said. "Good morning, Rowan. We've got some pretty heavy stuff to shift."

She glared at the Capellan, knowing he was right. And yet, if she didn't take the plunge, when would she? Why shouldn't she—if she was only reacting to a conditioning? But his caution, and his obvious concern, deflated her impetus. She was not all that sure of her reconditioning—not just after one swing to Demos. Her glare was the signal for everyone to become intensely interested in lists or keyboards or any task that took them out of her immediate vicinity.

"Now listen up, you lot. There's two hours and fifty minutes before Callisto clears Jupiter. You all know how to set up the day's shifts without Afra and me. Afra," and she intensified her glare, "I want to go back to Demos again. Now!"

"As you wish," he said in an unexpected capitulation. She caught a very suspicious glint in his yellow eyes before he turned his head away. And his shields were up tight as air-lock seals. She decided to ignore him and marched back out of the Tower and down to the launch.

This time, though she strained her eyes wide to catch any motion, Afra's lift was so smooth that she had the bulk of Demos before her eyes again. This time she did look about her, and if her breathing quickened, she initiated control and steadied herself. The view was rather spectacular.

Is Earth visible from this position? she asked Afra. She caught her breath again as her capsule altered direction.

Cut in the visual magnification. Second position on your right finger-board, Afra told her.

Four taps and the cloud-swirled marble of Mankind's world became clearly visible. Its moon hung like a milky pebble, fully lit by the distant sun. Awesome to think that the insignificant speck in the vast space-black panorama had spawned those now inhabiting the planets of far distant suns.

Suddenly she became very conscious of the blackness around her: too much dark and she was confined in a very small space . . . And she didn't even have Purza for comfort!

Easy, Rowan! And abruptly she was back in the launch site on Callisto, Afra unsealing the lid of her personnel carrier, his yellow skin sallow with anxiety.

Shaking, she held her arms out to him. He lifted her out of the capsule and ran with her back into the Tower, yelling vocally and mentally for a stimulant.

Blackness! Why blackness, Afra? I was all right, truly all right, until I thought of the blackness . . .

And claustrophobia, Afra added. He took the glass Ray offered and held it to her lips. She was shaking too much to hold it herself.

ROWAN! Jeff's anxious shout made her wince.

I'm all right, Jeff. I'm all right.

Blackness. Why are you reacting to blackness, Rowan? Why do I see the pukha in your mind?

I don't know, Jeff. I don't know. I'm all right. Afra's determined to get me drunk early today! She tried to lighten up her mind tone: she didn't want to upset him because she'd experienced a moment's silly panic.

Scared me half to death, you did! Jeff went on and she was as aware of the pounding of his heart as her own.

Jeff, she's all right, Afra said, initiating metamorphic massage to reduce her tension.

"It wasn't space. It was the blackness. The awful blackness."

Damn it! I've had just about enough of this! Jeff Raven said, his tone incandescent with fury.

DENEB! and Reidinger's roar made even the Rowan's skull vibrate. Afra rolled his eyes in intense mental pain, clutching at his head. *Primes don't have privileges! She's only shaken. And there'll be no more of these experiments, Rowan. YOU HEAR ME?*

Even I can hear you, said David of Betelgeuse sourly.

I think you're being extremely selfish, Reidinger, came from Capella.

I told you this could be fatal, was Siglen's moan.

Leave me alone! the Rowan said, furious at being the center of so much unnecessary attention. *Go away and get back to business. Reidinger's made his point!*

Jeff's parting phantom caress did not make it any easier for the Rowan to ascend to the Tower, and her couch, and try to focus her thoughts on the day's business. A steaming cup of java appeared and she reached for it gratefully. Deep inside her something was frozen, some black . . . something odorous? A whiff that she couldn't identify—a reek that was connected with the frightening blackness. Not today's darkness, a smelly, clanging, *revolving* darkness. That was what had set off her panic—revolving around to see Earth . . . Just as the bucking *Miraki* had panicked her with Turian sailing up the Straits that time. But it had been a "spinning" motion that had triggered her on the *Jibooti* on her first space voyage.

Cargo coming in, Afra said, bringing her back to her responsibilities.

Once again Callisto Tower staff moved with dull efficiency through the day's tasks, with none of the livening humor or even bad temper that signalized an off-day for the Rowan.

Callisto was space-side of Jupiter and receiving the last of the inbound receipts, which would be downshipped once the Moon was again Earth-side, when an emergency signal for live cargo lit up the board.

Live one coming in, Rowan, Brian Ackerman warned her in his capacity of Stationmaster. She'd lost her deft touch in the late afternoon, unusual enough for her, but as the packets were not marked fragile, he hadn't remonstrated.

Now what? she demanded but she retrieved the capsule with more care.

Some Fleet nerd to judge by the ID . . . Brian began and then broke off.

At first the Rowan did not notice the silence from her staff. It was day's end and, with that tardy capsule, the generators were growling down to rest. She was making a neater pile of deliveries and transshipment copies when she heard someone taking the Tower steps two at a time.

"Tut tut, I didn't think I could really put this over on you so easily!" And it was Jeff Raven who swung the door wide, his blue eyes brilliant with teasing—and his love. "I don't think you've missed me at all!"

The Rowan didn't bother to answer his jibe. She grabbed his hand and launched them into her quarters, into her bedroom, out of their clothing, proving in every way possible just how much she had missed him and exactly what she had missed the most of him.

At several points during that magical night, they had time to exchange words rather than emotional extravagances.

"I've a new nephew, you see," he said, cuddling her against him, her head on his shoulder, her body edged as closely to his as was possible, her legs entwined about one of his. With one ear on his chest, she could hear his voice rumbling up from his diaphragm. "And I was congratulating Mother when she reminded me that a day of rest from hard labor has long been ordained. So, with the impetuosity for which I am known on

Deneb, I tagged an assortment of reliable people to hold the planet secure for at least one day, and came back for what I've been aching for!"

"I shall bless your mother forever!"

"She's mighty curious about you, I will say. I have informed her that holograms do not do you justice."

"Does she have any Talent?"

"Oh, masses, but she's never trained much, so sometimes her use of what she has can be quite devastating," and Jeff's chuckle began where her left hand rested on his flat belly. There wasn't, the Rowan realized, a spare ounce of flesh on him anywhere. He was much too thin. *Eating's the last thing on my mind, love!* "I don't think she has enough range for Callisto but, if she put her mind to it, she could blast a message to us anywhere in the City and down on the farm." His chuckle turned rueful. "Could never put anything over on our Mom."

"I never knew my mother!"

Jeff's arms pressed her lovingly. "I know, pet. I know." He shifted suddenly, raising up on one elbow, breaking the physical closeness that the Rowan was reveling in. "Why is that Purza on your mind again? I know the function of a pukha, but it's no surrogate mother!"

"You're digging deep."

"No," and Jeff frowned slightly, soothing her hair back from her face and gathering up a handful from the pillow, fascinated by its paleness in the dim light of the room. "I'm not. Not half as deep as I intend to dig. And speaking of digging, or delving . . ."

And that ended that conversation though the Rowan was fleetingly aware as Jeff stroked her body with deft erotic caresses that the interruption was deliberate. She was soon too involved on too many levels of exquisite lovemaking to complain. Jeff was incredible and kept urging her on to new delights.

When at last they moved apart an inch or so, Jeff's stomach emitted a rolling growl which the Rowan's answered.

"By God, we've even got compatible digestions."

"And you need feeding up. Does no one take care of you on Deneb?" she demanded, half her attention on manipulating food items from freezer to heating chamber.

"Got any Terran beef steak up here?" he asked, following her efforts. "We lost most of our food animals in the bombardments and we can't really plant until we clear the fields of metal objects. I don't care how nutritious the processed stuff is supposed to be, it tastes bloody awful. Oh," and he inhaled the aroma of grilling meat that wafted into the bedroom, "and never smells right. What a talented woman I've found!" And he expressed his appreciation in the most delightful way.

"Jeff! The meat'll burn!"

"Oh, a little charcoal does you no harm! Got to eat a peck of dirt, you know . . ."

"JEFF! That's the only decent steak I have right now!"

"Oh, in that case . . ." and he desisted.

After they had ravenously consumed a huge meal—with the Rowan going back again and again to her larder to supply them with the high-protein substances they both needed to fuel their ardor—they made love again. They slept so soundly that neither heard Afra's discreet knocking, nor the ringing of the comsystem.

I do beg your pardons! Afra inserted the phrase politely in each mind, repeating it with more mental force until the Rowan roused.

She felt deliciously rested, totally sated . . .

Rowan! You're broadcasting . . . Afra said with a discreet mental cough.

Startled into full consciousness, the Rowan felt the unexpected heat of a blush. Afra would never "look" but nonetheless she covered herself with a fold of the thermal sheet. Jeff Raven grumbled sleepily, one hand searching for a touch of her.

"Jeff! Wake up! We've overslept!"

"Nonsense. Today's my day off!" He opened one eye.

"I think that was yesterday, Jeff."

She's right! Reidinger doesn't know you're here . . .

Why not? Jeff pulled himself to a sitting position and then hauled the Rowan back into his arms, his hands lightly caressing her.

He's not . . . Afra faltered. *He's in a very touchy mood.*

That's not unusual! Jeff refused to be cowed. *He threw us together on purpose and now I'm here on purpose so he can like it or lump it.*

Tell him the truth, Afra, the Rowan added. *I overslept and I'll be back at work as soon as I've had a decent breakfast.*

Aware that she had, indeed, been delinquent in her own responsibilities, the Rowan tried to wriggle free. But Jeff merely tightened his arms, keeping her close.

Trouble with Reidinger is, he says jump, *and every single one of you ask* how high! *Well, this Denebian lad doesn't!* "*IS* there anything left to eat in the house, dearling?" And, as if he hadn't a care in the world, Jeff grinned fondly down at the woman held firmly against him.

The Rowan swallowed, both appalled by and admiring of Jeff's nonchalance.

"I think, lovey, it isn't only Siglen's conditioning you must slough off." His voice was soft, very gentle but with an edge in it that gave her another, totally new perspective on Jeff Raven of Deneb. "That FT&T of yours has exploited you for such a long time that you've never stopped to realize that you, as a Prime AND a citizen of Central Worlds, have certain inalienable rights that you haven't even bothered to exercise!" He dropped an affectionate kiss on the end of her nose. "And it's time to exercise! Last one in the pool has to take the day off." He began to unwind himself from her and the covers.

With all respect, Rowan, Raven, Afra said, still standing outside the dwelling, *we managed well enough yesterday but there's a passenger carrier coming in that needs the Rowan's gentle touch.*

So it has to stay cradled for half an hour, Jeff replied, employing his mouth to plant kisses on places of the Rowan that he had somehow missed earlier. *Tell the Captain it's generator trouble. I have it all the time on Deneb. No one minds!*

"But, Jeff, not a passenger ship. That's a contractual violation . . ." the Rowan began.

"And violating the contract we've been forming is a far more heinous crime in my eyes," and he leered at her, his black hair hanging over his eyes to give him a very piratical appearance. *We shan't be* that *long, Afra! Tell them they have to give way to a priority shipment. Me. And it's not ready to launch yet.*

Their swim was less than brisk but more than languid, interspersed as it was with loving kisses and caresses. Just the touch of his hand roused the Rowan, so totally unused to any physical contact. She kept in tactile contact as if loosing touch would somehow lessen their incredible rapport.

Between them—for Jeff was becoming familiar with the storage and cooking facilities in her kitchen—they had breakfast ready by the time they had dressed.

On their way to the launch pad, the Rowan's hand tucked and held against Jeff's arm, Reidinger's angry shout made her wince.

No need to shout, Jeff Raven replied mildly.

WHAT ARE YOU DOING THERE?

Spending my day of rest . . .

HA!

Now, now, Reidinger, there is a long-standing precedent for rest days, and I haven't had one, and my lovely Rowan certainly hasn't had one . . . Jeff looked down at her, his blue eyes glinting with pure mischief and a broad grin spreading across his mobile features. He restrained the Rowan from quickening her pace in her obedient effort to placate the angry Earth Prime and held her to his lazy saunter.

You have a contract with FT&T . . .

So I do, so do you, and does the Rowan, but nowhere in that contract does it stipulate we are obliged *to work a seven day week, twenty-four or twenty-six-hour day.* His tone abruptly changed. *Now butt out, Reidinger. You're invading our privacy. And that IS a contract violation!*

Some kind of a sound, initiated and abruptly severed, similar to a gargle of pure rage, echoed in their heads. Jeff grinned and the Rowan looked anxious.

"Honey, don't let him exploit you anymore. We can do without him, but he and the mighty FT&T can't do without us! Remember that. Stiff upper lip and all that guff." They had reached the battered personnel carrier, in which he had made his surreptitious arrival. Now he took her into his arms again, tucking her head under his chin, their bodies as close physically as their minds were. He said nothing, savoring the contact. Abruptly he released her, kissed her cheek, and stretched himself out in the carrier. "Same time six days from now, dearling." The hatch covered his reassuring grin.

Scurrying to the Tower, the Rowan pressed her lips tightly against the pain of this farewell, somehow more intense than when she hadn't known what she would be missing.

Now, then, honey, neither distance nor time can really separate us! And he gave a quick demonstration that made her gasp. *See what I mean?*

Her cheeks were burning in the cooler air of the passageway. Ducking her head so that none of the Station personnel could see her face as she entered the Tower, she took the steps two at a time. By the time she had taken her place, the generators had hit their peak whine.

Safe trip! she said, as she spun his shell back to Deneb. A kiss that lasted beyond the moons of Neptune brought a smile to her face. Then she flipped up the com to the waiting passenger liner. "I do apologize for the slight delay, Captain, but if you are prepared, we can launch at your convenience."

Either he was an unusually tolerant master or someone in the Station had dropped a discreet word, but he made no more comment than to request the lift at the mark of five minutes.

All that day the Rowan half expected a blast from Reidinger, so she took particular care to keep incoming and outgoing shipments moving in a steady flow. Nor did she receive any word from Jeff over the next five days. She was, however, in very constant and reassuring touch with her lover:

his presence palpable in her mind, like a silken touch in the corner of her mind, a feather-gentle caress.

That was probably why it was such a shock when abruptly she became aware of the absence of that touch.

Jeff? She felt more alone than she had when Purza had been destroyed, than when she had been . . . in the tumbling blackness. *Jeff!* She strengthened her mental shaft, swiveling in her chair in Deneb's relative direction. *JEFF!* Anxiety took the place of surprise. *JEFF RAVEN!*

What's the matter, Rowan? Afra asked, now aware of her concern.

He's gone. His touch is gone!

She heard several people rushing up the steps to her Tower.

We'll link! Afra suggested as he, Brian Ackerman, and Ray Loftus entered the room.

She opened to them and, tapping the generator power, called again. Panicking, she turned to Afra.

"He isn't there! He's surely heard us!" She tried to keep her voice steady, but Afra was far too sensitive not to feel her growing terror.

The tall Capellan took hold of her hands. "Breathe more slowly, Rowan. There can be many reasons . . ."

"No! No, it's as if he'd been blotted out suddenly. You can't understand . . ."

Rowan? The mental call was faint, heard only because the Rowan was linked with the others. *Rowan . . .*

"You see, I told you . . ." Afra began and she yanked her hands out of his.

"That's not Jeff!" *Yes?*

Come at once! Jeff needs you!

"Now, wait a moment, Rowan," and Afra caught her arm as she started out of her chair.

"You heard! He needs me! I'm going!" *I want a wide open mind from everyone on Station,* she added, jumping herself out of Afra's physical grasp and to the launch. She flipped open the canopy and settled herself within. *Where's my linkage, Afra?* There was a long pause, although the Rowan could feel each new mind of the Station's personnel adding strength to hers, Mauli wishing her luck as Mick echoed it. *Afra, do it now! If Jeff needs me, I must go! Do it before I realize* what *I'm doing!*

Rowan, you can't attempt . . . Afra began, desperately worried for her.

Don't argue, Afra. Help *me! If I've been called, I must go!* She already was consumed with anguish by Jeff's absence in her mind: she would go mad with the uncertainty of *why* his touch had been so abruptly withdrawn.

I will be watching for her at the usual point . . . came that faint firm mind-tone.

With her own abilities augmented by all those on the Station, the Rowan overrode Afra's hesitation, bringing him so firmly into the merge that he could not resist or alter it. Then, with the coordinates of the dwarf star firmly in her mind, she pressed against the generators, too, and launched her carrier.

PART THREE

DENEB

It was black, yes, but the capsule made the jump with no rotation to remind her of an old terror. She felt the unfamiliar multiple-mind touch hers, felt both urgent need and gratitude. Inclining to it, she followed the path it showed her.

Her carrier rocked as it landed roughly in the cradle. Simultaneous to the apology for the landing, she heard the gasping, clanking off-torque rattles of a malfunctioning generator. If the multiple-minds had gestalted with that, she was bloody lucky to have reached her destination at all.

Opening the canopy, she lifted herself out of the carrier, fighting to hide additional dismay at what she saw. The generator, apparently hastily installed at the side of what had once been an airfield control tower, gave one last wheeze as a stanchion collapsed. A cloud of black, oily smoke rose to obscure the mechanical corpse. From the temporary tower a group of people emerged, one of them carrying a child across her shoulder.

The Rowan reached out and recognized the dominant mind of the merge: Isthia Raven, Jeff's mother. Of the ten minds which had participated, only hers remained relatively unstressed by what the Rowan knew would have been a tremendous effort for a novice team.

My profound gratitude, she sent gently to them all. *How badly is Jeff hurt?* she asked directly of his mother.

Isthia Raven looked to her right, to an older man with such a strong resemblance to Jeff that she wasn't surprised to discover that he was an uncle.

"A freak accident," Rhodri said, guilt/grief/concern vivid in his mind as he spoke. "We'd found an unexploded beetle bomb. We're supposed to let *them* . . ." (and a thumb jerked skyward indicated the Fleet in orbit above Deneb) ". . . neutralize 'em but the fardling idiots set their great flaming pod down so hard it jarred the detonating mechanism and it exploded. Jeff tried to shield *us* and forgot to duck! Damn fool altruist. I told him and I told him that you gotta think of number one first."

As he spoke, she caught a replay of the scene from his mind, which was an orderly one for all the present turmoil of self-recriminations. She saw the cylinder uncovered in the trench it had plowed on the edge of the City; saw the disposal group's tentative investigation; saw the large armored Fleet pod come down, displacing dust and dirt in the ungainly landing, heard the shouts, saw the bomb's disintegration, and the searing rain of fragments and even their deflection. Then she saw Jeff's body start to rotate, stagger, and fall.

"The worst is the chest injury," his mother said. And from her clear mind, she showed an all too graphic image of Jeff's lacerated body and the long deep wound across the left pectoral. "The medics say it's only shock but I couldn't reach him. I thought you might be able to. Time is critical."

"Where is he?" the Rowan replied with a calmness and assurance she did not feel. Especially as she sensed that Isthia Raven was withholding some information. Something else had gone horribly wrong with Jeff. She must deny despair as long as she could.

She paid strict attention when Isthia projected an image of an underground facility, the only still functioning medical installation in the battered City. A large "7" was painted on the pillars outside a lighted entrance. "We'll follow," Isthia added, nodding toward the assortment of groundcars.

The Rowan nodded understandingly, for the kinetic effort had drained energy from everyone in that makeshift team.

She concentrated on her destination's coordinates and teleported herself as close to the 7 pillar as possible, making it less likely that she would collide with a person or an emergency vehicle. Her nose was only an inch from the pillar. She turned herself toward the entrance. Immediately she felt the presence of more Talents, Talents of varying strengths and most of them trying to cope with grief and anguish. Well, this was a hospital! What else did she expect as its aura? Jeff Raven might be the most important one to her personally, but she had caught sight of peripheral victims in Rhodri's vision.

The doors into the Level 7 facility whisked apart for her. She was surprised to find people alert to her arrival, pointing directions to the intensive-care facility where Jeff Raven lay.

She paused long enough in the anteroom to let the sanitizing panels purify her. As soon as that procedure was finished, the inner door slid aside. The recovery room was circular, split into ten wedge-shaped cubicles, several of which were curtained with patients already installed. Against the wall above each section, easily visible to the nursing staff seated at the central hub of the facility, were banks of screens, monitoring the vital signs of the injured.

Jeff was in the fifth cubicle, four medics and a nurse watching his screens, murmuring occasional comments. Their mental comments over the erratic behavior of his life signs told the Rowan that two despaired of his recovery: Two more were Talents, and one was desperately trying to think of something more to do for Jeff. Her approach was noted and room was made for her at the bedside.

Despite what she had gleaned of Jeff's injuries from his uncle, she was shocked to see him, his tanned face bleached by the powerful surgical lights, his left side showing nearly a dozen wounds in an almost stylized pattern along his upper arm, chest, hip, thigh, and calf where fragments had been removed. But the chest wound was the deepest. She could follow it, through the layers of skin, muscle, and bone, right to his heart and see where the damage had been repaired.

"Asaph, Chief Medic," said the older man. His mind still sorted out alternative treatments but he looked to her for some "miracle." "They got you here in record time. We've only just come down from the theater." He paused and the Rowan had no need of her Talent to recognize his reluctance to proceed.

"Your prognosis?"

He sighed, choosing his words, but the Rowan followed those he discarded and those he used. "He has suffered massive shock and insult. It was touch and go despite the fact they 'ported him directly here. The Admiral sent down two of his best surgeons," and Asaph indicated two of the other medics.

The Rowan's swift probe told her that the naval medics were amazed the man had lived through surgery and didn't give him a chance of survival. Their doubt stiffened the Rowan's purpose.

"Shock can be reduced, and major bodily insult," she said with such confidence and assurance that she surprised herself. But this was Jeff. Jeff Raven, her lover.

"Get him through the next few hours and he *could* stabilize," Asaph said, somehow taking heart from her positive attitude.

"It'd be a miracle," one of the naval men said, shaking his head. "There should have been a response by now . . ."

The Rowan ignored him and looked at the two Talents—the nurse, whose mind identified herself as Rakella Chadevsky, Jeff's aunt, and the medic, identified as his surgeon brother, Dean.

"Have either of you *tried* for a response?"

"Tried, yes, when he was first brought in . . ." Dean admitted.

There was not so much as a flicker, Rakella said, *and a great deal to be done physically before it was too late. At that, I only just managed to restart the heart!*

No delay? the Rowan asked, refusing to panic for that was what Isthia Raven had withheld from her. Hearts can be repaired, replaced if necessary, even in this temporary facility. As long as the brain had not been deprived of oxygen, a heart wound was not as serious as a major head wound would have been for a Talent.

None, Rakella reassured her. *I was monitoring his heart closely because of the wound . . .* she gave a tremulous smile, *I caught it before the EEC could register it!*

Then no one's tried to reach him on the metamorphic level. . . .

Neither of us *know that technique,* Dean added.

"Then you're about to learn," the Rowan said, wondering just what Talent medical staff *were* taught on Deneb, apart from reviving a faltering heartbeat.

Suppressing the fears which his moribund appearance had raised, the Rowan moved to the bed and placed her hands on Jeff's ankles. The slight chill of the skin was only normal, she told herself, and pressed deeper, feeling the faint shallow pulse at the meridian point. With fingers and mind she could feel the congestion there, as Jeff's system began to close down prior to cessation. She dug her thumbs deep into the soles of his feet, in the solar plexus correlation point, rubbing with a hard, circular motion. Then she pressed hard on the top of each big toe, again, and again. Then back to the solar plexus reflex. As she pressed again, she heard Rakella's quick inhalation.

There's a response. Whatever it is you're doing got a response!

You've repaired him on the physical level. I will deal with the metamorphic.

May I assist you? Rakella asked.

By all means. Copy my manipulations. I admit that I've had few occasions to use such treatment, but it can be quite effective. Any stimulus could make a difference. Right now, time would have no meaning for him so we use that timelessness to develop a support level strong enough to sustain his life force and restore balance.

She was startled by the muted wail of an angry baby.

Balance yourself, Isthia Raven said in a dry tone, entering the room. Grateful for the tonic of Isthia Raven's presence, the Rowan did. *I think, Asaph, that there are far too many unnecessary bodies crowding around my son. Do thank the Fleet men and send them on their way. Their thoughts are too negative, and that's a bad aura to have in here.*

With Rakella now following her every move, the Rowan repeated the hard pressure on the sole, began to massage the whole foot, warming the flesh, then gently and lightly rubbing the main bones from toe to heel bone. She worked longer at the groove between the internal cuneiform and navicular bones, which should quicken his flagging energies. She moved on to the calcaneum, massaging the side of the heel back to the Achilles tendon. Lightly her fingers crossed the top of the foot, down, and under the outer ankle bone. Then she repeated the sequence, using hard strokes only on the sole and the big toe, before lightening her pressure up the bony ridge of the arch.

Rakella had acquired the rhythm of the massage now, and they worked in unison. Occasionally Rowan tested the meridian above the left ankle, willing the tempo of her own measured heartbeat to echo in Jeff's arteries, willing him to rally, to respond, however faintly, to show them that he clung to life.

The superfluous bodies out of the way, Isthia moved to Jeff's head, smoothing back his sweaty hair. Then she placed her fingers lightly on each temple and looked up at the Rowan. Jeff's mother had the same startlingly blue eyes, the same direct, honest gaze. But neither of them could "feel" his mind.

We Ravens have hard heads, Isthia said, closing off her emotions to the hope still deferred.

And callused feet, added Rakella.

As the Rowan kneaded the sole, she suddenly felt the breakup of that awful congestion. She glanced at the monitors and they confirmed a slight but measurable improvement. Yet still, there was nothing of Jeff to touch in that special area in which all Talent dwelt.

We will not let him go! Isthia said softly. Her eyes held the contact with Rowan.

No, we will not! And the Rowan renewed her ministrations, sliding her hands up his legs to his knees and the next major meridian. Even lax in his present condition, she could feel the muscular strength of him—memories flooded back.

Even those could help, his mother said drolly.

The Rowan looked up, caught off guard.

Jeff said you had a loud voice, the Rowan said respectfully, gently stroking the bony ridge down the arch. The lightest of caresses now to coax his return. *He didn't mention you had a long ear.*

Isthia smiled. *I'd heard about this sort of hands-on techniques. Interesting!*

It might take time to show results . . .

It takes time for most healings, Rowan. And I "feel" that this is working even if we don't see much progress.

Suddenly Jeff's foot gave a feeble twitch. The Rowan started in surprise.

Now that's a definite reaction, Rowan! Rakella said, looking much encouraged.

So the Rowan pressed deeply in the pad of his left big toe and saw a wriggle in the Alpha line and a minute shudder in the Delta. Rakella gripped the right toe, and again there was a brief response.

"How long do you keep this up?" Medic Asaph asked, returning. He was deeply anxious about Jeff, his broad face reflecting concern and fatigue.

"Until we bring him back," the Rowan stated flatly. "There is no time where he is now."

Asaph gave a snort. "Time? He gave us a time, I'll tell you! Worth it, though. Jeff's sort of special to us here on Deneb." Then he added hastily, "Unfortunately, I need Rakella. Jeff wasn't the only one injured."

Isthia touched the Rowan lightly on the shoulder. "I should feed the baby," she said, and through her mind the Rowan could hear the now frantic cries of a very hungry infant. "If it's necessary he can wait a while longer . . ."

The Rowan could also feel the dichotomy of her needs: two sons to succor.

"Feed the child!" she said. She could concentrate entirely on Jeff, then, free of the anxieties of others; alone with Jeff, who was her responsibility right now as no one else had ever been.

Isthia slipped away through the curtains. The patient in the next cubicle groaned, and the Rowan heard the quick, soft steps of the nurse coming to attend him.

Then, in privacy, the Rowan forced herself to look at Jeff's face again, so sickly pale beneath the tan. For a man of such mental and physical strength and vigor, he looked boy-like when unconscious, as if injury had wiped clean all traces of his charismatic personality as well as health. The ache within her grew to alarming proportions, an insistent pressure of tears behind her eyes and her throat so clogged that she had to force breath out and then down.

Easy! Isthia's touch, stemming as it must from a pain as severe as her own, soothed her. *Do not compromise the good you've already done with negative emotions.*

Such a long ear his mother had! The Rowan was both resentful and grateful for that reminder. She paused long enough to bring the stool, the one other piece of furniture in the cubicle, to the foot of the bed. And then renewed the metamorphic treatment. Lightly, lightly, stroking endlessly. Occasionally she placed her fingers on the meridian point, feeling the beat of the arterial blood flow, and trying to bring the tempo up to her own circulatory level.

"Are you there, Jeff? Are you still there?" she whispered, willing him to hear her voice, if not her mind. And as she continued to stroke his feet, she talked to him in that whisper, so low that it would not reach past the privacy screen. Oddly, the sound of her own voice soothed her.

The Rowan had never sat in vigil. Nor had she ever—no, once before, a long, long time ago—felt so helpless. In a tumbling stinking darkness? But never had helplessness been so bitter a state. What good did Talent do her now? And yet it had! His mind might not know that she was there, but his body did, borrowing her physical strength to bolster his faltering grasp on life. She placed her hand on his wrist, her fingers monitoring the slow but not so faint beat. Yes, his body knew that she was there, even if that could not be recorded in the green lines wavering along the screens.

Through her hands she continued to let her energy flow to him. When Jeff . . . yes, *when* Jeff was well . . . she promised herself she would take additional training in the metamorphic from those Earth Talents whose healing abilities produced effects close to the miraculous. A miracle was certainly needed here. How long did miracles take on this alternate level?

Had she truly reached it? Be positive! Jeff would live, would revive, be wholly himself again. She flowed life from herself into Jeff Raven in a calm and even stream, laden with love and dedication.

Despite herself, despite her uncomfortable position on the low stool, despite her continued gentle massage, the Rowan must have dozed.

For her head was resting against one foot. She shook herself awake, ashamed at such weakness, which was negative, when positivity was so essential. Apprehensively she glanced at the monitors: all registered stronger functions.

The shout that then burst from her, bringing both nurses to the cubicle, was sheer exultation.

Rowan! cried Isthia, hope bursting like a meteor tail through her voice.

Back where she had missed it was the light but tender touch of Jeff Raven's sleeping mind.

He's there! He'll live! He's there! He'll live! she chanted, sobbing with almost unbearable joy and relief.

She intensely resented the nurses who shoved back the curtain and brusquely motioned her to one side.

Let them do their job, Rowan, said Isthia in a tone of mild rebuke. *It's not as if* he *could help raise his endorphin levels and reduce pain. Which I guarantee you he'll feel soon. He was brought in unconscious, bleeding to death, so there was no time to use less stringent methods of anesthesia. It'll take him a while to revive from the chemicals. But at least now we know he will! You have my eternal gratitude.*

The Rowan did not like being pushed to one side so arbitrarily, having to watch while necessary things were done to the body of her lover. Then the nurses, with no more than a curt nod to her, left the cubicle, twitching the curtains back in place.

"Don't jump before you can walk, girl," Isthia remarked dryly as she entered. "In case you're thinking of single-handedly nursing him from now on. Frankly, you may know how to deal excellently with the metamorphic levels but not the medical, even as deeply as you can experience. And don't glare at me like that, child! I willingly accept that my son has chosen you as his life mate but," and Isthia raised a warning hand, "you *don't* try to own a man like Jeff."

The Rowan found herself resenting Isthia's presence because it impinged on her privacy with him. She resented her cautions all the more because she recognized their validity. She did not wish to share Jeff, injured or sound. She hadn't realized just how much their necessary separations had rankled in her mind and emotions.

"Sort it out in your head now, Rowan," Isthia continued, ignoring thoughts which the Rowan didn't bother to shield. "Don't let petty jealousy and other unworthy notions tarnish what you and Jeff share. Nourish your bond, don't stifle it."

When Isthia placed a reassuring hand on her shoulder, she almost jerked away from it, unused to casual physical contact. Isthia's hand tightened.

Well, we Denebians use a lot of tactile contact, so that's another thing to get used to. It helps us lamebrains to function on the mental level.

"You're no lamebrain," the Rowan flared, her basic sense of justice denying Isthia's self-deprecation. But in rejecting that, she made eye contact with Isthia and the older woman caught and held hers, using the anger to project a searching shaft past the Rowan's guards.

You have never had it easy, have you, child? Isthia's mind brimmed with compassion and a generosity of spirit that the Rowan had not encountered since Lusena's death and which dissolved her immediate resentments. *You love Jeff but so do most of the people left on Deneb. You can't deny them their share of his attention. I wouldn't try. You're smart enough to know what I mean. Be wise enough to accept it. You hold most securely what you are willing to let go.* Then Isthia frowned slightly. "Who is Purza?"

"Jeff said you had a devastating Talent," the Rowan said, stunned that Isthia had "seen" Purza. "And I cannot imagine how you managed to access that bit of ancient history."

"It's right there at the top of your mind, my dear," Isthia said gently and pressed for an answer.

"Purza's not a who, it's a what. A monitoring device in any one of a number of comfort forms for a troubled child."

"Which you certainly were—also very much on the top of your mind. You've too strong a mind for someone untrained like me to pry into very deeply."

The Rowan gave a short ironic laugh.

"That's better," Isthia said, smiling back. "You'd got locked into a very bad mind loop there, doing you no good when Jeff is still going to need you. I'll have a meal brought in to you, and a more comfortable chair." With that she left.

Both the meal, which the Rowan forced herself to eat, and the chair, which was an improvement on the stool, were welcome. The monitors above Jeff's bed all indicated much stronger body rhythms, good Alpha and Delta responses. His light contact remained in her mind but it was still a passive one.

It was another hour before he revived enough to recognize his surroundings. At the sight of the Rowan beside his bed, he gave a weak grin which turned into a grimace of pain.

"Rowan?" and he reached for her hand, "I thought it was you, but I didn't know how you could be here." His voice was a dry whisper.

Sensing his thirst, she brushed his lips with water as she had seen the nurse do, then dribbled a teaspoonful into his mouth. *In fact, I argued with myself that I had imagined you from a deep subliminal level.*

"Hush, love. You needed me. I'm here."

You made it on your own? His mental tone was far stronger than his physical voice, and his fingers clutched hers with more force than she had expected.

Your mother . . .

Trust her to call in the cavalry. But you came? His astonishment and gratitude washed her mind.

Isthia had assembled a team. And then the generator fell apart! Relief made her silly.

Reidinger let you come?

Hush, love. I hear the nurse coming.

"Well, back with us again, huh, Raven," said the sandy-haired older nurse who flicked back the curtain. She nodded approvingly at the Rowan. "Medic Asaph will be very pleased." Then she turned squarely to the Rowan. "*Now* will you leave his bedside and get some rest before I have to clout you on the head with that hardwood bat I keep for obstreperous bedside leeches?"

"I'm fine," the Rowan said and her voice cracked with fatigue.

The nurse cocked one eyebrow skeptically. "Ha! You've done two and a half shifts already. Raven, you manage her."

Go and rest, dearling! Jeff urged. *I'll keep you in mind, you know.* And he gave her the tender smile that was hers alone.

Over the next two days, now that Jeff was on the mend and she had time to observe her surroundings, the Rowan was increasingly amazed by the resilience of the Denebians. The planet had lost over three-fifths of its population, its two population centers had been demolished by bombardment, farming communities burned out, and the mines, on which Deneb depended for outworld supplies, were all but useless.

All known survivors of both plague and attack had long since been centralized, along with available supplies and skills. That had happened even before Jeff Raven had contacted the Rowan for assistance.

Between their first momentous meeting and now, the City's ruins had been leveled, and temporary living quarters erected: rudimentary, to be sure, but supplying shelter for all. The hydroelectric plant, deep in the cliffs through which the broad Kenesaw River surged down to the distant sea, had escaped damage but it was the planet's only operating power source. An immense communal kitchen fed everyone and four facilities scheduled time for personal bathing and laundry. Except for toddlers and infants, even the children spent half their day on work teams, and schools for the older ones were devoted to on-the-job training.

While the Fleet had generously given urgent medical supplies and freeze dried emergency rations to the battered colony, the Rowan began to notice critical shortages . . . such as work boots and warm clothing now that the Denebian winter was closing in. Though the City was located in the temperate zone, winds with bitter chill factors were known to buffet the plain and the hunters could not bring in sufficient pelts from the meat animals they killed to clothe everyone.

The Rowan knew she would receive private assistance from Capella and Betelgeuse as soon as she asked, but until she had a functioning generator, she couldn't bring any of it in to Deneb. She 'ported herself out to the dilapidated facility to see just what was needed to make it functional. The cracked housing, still on the ground, was not a priority repair. The generator itself was jerry-rigged. Two slip rings had cracked, there were only the holders of the carbon brushes left, and the drive shaft looked doubtful. She lifted the housing back into place, wondering if anyone in the City had pyrotic Talent to mend the crack and if there were any spare generator parts left on Deneb.

When she entered the shaft (she couldn't give it the title of Tower), she realized that sheer blind luck must have been the guiding factor: the instrumentation was minimal, contrapted together out of spare parts not all of which seemed to perform any function when she tried to trace it. She thanked Gerolaman from the bottom of her heart for teaching her so much about the mechanical and electronic workings of a Tower. She might have passed the first essential lesson in 'porting herself in her frantic dash to Jeff's bedside, but she couldn't—wouldn't—attempt a return without more sophisticated safeguards than these.

Isthia had helped her convince the pro tem Council that the Tower facility was a priority.

"We're sort of used to doing for ourselves, you know," Makil Resnik, the provisional Governor and Labor Manager, had told her. "Anything we can't make ourselves, we do without."

Hold it, Rowan, Isthia advised when she felt the surge of the Rowan's protest. "We can make a great deal ourselves—mostly, Makil. We may even get through the winter without suitable clothes. But we must import seed and medical supplies. We've got too few survivors to risk any on the horns of false pride."

"You got a point there, Isthia. Even so, can't spare a big team to help. Got to open the Benevolent Mine right soon. They'd just hit a big seam of platinum."

"I can do a good deal of the contrapting myself but I need someone with electronic skills," the Rowan said, managing a calm tone.

Resnik consulted his compack, tapping keys with a blunt thick forefinger.

"Zathran Abita's the one she needs," Isthia said calmly. "She knows more about Towers than Jeff did. Give her a team of kids to scrounge. With any luck, she'll find most of what she needs in the salvage sheds. Oh, and Jeff has those I-beam specifications for you."

You've all this down to a fine art, haven't you, Isthia? the Rowan said, appreciating such deft manipulation. *Was it you who taught him how to charm?*

No, I learned in self-defense against his father. Bear that in mind! Isthia turned her smile from the Rowan to Resnik, her manner acquiescent and grateful.

"Little thing like you can refit a Tower herself?" Makil asked, peering at her appraisingly. "Hmm. When d'you want to start?"

She who hesitates loses her advantage, Isthia drawled. *Jeff's occupied at a suitably sedentary task that'll keep him out of mischief. A little fresh air and exercise will do you good.*

"No time like the present," the Rowan replied, deciding to ignore the fact that Isthia was manipulating her as easily as she did everyone else around her. *Why weren't you made Governor?*

The rich sound of Isthia's chuckle echoed in the Rowan's skull. *A nursing mother would make an awkward Governor. Otherwise . . .*

"I can detach Zathran only two days. Then he'll be needed at the mine, when we've got the adit cleared. Sooner we get a mine running, sooner we'll have something to cheer about."

"You've already done marvels," the Rowan assured him, slightly distracted by Isthia's asides. Then she wondered if she would manage. She'd never done anything like this before.

You'll do fine! Jeff told her. His mental tone was considerably more vibrant today than his physical condition. The Rowan knew that he struggled to overcome his injuries. *And when you're stuck, you can always call on me to bail you out!*

Ha!

By the end of the first day the Rowan found herself exceedingly encouraged by the result. With a half dozen midteens, she had gone through the open sheds where the salvaged items were stored. She had reviewed her requirements with Jeff, to see what he thought she might be able to find among the salvage. Having quick-witted kids who knew where to look among the bewildering aisles and sheds was one advantage: being kinetic and able to shift what was found immediately out to the Tower shack was another. The list of needed parts was reduced drastically by the end of that day. But before she could make the best use of Zathran Abita, she needed items like carbon brushes, two more large magnetic coils and slip rings, as well as small transducers and some circuit boards, which she could only get with Reidinger's assistance.

The unexpected fillip in the day was discovering three burgeoning Talents in her young team. The oldest girl, Sarjie, had a definite metal affinity and could assay metallic content, discern metallic fatigue or flaw in any piece she handled. She tossed more into the meltdown bins than on the pallet for transfer to the Tower. Fourteen-year-old Rences could snatch the shape of what the Rowan wanted from her mind and unerringly locate it among hundreds of rods, pipes, fittings, coils, and other "junk." Morfanu was struggling to understand a kinetic ability and the Rowan deftly guided her efforts into more positive channels. Sarjie had no telempathy: Rences' was limited to shape-finding (he preferred to see drawings or pictures of what was required), and Morfanu could not project. They needed years of training to refine their innate abilities.

For someone who had always worked with mature, trained Talent, and those mainly kinetic or telepathic, the Rowan found the association with new abilities a fascinating experience.

You've got a lot of patience with them, Jeff said approvingly.

You've tired yourself out, the Rowan accused, furious that she hadn't been keeping a watch on him along with her salvage operations.

It wasn't my head that was opened. Jeff sounded irascible and, remembering Isthia's cautionary words, the Rowan aborted a scathing retort. *Sandy's read me the riot act. But the drafts for the mine reopening are finished.* She felt his sense of satisfied achievement. He was a difficult patient, hating to be incapacitated when he was most needed, railing at medical restrictions and supervisions.

The day after major surgery, he had insisted on taking on paperwork: freeing up uninjured personnel. Sandy slipped enough of a sedative into a "restorative" drink to send him to sleep for several hours. That night, fretting because he hadn't finished the task he'd set himself that day, he refused to stop work. So, the Rowan simply shut him down into sleep.

In the small hours of that night the Rowan, tapping as lightly as possible into the generators that supplied the hospital's power, contacted Afra with the order for the most urgent items. He was reassured by her touch and reassured her that all was still functioning smoothly there, but he wasn't certain how long that would last. Relieved, the Rowan then curled up on the cot beside Jeff's bed and told herself to go back to sleep.

Don't try that on me again, Rowan, Jeff told her when she finally let him wake up late the next morning. He was livid at her high-handedness.

At least you've the strength today to get *mad,* she replied, unrepentant. There was more color in his face and more vigor visible in the monitoring graphs. *And quite likely strength enough in that fist of yours to handle a spoon. Your breakfast's ready.*

He glared at her, his eyes glinting as he imaged what he would like to do to her.

Tsk, tsk! How bizarre! she responded very sweetly. With careful kinesis, she lifted his upper-torso, inserting several pillows behind his back before she spread a napkin over his chest. *Any day now you're strong enough to try that, my own true love, I shall give in gracefully to the inevitable. Will you return the compliment now? Here's your breakfast!*

"Now," she went on pleasantly, "I have to figure out when is the best time to use the tower, so as not to brown out."

Reidinger caught up with her on her fourth morning on Deneb.

ROWAN! HOW IN HELL DID RAVEN GET YOU THERE WITHOUT MY PERMISSION?

It was as well, the Rowan thought with grim humor, that she was on Deneb instead of Callisto. He'd have singed her shields out with that roar.

Perhaps I was wrong to assume that you would prefer Jeff Raven alive? she asked acidly and grinned at such a suave throttling of Reidinger's officious outrage. She wished she could have seen his face at that moment. She followed up that shock by a clear image of Jeff as she had first seen him, adding a macabre view of the gaping chest wound. She followed this with Jeff's current appearance, palely sleeping after his chest wound had been dressed. Even with her assisting Rakella's kinetic manipulations, it hadn't been an easy ten minutes for Jeff. *The medical facilities here were reduced to the medieval by the bombardment. Which reminds me . . . I sent in a Top Priority Emergency order for replacement parts and unless you want me lodged permanently here on Deneb, they'd better be 'ported out this way NOW! At that it will take me another six days to organize a Tower I'd risk myself with. It is also,* she added, suppressing a desire to smirk, *too far for you to lift me.*

She knew that Reidinger was listening, and hard, for she could feel the throb of continued contact between their minds. Since she had his attention, she continued.

What you cannot have appreciated, as you haven't been on this planet and none of that irrelevant armada on retrieval patrol would think to mention it, is that Jeff Raven had only a very elderly jury-rigged generator for his gestalt when he was lobbing back missiles and repelling three alien vessels. Just think *what he could do with the kind of equipment most Primes consider absolutely essential before they tax their lobes.*

Deneb's broke, Reidinger roused sufficiently to growl at her.

I'm not, the Rowan replied in her sweetest tone. *That order's paid for and should be ready for shipment today. Any time you have a spare moment. Oh, and if you'd send Afra a couple of T-2s, he'll see that Callisto Station operates as efficiently as if I were there.*

And how long, came the slow acid tone of Earth Prime, *do you feel this new Denebian emergency is going to last?*

Well, until I have a Tower facility of an operational standard.

If Raven was that badly wounded, who brought you in? Reidinger's tone was suspicious.

Pure luck, I think, she replied soberly now that she had had plenty of time to poke about in the tower. When she realized what little formal kinetic training Isthia Raven had had, and all the things that could have gone wrong, she'd been horrified. Desperation can produce amazing stimulae. *I'm not about to risk a return without properly drilled personnel.* She felt curiously reticent with Reidinger and unwilling to disclose just how many strong Talents existed on Deneb. If Jeff Raven had not informed Earth Prime, she wouldn't. *There are some Talents with enough range for short-range stuff. But nothing is really short-range to Deneb, is it? Not until Jeff is recovered. Desperation got me here but calm, cool reflection is unlikely to get me back to Callisto!*

That was little more than the truth. In the first place, she was not leaving Jeff until she was certain of his complete recovery. In the morning he would be transferred to a private room. He had already taken a very short walk, gritting his teeth until his endorphin level compensated for the pain of sore tissue and muscle. The Rowan had had to exercise a stern control over the almost overpowering desire to support him kinetically. But Isthia flicked her a warning glance so the Rowan had endured the mental echoes of Jeff's discomfort without interceding.

In the second place, she wasn't at all sure that she was sufficiently confident enough to push herself, cold-mindedly, out on such a long kinetic haul. She wondered if she could try Reidinger's patience enough to wait until Jeff could handle gestalt again.

If you don't have a generator, Reidinger said with dangerous logic, *how can you expect to catch a shipment?*

My immediate need is light stuff. I've access to a small generator. Toss it out to reach here at 0300 Deneb time, and I'll catch.

If you're trying an unpowered catch, you little . . .

Burning my mind out is the last thing I want, I assure you, Reidinger, but I must have those parts or we don't get the tower functioning. If there isn't a proper tower here, you don't get me back at Callisto! Understand?

I'll deal with you later, you may be damned sure of that, Rowan child!

Despite her valiant words, the Rowan shivered delicately at the malice in those last two words. A Reidinger threat was never idle. But no threat could be severe enough to remove her from Deneb right now. Besides Jeff Raven, the planet was eminently worth any effort on her part. Like her devoted team of scroungers, Isthia, and other intangible things, like sunsets.

For ten years, she had seen none. Here, Deneb's primary went down with blazing red and orange clouds, the hectic colors fading slowly to a bleached-blue sky until the sharp peaks of the mountains that ringed the plain stood out with incredible clarity. Though starscapes were nothing new to her, the night sky was equally brilliant. Deneb VIII had three small moons whipping about it and an asteroid belt beyond their orbits that was the remains of a fourth. But it was the crispness of the night air, scented with pungent and unfamiliar fragrances when the wind blew down from the mountains, which the Rowan found truly remarkable. She liked the feel of it riffling her hair, caressing her face, pressing gently against her raised hands. Callisto had no breezes. She hadn't realized how much she had missed them until now.

So she didn't mind standing out in the dark, waiting for the shipment, ready to gestalt with the hospital's generator, taking an atavistic pleasure in the night.

Reidinger sent exactly what she ordered: not a brush, bar, or board more. It took the Rowan and her team a long day to get the generator cleaned and repaired, to reconfigure the control panel, and strengthen an adequate link to the Kenesaw hydroplant. Scarcely an aesthetic installation when finished, but it worked. Zathran Abita worried about the drain on the City's power. As the electronics expert had no notion of how Talent worked, she had to explain that the tight focus of gestalt required a short burst of power: Flow rate and pressure altered slightly with the distance and/or the weight of the object 'ported, but the actual "use" of power was split-second.

Finishing the Tower gave Deneb one more short step toward independence. The Rowan's team had broadcast her efforts so that she was greeted wherever she went on the streets or in the hospital. She was both slightly embarrassed—since Talents preferred nonentity—and delighted. Morfanu followed her about, which could have been a nuisance, except that it allowed the Rowan more opportunities to train the girl's innate Talent.

Had every single Talent instructor been killed? Or was it a result of Deneb's rather offhand colonial mind-set? On Central Worlds, parents had their children tested at birth for any sign of viable Talent. (Birth trauma often produced a measurable spark even if the ability did not mature until adolescence.) Talented children were assiduously guided and trained, even as she had been.

So far only Jeff Raven was formally contracted to the FT&T, and the Rowan knew that he was determined to keep it that way. It was also obvious to her that Deneb needed to keep every useful citizen on the planet, to ensure its revitalization. But they *ought* to be trained.

Was it fear of the exploitation by FT&T that Jeff had mentioned to her which inhibited training? But if you liked what you were doing, did it well, was that really exploitation? She had everything she wanted, anything she asked for, including tonnes of generator parts and comm equipment. Apart from her intense loneliness and isolation—which had always been with her—as Callisto Prime, she enjoyed enviable privileges along with her responsibilities.

Once Jeff was in a private room, he had almost nonstop visitors: additional workspace had to be sent for to accommodate files and monitors. He seemed always to be conferring with some group or other.

"I thought Makil was Governor," the Rowan remarked acidly to Isthia, seething with worry that Jeff would work himself sick again. "Can't *you* do anything to curb him?"

"He's one of the best engineers we have," Isthia said, though her thoughts echoed the Rowan's worry about Jeff's stamina. "So much needs to be organized for us to get through this winter. You know how short his time is."

Short? the Rowan demanded of Isthia with sudden panic, probing to comprehend her qualification.

Easy, girl, and Isthia bounced the probe back. *You know he's under contract to FT&T. When the Fleet is satisfied they've swept sky and surface clear of alien artifacts, they'll go and Jeff will be transferred elsewhere. Deneb's not due for a Prime. Reidinger made that clear to Jeff in their initial interview.*

The Rowan had forgotten about that. *If he's trying to work himself into a relapse to stay here longer, Reidinger can invoke punitive measures. He wouldn't like that. I wouldn't like that for him.*

Then make him stop working, my dear. I'm only his mother! And, grinning at the Rowan's astonishment, Isthia left the room. *And you have measures that I can't use!* Then her laugh echoed merrily in the Rowan's ears as the girl suddenly realized what she meant.

The Rowan waited until the current delegation left, then she closed and locked the door.

"Now don't start on me again, Rowan," Jeff said, looking up from the files he was scanning preparatory for his next appointment.

"You have ten minutes free-time right now," she began, affecting a provocative posture, "and it's mine!" She snuggled up to him in the bed. "Everyone on this planet gets a piece of the action but me," she went on, "and I protest."

"Rowan," he began, not quite masking irritation at her form of interruption. Then, he took a deep breath and smiled. "I do have a lot to do."

"You'd do more if you give yourself a chance to rest . . ."

Was rest what you had in mind? His startlingly blue eyes began to sparkle.

Well, it's plain you've got your mind on many things far more important . . .

He laughed then, and dropped the films onto the bedside table, putting his good right arm about her.

And while cerebral activity is all you're able for . . .

"We've got ten minutes alone and I'll just prove what I'm able for, my dearling," and that is just what he did, with considerable invention to overcome the handicap of his injuries.

When he was totally relaxed, she subtly nudged his mind into a sleep pattern and postponed his next appointment. His nap was brief but he ruefully admitted that it had done him so much good, he wouldn't fight her on that point again.

By the end of that week, healing had progressed so well that Jeff was allowed to move to the Ravens' accommodation. The Rowan was amazed to see so many people living so congenially in such cramped quarters. The room she shared with Jeff was smaller even than the one she had occupied in Lusena's neat apartment. There was space for the bed, a workspace and monitors, and one had to step around the foot of the bed to get in and out of the room.

"Of course, we don't need much space," Isthia remarked as she easily read the Rowan's dismay despite a quick shield to hide it. "We don't have much in the way of possessions at the moment," and she gave a wry laugh. "Except for Ian, none of us have more than one change of clothes right now."

At the best of times the Rowan rarely paid much attention to what she wore, but footwear, appropriate for walking between Tower and her quarters on Callisto, was coming apart at the seams.

"I think I can help you there," Isthia said and passed Ian over to the Rowan who had never held a baby in her life. The child regarded her with solemn wide eyes and his fist crept up to his mouth.

You can trust me, the Rowan said carefully, wondering how you reassured a nonverbal infant. She was rewarded by an astonishingly jubilant smile so infectious that she grinned back in an idiotic fashion.

"Yes, he has that effect on one," Isthia remarked, rummaging in a small chest that also served as seating. "Ah. You've small enough feet. Maybe these will fit."

The Rowan had grown accustomed to Isthia's openness so that when it shut down completely, as Isthia handed her a pair of country boots, she looked at her questioningly.

"A granddaughter's," was Isthia's terse response. Then she repossessed Ian, who squirmed about to watch the Rowan try on the boots. "She'd be thrilled to think her beloved uncle's wife could use them. Put them on." The moment of closure passed, but the grief behind it had not.

The Rowan carefully put them on, folding over the flap and standing up to test the fit. A little loose but a thicker pair of socks would solve that problem.

"I should have some socks around here, too," Isthia said and those, too, were passed on to the Rowan.

"This is becoming a most salutary visit for me," the Rowan said. "One gets accustomed to taking ordinary things for granted, like socks and shoes and a change of clothes."

Isthia smiled warmly at her, taking Ian's fist out of his mouth. "A new baby helps, too," she added in the same thoughtful tone. "A new life means continuity. In one way I'm sorry he's the last of them. However, an even dozen was all I promised their father."

The Rowan felt an unexpected shaft of pure envy for Jeff. To be one of a large and, from what she'd now seen, extremely congenial, loving family was truly enviable. Lusena's two children, Bardy and Finnan, had been much older, so she'd missed a true sense of family. Turian had also had a similar deep familial attachment.

"You had no family at all?" Isthia asked, surprised.

Shaking her head, the Rowan dropped the eye contact.

"I was the sole survivor of a mining camp that was buried in a freak mud avalanche," the Rowan said quietly. "The Company office narrowed it down to three possible sets of parents . . ."

"But surely, you'd remember?"

"I was three. When I cried for my mother, an entire planet heard me." The Rowan managed a weak chuckle. "They had to shut me up so all memory of the tragedy was blocked out."

"And no one's removed the block?"

"Yes, they tried once," the Rowan said, frowning as she remembered the occasion. "The block was well constructed. I resisted and they couldn't go deep enough. So," and she firmly changed mood, "that's it."

"Is it?" Isthia remarked cryptically as she left the room. Startled, the Rowan probed but she came smack up against Isthia's formidable shield.

It took the concerted effort of his entire remaining family to get Jeff, complaining that he had a lot of catching up to do, to retire at a reasonable hour. But he surrendered gracefully. "Not that I had any choice," he muttered to the Rowan as she preceded him into their room. "At that, we're lucky," he added.

"We are?" and the Rowan heard the faint sibilant shushes and loud whispers for "silence."

"We've got a room with a lock." He yawned mightily, wincing. The wounds across chest and ribs remained tender. Cautiously he lay down on the bed, then negligently reached out to draw her close to him. "I made them all promise to knock, too."

"Will they?" the Rowan asked, experiencing a sudden inhibition. She'd been looking forward to some privacy after the comings and goings of the hospital. "Will they, Jeff?"

A gentle snore informed her that the convalescent was already asleep.

Living in the boisterous Raven household was at first a novelty for the Rowan, totally foreign to anything in her experience. His various brothers and sisters, their mates, children, occasionally in-laws, orphaned nieces, nephews, and some elderly relations of both Isthia and Josh Raven lived happily in each other's pockets. The accommodation wasn't even quiet late at night since some of the residents worked late shifts. While there may have been an understanding about knocking on the door, in practice a knock was usually immediately followed by the door being opened to admit anyone who wished to speak to Jeff.

The first day, the Rowan took it in good part: she remembered what Isthia had said about "sharing." But she was unused to continual babble and certainly all the touching that went on, friendly though it was and meant in the nicest possible way, made her edgy. She firmly suppressed the irritation and sublimated it into hard work.

Along with manning the Tower for 'porting men and supplies out to the platinum mine, the Rowan did some judicious investigation into what could not be found in the salvage sheds. No one had fully inventoried what had been saved from the ruins so, when she learned from Rences that he had spent fruitless hours trying to find certain unusual bolts and fasteners, when she heard Rakella complaining about the lack of some surgical instruments, or from Isthia which size of work boot was no longer available, she discreetly contacted other Primes and, pledging her credit, made up the shortages. She respected the fierce independence of the Denebians but they could carry it too far, even if the planet was poor. A few bits and pieces could be added without offending anyone's pride.

Then Jeff paid her a surprise visit at the Tower while she was shifting some internal freight, including two crates of tools which she had discreetly brought in from Capella. The kinetics she was training for in-planet freight never questioned what she asked them to 'port. Jeff was another matter entirely. Unfortunately, not only was the origin of the crates clearly stenciled on the side, but also they were far too fresh-looking to have been miraculously "unearthed." There were also two inbound shipments still in their cradles, waiting to be dispersed.

Where *did all that come from?* Jeff wanted to know, striding into the Tower room. He halted, staring about a facility which bore little resemblance to its previous appearance. He whistled in apparent appreciation which made the three youngsters grin, but the Rowan had no trouble sensing a growing concern and anger.

"All right, Tony, you and Seb link and send Cradle 4 to the mine," she said, continuing the procedure. "Good," she added as Seb punched the appropriate coordinates up on the screen. "Touch the gestalt . . ." The generator's whine peaked. "No, don't look at me for the go. You have to know yourself *when* it's go . . . that's right. On the button! Good transfer!"

Jeff found himself a seat and, if he seemed to be interested in how the three trainees were teleporting, the Rowan was all too aware of the tension building in him. His eyes were brilliant with what she identified as suppressed outrage.

"That's all for today, crew," she said. "Now, why don't you take all you've learned 'porting inanimate objects, and take yourselves back to the City while the generator's still running sweetly." She added that impudently.

"You'll never know until you try," Jeff added with a hearty enthusiasm for them to be well gone from the tower. "Out you go. You've thrown heavier stuff than yourselves. And you ought to know where home is by now. Off with you."

One by one they managed the feat, echoes of astonished delight from each of the three minds before their touches dissolved.

"And why are you annoyed, anxious, outraged?" the Rowan demanded because she couldn't bear his displeasure.

"Deneb's bankrupt!" The words exploded from him and his eyes seemed to shoot sparks at her. "How're we going to pay for all this? Hire more kids out to FT&T when we need every survivor we've got to rebuild?"

"It's all paid for," she said, clamping down but not quickly enough for someone as swift to see an opening as Jeff Raven. *Why not? I never use half my contractual monies anyway. I called in a few favors . . .*

Deneb isn't your planet, isn't your problem . . .

Don't be so damned proprietarial! It's my problem if I make it mine. I've great respect for this planet's people. I admire your family tremendously . . .

Family's the keyword, isn't it? Jeff's tone had abruptly altered and his eyes narrowed. He caught her by the shoulders then and before she guessed his intention, he had pierced through every layer of privacy in her mind. She cried out at the force of his mental penetration as he also broke through the block that had remained intact against every other invasion.

Trembling violently, she clung to him as his intrusion restored the memory of that horrendous time. Then slowly, with infinite tenderness, he withdrew, soothing away forever the terrors of a three-year-old girl, battered about in the dark of a rolling, plunging vehicle.

They stood a long while locked in each other's arms, until the glorious sunset colored the sky and they realized just how long this passage of restoration had taken. Rowan's tears were dry on her cheeks and she was no longer racked by shudders.

"I was named Angharad Gwyn. My father was a shaft supervisor and my mother was a teacher. I had a brother named Ian . . ." She looked up in amazement.

"We have something else in common then." He tucked her head under his chin again, holding her more firmly now. "It was a rough trip all

right, enough for one small, lonely girl." He pressed her tightly when he felt her begin to shudder again. "You know, I don't think that it was all Siglen's fault that you were afraid of big, black holes in space. Not after that trip!"

"You know, you might be right," the Rowan said slowly, for she remembered all too clearly her terror at being propelled toward the shuttle that was to have taken her to Earth for training. She'd been so frightened that she'd even dropped Purza as she 'ported herself back to the one safe place she knew. "I couldn't think of anything but you on my way here." She gave a convulsive shake at the memory of her first glimpse of Jeff.

"I was really messed up, wasn't I?" he said in a thoughtful tone as he caught the image in her mind. "It's probably a very good thing that patients don't see how they look to observers."

She hugged him as hard as she could. "So, if you don't object, may I please contrive in my own small way to be of assistance to the beloved planet of your birth?"

Jeff cocked an eyebrow as he looked down at her. "You do mean well. And Makil and the Council are about to give you honorary citizenship for getting this facility working again, so I'll trust your discretion. Now, since the Tower is functional, how much longer do you think Reidinger is going to allow you a leave of absence?"

The Rowan smiled beatifically at him. "Oh, as long as I can make him believe you're still recuperating."

"Oh?" and Jeff was highly skeptical.

"It's nice and quiet out here," she said, pulling him toward the long bench under the windows, "and no one will knock on the door and then just . . ." she halted, hearing the edge in her voice.

Jeff chuckled understandingly. "I thought it was getting a bit much for you—all the Raven togetherness. You have to grow up in such bedlam to be able to ignore it, and you never really had much childhood, did you?"

"Don't patronize me!"

"Temper, temper!" And he kissed the corners of her mouth in a way that put all trace of temper out of mind.

AND JUST WHAT DO YOU THINK YOU'RE DOING, YOU WHITE-HAIRED, BUG-EYED ALTAIRIAN LOON . . .

An empath with half your range should instantly perceive that I am

feeding my nephew his breakfast, she replied equably, as she managed to get another spoonful of thin cereal into Ian's mouth.

Jeff, hands cupped under his chin, was closely observing this totally unexpected facet of his lover. *Ah! Our master's voice. Glad it's directed at you!*

NOW, LISTEN YOU, YOU UNREGENERATE . . .

You know I'm immune to flattery, the Rowan replied.

You're not immune to contract penalties. And that goes for that culchie whom I sense is in your immediate vicinity. If you and that bondmate of yours are not back at your respective stations by the end of this day—this Earth Day—you will both suffer the maximum deductions for dereliction of duty. And that *should put a crimp in this altruistic spending spree of yours, Rowan of Callisto!*

"I think he means it," the Rowan told Jeff, giggling.

"I *am* sufficiently recovered to shove you back," he said ruefully, for the past week had been one of joyful discoveries about each other. Despite busy-ness requiring long days, they had managed to work in tandem now whenever possible. And they had managed to get sufficient sleep at night to work equally hard the next day.

"I'm secure enough now to do my own 'ports," she replied, deftly scraping up the residue of cereal around Ian's mouth and popping it in again. "This doesn't seem to be too arduous a task."

The first time, no, Isthia Raven said from another room. *By the twelfth, you, too, will be delighted to have volunteers.*

My, what a long ear you have, Granny Raven, Jeff said.

I can hear with it, too, she added drily. *Or are you two so totally engrossed in each other that you can't tell when you're speaking or minding it?*

"I'll mind leaving here," the Rowan said with a deep sigh, mopping young Ian's mouth clean. Her brother's namesake was twice as precious to her for having had the brief care of him. The baby waved his arms vigorously, a deep scowl on his little old man's face which utterly entranced the Rowan. She lifted him over her shoulder, patting his back.

"Anyone would think you'd been handling babies all your life," Jeff remarked with a snort though he regarded his littlest brother with great affection.

"A natural talent," was her quick retort. Simultaneously each realized that their inane remarks covered the dismay both felt at the imminent end of this idyll.

It's not an end at all, Rowan, Jeff said, his tone infinitely tender and his blue eyes ravishing her with love.

It's a separation! she said rebelliously.

For six days? He raised both arms, to dismiss such a minor parting. *Your place or mine?* His eyes glinted mischievously.

I'd prefer to come here, but it might be more politic to remain at Callisto after being away over three weeks.

The first vacation, may I point out to you, my love, which you've had in the ten years you've been Callisto Prime!

Ah, but I never had vacation plans before now! And I suspect from the depths of our Master's anger, that it had little to do with my *absence.*

Oh??

I may, of course, be doing Reidinger an injustice . . .

That's hardly likely, love, considering the terms of the contract he made me sign—in heart's blood.

Just keep everyone at their exercises while I'm gone, Jeff. I know Sarjie's young but she should be at the mines, learning all she can about metals and mining. She should go to Earth for training. Especially since mining's Deneb's main source of income.

We can't afford to send her away. She'd hate Terra, Jeff added. *We Denebians are real homebodies and don't like leaving our birthplace.*

You did!

I, my love, had devious ulterior motives . . . and besides, I lost the toss. He grimaced in mock horror. *However, lest he chastise me by sending me somewhere too remote from Deneb . . .*

Nothing habitable is remoter than Deneb . . .

Checking appropriate times, the Rowan and Jeff decided it was best for her to arrive at the beginning of Callisto's working day, when shipments would be forwarded from Earth. For the first time, the Rowan could enter her personal capsule without a single vestige of the old inhibiting terror. In fact she was eager for the challenge.

That's the girl. And aren't you going to surprise Reidinger!

Through him she felt the generator whining up to full power. Jeff had done some fine tuning, though he had been full of pride in how she had effected the initial repairs. Closing off the fierce regret at having to leave him for even six days, the Rowan settled her mind against his and readied herself to exert their mutual gestalt.

The voyage was accomplished in a mood of high elation, for Jeff followed her all the way back. As she felt the slight jar of her carrier settling back into the cradle it had left twenty standard days before, she felt another of his special phantom caresses.

ROWAN? Afra's incredulous shout was accompanied by cheers from every other empathic Talent in the Station.

Those who could teleported to the landing area. Protocol and privacy was forgotten as she was grabbed, hugged, slapped, and made to feel royally welcomed. She found herself unexpectedly warmed by such a reception and felt color flooding her cheeks.

"We'll lay on a real celebration later, folks," Brian Ackerman said, "but we got a heavy morning's work. Boy, am I glad to see you, Rowan! You'll just never know!"

"You know," she said with a surprised laugh, "I'm glad to be back, too!"

When she reached her Tower, with all the sophisticated technology which the makeshift one on Deneb lacked, she was surprised to see two couches in place. And then turned to meet the T-2s who had replaced her. The rising whine of the generators reminded them all of duty.

We'll talk later but you have my deepest gratitude and appreciation, she told Torshan and Saggoner. She realized from a quick "look" that their deep, personal attachment raised their efficiency to a level close to Prime.

The entire Station knew the difference when the Rowan began to spin outbound materiel in or launched waiting inbound shipments. Deneb's facilities would need to be quadrupled to match Callisto's, she thought with the part of her mind that was not needed in these routine shunts. There was so much still to be done there: so little more that would be wise to do without giving offense.

Finally back at work, are you? demanded Reidinger as she deftly caught a "fragile" shipment directly from him.

I thought you'd never notice!

I'll have a few private words with you later, girl! he said in a tone that once might have distressed her.

Deep down inside herself, she chuckled. He'd have those words. In private and in person.

Then, one by one, the other Primes contacted her with welcoming thoughts. David remarked rather caustically that she had finally found out what it was all about, and did she like it? The Rowan had forgotten how clever he could be. Fortunately Capella had so many complaints about "inefficiency" from Callisto that she didn't bother with personal remarks. The others were courteously glad to have her back in her Tower and relieved that Jeff Raven was able to resume his own duties. Siglen alone sent no greeting, but the Rowan wasn't particularly surprised by silence from that quarter. Siglen would not have understood *why* she'd jeopardize everything to go to a sick man!

Once outward bound freight had been received, and inward stuff dispatched, there would be a four-hour period in which Jupiter's bulk still shielded Callisto Station from deep space. As the Rowan figured she could complete her "talk" with Reidinger well within that time frame, she spoke in a tight shaft to Afra.

I've a few things to discuss with Reidinger, old friend, she began. And felt his astonishment. *Yes, of course, I'm going to Earth! I can make my points a lot stronger in person. And, it's about time we met face-to-face.*

Is that wise? Afra asked noncommittally. He had met Reidinger on a number of occasions and was always relieved to escape unscathed.

He can't be that bad! He's got no call to discipline me for responding to an emergency. The Station was covered. I've just had a look through the records, and you've managed quite nicely without me: Nothing got cracked or spilled and no freight got misdirected. What's his problem?

The risk to Callisto Prime, Afra replied, his tone dry and his yellow eyes sardonic.

He gained a lot more than I risked, she said tartly.

I know, Afra answered with gentle emphasis.

The Rowan grinned. *I'd like to surprise the old geezer.*

Geezer? Afra sputtered at her impudence.

You've contacts at Earth Prime Headquarters. Can one of them sneak me in without having to announce my arrival?

Hmmm, that's not the easiest thing to arrange, you know. Callisto keeps you secure but there're still a lot of crazies on Earth. Reidinger's pretty heavily guarded.

Guarded?

Guarded!

But surely a Prime is able to defend himself . . .

A waste of energy that could be expended elsewhere on FT&T's behalf, Afra remarked dryly.

The Rowan snorted. *Well, can you help at all?*

There's a T-4 I trained with: one of Reidinger's trouble shooters, a Terran named Gollee Gren. I'll see if he can oblige . . .

Don't tell him who I am!

At that Afra laughed. *I doubt there's a single Talent who doesn't know who you are, my dear Rowan.*

Oh! And when she had absorbed the implications of that, *What if I shield tight? And if he's not expecting the Rowan, why would he* know *my identity if he can't read it?*

A point there but you still have to pass Security to get into the FT&T cube. A routine check will reveal your identity.

If a Prime can't manage a minor formality like that . . . The Rowan was dismissive.

If you want to get in quietly, to surprise Reidinger, it'll take managing. Let me check with Gren. There was a fairly lengthy pause before Afra came back to her. *Well, he's agreed on my especial request to escort my anonymous young friend as far as he's able but Security has to be placated. He'll meet you at the landing entrance.*

The journey was so effortless that the Rowan wondered that self-portation had once seemed so arduous and terrifying. She wondered if there was anything to be done to release Capella or David from that imposed travel fear. She indulged in a projected scene, where she just waltzed into Altair Tower and told Siglen that she had just come in from Callisto Station. The old dear would probably faint.

She settled her carrier at 14.30 Earth time in one of the single cradles just outside the reception building. She had always known what the main FT&T facility looked like, having shifted carriers, pods, and vessels of all sizes in and out of the great landing field. But standing in the center of it, dwarfed by the immense cube to her right that was the Headquarters building on a field of twenty-square kilometers, gave her the proper perspective.

Cradles, scarred by long use and rough handling, surrounded her, from the singles and doubles nearest the building to those looming on the edges of the field that could receive the largest freighters, passenger and naval craft. To the east she caught the glint of water. Surrounding the field on its land sides were rank upon rank of buildings, starting with low industrial complexes. Behind them, in seried ranks of varying height and bulk, the business and residential towers of the largest single metropolis of the Central Worlds receded into the distance.

The Rowan knew from childhood lessons that The City was unbroken along the coast of the Atlantic Ocean and each decade penetrated farther inland. By the turn of the next century, The City would inexorably engulf the entire continent as the western habitations expanded eastward to meet it. What a contrast to Deneb!

Beneath her feet she could feel the rumble of immense generators, and the wind carried the high pitched whine of hard working turbines. A light sea breeze ruffled her hair, bringing with it the taint of brine. That was almost a welcome change from the metallic stink of air that caught at the back of her throat. Even Callisto's recycled atmosphere was better than this. She began to cough as the acrid air irritated her throat.

"Hey, where did you sneak in from?" asked a man in the bright orange of a cargo handler, appearing from behind a rack of single carriers.

"I didn't sneak in," the Rowan replied. "I've come from Callisto with orders to report to Reidinger."

"Prime Reidinger to the likes of you," he replied with a sneer. He peered at the number of her shell and consulted a wrist-unit. "Hey, your carrier's not listed."

"T-4 Gollee Gren has been delegated to escort me," she replied. So much for Afra's contention that Callisto Prime was well known.

"Talent Gren? Well, now, we'll just . . ." Suddenly his expression altered to nervous surprise and he straightened, giving her a strange glance. His right hand went to his ear and it was then that the Rowan noticed he was wearing a comdevice. "Yes, sir, Talent Gren. A carrier of that ID has arrived. Yes, I'll direct her." With a much altered manner, he pointed toward the FT&T building. "You go there. Talent Gren's waiting for you. And you don't keep Talents waiting. Not around here you don't."

He jerked his head toward the airy shell of concrete and plasglas that extruded from this facade of the vast opaque cube of the Federal Telepathic and Teleportation Agency. From the sides of the great cube she could see transport cables stringing out to the edges of the great portfield and the dewdrop vehicles speeding along them.

Housed within Earth Prime Station were the administrative and training facilities of Federal Telepath and Teleport, and somewhere inside was Reidinger. The size of the place was daunting. Her whimsical notion to surprise Reidinger would tax her ingenuity. She ought not to have dismissed Afra's mental reservations so airily. How had Jeff got in to see Rowan? She pressed her lips together: that man could charm his way anywhere in the galaxy. But if he could, so could she.

The Rowan straightened her spine, rejecting the grandeur and sheer size of Earth Prime Station. Would Reidinger be as grand face-to-face? How truly realistic had that hologram cube been? She squashed notions of inadequacy, and impudence, and walked as briskly as she could, considering the difference in gravity between Callisto and Terra, toward the shell entrance.

As she neared the entrance, she saw a lone figure waiting by the door, highly visible in the deep crimson suit he wore. Suddenly she wished she had taken time to plan this expedition, for she was in rather drab work clothing. So much for impulsive decisions. Perhaps. But she was here on Earth and that was a positive action . . . and long overdue.

The central door panel of the plasglas facade whooshed open and the man stepped forward smiling, hand extended. She battened down her shields.

"Good afternoon, Angharad Gwyn." The Rowan took a second to

recognize her birth name. That was clever of Afra. Had she actually *told* him or had he accessed that discovery from her mind? Sometimes she wondered if Afra had not improved beyond a T-4. "I'm Gollee Gren. Afra of Callisto requested that I escort you to the Prime's offices."

Smiling, she shook the offered hand and deflected the tentative peek which the physical contact allowed. She permitted him to glimpse an inexperienced mind awed by its present surroundings. In return she extracted a good deal more from the T-4's mind.

"I appreciate your escort, Gollee Gren," she said in a breathless manner. "I had not realized how massive the installation is."

He hesitated, holding her hand longer than the courtesy required, and he frowned slightly. "Have we met before?"

"I doubt it. This is my first trip to Earth."

"I see. Well, let's get inside, shall we? That air's bad for the lungs," Gren said with an ingratiating smile as he gestured for them to proceed. "I've always been in Afra's debt," he went on, "but I'm not at all sure that I can assist you very much, no matter what Afra may have hinted. Especially today with all that's happened." He led her to a bank of shafts, set in the rear wall, on one side of the main exits. "Once we've got your Security Clearance," and from his mind she neatly picked all she needed to know about that procedure, "I can, of course, escort you to the Prime's office."

"I'm properly cleared," she said and showed him the Top Security Clearance badge which she had just procured for herself. "Afra took care of everything." She stepped into the first vacant lift.

"Oh?" Gollee was amazed. "I didn't realize . . . well, never mind. But even with that, it's still not going to be easy to see Prime Reidinger today. You'll have to be content with an appointment for another day." Then he placed his hand on the palm plate marked "Restricted" and the door closed and the lift rose.

"I heard," and she stressed the verb, "that the new Deneb Prime didn't have to wait."

To her surprise, Gollee Gren gave a hearty chuckle. "How that lad knew where Reidinger's real office was located has given the Security Talents bad nightmares."

So, because that location was very much in Gren's mind, Prime Rowan had no difficulty extracting it. Jeff Raven, with that charismatic charm of his, had probably used the same trick.

They stepped out of the lift into a handsomely furnished lobby, with wall hangings of exquisite design and vivid colors. Elegant hardwoods in an intricate pattern covered the floor although corridors branching from the big room were carpeted. There were finely wrought seats, couches, and some odd resting pods to accommodate nonhuman forms. Two women, elegantly dressed in wildly striped, tight-fitting body-suits with their hair in intricate braids, seemed intent on the monitors of their consoles. Both had instantly identified and made mental notes of the new arrivals, slightly uncomplimentary about the Rowan. A man appeared at the side of the main desk complex, smiling at Gren and attempting to read her. A T-3 had no chance of doing that.

"I'd like to freshen up before . . ." the Rowan said in a meek tone after looking about her with suitable awe.

Gren pointed to the green carpeted hall directly to their right. "I'll wait for you," he said and walked jauntily to the front desk to speak to the man.

The Rowan heard him greet them by name as she moved out of sight. In the toilet she did give her silver hair a brush and washed her hands. The T-3 had kept a loose touch on her as she made these ablutions. He broke that light contact with propriety as she entered one of the stalls. Then, grinning at such a splendid opportunity, the Rowan teleported herself down three stories and into the southwest corner of the great cube, right into the center of the spacious suite that was the operational "tower" of Peter Reidinger IV. She blanked herself out totally as she emerged so that not even Earth's Prime would know she was there, since he didn't waste his energies on personal safety.

His contour chair was similar to her own, but larger, to accommodate his heavier, taller body. In front of him was a console, far more extensive than hers on Callisto. Like a shadow she glided to a point where she could see his face in profile. His hair was black, with just a touch of white at the temple. She had thought he'd be younger for his mental tone was so forceful, reeking of authority and vitality. His beard must be a recent affectation, for he had been clean shaven in the holos she had of him. But the beard was cut close to his jaw and, oddly enough, was dark red as was the carefully trimmed moustache on his upper lip. Standing he would not be as tall as Jeff Raven, but he was more powerfully built. He wore an ordinary worksuit just as she did. He was frowning in concentration and the dials reflecting generator power were jumping toward the right-hand sides as he exercised considerable gestalt. Since he was obviously in mental contact, she would not commit the worst solecism of her kind.

Suddenly a long, red panel flashed wildly across the top of his console and a weird hooter broke the silence.

"Heat readings detect an intruder, Prime," said an agitated male voice.

"Well, I am glad that people can't just sneak up on you," the Rowan said with a laugh, opening her mind enough for him to recognize her, as he swung his chair about, glaring savagely.

His eyes quite literally bulged as he recognized her. She continued to laugh at the conflicting expressions mirrored on his face and did not intend to establish a mental contact until he had calmed down.

"Prime? Answer! Are you all right?"

"Abort measures." Reidinger continued to stare at her.

"But there are two heat sources . . ."

"Identify the second as Prime Rowan of Callisto and leave us alone."

There was an audible click as the comunit went silent.

"So true love really works," he said. "Which is serendipitous and saves that wretched Denebian for other duties. Since you have mastered the inhibition, you will in fact do far better than Raven." There was a smug look on Reidinger's heavy-featured face. He steepled his fingers and actually smiled at her. She did not *like* that smile. "Yes, by far the better since you're familiar with the Altairian Tower."

She caught his news then, and realized she had not only misinterpreted Siglen's lack of greeting but Gollee Gren's remark about recent developments.

"Siglen?"

"She's had a massive coronary and it would be kinder if she didn't survive." To do him credit, Reidinger deeply regretted her illness. "I didn't fancy putting Raven in charge of a Tower . . ."

"He's more than capable of it," the Rowan interrupted, with fierce pride.

"Have the courtesy to be silent!" His vocal bark was quite as severe as his mental chastisements. "Capable, yes, but unfamiliar with procedures and rather rough and ready in deliveries. As I recall it!" He cocked a heavy eyebrow at her.

"I think he's done exceedingly well considering the fact he's only just emerged."

"How is his convalescence progressing?"

The Rowan suppressed the biting answer that was her reaction to his acid tone and shrugged noncommittally. How could she have been naive enough to believe she could best Reidinger. Except . . . and her swift mind caught a wisp. So! Prime Reidinger could be read. He wasn't used to the shielding needed in the presence of another mind as strong as his own. To distract him she brought over the most comfortable of the few chairs in the big room and arranged herself languidly on it. A Prime need not stand about shifting from foot to foot like a lackey.

"His injuries are healing well but he doesn't have much stamina yet, no matter what he thinks! I set up a fairly decent Tower facility, and he did a rather nice job of fine tuning the components. Deneb's effectively back in full contact."

Reidinger waggled a finger at her. "Deneb's also broke and Central Worlds has no intention of planting a Prime Station there no matter how many Talents you discovered out there in the boonies."

"They concur completely, Peter," and she smiled when her use of his first name caught him off guard. *Is everyone and his brother awed by Earth Prime Reidinger? Surely your wife . . .*

If you don't get personal, neither will I, you white-haired scut . . . He scowled, his eyes glittering.

She laughed. "In fact, it was all I could do to muster the Talent I needed," she added which was true enough, "to repair the Tower for *my* uses."

"Speaking of use, you've exhausted all your private funds . . ."

"And borrowed as much as I could," she added, airily. "In an excellent cause. You may not have bothered to find out," and then she realized that Reidinger had been well briefed, "that that aborted invasion cost Deneb three-fifths of its population and every single installation."

Reidinger shrugged. "Colonists know the risks. They get what they can pay for. And you . . ." he shook his finger in her face again.

Don't tell me what I can or cannot do, Reidinger, she darted at him before he continued. "Nor would I humiliate such valiant people with spurious assistance. They'll do fine on their own . . ."

"Great! Because you'll be too busy at Altair Station from now on, and that man of yours is going to learn about contractual obligations."

"He'll honor them," the Rowan began, incensed by the slur implied.

Now Reidinger laughed. "And he'll learn how to function as a Prime."

"He already does!"

"No Station discipline. You," and Reidinger picked up a jade statuette and began toying with it, "will go to Altair and he will work Callisto, right where I can keep track of him."

The Rowan deflected the quick lance of Reidinger's querying shaft so that he wouldn't see her delight. She couldn't have wished for a better situation. Reidinger would soon learn more about Jeff Raven than he wished.

"Callisto?" She kept her voice neutral, with just a tinge of surprise and consternation in her mind. "How are you going to get those naval units back from Deneb then? He's good but even I can't reach that far from Callisto. Nor you!"

"Torshan and Saggoner managed quite well at Callisto in your unavoidable absence." Reidinger made no attempt to disguise how much that absence had rankled. "You say you made a working facility there? That'll be sufficient for the naval displacement. Then Deneb will just have to rely on its natural resources." And he dismissed that battered planet from further FT&T considerations.

Very privately the Rowan thought that Torshan and Saggoner would do very nicely to carry on the training she had started. Or was Reidinger better briefed about Denebian Talent potential than she could discern?

"You'll have to 'port out to Altair . . . you are able for distance now, I believe," Reidinger continued to poke subtly at her mind.

"Home the Conquering Hero comes!" she replied flippantly. Then abruptly altered her tone. "There isn't any chance that she'll recover?" She owed Siglen some compassion.

"None!" Reidinger interrupted her harshly. "We owe her surcease now, Rowan," he added in a kinder but still gruff tone. Then, for the first time, he really looked at her, his eyes falling to the security badge. "Angharad Gwyn?"

The Rowan chuckled for his surprise was genuine. "My true name."

For the first time, Reidinger's expression was respectful. "You let him read that deeply?"

"Of course." She did not bother to mention the circumstances. "Dai Gwyn, a mining supervisor, was my father, and my mother was Marie Evans Gwyn, one of the camp's teachers. I had an older brother, Ian. You may wish to correct the records."

"Why?" And Reidinger was his truculent self again. "Everyone knows you as the Rowan. You won't ever turn into an Angharad Gwyn at this late date. Now, finish the inbound stuff at Callisto. I've already called that impudent manipulative Denebian in. But, if you hang about to have a snuggle on Prime time, I'll blast the pair of you so hard where it'll hurt, you'll neither of you want to sleep together for a month. I've allowed you two far more leeway than you deserve."

"I wonder I don't see it that way, Reidinger," she said with a laugh, "considering all that our association has achieved." Reidinger probed swiftly and she countered, laughing. "Don't bother to see me out." She could afford to be gracious. "I know the way."

She put herself back into the reception area to find Gollee Gren in a heated argument with five angry men in Security garb.

"I completed my errand, Talent Gren," she said, interrupting the dressing down he was getting. She lifted enough shielding for every one of them to realize who she was. "I didn't mean to get you in trouble but I considered it necessary to speak with Earth Prime as quickly as possible."

"Couldn't you have done it the normal way?" asked Gren, understandably aggrieved.

"No," she replied without remorse. "But don't fault Afra. He could only comply with my wishes. You were most helpful and courteous." Gren gave an audible groan of resignation. Then she smiled winningly at the Security team who were considerably less forgiving. "There really is no way to keep one Prime from seeing another, you know, though the heat sensors relayed my presence. I promise that the next time I call in, I'll do so strictly by protocol. Come, Gollee, escort me back to my carrier."

PART FOUR

ALTAIR AND CALLISTO

For the Rowan to return to Altair Prime Station under her own power was cause for considerable surprise, elation, and pride. The hastily assembled reception committee included many people known to her; among them her foster brother and sister whom she was very pleased to see again. She suppressed a surge of pain that Lusena was not alive to see this day. Nor Siglen, for between her interview with Reidinger and her departure from Callisto at the end of the working day, the old Prime had, mercifully, died.

Foremost of the welcoming committee was the Secretary of Interior, who abandoned protocol to embrace the Rowan, crying happy tears.

"Oh my dear child, it is such a *blessing* to have you back with us!" Holding the Rowan away from her, she gave her a quick, satisfied appraisal, and then hugged her again.

The Rowan returned the embrace willingly, warmed by the Secretary's spontaneity. The woman had perceptibly aged in face and form but her mind was as lucid, open, and kind as ever, her touch a cheerful bright green. In that contact, the Rowan understood even more: that Secretary of the Interior Camella had hated turning the Rowan, as a child, over to

Siglen's cheerless establishment; that she had often felt guilty that she hadn't been able to keep a closer personal contact with the orphaned child. The Rowan was also aware of the Secretary's enormous pride and relief that the Rowan had returned to Altair as their Prime.

"And I wish I could have returned in less urgent circumstances," the Rowan said, replying to the spoken welcome.

Dismay colored the Secretary's face briefly. "Oh, poor Siglen. At least she was spared undue pain and never knew the ignominy of her condition. It's such a relief to have you: so fitting that Altair's native Prime should take over."

The Mayor and Governor were introduced, both new to their offices, though the Rowan recognized their faces from earlier service in less exalted roles. They observed scrupulous protocol with respectful bows. Gerolaman came forward then, beaming with pride. For such a splendid occasion, he had dressed in the formal deep-green FT&T uniform. He then introduced to her the four Talents new since her time there. The rest of the station staff she greeted by name, feeling this odd sensation that she hadn't been ten years gone from Altair.

Bralla? she asked Gerolaman privately when she noticed another missing face.

She had to retire from active service last year, Gerolaman replied testily, which suggested to the Rowan that he felt Siglen might still be alive if Bralla had been on duty. *And she deeply mourns Siglen's death.*

"We've arranged a proper reception for you later, Rowan," the Secretary of the Interior said, and then added hesitantly, "that is, if you wouldn't mind attending." Siglen had rarely responded to invitations. Nor allowed the Rowan to.

The Rowan laughed. "I'd love to come. I've been mewed up in the Callisto Dome quite long enough. It'll be a real treat to have a planet to range."

"When work's over," Gerolaman said with a discreet cough.

"Oh, dear, yes," and the Secretary was briefly dismayed. "It seems so uncharitable to shove you into the Tower as soon as you've arrived. Stationmaster and the others have done a magnificent job coping . . ."

"I can see the loaded cradles, Secretary," the Rowan said, grinning. "It won't take me long to shift it all."

The Secretary's dismay melted into a relieved smile. "Then just send word when you're free, Rowan . . . or should I call you Prime now?"

"My *name* is Angharad Gwyn," the Rowan said, grinning impudently and enjoying the shock on the Secretary's face. "I prefer being the Rowan. I'll send word," she added and walked briskly into the Tower.

Towers followed the same basic design throughout the Central Worlds' sphere of influence but the Rowan quickly noticed both subtle and obvious differences in the Altair Tower since she had last occupied it. The new generating system was three times as powerful now. The console had been updated, quite likely to compensate for Siglen's depleting energies. She noticed the overrides in every system and realized that Gerolaman and the T-2s, Bastian and Maharanjani, had discreetly monitored the old Prime.

Briefly glancing through the stack of manifests to check for priorities, the Rowan settled in the chair and ordered the generators powered up.

This is a grand new system you've got, Gerolaman, she said appreciatively for the warm-up was accomplished in seconds. *That blasted Reidinger gave me substandard junk to use on Callisto.*

Gerolaman's chuckle echoed in her head. *You didn't recognize them? The old Altairian system was sent to run Callisto!*

I don't know why I work for FT&T! Cheap outfit.

Only one in the Galaxy.

The Rowan smiled to herself and, deep in her mind, heard Jeff Raven's chuckle. Then, picking up the power of the generators, she sent cargo spinning out of their cradles in a steady stream.

I taught you well, Gerolaman remarked smugly and settled in to work.

Later the Rowan teamed up with Bastian and Maharanjani to get accustomed to their minds and methods. Both were capable, if at first very formal with her, but they relaxed as the day progressed. It was an advantage that they'd all been taught by the same Prime.

That first six days were occasionally upset by minor adjustments which the Rowan would have solved much differently at Callisto, and in the days before she had met Jeff Raven.

You've had a soothing effect on me, love, she told him in one of their conferences. Late night Altair was often early morning on Callisto and she easily pictured him in her bed, hands clasped behind his head, blankets pulled up to his chin.

One day, he began, his mind tone deep and sensual, *I might be able to enumerate the colossal alterations you've effected on this poor li'l boonie boy. What mischief have you been up to today?*

Mischief? When was I ever allowed to get into mischief? But I did clear all of Siglen's junk and got the bedroom repainted. So tonight I'll have no more nightmares about those ghastly vines and flowers trying to eat me alive.

The Rowan had not wanted to take the Prime's accommodations. Not after her first horrified look at the main lounge. Siglen's bizarre tastes had never improved and the Rowan wondered how the crippled, obese old woman had managed to move about without knocking things off tables. Shuddering at the clashing colors and hoarded junk, the Rowan had closed the door, whooshing some of the heavy musky scent Siglen had been fond of into the hall. She would have preferred to move back into her old accommodation, now occupied by Bastian, Maharanjani, and their two children. But Siglen's quarters had to be redone for the Rowan to feel comfortable in them. At that, about all she could afford was to strip off the ghastly wallpaper and paint the rooms. She had spent well into next year's salary on Deneb's needs.

She was touched to learn that Gerolaman had saved those furnishings she had not had sent on to Callisto. Despite fresh paint and sparsely furnished rooms, the Rowan spent a few uneasy nights before she settled in.

You're sure you don't want any thing from here? Jeff asked. *I can ship you anything you want.*

I'd rather see you enjoying them, Jeff, she said in a wistful tone.

Oh, I do! Though it's your Station equipment that I really covet! He imagined himself, rubbing his hands, a caricature of a greedy expression and an unctuous grin.

Don't bother. Covet Altair when you get here. Though anything would be an improvement on what you made do with on Deneb. HOW you managed so much with that one puny little generator, I'll never know. Reidinger doesn't realize just how powerful you are!

Me? There was such genuine surprise in Jeff's tone that the Rowan stifled a flash of envy. Her lover really didn't appreciate his unique strength.

The way Reidinger referred to Jeff in such uncomplimentary tones, the old man evidently hadn't realized Jeff's full potential. Odd that Reidinger, usually so quick in matters of Talent, should have missed it. He'd been in the mind merge, too. Or had he simply assumed that the merge had made Jeff Raven so omnipotent?

Yes, you, love. You're a Prime and a half. I realize it if no one else does. But don't let any one else realize it. Not yet, at any rate.

Which reminds me: it's a good thing I've got Afra and Brian coaching me on all that FT&T protocol nonsense . . . The Rowan grinned at his disgust: Jeff found those nuances and niceties the hardest part of his new duties. Deneb was too young, raw, and struggling a colony to waste time on conventions or unnecessary priorities of rank and precedence. *Otherwise I'd have made a right drone-brain of myself!*

May I live to see the day you're really droned! The Rowan knew from a chance comment of Afra's that the Callisto crew found him a lot easier to work with than she. He had assimilated procedures and the subtleties of dealing with freight and passenger captains as if he'd been trained as Prime since his early teens. He was adapting more easily to Callisto than she was to the greater responsibilities of Altair. But then that ineffable Raven charm was a considerable asset.

Are you coming home this weekend?

I really shouldn't. I'm still settling in. The Rowan remembered with a twinge of conscience the bruising schedule that Siglen had maintained.

That got her dead, didn't it? Jeff remarked, reading easily into the more private areas of her mind. *Come to think of it, it* would *be more educational for me to visit Altair. Reidinger is so hot on extending my abilities and horizons,* and Jeff chuckled with pure malice, *I'm only too willing to oblige. Besides, this weekend, I have a whole big thirty hours to "rest" unless I've misread Callisto's orbit.*

He hadn't and arrived just as she told Gerolaman to turn off the generators. He did a repeat of his act at Callisto Station, only this time the Rowan listened in. Just to see how he managed to charm so many people so completely in so short a time. He imaged her as a tiny mascot tucked over his ear as he talked Gerolaman into a buoyant mood. He was nearly as fast charming both Bastian and Maharanjani, despite the fact that they had recognized him as heavy Talent and suspected his true identity.

When she heard him meekly admit that the Altairian Prime had sent for him, she responded with a mocking laugh that preceded her into the main office.

"And if you believe everything a Denebian tells you," she said as she entered, "I'm thankful there's only one in FT&T."

When she saw Maharanjani blush furiously, she knew the woman had caught some of the very vivid, naughty imagery which was Jeff's response to that insult.

"So you're Deneb's Prime?" Gerolaman asked, too bemused by the Raven charisma to take offense at the little charade.

"Callisto's," Jeff said with a little bow. "I take whatever leavings that drop from this one's fair hands." His blue eyes were glinting with such mischief that the stationmaster chuckled. "Can I help you clear up any last little chores, Rowan?" he asked, all politeness as he gathered her proprietarially under his arm.

"I do believe," and she announced magnanimously, "that our work day is finished. Altair will resume operations in thirty-two hours. Enjoy your respite." They exited, leaving the Station crew bemused by their vivid delight in each other.

Halfway through the next day, the Rowan asked Jeff to accompany her. He knew instantly where she meant to go and kissed her gently on the cheek, compassionately supporting her.

At their destination, the smell of the *minta,* heavy in the air, made the Rowan shudder with memory.

"Rather a remarkable odor. Hard to forget." Jeff's nostrils flared at the reek.

In the quarter of a century that had passed since the devastating mudslide, *minta* had grown to formidable size on the mud-filled valley that had once been the site of the Rowan Mining camp. She found nothing to recall here, yet somewhere, fifty meters below where they stood, Angharad Gwyn had lived for three years. Though Jeff had fractured the mind block, she remembered little more than her name and an impression of faces peering down at her, no sharp details at all, though she knew some of the faces had to be her mother, father, and brother. She remembered the rag rug on which she had often played in front of a screened fireplace. And the permeating stench of *minta.*

"Not much truly memorable happens to a child of three."

"Unless she gets very unlucky," Jeff said gently. "Where did they finally locate you?" Jeff asked, knowing this return had to be played out in its entirety.

She took him down to the Oshoni valley, to the ledge where her rescuers had landed. The little hopper had long gone to scrap. The tongue of mud had dried in the ensuing years and was much eroded by rain, sun, and wind. She had a more vivid, if brief, memory of her release from the little broached hopper.

"There should be something more than this," she murmured, unable to express her unease on any level. "I don't even remember more of that awful journey than the rolling and bumping and then I was knocked unconscious."

"You were lucky in that," Jeff said, trying to fathom the nebulous disquiet which she could not express. "Coming to, with mud oozing in on you, scared, cold, hungry, and thirsty and no one to reassure you was surely the ultimate horror for a three-year-old child. But that's over and done with. Long done with," and he put his arms around her, resting his chin on her silvery hair. "I don't know what you were hoping to see, or find here, love," he added in a caressing tone, his mind soothing against her frustration. "The miracle is that you emerged alive and had a future which no one else in the Rowan Mining camp did. Don't keep looking at the past: that can't be changed."

"I checked with Immigration, you know," she said, still depressed. "There were three families with the same surname, an older couple and their two sons and wives, so I still have a choice. The Rowan Mining Company was only too willing to open up their records for the Prime," and she muttered bleakly. "I could be the daughter of Ewain and Morag Gwyn or Matt and Ann Gwyn. Both Ewain and Matt were mining engineers and the occupations of their wives was not given. So, although I do remember that my mother was a teacher, I still don't know if she was Ann or Morag."

"Does it matter very much, love?" Jeff tipped her head up to gaze with the intense fondness that his blue eyes could reflect.

"I don't know why it should since I know a lot more about my background now than I ever have, but it does. Especially when I see—and envy—your big family."

Jeff threw back his head and laughed aloud, the sound spun away on the wind that soughed down the valley. "Didn't a large family put you off back on Deneb?"

"You Ravens take getting used to," she admitted, burrowing into his shoulder. "I want as many children as I can have."

"That's one way of redressing the balance," he said with a chuckle.

"I also want them to know as much about my side of the family as they do about yours."

"Don't tell me you intend waiting until you do?" Jeff pretended dismay.

"I can't." And she opened her mind to reveal what she was only beginning to suspect.

"Rowan!" Then he whirled her about, his mind reverberating with his elation.

Easy on me! I'm having enough trouble with vertigo without you spinning me about like a wheel. But she clung to him and grinned at the effect of her marvelous secret.

When he deposited her gently to the ground again, he pressed her as close to him as possible, and she could feel his mind trying to reach the new life in her womb.

"Not yet, dear," she said in gentle amusement. "At a bare three weeks, it's no better than a tadpole."

He held her from him with mock dismay. "My son, the tadpole."

"We don't know 'son' yet awhile. Be patient!"

"I don't *feel* like being patient."

"Mankind's been able to do a lot of things, but no Talent has ever been able to speed up gestation."

"My son," Jeff insisted, his eyes shining as he looked to the future, "the new Deneb Prime!"

"Give the child a break!" the Rowan protested.

"How else are we going to get a Prime on Deneb unless we produce one between us!"

The Rowan's mood altered abruptly and she said in a querulous voice, "That's exactly what Reidinger's been counting on. Damn him. I *hate* to find myself doing exactly what he wants."

"Aren't you happy for yourself, love?" And Jeff turned her face up to his. "I am!"

"Yes, I am." But in the deepest part of her, something was not so certain.

"Your own mother says that she never heard of a kinetic having trouble during pregnancy," the Rowan said heatedly, trying not to let her anger get out of hand. Jeff didn't deserve her temper, even if his attitude was infuriating her. "She says that you're behaving exactly the way your father did for your oldest brother, proprietary, protective, paternal and a pain in the neck!"

"And I shouldn't be worried about you?" Jeff demanded, pacing her room in Altair Tower. "You're rail thin, you work long, hard hours, and you don't really feel comfortable taking a day off to get the rest and relaxation you need right now."

"You saw the food I put away at dinner? You know I've always done just fine on four hours' sleep. And I do take a whole day off . . . you won't let me do anything else."

Jeff halted midstride, fists planted against his hips: he cocked his head and that sudden marvelous smile of his erased the glower. *Why on earth are we fighting with each other?* And he held out his arms.

"I don't know," and she gratefully entered his embrace, laying her cheek against his chest. As he usually did, he tucked her head under his chin, one hand gently ruffling her hair. "Except you suddenly won't let me go on as usual just because I'm five months' pregnant. And the baby tells me he's fine."

"You're both precious to me, you see," he said, his intense feelings vibrating through her mind. "I'm new at this fatherhood game."

"With your mother, aunts, and sisters shelling babies like peas?"

This time it's my heart's darling who's gestating and that adds a totally new perspective. D'you know they're taking bets on the date Reidinger finds out?

"Who's doing a thing like that?" The Rowan was outraged. "How did they find out?"

Jeff threw his head back, laughing uninhibitedly. "My darling, you haven't really looked at yourself in a mirror, have you? You positively glow. And besides, that baby's loud. Maharanjani heard him, I'm sure, which means Bastian does, too. Gerolaman smiles fondly at you when you don't notice it. Most of the other Tower staff have suspicions, especially the way you're eating. And Afra asked me point-blank when you're due."

The Rowan made a face. "Trust Afra to know."

"Are you certain he's only a T-4? And were you aware that he has always loved you?"

"Yes," she said with a deep sigh. "I'm very fond of Afra: I trust him at the deepest level but . . ." She fell silent for a long moment. "If you hadn't made yourself known . . ."

"My timing has always been superb," Jeff replied in a tone of ineffable superiority which dissolved into one of his infectious chuckles. "You could have done a lot worse than Afra." His embrace assured her that Afra had never had a chance.

"Do let me come to Callisto next week. I haven't been back since you took over."

"You don't trust me with your ratty old dome?"

"You're dodging, Raven," she said with some heat, trying to wriggle free of his grasp. "It's my body that's pregnant, not my head—if I may hand your own words back to you—and my head is what gets me from Altair to Callisto. It took me long enough to know I could travel: don't restrict me."

"Our child is very precious to me, Rowan," Jeff said firmly. "How can you risk him?"

"I don't see any risk involved! Oh, you can be infuriating."

"I'll make one more point, dear heart. On Altair, Reidinger rarely needs to contact you. On Callisto, he will certainly exchange courtesies . . ."

"How will he know I'm there if we don't tell him?"

Jeff cleared his throat, amused. "I remember once suggesting that I could manage Reidinger. I take that back. To the nth power. That man knows *everything* about everyone connected to FT&T. He'll *know* you're there and once he establishes contact, he'll know you're pregnant. When he knows that, he's not going to let you go anywhere."

"Nonsense!"

"So be it!"

And it was. Within an hour of her arrival at Callisto, Reidinger was in touch with her.

"Now, listen here, Rowan, it's one thing for that assered Denebian to ricochet about the stars like a . . ."

Aware of the contact, Jeff had covered his face to conceal his "I told you so" grin. As Reidinger's voice broke off, Jeff raised his hand and began ticking off seconds with his fingers. He had just added the fourth when Reidinger came back.

YOU'RE PREGNANT? And you RISKED yourself 'porting from Altair? Shock, horror, and fury reverberated so violently in her mind that the Rowan exclaimed.

Reidinger! Jeff's stern voice cut through even as he jumped from his chair to put protective arms about his shivering mate. *Ease up!*

BY ALL THE HOLIES, RAVEN, I thought you'd have more sense! How COULD you permit such a risk?

No risk was involved, Reidinger, the Rowan snapped, furious that Reidinger could startle her so badly. *I'm quite capable . . .*

CAPABLE? You're no more capable . . .

That is quite enough of that, Reidinger, Jeff intervened in a tone that halted the Earth Prime mid-fume. *The Rowan's in excellent health and the pregnancy is proceeding normally. Not that that is YOUR business.*

It is MY business if a Prime jeopardizes herself . . .

Especially one who can breed for you and FT&T! the Rowan angrily shot back at him. *Well, I'm NOT breeding for you and FT&T. This is between Jeff Raven and me. There's nothing in my contract that says FT&T*

controls the produce of my womb! Get that straight, Reidinger. My son is not automatically indentured to FT&T.

A long pause. *A son? You know that already?* Something akin to awe replaced the bluster. It wasn't just that Reidinger had abruptly discarded anger as a useless tool against the partners he was trying to dominate. It was something more but *what* eluded the Rowan.

Yes, and the Rowan, too, reduced her tone to the conversational. She didn't really want Reidinger angry with her. Or with Jeff.

You're in contact with him? The need to know came across as a painful urgency.

Jeff raised his eyebrows in surprise at the near plea.

Five months into the pregnancy, we both are, Jeff answered when he felt the Rowan was spinning out the silence too long.

Why did you tell him that? she said in a private shaft at him. *He doesn't deserve it.*

We've had our fun with him, Rowan. I've been listening on another level. Reidinger's a tired, worried old man and you've just given him something to hope for at a time when he needs it.

What does he need hope for?

I don't know, and Jeff was baffled. To Reidinger he said, *It's a nebulous contact, of course, at this stage of fetal development . . .*

And what do you *know of fetal development?* the Rowan asked again on the private level.

Jeff grinned at her. *I didn't have six sisters without picking up some dribs and drabs of obstetrics!*

Suddenly both realized that Reidinger had broken off contact during their swift mental exchanges.

"Well, that was sudden!" the Rowan said, piqued.

Jeff chuckled. "We gave the old boy something to mull over."

The Rowan let out a long sigh then. "I'm glad it was a short inquisition. Now, whose turn is it to cook?"

"Ah-ha, I decided neither of us would waste time on mundane chores so scan the list of viands made ready for your arrival!" He tapped up a menu which used such an elegant archaic script that the Rowan had trouble deciphering it.

"I could probably eat all of it!"

"And grow to Siglen's size over the next few months? I won't permit it," and with the foolery that followed, it was nearly an hour before they returned to the menu again.

They were sitting in front of the artificial fire which was, as Jeff reluctantly admitted, a very good simulation, when the comunit gave a discreet burp and tripped the green flash all over the house.

Raising her eyebrows in surprise at such a discreet summons—both she and Jeff were accustomed to a direct mental inquiry—she opened the channel.

"Prime Rowan?" asked an unfamiliar feminine voice, a warm and kind voice, "I am Elizara Matheson, T-1, Medic/Ob. With all due respect, I request an interview."

"Not on my day off!" The Rowan's finger was halfway to the disengage when Jeff caught her wrist. "Damn Reidinger! How dare he presume!"

"What harm does it do?" Jeff asked at his most disarming. "You're going to need a T-1 during the delivery of a Talent. They can be most obstreperous about leaving their safe haven. At least Reidinger cares enough to send the very best." When the Rowan regarded him with amazement, he grinned. "I don't think you accessed the right prenatal information. And if that lad of ours is half as stubborn as either of his parents, you may need all the persuasion you can muster." He leaned across her. "By all means, Medic Elizara. Please proceed to the residence."

Every now and then the Rowan came smartly up against the realization that she couldn't argue with or wheedle her way around Jeff Raven. He was steadily becoming stronger and stronger in all areas of his Talent. If sometimes a part of her resented that strength, at others she felt tremendously comforted and protected. Or, as right now, in complete rebellion. But she rebelled right now, not against his common sense, but against an intrusion of the short hours when they could share each other on the deepest possible levels, physical, mental, emotional, and spiritual.

But she acquiesced. *You give me no option, do you?* she shot at him as they waited for the unsolicited visitor.

I'm far more careful of you than Reidinger gives me credit. There was no flexibility in his gaze, or mind. *You are not the obstetrician's ideal proportions for easy birthing, you know. Let's take every precaution.*

Medic Elizara's personal appearance was a surprise to them both as she was a slender woman, no taller than the Rowan, and looked far younger. Her smile as she felt their astonishment was vastly pleased with her effect on them.

"I have heard so much about you, Prime Rowan," she said with irrepressible mischief in her wide-spaced, light-green eyes, "that I elbowed my way right past everyone with far more seniority than I have. Then, too, your reputation . . ." and her marvelous smile deprecated the Rowan's reputed temper, "made others demur. Gollee Gren solemnly warned me that you're more devious than Reidinger."

At that remark, the last of the Rowan's resentment evaporated. "Gollee warned you, did he?"

Reidinger's positively Machiavellian, isn't he? Jeff said to her privately. *What a choice!*

Oh, no, came from Elizara, *the choice was mine, though when Earth Prime interviewed me, I could tell he thought that I would suit.* "I shan't take more than a few moments of your time right now, Prime, but I need to update the Altairian report."

"Not a moment has been wasted," the Rowan remarked sardonically.

"No!" And Elizara's eyes twinkled.

She did not indeed take more than a few moments. The Rowan had never met a T-1 in another field and was very much reassured by her competence and deftness.

"The pregnancy is proceeding nicely. I have nothing further to add to what the Altairian medics told you," Elizara said in conclusion. "The boy child is not far enough along for us to make a worthwhile contact. *That's* when my particular Talent becomes useful and I can assist you both in the preparations."

"My mother had no trouble with any of us," Jeff said, and the Rowan heard the first tinge of uncertainty before he could dampen it.

"True enough," Elizara admitted, "probably because *her* mother was her constant companion during the final month."

"How on earth did you know that?" Jeff asked, surprised but he found out before Elizara could prevent him. "Reidinger has been very busy, has he not?"

"I think you both must appreciate why and allow him his prerogatives," Elizara said with gentle dignity and a hint of reproach.

"This is our child, not Reidinger's. And he's no relation to be prying into . . ."

Easy, love, Jeff said, reaching with hand and mind to soothe her.

The fetus will react, you know, Elizara said mildly. *The calmer you remain, the easier it will be for you both! The stronger a bond of trust you make right now, the easier the birth will be. The child will need to trust you then.* "But the main reason I was acceptable to the Prime, and you may find this so, too, was that I had easy births with my own two Talented children."

That reassured the Rowan more than anything else about Elizara, though at that moment, she did not *want* to feel calm, even to reassure her unborn child, but she could not evade Jeff as easily as she could Elizara. Nor could she evade, or disobey, any of Reidinger's subsequent safeguards which she found intrusive, impudent, arrogant, unnecessarily restrictive, and too authoritarian by far. Unfortunately, Jeff Raven was in total agreement with the Earth Prime. She was never sure if Elizara truly disagreed with the two men on the subject of her return to Altair or was "humoring the pregnant woman."

The upshot was that the Rowan was not permitted to return to Altair and was reinstalled as Callisto Prime. Jeff went off to Altair until two appropriate T-2s could be found and integrated with Maharanjani and Bastian at Altair. When that task was completed, what Jeff termed his galactic peregrination began. Reidinger sent him to each of the other Prime Stations on various errands of high security importance.

"I don't know what could be more secure than a mind-to-mind contact or why he has to shoot you all over the place."

"Oh, I find it incredibly fascinating, love. I've met all the Primes, now, and I really did pick the best of the lot of you," he said with an outrageous glint in his eye. "That Capella!" He raised eyes and hands in such comic dismay over that confrontation that he made her laugh.

While the Rowan could appreciate just how valuable Jeff was to FT&T as the only peripatetic Prime, she resented his absences even though Jeff always took several days rest on Callisto between jaunts. On the other hand, Jeff returned, stimulated, excited, and highly pleased by his reception at every tower. She did like listening to him discuss his perceptions of the other Primes, the diversity of the planets linked in the Central Worlds: once she would have envied him his fearless ability to transverse those immense distances, but she formed a secret intention, when her pregnancy was over, to join him in these tours. But the traveling, despite Jeff's innate strength, took a noticeable toll of his energy. She worried about the alarming signs of deep fatigue which he dismissed lightly.

"Sure it takes effort, love," Jeff told her as they sprawled together in their favorite spot in the lounge before the artificial fire. For the Rowan, being close to him physically was in many ways far more satisfying than the more intimate mental contact. As much, she thought, because she had had so few physical relationships that she found their intimacies especially rewarding. "And it's tiring, but a few days with you and I'm rarin' to go again. This galactic touring's quite an eye-opener for this poor li'l ole Denebian farmboy."

"Don't you say that about yourself!" The Rowan bridled at his phrase, punching his upper arm to emphasize her annoyance.

"Dearling, I *am* poor," he reminded her. "Mind you, the bonuses

I've been extorting from Reidinger for doing these leapfroggings is bringing me out of debt much faster than if I just drew stationary Tower pay."

"Nor are you little . . ." The Rowan was not letting him belittle himself in any way.

Jeff let out a hoot of laughter. "Honey, I love your sense of loyalty but have you seen the guys they grow on Procyon? And Betelgeuse?" He shot her a glance for comparison's sake and she saw that he had felt dwarfed in their presence. "And I AM a Denebian farmboy." He grinned in his roguish way. "Keeps me from getting above myself."

"Oh, was David being difficult again?"

Jeff ran a few scenes of the Betelgeuse Talent's arrogance through her mind and she was both appalled and amused.

"If I'd ever met Siglen, I'd've had a few cogent remarks to make to her about her notions of 'training' Talent," he said, serious for a moment. "And Primes are unquestionably the vital links between Central Worlds, but there are T-1 ratings in every other Talent that make some of us stevedores look rather limited. Still," and he sighed for he was at heart a generous and forgiving person, "she got the basics right but we'll train our own kids the way they ought to go."

"Indeed we will!"

Jeff tightened his arms about her, kissing the side of her neck tenderly. "And none of our kids will need a Purza."

"Was the pukha on my mind again?"

"She keeps lurking there, where you can't see her."

"I can't imagine why. Not after I've been back to Altair, and the Rowan mining campsite. Not with you doing far more for me than any construct could ever do."

"I can't read why she keeps surfacing, love, except that Purza was the most important thing in your young life. I'm not exactly sure I like competing with a pukha."

No way! Then the Rowan let out an exaggerated sigh and then a self-deprecating chuckle. "But for ages there, that pukha was the only thing in the world that truly understood the young Rowan child . . . or so she thought." She paused, frowning. "You know it's very odd, your mother asked me who Purza was, too. That caught me off-balance."

"I think we ought to get Mother to train her mind."

"Oh, she wasn't being intrusive. It's as you said, she has a long eye. I've never met anyone quite like her before. She was so calm and reassuring, even when . . ."

"When everyone thought I was dying?"

"You were never dying . . ." But a shiver caught the Rowan even as she repudiated the mention.

Jeff cocked his right eyebrow, a droll expression on his face. "Not the way Asaph and Rakella tell it, my love. Well, I suppose Purza would surface at a time like that. When you need support the most."

The Rowan nodded, nestling as close to him as her altered shape permitted.

"I think we, all of us, have someone," Jeff went on, "or some place, we retreat to in times of stress: a known comforter, adviser, confidante, who never fails us."

"You never needed one." The Rowan was beginning to wonder about the odd resurgences of Purza. She felt the unexpected embarrassment in Jeff's mind.

"I haven't got you fooled, too, have I, love?" And Jeff gave her a quick hug, laughing. "Believe me, dear heart, the only advantage I have over others is that I learned to read minds quick enough to correct my follies before they got out of hand. That's all."

"But did you?" She needed to delve into that curious embarrassment, so unusual in her self-possessed and reliant love.

"Yes, I did," and he gave a funny chuckle. "Your Purza was at least a *visible* creature, properly programmed to respond to certain infant and pre-adolescent needs . . ."

"What's wrong with an invisible friend?" The Rowan now plucked that easily from his mind.

"Nothing. Until your younger sister finds out about it and the whole family gives you an unmerciful ragging."

Does your friend have a name?

Jeff stroked her head. *Bagheera.*

Oh?

It's been so long, love, but you know, it's rather odd that he was also a feline, like your Purza. Big, black, powerful: he loved to lie on branches high up in trees which was not surprising as I was always climbing trees myself, or lurk on sunny rock ledges because I used to hide from chores on such places, and he hated water! Which I did not, actually. I loved to swim but I could never get him to join me. He had yellow eyes—like Afra . . . Jeff's tone was amused/amazed that he had found one point of resemblance with anyone of his acquaintance. *We spent a lot of time discovering unexpected treasures in caverns and mines and other unlikely places. He was good protection against all the terrors of wild, raw Deneb. And we'd make fortunes for our planet and bring it into the Central Worlds Autonomy faster than any world had ever been admitted.* Jeff chuckled. "You know, I haven't thought of Bagheera for years! He was, I think, a character in a children's story. I preempted him for my own special use. He was invincible. *Hey, are you falling asleep on me again?"*

"Not really," and yet a massive yawn caught her. "We don't need to move from here, do we?" She snuggled up against him, finding the right hollow in his shoulder for her head. He brought a warm blanket from their bed to cover them so there was no need to rearrange themselves.

Despite what the Rowan saw as Reidinger's intrusiveness, she looked forward to Elizara's visits. Gradually the T-1 Medic appeared on Callisto twice a month and then weekly. At the beginning of the last semester of the pregnancy, Elizara came to stay until the delivery.

"But I'm fine, and the baby is developing perfectly," the Rowan protested, "or so you've told me."

Elizara grinned. "You know it to be so yourself, Rowan. Call it an old man's foibles. A young man's too, considering Jeff's state of mind."

The Rowan grunted and felt her baby react. To save herself violent convulsions of her womb, she had learned to restrain untoward responses to each new imposition.

"Jeff knows how much family means to you," Elizara said.

"Family?" The Rowan found the wording odd. Jeff never referred to their unborn as "family": usually it was "his" or "their" son, or Jeran when they finally decided on a name for him. But the child's arrival would indeed make them a family!

"There was once a time," Elizara went on in her lilting voice, "when the mother and father of a newborn were totally unprepared for it, or the effect it would have on them and their own relationship. Of course, parenting has become so much a part of early education, that many of the iniquities of earlier centuries can no longer be perpetrated on young, unformed minds. But the high-potential Talent child needs special care and handling, especially at birth and in the first three months."

"I know that. I know that! I've been made aware of that by just about everyone in the whole damned Central Worlds. The only one who hasn't alluded to this is Capella and right now I could almost trade places with that dried-up old virgin!"

"Rowan! If she should hear you!"

"She is," the Rowan acidly replied, "probably the only Talent in the entire FT&T network who doesn't contact me half a hundred times a day to ensure I'm still all right and the child is alive and kicking! Which he is right now!"

"Then calm down!"

Elizara exuded an authority that the Rowan found as impossible to evade as Jeff's. So she found herself initiating meditation in obedient response. Elizara's inner serenity extended itself to the Rowan and the flare of anger and frustration was soothed away.

"Oh, by the way," Elizara said when the Rowan was tranquil again, "I took another liberty on your behalf." She hesitated.

"Why not?"

Elizara touched her hand in gentle rebuke. "I've managed to trace the Gwyn family. Just in case there might be some genetic flaws that we should know about in advance."

"You did?" the Rowan exclaimed. "But I tried . . ."

"Yes, you tried from Altair," and Elizara gave a little smile, "but not from Earth. And not consulting the original immigration files, only the Altair entries."

"They were useless. And?"

"Genetics prints were made of all outgoing settlers; genotypes and blood profiles. You could only be the child of Ewain and Morag Gwyn." Shyly Elizara slipped two small holograms from her pouch to the table. "As you'll notice, the tendency to premature silver hair affected both parents."

With a reverence akin to awe, the Rowan looked down at the two faces: Despite the fact that her father could have been no more than thirty, his hair was silver while eyebrows and moustache were as black as coal. He had a strong face, and his brows were drawn in a faint scowl. Her mother's hair had silver streaks from a center parting: she looked more worried than anxious, but she had bequeathed her gray eyes to her daughter and the narrow face.

Elizara, if you knew what this gift means . . .

Ah, love, I do! And Elizara laid her hand gently on the Rowan's bowed head.

What's wrong? was Jeff's sudden demand. He was never out of touch with her and he was as grateful to Elizara as she was. *That girl's a wonder! Give her a hug for me! I don't dare do it myself or I'll have you to answer* to!

I'm much too happy at this moment to deny you that, my love!

In her mind was a fiendish chuckle. *Warn her!*

The Rowan didn't, but smiled happily to herself, her eyes resting on the two holograms until they were indelibly imprinted in her mind. She had parents now: and it was enough to know that she had had a brother. She could console herself wondering whether he had resembled father or mother more. Maybe Mauli, who was deft with pencil and paint, would draw her a likeness of what her brother might have been.

On one count did the Rowan prevail against Reidinger's over protectiveness: she was allowed to continue working Callisto Station. Torshan and Saggoner were needed on another colonial outpost, and Elizara, backed by all other medical consultants, reassured Reidinger that the Rowan's mental abilities were in no way affected by the pregnancy. Nor was her normal occupation affecting her unborn child. The Rowan proved that more conclusively by a suspension of the pyrotechnics which had often disturbed the Station personnel during her moody periods. For this everyone on the Station was grateful.

As soon as her pregnancy became common knowledge, Brian Ackerman had braced Afra, wanting to know if the Rowan would be "okay."

"If by okay you mean is she likely to be as difficult as she was before Jeff arrived," Afra replied in a droll tone, his yellow eyes reflecting considerable amusement at the question, "I'm told that pregnant women are often more quiescent and docile."

"The Rowan docile? I'd find that hard to believe," was Brian's reply. "But that Elizara's sure a nice person. Does the Rowan like her?"

"I believe they are compatible personalities. Elizara is an extremely gifted practitioner. If I were having a baby, I'd like her beside me."

Brian regarded the Capellan with a startled glance. "You're no mutant!"

"No, and I'm as male as you are!" Afra stared back at Ackerman.

"I didn't mean . . . I mean, I know you . . . Oh, hell. I figured you were gone on the Rowan . . . Elizara's pretty, young, and . . ."

"I'll make my own match, if you don't mind, Brian, but I appreciate the concern." And Afra retired to his own quarters, leaving Brian wondering if he had mortally offended him and wishing he'd never started the conversation in the first place.

As the delivery date approached, the Rowan spent a lot of time in the Dome's pool. It was the only place she did not feel awkward and unwieldy. She had even discussed a water delivery with Elizara.

"Wherever and however you feel comfortable," the Medic replied.

"This isn't going to be a huge production, is it? I'm not going to have Reidinger shooting more experts up the moment I go into labor?"

"Whenever, however, and whoever you need to make birth easy for you and the young Raven," Elizara assured her so firmly that the Rowan let herself be convinced. She appreciated the irony of Reidinger's ban on any travel that precluded her having the child in one of the highly specialized clinics on Earth.

She was aware of all the discreet monitoring devices that had been installed; in her couch in the Tower, her quarters, lining her bed, the pool, the rocking chair which Jeff had made for her with his own hands, the couch in front of the fire, even in the food preparation area. That was quite enough surveillance but having a baby should be a private affair, not a matter of interest to the inhabited galaxy.

The Rowan suddenly knew of one other presence she wanted very much to have with her: Isthia Raven, with her deep ear and her loud voice. The notion surprised her and yet it had a calming effect on her. A matter of continuity . . .

"Whoever you need," Elizara repeated, tactfully advising the Rowan that her thoughts were clear.

"But would she come?" The Rowan was inhibited by an odd reticence. Isthia Raven would be harvesting Deneb's first post ET crop on the family's holdings.

Ask her, Jeff advised when the Rowan timidly tested the notion on him. *She'd be honored, and she'd be helpful. She's been taking instruction on that metamorphic-level treatment that worked so well on me. Does that stuff help in childbirth?*

Would you ask her for me?

What? The redoubtable Rowan is afraid of her mother-in-law?

Well, you are!

Not often. Not since I met you. There was a snide chuckle at the end of that thought.

I don't know why I put up with you!

Because you adore me, of course! Which is reciprocal. The chuckle was replaced by a vision of him as a callow moon-calf.

Isthia Raven was flattered by the Rowan's request and exchanged considerable information with Elizara. She had been rather worried about the Rowan who was, to her mind, not the optimum shape for easy childbearing. She said that she would come as soon as she was needed.

You're needed now, Jeff told his mother. *By me, if no one else.*

I thought it was the Rowan who wanted me, she replied teasingly. *You know perfectly well that she and your son will be all right. How many clairvoyant Talents have you asked already?*

I see no reason not to avail myself of professional courtesies, Jeff said in a testy tone.

Isthia chuckled and changed the subject, arranging with him to bring her to Callisto a few days before the Rowan's due date. Her own worries ceased the moment she saw the mother to be, radiant and, as the Rowan put it, bulging in all forward directions at this late stage of pregnancy. Isthia sincerely admired their living quarters, remarking drily that she had never expected dome living to be quite so spacious. She paid very close attention when the Rowan and Jeff explained all the safety features, and held a drill for her.

"Planets at least give you lots of places to hide," she remarked in her droll fashion. "Could be awkward if there was an emergency just when Jeran chooses to arrive," she added, as she peered into one of the safety chambers. She made a pantomime of the Rowan attempting to fit inside.

"The house has triple seals," Jeff remarked. "The Prime cannot be risked."

"I'll stay very close to you then, daughter," Isthia said. "But you certainly have an elegant residence. Ah, well, we'll soon set matters right on Deneb."

"Doesn't that ever bother you, Rowan?" she asked after dinner when Jupiter rose, filling the skyview. She eyed the massive planet warily.

"What? Him? I'm accustomed to it now," the Rowan replied, trying to settle herself on the comfortable couch in front of the fire.

"Levitation?" Isthia suggested, glancing at Elizara for her opinion.

"We've tried that, too," Jeff answered with a rueful grin for the Rowan's dilemma. "Not much longer, love."

The Rowan gave a skeptical grunt.

"Elizara, if you're a T-1 Medical, can't you establish a time, or at least a day?" Isthia asked.

"We have been able to improve prenatal care to insure almost one-hundred percent normal healthy babies," Elizara said with a slight smile, "and we can induce labor if the term runs over a normal gestation, but we're still unable to dictate the ETA."

"I wish this one would consider an early appearance," the Rowan remarked wearily.

"It's your first," Isthia said in a dry tone. "The way out is not so obvious."

"I've told him and told him," the Rowan replied, "to get his head down and dig in."

"Had any effect?" Isthia asked, amused.

"He responds with sentiments of complete satisfaction in his present environment and sees no need to make any alteration."

"In that many words?"

The Rowan laughed, delighted to have startled Isthia. "Hardly. I just get an impression of complete contentment."

Isthia turned to Elizara. "What about a hands-on? Of course, Rowan isn't overdue . . ."

Elizara smiled gently. "We wait. Time enough for hands-on if labor stops and we sense a complete reluctance to leave the womb."

Then, abruptly, Isthia sat straight up in the lounger which hastily rearranged itself to her change of position. She cocked her head, listening.

"What's the matter? What do you hear?" The Rowan asked. "Ian?" They might tease Isthia for her "long ear" from time to time but it was always respectful.

"I thought I . . ." Isthia faltered and looked keenly at Elizara. "Did you catch anything?"

Elizara frowned but she was patently sharpening her senses, listening with that other sensitivity which all three women had in generous measure.

There! Isthia said.

The Rowan had felt something, just at the very edge of her own deep range. *Too distant. Anger! Pain!*

Whose? Isthia added in a very thoughtful tone. *The source defeats me. I don't think it was human!*

Elizara regarded her with surprise. *How could you hear it, then?*

"I heard it, too," the Rowan reminded the medic. She grimaced. "None of our kin at least," she added to reassure Isthia. *Or shall I give a shout and be sure for you?*

Slowly Isthia shook her head, frowning with puzzlement. Then, shaking off the brief thrall determinedly, she smiled at the other two. "If it had been you, Rowan, we could put it down to prenatal nerves."

The Rowan sighed with deep exasperation, and stroked her extended abdomen. "C'mon, now, son, get in to position and let's end this waiting. You're old enough to be born now."

Two days later, as splendid Jupiter rose to obscure deep space from those in the Callisto dome, Jeran Raven decided to take his mother's advice. The baby dropped his head into the birth canal, precipitating the breaking of the Rowan's waters, and almost before Elizara could help the Rowan block the pain, long and intense contractions began.

Just off duty from the Tower, Jeff arrived as Isthia and Elizara were making the Rowan as comfortable as possible.

"Now is the time for hands-on," Elizara told him, "to reassure your son. This is the difficult part for him and he must not draw back or resist."

It comforted the Rowan tremendously to have Jeff's strong body supporting her, his hands stroking her; to join mental forces in urging their son to endure this brief discomfort and be made welcome in the world of the living.

Isn't it a shade hypocritical of us, the Rowan said very privately to Jeff, *to require him to leave the safety of the womb, for how can we promise him safety when we've never known it?*

So you want to stay pregnant for the rest of your life? Was Jeff's reply as he smoothed back silver hair already damp with sweat.

NO!

Then push! Elizara urged. *Take Isthia's hands!*

Isthia's strong hands anchored her through the massive contractions that followed: hands that also soothed and eased the involuntary spasms.

"Those contractions are fierce," Isthia remarked.

"Not unusually so," Elizara replied, "and at five minute intervals."

"Is he resisting or is it me?" the Rowan asked, panting with relief as a particularly severe contraction ended.

"A little of both," Elizara replied, and the Rowan could find no qualification in the Talent's mind. *I never lie to my patients!*

Not to this one, you couldn't!

Nor in the present company she's keeping. Elizara added, her tone amused. "All right, now, here comes another one."

They all sensed the child's sudden reluctance as the pressures of his mother's womb caught him in an inexorable rhythm. He disliked the sensation: it frightened him. He was instantly reassured of warmth and love and comfort if he did not falter. He did not like this experience at all.

I'm not much enjoying it right now myself, my son, the Rowan told him and then could not even think as a particularly hard contraction seized her. She clasped Isthia's hands in a grip that she feared would bruise the flesh.

Hold hard!

To the Rowan, caught by the inexorable process of birthing, the struggle with her son seemed to go on interminably. The contractions came more frequently, lasted longer and but for the nerve blocks she would have been in some agony. As it was, the muscular strain wearied her.

Please, Jeran, please! she cried, wondering how much more of this she could endure.

Gripped by yet another massive contraction, she felt Elizara and Isthia place hands on her heaving abdomen, and this contraction seemed to be abetted by their minds, overruling Jeran's resistance. As the boy's head passed out of the birth canal, he gave a terrible cry, mental and physical, of protest, of resentment, of fear.

"You are born, my son," the Rowan cried with mind and mouth as she opened her eyes to see Elizara receive the baby's wet and wriggling body in her hands.

Jeran wailed again, a confused and angry cry at the difference of environment, the noise, the cold, the disorientation.

There, there! three adult minds consoled him. *There, there. You are loved, you are wanted. Here, now, you will be warm. You will be comforted.*

Elizara deposited the baby on his mother's newly deflated belly while she performed the necessary post natal offices.

"Even upside down, you're beautiful," the Rowan told Jeran, intercepting one of his violently waving hands as he continued to complain on several levels about the brutal treatment he had just been through. *He's so strong!*

So angry! and Jeff's tone was infinitely proud and relieved. *Now, now, my beautiful boy! It's all over.*

Lord no, it's just starting, Isthia replied. "Good lungs on him," she added approvingly.

He has obviously inherited your voice, mother, Jeff said. *That birth shout was loud enough to reach Deneb!*

And you're soft-spoken? Isthia teased back, beaming with joy at the successful birth.

"Just over four kilos," Elizara said, pleased. "You wouldn't want any heavier a child, Rowan. And no worse for the passage. *Now we will* all *soothe him on the most primitive levels.*

Ganging up on my poor son? asked Jeff, fatuously smiling down at Jeran.

Soothing your not at all poor son, Elizara rebuked him. *This is the most important part for a child as obviously Talented as Jeran is. Hands-on! Isthia, begin on the metamorphic levels. Rowan won't want him operating on a psionic high over the next few months.*

As Isthia stroked the sturdy little feet, she began to croon softly. Elizara and Jeff sponged him clean, all the time soothing him with touch, mind and voice. Soon he was yawning and quite willing to drift off into sleep.

When the afterbirth was delivered and the Rowan made comfortable again in her bed, the sleeping child was placed in her arms and Jeff stretched out beside them both, his eyes dark and brimming with love.

I never thought I would feel quite this *intensely about a baby who will shortly drive us both demented with infantile needs,* Jeff said. On his forefinger, he tipped up Jeran's little hand which opened to curl about it. *I'll be the most impossible father in the galaxy.*

Jeran IS *quite the most marvelous baby,* the Rowan agreed, as fatuous with pride as he was. "What . . . on . . . earth?"

At her altered tone, Jeff followed her startled gaze and saw containers and arrangements of flowers of every variation imaginable appear and settle themselves on whatever surface available until the room was almost filled with them.

"What is going on?" Jeff scrambled to his feet though what harm could masses of blossoms cause.

That young 'un has so loud a voice I knew before Elizara told me! said the familiar voice of Reidinger in an unfamiliar whisper. *Thank you!*

Jeff and the Rowan stared at each other for the uncharacteristic humility in Earth Prime's tone.

Rowan? Jeff? Isthia's voice, too, was hesitant but there was such an underlying throb of excitement that they both asked what was wrong. *Nothing except there can't be any flowers left on Earth for the masses that just appeared all over the dome!*

"You should see our room," Jeff called aloud. "Come on in, and where's Elizara?"

"In the pool—if there's room for her to swim among the water lilies I saw heading in that direction," Isthia said in quiet mirth as she opened the door. She halted, staring around her in amazement. "Who on earth . . . ?"

"Reidinger!" the Rowan and Jeff said in unison.

They heard a distant exclamation, and a much more audible *Grandfather, haven't you got a wit left in your head? So much floral perfume and pollens are not* good *for a baby!*

"Grandfather?" Now Isthia joined the Rowan and Jeff in chorus.

Oh, bugger, I blew it! Elizara sounded disgusted. *Just let me dress and I'll come clean.*

Come clean first, dress is optional, Jeff replied, doubling up in a paroxysm of laughter.

Don't laugh, Jeff! the Rowan said, wrapping both hands around her much abused abdominal muscles. *Please don't make me laugh, Jeff! Please!*

Isthia came to the Rowan's assistance with strong hands on her belly, trying hard to scowl at Jeff but grinning broadly at the same time. Then Elizara appeared, her hair still wet, swathed in a big towel, and looking chagrined.

"Reidinger's your grandfather?" the Rowan asked, wondering how she could have missed the relationship.

"Actually my great-grandfather, but that's a mouthful and makes him feel ancient. I buried that fact behind a shield before I came here. Grandfather impressed on me that you might resent my help if you discovered the relationship. But I'm also the best qualified person for such an important accouchement. And what I told you in our first interview was true: I offered to come but he was so dreadfully relieved that I had. He may holler and rant at you, Rowan, but, believe me, that indicated just how much he cares about you. And about Jeff. And now Jeran is added to his most special list."

The Rowan closed her arm protectively about Jeran and glared at Elizara. "I'm NOT breeding for FT&T."

"No more am I," Elizara replied with a laugh, "but children are part of being a woman. Can you deny that you feel more feminine at this moment than at any other time in your whole life?"

The Rowan considered this and had to agree. "In fact, now I've done it, I won't mind being pregnant often." She shot a sly glance at Jeff. "Only Reidinger must know it's because we *want* more children, Talented or not."

"I won't for a moment deny that my grandfather lives and breathes for the efficiency and continued success and expansion of FT&T." Elizara's eyes twinkled. "He was massively disappointed that I went medical but that's where my Talent lay. In fact the poor dear," and she grinned as she caught the surprise in their minds at her loving reference, "has been continually disappointed in his seven children and their progeny unto the third generation. He's the third Reidinger to be Earth Prime, you see. Not always consecutive. The Talent sometimes skipped one generation. He did so want to train up a fourth. That's one reason for his bad temper. He feels he's been let down by genetics. Oh, most of us have valid Talents but none of us are Prime candidates. It *is* the rarest combination of Talent, you know. And you both are, and so is young Jeran."

"Reidinger has an odd way of displaying concern," the Rowan replied testily. "When I think of the blastings I've received . . ."

"Come now, Rowan," and Elizara's tone altered, "surely *you,* of all the Primes, appreciate loneliness!" She paused while the Rowan did indeed feel the pinch of that accusation. "Grandfather cannot let personal feelings interfere with his professional responsibilities. Much as it might surprise you," and the gentle Elizara spoke with an edge to her voice, "he feels very deeply. He just hides it better than anyone else."

My apologies, the Rowan said meekly. *I know I'm self-centered . . .*

"Primes tend to be," Elizara said more mildly, "it's a hazard of the profession. And you mustn't change your responses to him. He'd be annoyed with me for even suggesting that there were chinks in his shield. But I'm a match for him. As you two are. And you, Isthia, are far stronger than I first thought."

Isthia had been watching Elizara's face intently. Now she shrugged noncommittally. "Deneb is my future. But I am interested in these insights on the formidable Earth Prime." Her voice ended on an upward note.

Elizara gave a brief warning flick of her hand. "Enough of banter. Let's move some of these flowers out of this room. Too many is just too many for newborn lungs."

"Not to mention the air conditioning units in this part of the dome," Jeff said.

"You know, it was really rather sweet of him," the Rowan murmured sleepily. And by the time the transfer was finished, she was fast asleep, one arm curled protectively about her son.

"He's rather a good baby, as babies go," Isthia remarked several days later when she was making her farewells. "I didn't think I'd miss Ian, but I do. And I've wallowed in luxury far too long." She ignored her son's snicker and laid her hand on her sleeping grandson's forehead. "He'll be a handful, Rowan, but you've started out right."

"Thanks to you, Isthia," and the Rowan's voice and mind were deep with gratitude.

Isthia gave her an understanding smile. "I stood *in loco parentis,* my dear, and we both know it. Nonetheless I was flattered." She bent over and kissed the Rowan's cheek. "Such a bit of a thing!" And quickly left the room.

The Rowan's farewell wishes followed her personal capsule all the way back to Deneb. Elizara stayed on another few days, to be sure the Rowan had completely recovered physically as the delivery had been strenuous despite its brevity.

"I'm telling Reidinger in no uncertain terms," Elizara said as she, too, prepared to leave the new family, "that you are to be on maternity leave until I approve your return to work. He'll growl and rage but I won't budge an inch. He loves it when someone stands up to him. You don't know how delighted he was when you popped in on him."

"I'd never have known," the Rowan replied drolly.

"Besides, he's not about to risk his pet Prime."

"I dislike being considered a 'pet' anything," the Rowan responded tartly. She was nursing Jeran and her expression was singularly at odds with her voice.

"I'll remind him," Elizara replied mildly. "You're a good mother, too," she added. "That will please him more," and she grinned as that brought a sharp glare from the Rowan. "You are, you know. It comes naturally." Then she frowned slightly. "Who is Purza? Your mother?"

The Rowan stared at her. "Will she never stop haunting me?"

"She wasn't haunting," Elizara replied, pausing to consider her next words. "She's far too happy."

"Purza," the Rowan said with some asperity, "was what I called the pukha they gave me on Altair."

Elizara raised her eyebrows slightly. "She's been more than that, Rowan." She smiled gently. "And right now, she's proud and happy for you, that alter ego of yours. As you are proud and happy after a very long road to find such emotions."

"My alter ego is a pukha?"

"Why not?" Again that slightly mischievous grin curved Elizara's lips. "It was very cleverly and ingeniously programmed, you know." She laid a reassuring hand on the Rowan's shoulder and with the tactile contact more of Elizara's professional approval flowed through to the Rowan's mind. "Purza's physical form was destroyed by that arrogant little bouzma but you never really lost her." She gathered up her things. "Remember now, I'm only a thought away and I will be open to you at any time."

With parents so closely in contact with Jeran's needs, he made excellent progress and was rarely troublesome without an easily discernible reason. The children in Callisto Dome were as entranced with him as the adults. The Rowan recovered her energy while Jeff twitted her about her "maternal" curves.

When Elizara arrived back at Callisto Dome for the six weeks' postnatal check, she pronounced both mother and son in excellent health.

However, no sooner was the Rowan back in the Tower, Jeran in a carrier by her couch, than Reidinger sent for Jeff.

"That's mean!" the Rowan complained, pacing up and down. "Your son needs your presence. *I* need your presence. I don't care what Elizara said, he's got no right to break up our family unit."

"Sweetheart, we don't know that that's his intention," Jeff replied.

She caught his not quite suppressed thought. "You! You *like* whizzing about, oozing charm over everyone! Traipsing about the galaxy like a . . . a . . ."

"Trapeze artist?" Jeff suggested mildly, not the least bit ashamed of his inclinations. "And you can't fool me that you like someone else, even me, managing your Tower. Callisto is your bailiwick: it works more efficiently with your mindset than anyone else's."

She eyed him. "Now, wait a minute, Jeff Raven, don't try those tactics on *me!*"

"The last person in the world I can fool," and he held out his arms to her. *We don't stay angry with each other, love. We know each other far too well.* He fitted his body to hers, her head under his chin and reassured her with every fiber of his being. "Besides, I'm curious as to *what* Reidinger has in mind for me now. I've been everywhere else and even I know that Central Worlds isn't planning to install a new Tower any time soon."

Faced with the inevitable, she lifted his capsule and thrust it efficiently toward Earth and, with a sigh, went back to work.

Jeff was absolutely correct about Callisto being *her* Tower. Being Altairian Prime had been a subtle victory and she had enjoyed working with old friends, and using her new awareness to facilitate a blending of the Talent required to operate such a major way point. But Callisto was hers, her home, where she had met and loved Jeff, and where their son had been born. The Tower personnel were an integrated team that had survived all her early foolishness and she now realized they had become the family she had lost. Afra was more younger brother than colleague. He honestly found Jeran an enchanting child which only reinforced her good opinion of him.

Live stuff coming in, Afra's thought broke through her musing and instantly she caught the large personnel carrier as it arced up from Earth Prime.

Hi, honey, and Jeff's mind, the initiating kinetic, met hers. *Breeding animals for Deneb! We got a bonus: maternity and paternity. FT&T policy, so don't raise your hackles. I just blew all mine to restock the farm. I'll be home tonight.*

She could hear that he had something of momentous proportions to tell her. It was a long day for her, part of it waiting, part of it attending to Jeran's needs, but most of it wondering what sort of an assignment Reidinger was now laying on Jeff. She'd be willing even to leave Callisto but she had to be with Jeff.

You will be, love! His quick thought answered her. His mind resounded with elation.

The Rowan was nursing Jeran when Jeff arrived back so surreptitiously that she didn't hear him until she felt his presence behind her. Jeran let out a frightened squeak. Then Jeff opened up the blaze of his exultation and his son's eyes grew as round as his mother's as the import of Jeff's news clarified.

"Earth Prime!"

"Shhh! Everyone'll hear you," Jeff said, sliding onto the bed beside her and kissing her neck.

"You mean, everyone'll hear you!" Then she absorbed the implications. "Earth Prime? Reidinger's Earth Prime."

Sadness tinged Jeff's face and mind. "Mother caught it from Elizara. We were too involved with Jeran here to notice. Did you realize that Reidinger is 110?"

"Oh!"

Jeff nodded. "Precisely!" And he opened his mind to all that had occurred during that momentous interview in Reidinger's spacious hidden office in the FT&T Cube. How desperately Reidinger yearned to retire and enjoy a few years free of the stresses of such high position: a desire made more urgent after Siglen's demise for Reidinger was very much aware that his mind faltered from time to time out of sheer fatigue and the debilities of his advanced age. Yet he could not relinquish command to an unsuitable personality.

It would have been me? the Rowan said, shrinking from the very notion of such onerous responsibility. Patently Jeff regarded it as a magnificent challenge.

Sorry to do you out of it, love . . . He grinned, knowing the depths of her relief. Idly he reached out to let Jeran's fist curl around his fingers, his expression dotingly tender for an omnipotent Prime-elect. *Up until my call for help, you were being subtly groomed for the job. David certainly wasn't capable, much less Capella. When I think what I can now do for Deneb . . .*

"For Deneb?" the Rowan echoed, startled. Then she began to laugh, loving him more devotedly than ever for that altruistic consideration. Small wonder he had become Reidinger's choice.

Jeff nodded, his brilliant blue eyes twinkling with delight in her appreciation. *It simply isn't on for Earth Prime's native world to be second-rate, now is it?*

You demanded a Denebian Tower as a condition?

Lover, and Jeff stretched out on the bed, punched a pillow comfortably behind his head, *I could have demanded the moons of the solar system on a diamond chain and had them. As you well understand, Central Worlds has to have the best Talent as its Prime.* His grin was particularly arch. *I don't think I was greedy or particularly difficult. But Deneb will have a Tower. You cobbled together the basic facilities: we'll improve them and send in teachers and assessors. Rakella's oldest boy bids fair to develop into a reasonable Prime. That is, until Jeran here is old enough to take over . . .*

The Rowan curled her arms protectively about her son. "My baby's not going to be marooned on Deneb! You said you wouldn't let him be indentured to FT&T."

Jeff flipped over on his side, stroking her cheek to reduce her wrath, grinning in a fashion that she could never resist.

"Love, the whole game plan just changed, in our favor. It'll be quite another matter if our children end up *running* FT&T, now won't it? We'll raise 'em the way Primes should be reared, in a large and loving family. None of them will have to make do with a pukha. Not while we live! We're a team, love, with strengths and resources not given to many. We'll make the best possible use of our Talents." His expression was both entreating and serious. "On that score, let us have a meeting of minds."

Loving him as she did, that is exactly what they had.

Jeran was a hearty six months old when the Rowan conceived again. She was amazed to be roundly scolded by everyone.

"It's my body!" was her response. "I feel fine so stop fussing at me."

Despite his increasing frailty, Reidinger's voice was not off a decibel in full bellow as he let her know in no uncertain terms that he considered she was putting both herself and the new child at risk by becoming pregnant so soon.

Reidinger, you will butt out of my private life. You are the last person who should have objections! she responded in icy tones. *You made it abundantly clear to Jeff by the tonne on the hoof how much you appreciated Jeran. What's your gripe?*

I will not have my best Prime . . .

The Rowan laughed heartily and without a tinge of jealousy. *Do get your facts straight, old dear. You told Jeff that HE was your best Prime.*

DON'T YOU DARE INTERRUPT ME . . .

No, I shouldn't, should I? the Rowan replied meekly. *It's sooooo bad for your blood pressure or heart or lungs or cranium or whatever. So you be a good boy and take some of that tonic and mind your Tower. While you still can . . .*

She felt him gathering himself for another blast and then suddenly, he was silent. For a heart-stopping moment, the Rowan wondered if she had gone too far.

No, I told him it was our business, Jeff reassured her, and then went on in another mental tone entirely, *but even Mother gave herself a year between pregnancies.*

The Rowan, rather too sweetly: *I thought you wanted to come home tonight to your loving wife and adoring son?*

There was another pause. *I will be home and I will discuss it with you.*

Another of those times, the Rowan thought to herself testily, when a man thinks he knows more about maternity than someone who has borne a child. So she decided just how to handle him this evening before he could handle her.

She hadn't *meant* to get pregnant again so soon, but Reidinger dispatched Jeff to check on this or that Terran installation, or to the Moon, and then the big Mars substation, and the more important Asteroid Wheels. Jeff had to be introduced to all the Governors as well as the more important members of the Nine-Star League. Consequently, when he *was* on Callisto, they tended to make up for opportunities lost.

"I've had to sit through some of the dreariest meetings," he told her wearily. "It ought to be a prerequisite to high government office that the incumbent be at least a T-4. That would halve the time spent in politicking and correctly aligning power balances."

"I didn't realize that Reidinger had to deal with that kind of administrative nonsense," the Rowan said. "No wonder the man is aged before his time."

"Oh, that isn't part of the FT&T Prime's function but as heir apparent, I have to be *displayed* to all those who worry about leaving FT&T autonomous. I've got to be shown to be the right sort of stuff and all that. As it is, not all the League Ambassadors are convinced that an ex-colonist is the 'right sort of person' to be entrusted with such grave responsibilities."

Jeff's mobile face ran a gamut of the lugubrious, skeptical, or censorious expressions of his various detractors and had the Rowan in whoops.

"Be glad you're stationed on Callisto," he assured her and then turned his attention to more pressing matters: such as showing her how much he had missed her.

Which was why she was pregnant now despite the fact that a Talent of her scope and strength was able to affect certain bodily functions. She had forgotten—well, neglected—to affect the possible outcome of the evening's pleasures. The two children—this one, by the Rowan's choice, was female—would be close in age, yes, but the Rowan and Jeff would make certain that they were close in affection as well: another fringe benefit of strong Talent when properly directed.

Rowan! Jeff's urgent call reached her as she was feeding Jeran his supper. Even her name was colored with excitement—and more. *Mother wants me to come out to Deneb. Something's troubling her. She said you and Elizara had a hint of it, too, just before Jeran was born. Do you remember?*

Suddenly the Rowan did, though she had given the incident no further thought, being involved in maternal duties.

Elizara felt something *but couldn't define it. Any more than I could beyond anger and pain. At the time, Isthia thought it wasn't even human.*

I'd better go and see what I can hear.

The Rowan gave a mental snort which Jeran picked up, regarding his mother with rounded eyes and a certain babyish pout of anxiety. She soothed him on one level and responded to Jeff on another. *Your mother's got the "long ear."*

Which, in her son, has been considerably refined, sharpened, strengthened, honed, and is completely operational. Maybe now is the time to pester Isthia to train properly.

Jeff returned to Callisto the following morning, arriving by his own gestalt with the first batch of inbound drones.

Hi, darling. Where've you stashed our son? Ah, with you. Look, I'm going to bathe and eat, then I'll join you. I'm twelve hours behind Callisto's day. His buoyant mental tone reassured her that whatever Isthia had "heard" could not be of any urgency.

Jeran was asleep when Jeff reached the Tower. She continued her grab and thrust, keeping the generators at a high peak. He waited to join her until she had handled the outward bound freight. He brought up cups of the sweetened drink she liked, handing her one, kissing her forehead, before pausing to stare down at their sleeping son, a doting expression on his face.

"He doesn't look like anyone in my family," he remarked and not for the first time.

"He looks like himself, Jeran Gwyn-Raven. Well?" She regarded him over the rim of her cup.

"Well, I don't know what upset my mother," and he perched on the console, one arm across his chest, the other supporting his cup. "I didn't hear a blessed thing. But Rakella said she did, too, and Besseva Eagle, who's been ninety-eight percent accurate in all her precogs, thinks there is trouble on its way to us." He made an immense circle with his free arm. "Immense trouble."

"The beetles wouldn't come back for more. Would they?" *That would account for the anger and pain I felt.*

"Beetle anger? Beetle pain?" Jeff was close to laughter at the suggestion. "Though they might well have been annoyed at the loss of two advance assault vessels. However, from what the specialists have deduced to date, they had a hivelike societal structure—our merge saw eggs in the ship, remember, and we found hundreds in the space debris—at various stages of larval development for different types of beetles. Hive societies don't tend to emotions: workers, drones, queens, whatever, do exactly what they were bred to do."

"Yes, but there was sentience of some sort directing the three vessels that attacked Deneb. That oversized beetle we saw in the protected inner chamber of the ship? The queen. Could it have been intelligent enough to direct the others?"

"Hmm. Tactics did change," was Jeff's grudging admission.

"Beetles tend to be tenacious," the Rowan added, though "tenacity" was certainly more of a trait than an emotion.

Jeff shrugged. "They can come back, angry, hurt, or merely tenacious, any time they care to have more of the same. And when they get anywhere near the perimeter of League Space, alarms will ring all over our sphere of influence."

"I'd've chalked it up to prenatal nerves," the Rowan went on, still trying to analyze the faint emotions she had perceived, "except that Isthia heard it, too."

"Isthia's maternal sensitivity is exceedingly acute," Jeff agreed but his tone also assured the Rowan that he was not going to make the mistake of dismissing the incident.

* * *

Rowan? It was Isthia's tone, stronger than her usual mental voice, *have I caught you at a bad time?*

Jeran and I are having a swim, the Rowan replied, not slow to catch the anxious undertones to that deceptive query. *What's wrong?*

Whatever IT is is getting stronger and more ominous. Her worry was deep. *Rakella and Besseva concur, and every woman with any modicum of Talent on this planet is beginning to display anxiety symptoms. You'd think the planet was populated by viragoes the way tempers are flaring for no reason at all. Rakella and Besseva are merged with me to make this contact!*

And here I thought you'd yielded and taken some training! The Rowan deliberately spoke in a light vein.

Now *I wish I had. I shan't be so perverse if we get out of this!*

Even as she spoke to Isthia, the Rowan had risen from the pool and thrown towels around her son's wriggling body and her own.

I take it no masculine minds have been touched by this phenomenon? the Rowan asked, deftly inserting Jeran into his padded pants. She also assembled some travel requirements for them both.

That's it precisely. Isthia's reply was grim. *The male minds don't hear a twitch. Not that they won't listen to those of us who do!*

Callisto is occluded right now so I'll call a day of rest. I think I'll bring Mauli with me. She's a keen echo finder even if Mick isn't present. Jeff's on Procyon. Be with you soon.

The Rowan did not find Afra or Ackerman as cooperative about what they termed a "rash and impulsive venture."

"Mauli will do anything you ask," Ackerman said testily, "but I'm damned if Afra and I will take the responsibility for you two, and Jeran, haring off to Deneb without at least checking with Jeff."

"I can't disturb Jeff in that meeting on Procyon right now. And if I have to, Brian, I can also launch myself and Mauli without a gestalt," the Rowan replied, gesturing for Mauli to settle herself in the double capsule. She handed Jeran over and faced her critics. "Now, will you stop being overprotective and run up the generators? You both know that Isthia wouldn't put me, or Jeran, in jeopardy but if she wants me on Deneb, she's earned the right to my assistance at any time. Hasn't she?"

"At least clear it with Jeff," Ackerman replied in a request that was nearly a plea.

Jeff! Isthia wants me on Deneb. The situation is hotting up.

Really? Should I come? She could sense that he was only half-listening to her. He was at a meeting but not bored.

I'm taking Jeran and Mauli.

He's old enough for a long 'port.

Afra and Ackerman had to accede to her orders then, but she knew both were uneasy. But then, they always were when she wanted to 'port anywhere: even when she was now undisturbed by the process.

Call this an inspection tour by the Denebian Prime-to-be, Afra, and don't worry, dear friend, the Rowan said, lightly touching Afra's forearm so she could impose assurance on him.

He gave a shrug and a wry smile, then helped her into the double carrier beside Mauli. Brian's scowl did not abate as the canopy locked shut. Then he turned on his heel and returned to the Tower, Afra following him.

Though this would not be Jeran's first 'port, for Jeff had taken him out beyond Jupiter on several occasions to accustom his son to the sensations, it would be his longest. He spent the transfer gurgling and enthusiastically waving his arms. He registered Isthia's welcoming mind-touch with an extra chirrup. He liked his grandmother and his mind associated her with soothing sounds and contacts.

Did you catch that, Mauli? the Rowan asked, sometimes unable to restrain her pride in Jeran's obvious Talent.

Mauli's smile broadened into a laugh.

Isthia brought them with no more than a light bump into the cradle at the fine new Tower, bathed in spotlights at this time of Deneb's night, its big, new generators humming idly. The Rowan had a nostalgic moment for what she had contrapted out of sheer necessity but then Isthia, Rakella, and a third woman whom the Rowan identified by mind-touch as Besseva emerged from the facility. Besseva reminded the Rowan so forcefully of Lusena, physically and mentally, that she experienced a brief jolt at the contact.

I am then doubly honored, Besseva said, inclining her head slightly toward the Callisto Prime.

"And no problems with this fellow in a long 'port, I gather," said Isthia, taking her grandson from his mother and settling him on her hip as she had her own children. "I am truly grateful to you, Rowan, and to you as well, Mauli, for humoring me."

"Humoring you? Spare me that, Isthia!" The Rowan let her exasperation color her mind as well as her voice. "Since you've obviously left the generators on, let's see what we can plumb out there. I brought Mauli for that echo effect she has."

"Night is the best time to sense the presence," Isthia said.

"And we have!" Besseva stated firmly, and Rakella gave a single emphatic nod of her head.

All three Denebians emanated a tenseness, a barely controlled fear that bordered on terror. The Rowan was seized with an urgent need to either deny or confirm it.

The Tower had been enlarged as well as modernized and, judging by the blank west wall, clearly the architect intended to expand in that direction when the time came for Deneb to have a full Prime Station.

"That's right, Jeran, look about you! This may one day be your domain," the Rowan said, grinning archly at Isthia, trying to neutralize their fears so she could be objective. They felt so strongly that it was, for once, difficult for the Rowan to maintain her integrity.

"Poor baby! What a fate!" Isthia stroked his cheek and then placed him in one of the spare couches, lightly strapping him safely in. "He shouldn't be bothered there." She gestured for the others to take the conformable seating grouped at the main console. Then she courteously gestured for the Rowan to initiate the gestalt.

As the Rowan felt the ready response of the bank of generators, she grinned again at the change from that poor wheeze of an affair Isthia had been practicing, for her mind smoothly blended with hers: then Rakella, Besseva, and a little timidly, Mauli merged.

Where? the Rowan asked.

Isthia pointed to her right, slightly west of true north, at one of the more brilliant constellations in the Denebian skies. The Rowan didn't know its astronomical designation for she was more familiar with the patterns in Altairian or Callistan skies.

Though I don't think that star system is where it originates, Isthia added. *But it is coming from that general area of space.*

The Rowan let her augmented mind range beyond Deneb's night horizon, beyond its moons, far, far out, past Deneb's heliopause, into the blackness of space. This merge was vastly different to the one she had led to Deneb's help nearly two years ago. This time she was the focus. Suddenly Yegrani's Sight came back to her, and the Rowan wondered if perhaps she had erred in believing that the Sight had been fulfilled with Deneb's trouble and Jeff's arrival.

You have not yet been the focus of which Yegrani spoke, said the quiet voice of Besseva, *nor was she ambiguous. Deneb's danger was not yours. This is!*

What the Rowan felt then was not prompted by Besseva's voice or words. There was inarguably something *dangerously evil* inexorably heading toward Deneb's system.

No, not evil! Determined! And determined in a sense that gives new potency to such a mind-set. The Isthian section of the mind merge qualified the emanation.

Rowan: *The emanation has no pain now. No anger.*

Besseva: *In time all pain heals and the anger has been sublimated into purpose.*

Rowan: *What IS it?* Though she could discern intense and unrelenting mental activity, she could "see" or "read" nothing: she could detect no string of thoughts being processed, only the moil of determination.

Rakella: *"It" is not single!*

Mauli, in a surprised tone: *"It" is a many. And they frighten me! They are . . .* oily.

Isthia, bleakly: *This "many" exudes a purpose of destruction. Enough to agitate even an insensitive mind.*

Rowan, recalling vividly that earlier merge: *The survivor was sent off in that general direction!*

Isthia: *The merge didn't follow it to its destination?*

Rowan, with a sigh for that error: *At the time our actions seemed sufficiently punitive.*

Isthia: *All should have been destroyed.*

Rowan: *Hmm, yes, a bad judgment error. We didn't succeed in scaring them off. We should have plunged all into the sun and saved a lot of cleaning up. Were you in that merge, Isthia?*

Isthia: *No,* and there was a thread of droll amusement in her tone. *I was otherwise occupied. This time we will see the threat removed completely.*

Rowan: *We will not err this time. Only what will be a sufficient deterrent?*

Besseva: *I respectfully suggest total annihilation.*

Rowan: *That notion will be totally unacceptable to the League Councillors. Even the aliens are nonviolent.*

Isthia: *Drastic measures must be considered. The hive mentality obviously didn't respond to a fear stimulus. Just what sort of intelligence guides this second assault?*

Mauli: *Would it be wrong to assume that, as in other insect colonies, the female, or egg-laying gender, is the guiding force? Ensuring the perpetuation of the species?*

Isthia: *A logical assumption since* we *apparently sense what the masculine mind does not.*

Rowan: *I resent reacting to a* beetle.

Isthia, drolly: *Did you see the reconstruction the specialists made of one of those "beetles?" BIG! Even one of the smaller types would be a formidable opponent! Don't think of them as beetles. Think of them as BIG, dangerous animosities. I should not like to have to defend myself against them on Deneb's surface.*

Besseva, in a dry voice: *Especially as Deneb has little in the way of defensive weaponry. Hunting arms wouldn't even dint their body covering. If we can assume that we are dealing with a hive society . . .*

Isthia: *I think we can. Remember the eggs among the debris of the ships that were destroyed . . .*

Besseva: *And with a species that will pour huge numbers of determined troops into a surface assault, they must be halted before they reach the planet! Or we'd better think of evacuating Deneb right now.*

Isthia, in unalterable defiance: *We are NOT abandoning Deneb.*

Mauli: *I sense something so massive . . .* and broke off, tucking her fear as far away from consideration as she could.

Rowan: *That has not escaped any of us, Mauli.*

Isthia, wryly: *D'you think we'll get the Fleet this time without a lengthy argument, Rowan?*

Rowan: *You better believe it! Even if I have to 'port every unit myself.*

Besseva: *Be a little more subtle, Rowan. Just tell Earth Prime that you refuse to leave Deneb until naval reinforcements arrive!*

Isthia, laughing: *Reidinger won't risk you!*

Mauli: *Shouldn't we withdraw? They might sense us.*

Rowan: *I doubt it, Mauli. There is no sense of awareness of anything other than their purpose. Deneb. And that's the reason we sense them: their purpose is aimed at us! Single-mindedness has certain disadvantages. I just wish I could perceive more details, unravel the mechanics of their thought processes. The Fleet will want details.*

Isthia: *So will Reidinger and Jeff. But there are none. They will have to trust our perception.* She sounded dubious.

Rowan: *Oh, they'll believe us! Why have a dog and bark yourself?*

Isthia: *Say what?*

Rowan, chuckling: *One of Siglen's little sayings.*

The Rowan began to relax the focus of the merge and was astonished to see daylight flooding through the Tower windows. Jeran was sound asleep, his right thumb pulling down his lower lip. A quick glimpse reassured the Rowan that his mind held no trace of any neglect, that he had fallen asleep unfretted.

"I hadn't realized we'd be gone so long," Isthia said with apology, looking at the station timer. "Five hours! You took us farther than we'd been able to reach."

The Rowan stretched, easing stiff muscles as she swung her legs off the conformer. The others were doing the same.

Rowan! Jeff's tone bordered the peremptory. *Where have you been? I couldn't reach you at all!*

Well, have a good look then, my love, because Deneb's the target once again. Only this time we won't stop with half measures, the Rowan replied and opened her mind to him.

That's fascinating! Jeff replied when he had absorbed the total report. *Nor can anyone ignore this as a case of mass hysteria if you and my mother are involved. And Besseva,* he added hastily, with a mental grin of apology. *These days I know* why *Reidinger couldn't just call up the Fleet when I wanted him to during the last invasion. But I also know which panic buttons to press to initiate a Red Alert.*

Isthia, at her drollest: *If what we sense about the incoming vessel is even marginally accurate, the Fleet wouldn't be of any use. Except psychologically.*

Jeff: *Mother! You'll crush their fragile egos! Surely they're good for something!*

Isthia: *Well, they might be able to spot the thing when it gets closer but, to be perfectly candid, I don't* want *that thing to get much nearer! It's causing sufficient havoc as far out as it is and I dread what it'll do up close.*

Jeff: *It would be wisest to nip its pretensions as soon as possible.*

Isthia, patiently: *It's not an "it," Jeff. It's a "many," a feminine "many."*

Jeff: *Then we are in trouble!* And he was only half-joking. *Are you staying on there, Rowan-love?* His thought was only for her and its wistfulness made her smile.

Rowan, with a quick look at Isthia: *No, I should return to Callisto. I can nag people just as easily from there. I'll leave Mauli to help keep in touch. But I assure you, if we don't get immediate action, I'll come right back here so the League will be forced to take this seriously. These creatures may be heading* for *Deneb, but to have such animosities anywhere in the League's sphere of influence endangers ALL!*

Isthia: *It's proceeding at a frightening rate of speed.*

Jeff: *I know. I'll persuade Admiral Tomiakin to lend me a fast scout ship for reconnaissance.*

Rowan: *With you on it?*

Jeff: *Who better?* A grin tickled the edges of her mind. *I didn't call "wolf" the first time so they'll listen to me.*

Isthia said aloud and screening her thought: "Men! They have to have their place in the scheme, don't they?"

Rowan: *You'd better be sure there's a large female complement on that scout. Or better still, take Mauli with you. She knows what to listen for.*

Jeff: *Your wish is my command!*

"I think *everyone* is going to have to be in on this defensive action," the Rowan said soberly, "or that thing is going to land on Deneb. And all too soon."

The Rowan knew she had only put into words what the others thought but saying it out loud did nothing to relieve the tension.

"I will arrange a watch rota," Isthia said. "There are enough of us to do that. And Rakella, you can see about some sort of medication to dampen the reaction."

"Not every woman is experiencing it," Rakella remarked.

Isthia grinned in sudden humor. "So we find out just how much of Deneb's female population have traces of Talent. 'Tis an ill wind that blows no one good."

Rowan, very privately: *You're amazing!*

Isthia, equally private: *Take the good with the bad.*

Then Jeran awoke to be fed, so Isthia hustled mother and son back to the rebuilt Raven Farmhouse, where the stock purchased by Jeff's paternity bonus grazed on the lush hybrid grass that had thrived in Denebian soil. What surprised the Rowan about the new residence was that most of it was built underground.

"Once bitten, twice shy," Isthia replied with a shrug and a grin, "as well as being sound home-engineering: energy efficient, cooler in the summer and warmer in the winter. And I feel a lot safer. Doesn't mess up the landscape either. You'll find more of Deneb City underground. We'll overfly it on our way back to the Tower. Now, let's feed this hungry young'un. And us! Those long night watches make me ravenous."

Once back on Callisto, the Rowan allowed Reidinger to scan her memories of the merge. That he was seriously disturbed was obvious by the fact that he hadn't so much as roared over her abrupt departure. When she mentioned Yegrani's Sight as verification, he became testy.

You were the merge, he said. *You saved Deneb and you've traveled.*

I was NOT the focus at Deneb. Jeff was.

Reidinger made a rude noise. *Damned clairvoyants are so clever with their ambiguities.*

REIDINGER, you are not ignoring this! It was her turn to bellow.

Fat chance I'd have of that when that aggressive Denebian husband of yours is agitating Fleet High Command as well as everyone he's ever met on the League Administrative Panel. Reidinger sounded disgusted yet there was a hint of pride in his protégé, which made the Rowan grin. *Should never have introduced him so universally. He's got Fleet in a flap but the units that were stationed around Deneb are insisting that they get the chance to reconnoiter.*

Rowan: *Jeff said he'd be leading the way.*

Reidinger was silent for a moment. *He hasn't wasted an ounce of that ingratiating charm of his over the last six months. He smothered exactly the right egos with it. Consequently he can manipulate the various authorities and agencies that would be involved in an operation of this magnitude. And cut through delays.*

The Rowan grinned to herself at Reidinger's grudging admission. She had learned a thing or two from Jeff about dealing with bureaucracy. More importantly, he could manipulate at a high level. With Deneb the ostensible target for this new assault, he had every reason to marshal his Talent.

Jeff was very effective: he managed a squadron to reconnoiter. And, obeying his wife's advice, specified a high complement of female crews on two of the ships.

Damnedest thing I ever heard of, Reidinger complained to the Rowan, *Jeff's the most perceptive, and certainly the strongest Talent I've ever encountered—and he had to go some to exceed you, Angharad—* Reidinger had taken to calling her by her real name since Jeran's birth because "Angharad" sounded more feminine than a tree name—*so he's got xenobiologists from all parts of the League screaming for details about these feminine menaces of yours.*

The female of the species has always been more deadly than the male, Reidinger, the Rowan replied, though she couldn't remember where she'd heard that maxim. It didn't have the same ring as one of Siglen's.

Defending its young. I suppose even beetles can have maternal imperatives! If it IS the same blasted beetles. His grumbling tone faded from her mind.

As the Rowan turned back to some minor domestic chores—'porting fresh water from a Welsh artesian well for the Callisto cisterns, the weekly supply of comestibles and special household orders of those who lived on the Station—she waited with half a mind open for Jeff's progress report.

We're beyond Deneb's heliopause by two AUs, he said. *I brought the squadron out myself. Fine Captain, excellent crew,* he added with a mental picture of the ZAMBIAN's bridge and the exceedingly handsome woman occupying the Captain's chair. The officers seated at consoles were all reasonably young and attractive, too. *Picked less for pulchritude and more for vestiges of Talent. You have no competition, my love!*

I won't dignify that with a reply.

Then shall I be magnanimous and say they confirm your perceptions about the approaching vessel? Not all the crew's female but those who are have exhibited the same symptoms Isthia reports en masse on Deneb. I'm feeling distinctly left out of all this and I'm supposed to be highly perceptive!

Be glad you don't pick up on the aura, Jeff! You can really call it evil, or even truly malicious, but it emanates an intensity—an anticipation of destruction—that is frightening. If I were a barquecat, every hair on my body would be standing stark out. And don't call the phenomenon "it." Mauli echoed a "many"—a many which will not be diverted from their purpose.

Exactly how Captain Lodjyn summed up her impression of the intent of this Many. And they're unequivocably headed toward Deneb. I may be slightly paranoid about what happens to my planet, but I really can't quite make myself believe the vessel is going through Denebian space for a short-cut when Deneb VIII will just happen to be in their way. What I can't understand is how they will avoid impaction at the speed they're going. It takes time to decelerate from the speed at which they're now traveling. Or maybe beetles stand multigravities better than us fleshy sorts?

Rowan, sensing suspicious peripherals from Jeff's mind: *Just what are you doing right now?*

Taking a look. Too much "noise" on the ZAMBIA.

She didn't like the thought of him in a vulnerable personal capsule, far from the nebulous safety of a multiweaponed scout vessel. *You should have taken the Captain with you. You won't hear a thing.*

I did and Mauli's along. And we're in the Captain's gig. I've some sense for a mere man, my love.

You reassure me no end!

Jeff's tone turned wry. *I thought this would, cariad. Mauli's echo is going to come in real useful.*

Like never before!

He was silent though his mind kept contact. So, putting everyone on the Station on a Yellow Alert status, she left the Tower, with Afra, Mick, and Ackerman in charge, to attend to her son. It was soothing to feed Jeran his lunch before settling him down for a nap. Most of the time she did not have to reinforce his natural rhythm with a mental suggestion, but he had been a little off normal schedule since the Deneb 'portation so she gave him a nudge. She gazed down at him for a long moment—he was endlessly enchanting. Then she stretched out on her bed, one arm flung across the side which Jeff usually occupied, and relaxed, clearing her mind.

WOW! The awe in Jeff's voice was sufficient to rouse her totally from the light doze she had entered.

Mauli's reaction was less awed and considerably more fearful.

Jeff: *We seem to have a lumpy-surfaced oval planetoid rolling towards us at speeds which make even gestalt-assisted movements seem crawler-paced. It is currently twenty AUs out but closing faster'n I like. That defense ring which Fleet is so proud of is going to be no use against a vessel this size. More like a flea trying to swat one of those large men Procyon breeds. Easy, Mauli. I don't care what instrumentation it might have, it can't see us. We're less than a mote. You may feel it, but if it had sensed us, we'd really be motes.*

The Rowan, briefly touching Mauli's panicked mind to reassure the girl, heard Jeff's chuckle.

This may only be a captain's gig but its scanner's the best so Fleet'll have the printout as confirmation. I'm getting no readings on mass or composition. Scanner says "no accurate assessment possible at this distance." That's a lot of comfort. Tut-tut! And it's running dark. Ignoring the basic laws of spacemanship! That seems to be upsetting the Fleet more than its size. No, that's a cover for the pure funk even admirals are feeling over my evaluation. They're making contradictory preliminary assessments, demanding that I increase the resolution. I did: it's on the max right now. What do they think I've got on this skiff? A portable sun for illumination?

The Rowan refined the contact with Jeff sufficiently to see, through his optics, what he and Mauli were viewing on the skiff's scanners: a darkness that flowed across the backdrop of stars. *Quite a Leviathan, isn't it? I understand why adrenaline is pumping through your veins.*

Leviathan? An interesting choice of phrase, my love.

Jeff Raven, if you go in any closer to that . . . that menace, I'll kill you, she added, abruptly seized by a gut-generated terror.

Jeff chuckled. *That'll teach me a lesson. Rest easy, cariad, I'm as close as I care to get, and closer than Mauli or the good Captain Lodjyn think wise.*

Do they hear anything useful?

Well, Mauli does and she doesn't. She's let me merge and I can sense great industry and bustle, orderly activity, and some areas with no sound at all. I think the damned planetoid was once just that and has been hollowed out for its travels. Mauli's picking up a lot more than I am: six or more different mental entities. His tone became attenuated as he spoke to her privately. *Mauli's in a muck sweat of terror from the level of "dedication"*

. . . purpose is too weak a word . . . that she perceives. I'm taking us back before the poor kid dissolves. Even the Captain's sweating and throwing out fear phenomes.

Rowan: *When Deneb was attacked, the merge didn't sense any great dedication, purpose, or intelligence from the occupants of those vessels.*

Jeff: *You're assuming that the ship we deported from our system went scurrying back to this big Mama?*

Rowan: *Why not? You thought then that they were softening Deneb up for an invasion. Why couldn't they have been preparing the planet for the arrival of what's bearing down on Deneb now?*

Jeff: *And the "mother" ship is why only females sense its intent?*

Rowan: *Don't you dare snicker!*

Jeff: *Believe me, dear heart, whatever reservations I might have privately entertained at the outset are null and void. We are in big trouble and I thank all the Powers of Balance for my mother's long ear! As it is, we're going to have to plan our campaign against that Leviathan very carefully. That's the hard place, and Deneb's the rock and we—Mankind—are between it.* There was a brief pause. *And so I've just informed Earth Prime!* This *time he also has no reservations.* In the second pause, Jeff chuckled wryly. *However the League may well just argue us all to our deaths. Would you believe it? They are now debating the ethical point of whether we have the right to interfere with the approaching vessel simply on the grounds that it* might*—get that,* might*—have hostile intentions?*

Rowan, aghast: *You can't mean it?*

Jeff, sardonically: *Now just how do we* prove *hostile intent? They haven't launched any missiles—yet—that I can lob at Earth and scare the doubters.*

Afra: *You said Leviathan is clearly on a course to Deneb, did you not?*

Jeff: *Yes, Afra, I did and the squadron's computers all confirm that. Unless this Leviathan decelerates when it reaches Deneb's system, present calculations confirm that it will smash right into Deneb VIII. Captain Lodjyn is extrapolating the repercussions of such a collision.*

Reidinger: *It will NOT come to that! Talent does not bust its balls for the Nine-Star League to have them disregard a considered warning of imminent invasion of a possibly hostile force of unknown potential.*

Jeff: *And what have you in mind, Earth Prime?*

Reidinger: *I am in conference with the Nine-Star League Councillors and you may rest assured that they will be persuaded to* act, *not argue. Ah, good! My first order from the Councillors is to dispatch the flagship* Beijing *to the Denebian system. It will deploy one-half AU beyond Deneb's heliopause, the Welcome and Identify modules which were so successful with the Antarians sentients not dissimilar to the beetle-type species of the first assault.*

Rowan, exasperated: *Of all the stupid face-saving ploys! Haven't we TOLD you that the main sentience of this vessel is motivated by destruction, the annihilation of Deneb VIII?*

Reidinger: *Oh, I agree with your evaluation, Angharad. I am further ordered to dispatch the* Moscow, *the* London, *and the* New-york *to redeploy defensive mines one-half AU inside the heliopause.*

Jeff: *Bluebells all in a row?*

Reidinger: *Under the premise that a warning shot across the bows ought to be universally understood.*

The Rowan snorted.

Jeff: *Remind the captains of those vessels to get the hell out of the way before that thing gets within fifty-thousand klicks of the space mines.*

Reidinger: *Now we wait!*

Rowan and Jeff in simultaneously expressed disgust: *Wait?*

Reidinger: *Wait! That's the trouble with you youngsters. You don't know when to bide your time.*

Jeff: *Not when it's my planet that's the target.*

Reidinger: *It was before and you were rescued. However, in addition to my official instructions,* and Reidinger paused significantly, *I have sent out a discreet alert to all Primes and Talent above grade 4, regardless of their discipline. Does that precaution reassure you?*

Jeff, diffidently: *Not exactly, for I fail to see what Talent will be able to do against that Leviathan!*

Rowan: *Alert for what action?*

Reidinger, malicious chuckle: *I thought you'd grasp the essentials more quickly. Mull it all over, will you, while we're waiting. And, in this interval, Jeff, I want you to proceed to Deneb. Angharad, please join him there but I would request that your son remains on Callisto.*

Jeff: *Now, wait a minute . . .*

Rowan, beginning to catch a glimmer of what Reidinger held so tightly in his most private mind: *No, Jeff. I should be on Deneb to augment Isthia. Then as soon as we know . . . and Jeran is safer away from the furor. It could overload him. And Reidinger most certainly doesn't want that, do you, Peter?*

Reidinger in a growl: *No!*

* * *

The Rowan did not *like* leaving Jeran behind: She would miss him keenly but, between the other women on the Station and Afra, he would be lovingly supervised. So she settled in her capsule and calmly waited for the generators to hit the proper revolutions before she, with Afra and Mick assisting, 'ported to Deneb. When she entered the Denebian Tower, she noticed the signs of stress in the faces of those who had maintained the Watch.

"If we swallow any more sedatives, we won't be able to hear a damned thing," Isthia said bleakly. However, as she gave the Rowan a quick embrace of welcome, her incredible energy seemed undiminished, bright red and tangy. "There's a bottom to the well and a long dry period if I dip in too often. But those things will NOT have my planet." The red of her deepened.

"What does Besseva say now?" the Rowan asked, missing the clairvoyant from those on duty.

Isthia gave a diffident shrug. "She's gone into a deep trance, trying to penetrate the shell of that—what did Jeff say you named it? Leviathan—" she went on when the Rowan put the word in her mind, "to see what's inside. It's damnably frustrating to have an unknown assailant."

"The Councillors wish to believe that they may not be hostile," the Rowan said in a saccharine tone of voice.

Isthia was not the only one in the Tower to have a poor opinion of that belief. Then the Rowan took a spare couch and joined the minds merged on the approaching vessel. It had shortened the distance to heliopause considerably.

Jeff: *Get set to catch me, will you, loves?*

Isthia, privately: *He must be tired if he's asking us for help.*

Rowan: *All right, then, my fine lad, into the cradle you go!*

Jeff's step had none of its usual spring as he entered the Tower and dropped into the nearest chair. Before Isthia could motion to one of the girls, the Rowan had obtained a glass of stimulant and, placing it in his hand, laid both of hers on his temples, transferring energy to him. Closing his eyes, he accepted her gift, a loving smile turning up the corners of his mouth. *You always know what I need, dear heart! My profound gratitude. I'll return the gift on demand.*

"How long before we get some action?" Isthia asked in a gruff voice.

Jeff shrugged. "The Fleet wants to make its war-game moves. They believe in their invincibility. I do not."

Rowan: *Could a focus protect them? Leviathan may have weaponry we can't perceive.*

Jeff: *Not over the area of space where they've deployed, and it'd be damned bad tactics to group them together where we might possibly be able to shield them.* He gave a mirthless laugh. *The Councillors are certain that Leviathan will respond reasonably to the Welcome & Identify modules. The Fleet are not so naive as to consider that likely. However, the good Admirals are confident that Leviathan will react to the presence of the mines. Once Leviathan has demonstrated its weaponry against the mines, they will know how to defend us against it.*

Rowan: *There are women Councillors . . .*

Jeff: *None with much more than an empathetical Talent and your report has frightened them from even the most discreet of direct contact. The W & I modules were only deployed to pacify the nonaggressive element in the Council.*

Rowan: *What if Leviathan is duplicitious?*

Jeff laughed: *What? Do you mean they'd respond sweetly to the Welcome and Identify and then launch missiles once we let them advance "in peace?"*

Isthia, consideringly: *The Many is definitely not as devious as that. Single-minded is what those things are! The Many all thinking along the same line. Destroying what is in the way of their objective.*

The other women in the Watch concurred immediately.

Isthia: *And where is Mauli?*

Jeff: *Resting. Which she needed, and an example that I should follow. Now, while I have the time.*

Jeff was back in the Tower when the first Welcome message was ignored. There were ten in the string, each comprising sounds, signals, and signs that were thought to have universal significance. He hauled the Rowan and Isthia away from what he called "their compulsive watching." He made them both sleep in the way that they had once forced him to rest and ignored their protests when they awoke.

"My squadron has taken up positions behind Deneb's moons," he told his mother and his wife as he watched them consume the hearty meal he had prepared for them. "It gives them a psychological sense of security!" He grinned. "Even the male complement on board all three destroyers are believers now! And Leviathan has passed into the Denebian system proper, closing fast on the minefield." He rubbed his hands together, his blue eyes sparkling with anticipation.

Isthia regarded the Rowan drolly. "They're all alike!"

"I beg to differ, Isthia," the Rowan replied with great dignity, "this one has a few redeeming features."

"Yes, he has learned a thing or two from us, hasn't he? And I don't mean cooking."

"Why didn't you think to arrange a sleeping facility here, Mother?" Jeff asked as they 'ported back to the Tower. The watch was just changing, but the outgoing crew showed no signs of dispersing to their homes.

Besseva: *What is really needed is enough seating for those who don't wish to miss the action shortly to begin.*

Isthia: *Oh, is that all?* Stacked metal chairs arrived on the landing. *Need more?*

Rakella answered this time: *About a dozen more, cups, and say a case of a caffeine beverage and several of fruit juices. It's going to be exciting and we'll need to keep blood sugar levels up.*

As well, the Rowan thought, entering the building, that the west section was empty of equipment for it shortly became a spectators' gallery. They were quiet and their presence supportive. Jeff sat at the console where screens linked up the three reconnaissance ships and two of the closer dreadnoughts, the *Moscow* and the *London.*

Once she was settled in her couch, the Rowan nodded to Isthia and the two women, their minds strengthened by the gestalt, reached out into space. Unerringly now they perceived the intruder. It had reached the last of the Welcome devices.

Isthia: *Well, that's that.*

Rakella, tentatively: *Maybe they just didn't understand any of the programs.*

Isthia: *That's immaterial. A pointed attempt to make communications deserves the courtesy of some response.*

Rowan: *So much for the pacifist Councillors' good intentions.*

Reidinger, gently insinuating an ironic voice in both minds: *It was worth a try, wasn't it?*

Isthia, giving a mental shudder: *I suppose it salves conscience and looks good on the record.*

Reidinger: *There was rather a large segment of our populations that bet that the intruder would shoot the devices up.*

Jeff: *Thereby establishing a clearly hostile intent!*

Isthia: *I keep telling you that hostile intent has already been unequivocably established! Those beings are really alien.*

Jeff: *Who's taking bets about their firing on the mines? Whoops! I never laid any credit on that bet!*

In the next few moments the screens were hectic with reports from the dreadnoughts and the smaller courier ships. The seeded mines were being demolished but not by Leviathan. Scanners now registered the appearance of mobile units, originating from Leviathan and speeding toward the mines.

The Rowan and Jeff simultaneously: *Same sort of craft we destroyed two years ago!*

Reidinger: *Score a point for Talent! Fleet took nine seconds longer to identify. ZAMBIA and her sister ships are demanding the chance to retaliate!*

The Rowan and Isthia: *Do NOT permit them to engage!*

The Rowan: *We'll need their minds!*

Reidinger: *You figured it out then, Angharad?*

The Rowan: *I did indeed! But Leviathan must get close enough to hit the gravity well before it can be swung away from Deneb VIII.*

Jeff, grimly: *And we wait?*

Reidinger, equally as grim but with such a strong vein of assurance that the Rowan could feel Jeff relax: *We wait for the* right *moment!*

Jeff composed a graphic display, the Fleet deployment and the Leviathan's mobile units, added the now measurable speed, mass, and composition of the invader, and grunted when the projection appeared. "Closing too bloody damned fast. And if this master strategy of yours doesn't work?"

Reidinger: *Fleet elements have already destroyed or disabled seven of the fifteen destroyers Leviathan sent out. We've sustained some casualties.*

When he paused for too long, Jeff asked sharply: *And they're beetles, aren't they? More of those damned beetles!*

Reidinger: *So the initial unconfirmed reports suggest.*

Jeff let out a wild yell, startling everyone in the Tower. "They'll be making statues to your long ear, Mother," he cried, hauling her into his arms and whirling her about.

Isthia swatted futilely at him but his ebullience did much to lighten the tension in the Tower. "Silly boy! Hearing was the easy part!" She pushed herself out of his arms, but not before giving his face an affectionate caress.

The eyes of everyone in the Tower turned to the graph and the inexorable progress of the Leviathan past the cold and sterile outer planets of the Denebian system.

Reidinger, righteous but sad: *Two of our destroyers were wiped out. Got too close to the Leviathan when they chased its defenders back. Then it sent seeking missiles in the direction of the dreadnoughts. All sustained damage, fortunately none have been crippled.*

Jeff: *Does the Fleet still believe in the potency of its weaponry?*

Reidinger with a snort: Moscow *and* London *are bracketing the intruder and have launched their first salvos.*

Isthia: *They have to be seen to* try, *Jeff. Stop that pacing. My nerves are bad enough without you clomping about like that.*

The Rowan: *Save your energy, love. Talent has the big guns and you're the bombardier!*

Jeff's eyes sparkled and his grin was pure malice. *I figured it out. A bit slow, perhaps, but this local yokel finally caught on.*

I think, and the Rowan paused dramatically, *you got past Reidinger's shield and sneaked a peek.*

Jeff, wearing an innocent expression: *I? Invade our Master's privacy? I'm good but I'm not that good!*

The Rowan laughed aloud. "I think you're better than good, love. If you'd waited, you'd've figured out what Reidinger has in mind."

It wasn't easy for anyone in the Tower to wait, watching the invader making its way deeper and deeper into Denebian space, knowing that the intersection of the planet's orbit and Leviathan's path was steadily approaching. Isthia sent people home to rest, ordered food brought in, revised the Watch rota, sent Jeff and the Rowan to the Farm to sleep. She arrived at the Farm and sent them back to assume command.

Additional squadrons were dispatched to harry Leviathan. Though many strikes were made on the surface of the planetoid, the hits had no discernible effect on its inexorable path.

The Rowan, on a thin band to Isthia: *Those mothers must feel pretty invincible by now.*

Isthia: *I sense that they are aware of the attacks.*

The Rowan: *And smug! I dislike that attitude.*

Besseva: *It will suit our purpose.*

The hours dragged and the Rowan began to realize subjectively how Jeff must have felt during that first contact.

Jeff: *Bloody useless is how I felt.*

The Rowan: *That's not how you came across to me.*

Jeff, giving her his special smile as he swiveled his chair around to her: *And how did I come across to you?*

The Rowan regarded him for a long moment, smiling tantalizingly. *Busy. Preoccupied. Annoyed with bureaucratic inefficiency.*

Jeff said aloud, fidgeting, "I wish I was busy right now! Even a little bureaucratic inefficiency to maul would be a relief!" He sat bolt upright when he glanced at the monitor. "Hey, that thing has slowed. It's going to go into orbit around us!"

"Why?" Isthia wanted to know. "I will not believe its intentions are pacific!"

Jeff was busily adding equations to the graph. "No, not in that orbit. Just far enough away for its missiles to be effective and too far for any retaliation from the ground—if we had any missiles of any kind. Ruddy bitches are going to pound hell out of us again!"

No, they're not! Reidinger's mental alert was almost anticlimactic when it echoed through the minds of everyone in the Tower. *Angharad Gwyn-Raven, the A focus is yours. Gather it! Jeff Raven, collect the B focus. Prepare!*

With a single look of exchanged love, the Rowan and Jeff lay supine on their conformable couches and relaxed their bodies. They didn't notice Rakella motioning for medical orderlies to attend them.

Capella came querulously into the Rowan's mind first: *This is becoming a habit: twice in as many years. Really! I do trust that we can dispose of this intrusive type for once and all.*

The Rowan: *That is the intention!* The Rowan also read how nervous Capella was under the guise of complaint. She felt vulnerable, a sensation which the Talented rarely entertained. To herself, the Rowan realized how much she had learned of herself, and others, in the two years since the first merge.

With Capella came the surge of all the female Talents of her system. Then the T-2 Jedizaira at the Betelgeuse Station added her strength; Maharanjani from Altair and, among those who joined from her native planet, the Rowan felt the touch of her stepsister and welcomed her. Earth's Talents, Elizara leading as she was familiar with the Rowan's mind, swelled the force still greater. Procyon sort of stumbled into the focus, apologizing but Piastera was a T-3 and, with Guzman as Prime, had had little chance to do much merging off-planet. Other minds joined in large and small groupings, led by T-2s or T-4s, tentatively at first, then melding in more comfort as they were integrated into the whole of female Talent throughout the Nine-Star League. Their determination to halt the invaders vibrated more fiercely than the force that opposed them. The Denebians came in last, Isthia, Rakella, and Besseva down to young Sarjie, thrilled to be admitted into this experience. Then all were swallowed up in the final consolidation of the Rowan merge.

Reidinger, and his voice seemed nearly a whisper to the totality that the Rowan had become: *Now, Angharad, now! The Raven merge is available!*

Blazoned in the mass mind was the graph on the Tower's screen and steadily the Rowan merge moved out toward the invader. Like a laser stabbing through space, the Rowan-mind gathered speed and reached the planetoid. Various elements of the Rowan-mind noted composition, mass, confirmed that Leviathan had been made from a dead world, now a darkness reverberating with noisy machinery and the scuttling of myriad creatures, whose minimal understanding responded to commands directed at them from the central point in the cavernous vessel.

The Rowan-mind: *The "Many" are sixteen but some do not emanate much strength. We interrupt and distract the "Many"—NOW!*

There could be no defense against such a shaft of pure mental energy and the "Many" struggled briefly, withered and collapsed into mindlessness under the intensity of the force directed against them.

The Jeff-focus shouted: *NOW!* And every kinetic male Talent was joined with full gestalt from all available generators to divert Leviathan onto its final trajectory—straight toward Deneb's primary.

Later, in the many years of discussion provoked by an event which lasted six hours, it would be seen as the most perfect example of mind over matter: ineluctably simple when compared to weapon technology or the complexity of spaceship drives. Once the Rowan-mind merge distracted and destroyed the minds of the huge, female reproducers, Leviathan lost its directive force: the diverse subordinates aimlessly continued in the routines for which they had been genetically designed, movements that had become pointless.

Then the Jeff-mind merge exerted the kinetic energy to deflect Leviathan from its intended orbit above Deneb VIII. Together both mind merges concentrated on speeding Leviathan on its new course. When the gravitic pull of Deneb's sun caught the planetoid, the mind merges released it.

Leviathan's plunge into the solar incandescence created a brief flare in the corona, recorded as the finale to this astounding exercise.

The Raven-merge: *That's what we should have done with the first attackers.*

The Rowan-merge: *We did warn them!*

Slowly the individual minds retreated from their foci: slowly because the mass elation of success had bordered on exquisite ecstasy, too sweet not to savor; slowly because the communion of so many minds was in itself a rare and unique experience. Thanks were given and received. Farewells were tender between those who had just met; reluctant between old friends, united once again. The last withdrawals were almost painful and the Rowan felt totally drained, her mind barren and echoing after such a surfeit.

"Easy, Rowan," said Rakella in a muted voice. Even so, the Rowan winced weakly. "Just drift. Jeff's fine. Dean's with him. You'll both recover after a good, long sleep."

I'm here, Jeff said and although he was still on the couch not a scant half meter from her, his tone was a whisper. *This was a much longer affair than the first one. Sleep! I'll love you later.*

"I want the pair of you asleep by the time I count three," Isthia said, her doughty self.

That's not fair, the Rowan thought despite a hideous pounding in her reverberatingly empty head.

Why's fair?! One, two, three!

When the Rowan woke much later, revived and refreshed, she found she was alone in the bed at the Raven farm.

Jeff was called back to Earth, Isthia said.

Reidinger? The Rowan shot straight up in bed in her anxiety.

Back in form, aren't you, "but don't you dare reach for him!" Isthia added in a bellow from the kitchen area. *The man's all right. I can't lie to you.* And she couldn't so the Rowan *knew* that Reidinger had collapsed. *He is very much alive and kicking! Or so Elizara says, and she should know. But his efforts to move dreadnoughts and who knows what else out to Deneb at the last moment were too much for a man his age. He,* and Isthia's tone became scathing, *had to do it himself to be sure all was set up for you and Jeff. Elizara has* him *in hand and she said that you must rest today, too. You've the baby to consider. But you may rise and dress.*

"You need food first, talk later," Isthia said, when the Rowan managed a slow and slightly unsteady entrance, "but you'll be happy to know that one of the beetle attack ships was captured intact. When the boarding party cracked the main air lock, they found the creatures in some sort of stasis, frozen in position. Xenobiologists are of the opinion that they couldn't even perform routine tasks without ongoing contact with Leviathan. The biologists are ecstatic: they can study the species with impunity. The Fleet has a complete ship to disassemble and all that technology to dismantle. When I think that Jeff nearly died trying to collect just bits and pieces, I could spit acid!"

As the Rowan listened to Isthia, she ate ravenously and with a single-mindedness that appalled her. It was a trifle unnerving when she recalled a similar trait in the beetle "Many." Not that there was even the faintest possibility of contamination or even a transfer of mentality, the Rowan thought as she devoured the very excellent meal Isthia had prepared. Not between such disparate thinking mechanisms, despite that brief but devastating period of contact. She was just very, very hungry after yesterday's exertions.

Isthia: *Of course you are. Nothing more. Don't even think about it!* "You were splendid, by the way. In case no one thinks to tell you!" Then she touched the Rowan lightly on her shoulder. "That was two days ago, by the way."

"Two days?" The Rowan dropped her utensils and stared at Isthia.

"You're pregnant. You needed more rest. But I saw to it that Jeff slept a full twenty-four before I let them ship him back to Earth. He deserved that much!"

"He deserves a lot more than twenty-four hours' sleep!" The Rowan glared at Isthia and wished there was someone she could really tell off!

I'm that person, then, cariad! And Jeff's chuckle sounded in her mind, soothing her, caressing her as only he could. *Your part of the merge was the difficult one. I only had to push!*

"Yegrani *was* right," Isthia went on, "you were the focus that saved us all. The Leviathan 'Many' had to be immobilized first."

Suddenly the Rowan had had quite enough of Yegrani's Sight. "I suppose I should feel relieved that I've fulfilled it."

Fulfillment for you has only begun, was Jeff's fervent reply, suffusing her mind and body with his love—and his yearning. *Get yourself down to Earth as soon as you can, cariad.* And his bawdy chuckle gave her fair warning of his intentions. *This is the beginning of the Gwyn-Raven Dynasty: you, me, ours,* us!